The
Spitfire Girl's
Secret

Karen Dickson is the author of six novels and used to work at her local branch of WHSmith, where she was fondly known as The Book Lady. She lives in Dorset.

Also by Karen Dickson

The Shop Girl's Soldier
The Dressmaker's Secret
A Songbird in Wartime
The Strawberry Field Girls
The Strawberry Field Girls at War

KAREN DICKSON

The
Spitfire Girl's
Secret

**SIMON &
SCHUSTER**

London · New York · Amsterdam/Antwerp · Sydney/Melbourne · Toronto · New Delhi

First published in Great Britain by Simon & Schuster UK Ltd, 2025

Copyright © Karen Dickson, 2025

The right of Karen Dickson to be identified as author of
this work has been asserted in accordance with the
Copyright, Designs and Patents Act, 1988.

1 3 5 7 9 10 8 6 4 2

Simon & Schuster UK Ltd, 1st Floor
222 Gray's Inn Road, London WC1X 8HB

For more than 100 years, Simon & Schuster has championed authors and the stories they
create. By respecting the copyright of an author's intellectual property, you enable Simon &
Schuster and the author to continue publishing exceptional books for years to come. We thank
you for supporting the author's copyright by purchasing an authorized edition of this book.

No amount of this book may be reproduced or stored in any format, nor may it be
uploaded to any website, database, language-learning model, or other repository,
retrieval, or artificial intelligence system without express permission. All rights
reserved. Inquiries may be directed to Simon & Schuster, 222 Gray's Inn Road,
London WC1X 8HB or RightsMailbox@simonandschuster.co.uk

Simon & Schuster Australia, Sydney
Simon & Schuster India, New Delhi

www.simonandschuster.co.uk
www.simonandschuster.com.au
www.simonandschuster.co.in

The authorised representative in the EEA is Simon & Schuster Netherlands BV,
Herculesplein 96, 3584 AA Utrecht, Netherlands. info@simonandschuster.nl

Simon & Schuster strongly believes in freedom of expression and stands against censorship
in all its forms. For more information, visit BooksBelong.com.

A CIP catalogue record for this book is available from the British Library

Hardback ISBN: 978-1-3985-3101-7
eBook ISBN: 978-1-3985-3102-4
Audio ISBN: 978-1-3985-3103-1

This book is a work of fiction. Names, characters, places and incidents are either
a product of the author's imagination or are used fictitiously. Any resemblance
to actual people living or dead, events or locales is entirely coincidental.

Typeset in Bembo by M Rules
Printed and Bound in the UK using 100% Renewable Electricity
at CPI Group (UK) Ltd

MIX
Paper | Supporting
responsible forestry
FSC
www.fsc.org
FSC® C013604

*For all the men and women who served in
the Air Transport Auxiliary (ATA)*

(15 February 1940 – 30 November 1945)

CHAPTER ONE

1935

'Look how many blackberries I've got, Bella.' Sixteen-year-old Bella Roberts turned at the sound of her twin brother's voice, smiling at the sight of his beaming face.

'Wow, Arthur. You've almost filled your basket. Mrs Wilson will be pleased. Though I think you've eaten the same again, judging by your mucky face,' she grinned.

Arthur's purpled-stained lips widened in a cheeky grin. He was a beautiful boy, Bella mused, with his dark eyes and long lashes. His skin, like hers, still retained its tan, acquired from hours spent under the hot African sun. She knew a lot of people thought Arthur should be in an institution but, thankfully, her mother was progressive and had insisted from the start that Arthur would have the same opportunities as his sister and, contrary to the prognosis of various doctors and tutors, Arthur could read and write and reckon up. His kind nature and joyful disposition had endeared him to the locals, and any seasonal worker who might pass a derogatory comment would find themselves quickly reprimanded.

Bella had always been her brother's staunchest supporter and protector. Whether on the plains of the Western Cape, or in the green fields of Hampshire, no one dared mess with Arthur when Bella was around.

Her heart bursting with love for her brother, she brushed away a strand of dark brown hair from her face and straightened up. It was early September and the autumn day was warm. From beyond the hedge, sounds of conversation drifted from the strawberry fields. The harvest would be over soon, the seasonal workers would depart, and the sleepy hamlet of Strawbridge would settle down in preparation for the coming winter. Bella shivered. After spending the past five years enjoying the temperate climate of the Cape colony where her parents had served as missionaries, she certainly wasn't relishing the prospect of the coming winter.

'Come on,' she said, smiling over at Arthur who was working his way along the row of blackberry bushes, shovelling as many into his mouth as he dropped into his basket. 'I think we've got enough for Mrs Wilson to make her jam, and some left over.'

Grinning his wide, boyish smile, Arthur loped towards her, his dark hair ruffled by the warm breeze. Bella took his arm, and they started down the track that would lead them to the back of the vicarage garden.

The hedgerows resounded with birdsong, and high above their heads, a kestrel soared on the thermals. A cock pheasant burst from the hedgerow and dashed across their path, squawking loudly, wings flapping in panic as it sought a gap in the hawthorn hedge. Bella motioned for Arthur to stop, waiting for whatever animal was in pursuit to emerge. She had no wish to be knocked off her feet by a fox or dog blindly transfixed on its quarry but, to her surprise, there came some muttered cursing before a tall, dark-haired lad emerged from the hedgerow, a shotgun slung over his shoulder. He stopped at the sight of Bella and Arthur, seemingly equally as surprised to see them as they were him.

He looked to be about a year or so older than Bella, and his shirt sleeves were torn and splattered with blood.

'You're bleeding,' Bella said.

'I scratched myself on a twig,' he replied, with a shrug. 'It's nothing.' He scanned the track. The pheasant was nowhere to be seen but its panicked cries could be heard from beyond the hedgerow. He returned his gaze to Bella and smiled.

'I'm Will Mullens,' he said.

'Bella Roberts and this is my brother, Arthur.'

'Are you going hunting?' Arthur asked, pointing at the man's gun.

Will looked at Arthur and smirked. 'What is he?' he asked. 'The village idiot?'

Quick as a flash, Bella punched him in the face, sending him sprawling in the dirt. Will lay on his back, blood spouting from his nose, staring up at Bella in open-mouthed shock.

'I think you've broken my nose,' he said, clutching his face. Blood gushed through his fingers and onto his shirt.

3

'Don't you dare insult my brother,' she said, with a twinge of remorse. She hadn't intended to hit him quite so hard. 'Come on, Arthur, let's get home.'

'I think he was going hunting,' Arthur said, as he hurried to keep up with Bella. 'I think he wanted to shoot that pheasant.' His face fell. 'I wish we didn't have to kill things, Bella,' he said, looking back over his shoulder. Will was sitting in the middle of the track, staring after them. 'Mrs Wilson wrung Miss Liddy's neck this morning. She was my friend.'

'All the chickens are your friends, Arthur,' Bella replied kindly, as she unlatched the back gate. It swung open with a squeak of rusty hinge. 'That's why Father gets annoyed at the way you give them names. They're not pets, love, not like Barney and Sybil.'

'But I like them,' protested Arthur, as two liver and white spaniels came bounding across the lawn to greet them, feathery tails wagging in ecstasy.

'I know you do, sweetheart.' Bella sighed. She closed the gate and Arthur dropped to his knees on the grass. At once, the two dogs were upon him, barking wildly and covering his beaming face with slobbery kisses.

'Barney! Sybil!' a voice called from an upstairs window. 'Quiet!' The dogs immediately sat back on their haunches.

'Good afternoon, Father,' Bella called, shielding her eyes against the glare of the late afternoon sun bouncing off the windowpane, as Arthur got slowly to his feet, brushing ineffectually at the grass stains on his trouser knees. 'How is your headache?'

'Terrible,' Samuel Roberts retorted, rubbing his forehead as if to emphasize the point. 'And those blasted dogs don't help. Is it too much to ask for a man to have a few hours peace and quiet?'

'Of course not, Father,' Bella said, shooting Arthur a quick glance to make sure he wasn't about to set the dogs off again, but he'd been distracted by a fat bumble bee buzzing lazily around a gladioli bush. He crouched low, his gaze fixed on the insect as it flitted amongst the flowers. 'We're sorry.'

Her father grunted and slammed the window shut. Bella sighed. Her father was a difficult man. He'd suffered from shellshock during the war and, according to her mother, he hadn't been the same since. Most of the time, her father was a kind, mild-mannered man who would give the shirt off his back to someone in need, but when the melancholy took him, he became morose and angry. Then it was impossible to talk to him at all.

Bella watched her brother, his sweet innocent face transfixed on the bee, feeling the familiar twinge of sadness. Though he tried hard to hide it, and Bella was certain her father would die before he'd admit it, she knew he was disappointed in his son. Bella could see it whenever she excelled at anything – sailing, swimming, shooting, though only at targets. She would never dream of upsetting Arthur by shooting a living creature. While they were living in the Western Cape, her uncle had taught her to fly his twin-engine plane, much to her mother's horror. She'd taken her first solo flight at just fourteen, and had loved the solitariness of it, loved knowing it was just her and her machine. Looking down through the cockpit window, she'd waved at her anxious mother standing beside her car. Her father had waved back, proud of his daughter but, once she'd landed, and Arthur was hugging her and begging her to take him with her next time, she'd seen the look on her father's face. He was clearly proud of his daughter, but was thinking it should be his son taking to the skies.

'Let's get inside,' she said to Arthur now. 'You need to wash up before supper. And be quiet. Father's head is bad today.'

Obediently, Arthur trotted along beside her as they followed the garden path to the back door, the dogs following behind, tails wagging.

'I thought that must be the two of you, when I heard the dogs,' Ida Wilson said, dusting her rolling pin with flour as she prepared to roll out the pastry for the chicken pie. 'Have you had a nice afternoon?'

'A very worthwhile afternoon, Mrs Wilson,' Bella said, setting her basket on the table and motioning to Arthur to do the same. Barney and Sybil flopped on the cool flagstones, panting, noses quivering as they sniffed the air and salivating as the aroma of roasted chicken wafted from the oven.

'Is that Miss Liddy in the oven?' Arthur asked, pouting sadly as he slumped onto a stool. 'I don't want to eat Miss Liddy.'

'No, sweetheart,' Ida said, throwing Bella a wink. 'Miss

Liddy has gone to chicken heaven.' She paused in her rolling. 'Do you remember when your puppy got poorly, and the gamekeeper shot him?' Arthur nodded sadly. He'd cried for weeks over that poor dog, Bella recalled. 'Well, Miss Liddy was poorly, too. That's why I wrung her neck. To put her out of her misery, see?' Ida went back to her rolling, the lies flowing easily from her lips. 'We're eating a different chicken tonight. Not one of ours, all right?'

Arthur took a moment to consider. 'I suppose,' he said doubtfully. 'I wish nothing had to die. I wish we could eat grass like cows.'

'You'd soon get bored eating grass every day and don't pretend you don't love my chicken and leek pie.' The house-keeper grinned, her floury hands moving back and forth as she rolled the pastry. 'Bella, be a love and rinse those black-berries for me, please. Arthur, run over to the orchard and pick me a couple of nice apples. I've enough pastry left over to make a lovely blackberry and apple pie.' Arthur nodded and headed for the door. 'Take the dogs with you,' Mrs Wilson called after him.

'You looking forward to starting at the secretarial college next week?' she asked Bella, who was standing at the sink rinsing the blackberries.

'Not really.' Bella pulled a face. After spending the past five years in the African bush where she'd experienced a freedom seldom enjoyed by middle-class English girls, she did not relish the thought of being confined to a stuffy room learning to type and take dictation. 'But Father is insisting

7

I do it.' She turned off the tap and drained the fruit, patting the plump berries with a clean tea towel. 'I think he's hoping I'll find a good job and end up marrying the boss,' she grinned, placing the bowl on the table. Ida returned her smile.

'I should think that's very likely. A pretty girl like you will not be sitting on the shelf for too long.'

'Ah, Bella, you're back.' Alice Roberts swanned into the room; her navy calf-length dress hugged her slender figure. A few weeks past her forty-first birthday, Alice was an attractive woman. She'd recently had her long, dark-chestnut-brown hair cut and styled in keeping with the latest fashion, emphasizing her swanlike neck. 'Where's Arthur?' Her hazel eyes scanned the room.

'I sent him to pick a couple of apples, Missus,' Ida said.

Alice nodded. 'Apple and blackberry pie, Mrs Wilson,' she smiled. 'I shall look forward to that.'

'Will Father be joining us for supper, Mother?' asked Bella.

Her mother sighed. 'I don't know, dear. It depends on his head. He's suffering quite badly today. Do try to keep Arthur quiet when he gets back. Your father finds his exuberance a little wearying when he's having one of his episodes.' Alice crossed to the open doorway and gazed over the garden. The roses were coming to an end, their petals littering the lawn, the edges brown and curling. 'Sometimes I wish we'd never come back,' she said, almost to herself. 'Your father seemed so much better out there.'

She turned back to her daughter, looking pained. 'It's like his demons were waiting for him the moment we set foot back on English soil.'

'You know he can't help it, Mother,' said Bella. 'We just have to be grateful for the times when he can be himself.'

'Of course. You're absolutely right, Bella,' Alice said, with a tired smile. 'I shall let you know whether the reverend will be joining us for supper, Mrs Wilson. If not, I shall take him up a tray.'

'Very good, Missus,' replied Ida good-naturedly. In the two months since the reverend and his family had returned from their five-year mission trip, she'd grown used to Mr Roberts' erratic mood swings and bouts of melancholy. She felt sorry for his wife and the children, especially young Arthur. He was a delightful lad, despite his limitations, yet he seemed to bear the brunt of his father's temper. She could understand the boy was perhaps not quite what the reverend had hoped for in a son, but he was kind and helpful and he was reasonably well educated, which she gathered was down to the Missus's patience and sheer determination.

'Are you all right, Mother?' Bella followed Alice out of the kitchen. 'You look tired.'

'I'm fine, darling,' her mother replied, leading the way into the well-appointed parlour. 'I think I'm finding it difficult adjusting to being back in England, too.'

'It is different,' Bella agreed. She'd been a girl of eleven when her family set sail from Southampton. She'd matured into a young woman on the plains of the Western Cape, with the warm mountain winds in her hair and the sun hot on her skin.

Bella sank into one of the armchairs facing the empty fireplace. The gold-plated carriage clock ticked rhythmically on the mantlepiece.

'I'm really proud of the way you and Arthur have handled the recent changes in your life,' her mother said, crossing to the window and gazing out into the lane. A cart creaked past, bound for Botley railway station with its cargo of late-in-the-season strawberries, destined for the jam factories in Bermondsey.

'You had to give up so much and I know you miss your cousins, and your pony,' Alice said, her back to her daughter. 'And now, like the changing colours of the leaves, your life is changing again.' She turned to face Bella. 'You shall be off to secretarial college next week and Arthur will be starting his new job with Farmer Monk.'

Bella pulled a face. 'I think I'd rather work for Farmer Monk than sit in a stuffy office at the beck and call of some pompous manager,' she said, making her mother smile.

'I was the same when I was young,' her mother said, coming to perch on the arm of Bella's chair. She stroked her daughter's dark hair. 'I was working as a governess for two young girls, and I hated it, but when they moved away that's when Great-Grandpa Turner offered me the job working for your father.'

'So, you ended up marrying your boss,' Bella grinned.

'I suppose I did,' her mother laughed. Her smile faded and

she turned serious. 'I know you're not keen on secretarial work, darling, but your father is right, there aren't many choices available to you. It's either that or being a governess, or shop work.'

'I suppose I shall have to endure it,' Bella said, with a rueful grin.

'Oh, Lordy, young master Arthur!' they heard Ida exclaim from the kitchen. 'I asked for a couple of apples, not an entire orchard's worth.'

Exchanging amused glances, Bella and her mother hurried to the kitchen where Arthur stood beaming in the doorway, clutching an armful of apples, the dogs milling at his feet.

'Oh, Arthur,' Alice said, smiling indulgently as Arthur took a step forward. He tripped over one of the dogs and lost his balance. Careering into the table, he let go of the apples, the fruit rolling every which way across the dark slate floor.

CHAPTER TWO

The next morning dawned cool and overcast. Bella stood at her bedroom window watching a lone buzzard circling in the monochrome sky. She could hear Mrs Wilson in the kitchen below, busy with her breakfast preparations. Arthur, always an early riser, would no doubt already be downstairs eagerly awaiting his porridge and eggs.

She tugged her gown tighter across her chest, shivering in the cool air. The church bells chimed seven o'clock. In a week's time she would have to be at the bus stop by now, for her college classes started promptly at half past eight. Oh, well, she thought, turning from the window and opening her wardrobe. She would just have to make the best of it. Hopefully she would meet some girls of a similar age and make friends. The girls she'd been friendly with at school were working, either in the factories or as domestic servants. For the past two months, Bella and Arthur had only had each other for company.

Hearing her parents' bedroom door open and shut, and her mother's soft tread on the landing, Bella selected her clothes for the day – a pair of cream, cotton trousers and a blue and cream blouse, over which she tugged a navy-blue woollen jumper.

'Good morning, Mother,' she said, bounding down the stairs.

'Good morning, dear,' replied Alice, flicking through the morning's post Mrs Wilson had placed on the side table. She turned to look at her daughter. 'Oh, Bella, you know your father doesn't approve of you wearing trousers. He thinks they're so unbecoming of a young lady.'

'I wore them all the time back in the Cape,' Bella said, tying her long hair in a thick ponytail.

'Things are different out there,' her mother reminded her, leading the way into the kitchen. 'The people of Strawbridge are very set in their ways. They'll expect a vicar's daughter to uphold certain standards.'

'How is Father today?' Bella asked, sniffing the air appreciatively.

'A little better,' Alice replied. 'Good morning, Mrs Wilson,' she said to the housekeeper who was sliding two fried eggs onto Arthur's plate. 'Good morning, Arthur.' She leaned down to kiss her son's soft, downy cheek. 'Elbows off the table, please dear.'

'What do you want to do today?' Bella asked her brother as she took her place at the scrubbed pine table, thanking Ida as the housekeeper set a bowl of steaming porridge in front of her.

'Just a slice of toast for me, please Mrs Wilson,' Alice said, taking the lid off the teapot and peering inside. 'The reverend is still feeling a bit under the weather, so I'll take him up a tray.'

'Very good, Mrs Roberts,' Ida nodded. 'That tea's been made a while,' she said. 'It'll be stewed by now. I'll make a fresh pot.'

'So, what do you fancy doing today?' Bella repeated, as Arthur stared at the wall opposite him, his brows knitted together across the bridge of his nose, clearly deep in thought.

'Umm, I think I'd like to go fishing with Great-Grandpa,' he said, turning his attention back to his plate of fried eggs.

'Has he said he'll take you today?' Bella asked, reaching for the sugar bowl. Arthur nodded.

'He said Tuesday,' he replied through a mouthful of egg. 'Today is Tuesday, isn't it, Mother?' He turned to Alice for confirmation.

'Please don't speak with your mouth full, Arthur, and yes, today is Tuesday. Great-Grandpa is calling for you at nine o'clock.'

'I'll be ready,' Arthur beamed.

'May I join you?' asked Bella, smiling at him across the table. Arthur shook his head solemnly.

'Men only,' he said.

'Oh.' Bella sat back in her seat, feeling somewhat deflated. It was very rare for Arthur to go on an outing without her. 'I see.'

'I have some letters for posting, Bella,' said Alice, arranging her pretty rose-patterned cups and saucers on the breakfast tray. 'I feel I should spend the morning with your father so it would be a great help if you'd run to the post office for me.' She picked up a pot of Mrs Wilson's dark-orange marmalade and put it on the tray. 'And perhaps you might also go to the farm for some butter and eggs. Ah, thank you, Mrs Wilson,' she said, as Ida handed her the freshly made pot of tea. 'I shall take this up to the reverend. He should be awake by now.'

Bella and Arthur chatted amiably with Ida while they finished their breakfast. Bella offered to help with the clearing up, but the housekeeper shooed her out.

'I work better on my own,' Ida said, gathering up the dirty plates and bowls. 'If you want to make yourself useful, you can call in at the store on your way to the post office and pick me up a tin of Brasso. That front door knocker is well overdue a good polish.'

Bella waited until Arthur had left for his fishing trip before leaving on her errands. The clouds had thinned, and hazy sunlight shone through the veil of grey as she walked briskly down the lane, the lively chatter of the strawberry pickers drifting over the hedgerows. She moved onto the narrow verge as a heavily laden cart rumbled past her. The driver, a fair-haired lad of about fourteen, raised his hat at her in thanks.

Several passers-by nodded and said hello. Strawbridge was a small place and everyone remembered the vicar's family who had gone off to Africa.

'How's your father, dear?' a middle-aged woman asked, tucking her basket on her arm.

'He's not so good today,' Bella replied.

'Ah, it's a shame, isn't it?' the woman said. 'He was such a nice man, before the war.'

Bella smiled tightly. Bidding the woman farewell, she hurried into the post office where she posted her mother's letters before popping into the store for the Brasso and heading to the farm.

'Hello, Bella,' Nellie Monk said, striding across the yard in her men's overalls, chickens squawking and flapping their wings as they scuttled out of her way. 'You here to collect your order?'

'Yes please, Nellie,' replied Bella, leaning against the five-bar gate. Cows grazed in the field opposite, and, to her left, a dark bay mare nibbled gently on a bale of hay, her tail swishing at the flies swarming around her hindquarters.

'Here you go,' said Nellie, emerging from the stone farmhouse with a dish of butter and a dozen eggs. 'Sorry I couldn't deliver but with Dad laid up with lumbago and Mum off visiting her sister, me and the lads have been run off our feet.' She handed Bella the butter and eggs and, resting one foot on the lower rung of the gate said, 'Your brother's starting here next week, isn't he? He'll be doing the deliveries for us, so we'll be back to some semblance of normality.' She grinned. 'He's a good lad, your Arthur.'

'Yes, he is,' Bella grinned back. She handed over the money and set off back up the lane towards the village. The air smelled of freshly mown hay and resounded with the sound of birdsong. She'd barely gone a few yards up the lane when she heard horse's hooves coming along behind her. Without glancing around, she moved to the side to allow the horse and cart to pass.

'Whoa,' a voice cried as the cart drew level with her. 'Bella?'

She looked up, her friendly smile turning to annoyance as she found herself looking up into the face of Will Mullens, the boy who'd angered her so the day before. She looked away, feeling a flash of satisfaction that he was sporting a rather impressive pair of black eyes.

'Hey, it's me, Will.' He engaged the brake and jumped down off the cart. 'Look, I'm sorry about yesterday,' he said, hurrying to keep pace with her. 'I'm not surprised you thumped me. I behaved like a complete boor.'

Bella stopped walking. 'You insulted my brother,' she said coldly, regarding him with disdain.

'I know,' said Will, dropping his gaze. 'And I'm thoroughly ashamed of myself.'

Bella snorted. With a toss of her head, she carried on walking.

'Look, will you forgive me?' Will asked, keeping pace beside her. 'Can we start again? You've given me two shiners,' he grinned, pointing to his face. 'I'm a laughing stock round the village. Getting trounced by a girl, I'll never live it down.' He was in front of Bella now, walking backwards, his dark hair flopping in his eyes. 'Come on,' he pleaded.

'What do you say? Will you give me a chance to make it up to you, and ahhh . . .' He stumbled over a rut in the lane and went sprawling in the dust. Bella stood over him, grinning.

'Every time I'm around you, I end up flat on my back,' Will said, with a rueful grin. Reluctantly, Bella extended her hand and helped him to his feet.

'Thanks. Does this mean you've forgiven me?' He looked at her hopefully as his horse cropped the dusty grass along the verge.

'It depends,' replied Bella.

'On what?'

'On whether my brother is prepared to forgive you.'

'Would you ask him for me? Tell him I'm really sorry and I didn't mean it?'

Bella shrugged. 'No need,' she said reluctantly. 'I know what Arthur would say. He's the most forgiving person you'll ever meet.'

There was silence and then, 'So does that mean you will forgive me, too?'

'I suppose so,' replied Bella. 'As long as you never refer to Arthur as an idiot again.'

'I won't. I promise. Where are you headed?' Will asked as Bella turned to walk away.

'Just back to the village.'

'Would you like to ride with me?'

Bella hesitated. It was a tempting offer. Her purchases weren't heavy, but she still had a good half-a-mile walk ahead of her and it looked as though it was going to rain.

'All right, then,' she said, rather ungraciously.

Will helped her up onto the seat and clambered up beside her. He spoke softly to the horse, and it plodded onwards, the cart rattling noisily behind them.

'My grandma says you and I knew each other as children,' Will said, turning to Bella. 'My parents left the village when I was young, so I don't remember much. I was about twelve the first time we came back to visit Grandma. You must have gone away by then? Grandma said you and your family went abroad?'

Bella nodded. 'My parents were missionaries in the Western Cape. We've only been back two months.' She tugged her coat collar up around her chin. 'I'm still getting used to the change of climate.' She gazed out across the shorn fields. A man was standing on a cart, loading hay from a tall haystack into the back of his cart.

'Who is your grandma?' Bella asked.

'Hannah Hopwood?' Will raised an eyebrow, wincing slightly as the swollen, purple skin around his eye was pulled taut. 'Do you remember her?'

Bella nodded. 'My mother is quite fond of her, though she hasn't had the chance to visit since we've been back.'

'I'm afraid she's not very well,' Will said, his tone turning sombre. 'That's why I'm here. My mother isn't well herself now, so she sent me to look after Grandma.'

'I'm sorry to hear that,' Bella said, with genuine sympathy. 'I do hope she improves soon.'

'Thank you. I hope so, too.'

They were nearing the edge of the village. Bella could see the grey wall of the church through the trees. The vicarage was right next door.

'Thank you for the ride,' Bella said, as Will brought the horse and cart to a halt outside the vicarage door.

'It was my pleasure,' replied Will. He was about to help her down, but Bella jumped out of the cart before he could rise from his seat. She gave him a little wave.

'Bye.'

'What are you doing later?' Will blurted as she turned away. 'This afternoon?'

Bella thought. It was unlikely Arthur and their great-grandfather would return from their fishing trip before teatime and she envisioned the day stretching endlessly before her, empty and boring.

'Why?' she asked boldly. 'What did you have in mind?'

'Grandma usually naps in the afternoon,' he said. 'There's a little pond not far from here. It's a pleasant walk, if you fancy it?' His voice trailed away, as if realizing that a girl as exotic and exciting as Bella would never entertain the idea of spending an afternoon going walking with the likes of him.

'All right,' replied Bella, surprising him. 'Why not?' She looked up at him, feeling the first drop of rain on her forehead.

Will grinned. 'Shall I call for you about half past two?'

Bella nodded. 'I'll see you then.'

'Who was that young man?' her mother asked, looking up from the hydrangeas she was arranging in a vase on a small side table, as Bella let herself into the vicarage. 'Poor lad looks like he's been in the wars.'

'Will Mullens,' Bella replied, her purchases clutched to her chest as she pushed the door with her foot. 'He's Mrs Hopwood's grandson,' she explained, not noticing the way Alice flinched at the mention of Will's name. 'Arthur and I met him yesterday.'

She didn't relate the incident in which Will had insulted her brother, knowing it would upset her mother. And she certainly wasn't going to tell her how he got his black eyes.

'He's invited me to go walking with him this afternoon,' Bella said. 'I thought I would as I haven't any other plans, or is there something you would like me to do? Is there something wrong, Mother?' she added, puzzled by her mother's odd expression.

'No, not at all,' Alice said, with a shake of her head. 'You go off and enjoy yourself. Your father said he might venture down to sit in the library this afternoon, so I shall be occupied with him.'

'All right, if you're sure. Thank you,' said Bella, with a frown.

CHAPTER THREE

She was still pondering her mother's strange reaction when Will rang the vicarage bell. Casting a quick glance at her reflection in the hall mirror, Bella hurried to open it.

'You're very punctual,' she said, smiling at the tall, dark-haired boy standing on the step. 'My father will be impressed,' she said, stepping out into the cool autumn afternoon.

'How is your father?' enquired Will politely, as Bella shut the door and started down the path. 'Grandma told me he hasn't been well?'

'He suffers from his nerves,' Bella replied. 'A lot of the time he's fine but he has bouts of melancholy which make him ... difficult,' she said, hoping she didn't sound disloyal. She loved her father, but the continual walking on egg-shells around him in case he was having a bad day was very wearying.

'I'm sorry to hear that,' Will said, shoving his hands in

his trouser pockets as they strolled down the lane. Some of the strawberry pickers were singing. A crow flew overhead, cawing loudly, its shadow flitting across the ground.

'So, do you go to the pond often?' he asked.

'Not since I was a child,' Bella replied. 'I was eleven when we moved away.'

'Yes, Grandma said. What was it like? Africa?' he asked.

'Hot, sunny, magical,' Bella replied. 'A land of vast, open skies and empty plains.' As they walked, she regaled Will with tales of growing up on a lonely mission station deep in the heart of the Western Cape.

'You can fly a plane?' Will stared at her in disbelief.

'Yes, my uncle taught me. He has his own plane. All my cousins can fly.'

'Wow!' Will said, impressed. 'I've never met anyone who can fly, never mind a girl.'

'My uncle said I was a natural.' Bella's trousers brushed the long grass as they followed a narrow track through the under-growth towards the pond. 'I loved it. It's the most amazing feeling in the world, just you and your machine, high above the world.' She sighed. 'I don't suppose it's something I shall experience again,' she said wistfully.

'I must say, I'm envious.' Will pushed aside a willow frond and the pond lay before them, shimmering in the September sunshine. A moorhen drifted across the smooth surface, its little head bobbing comically. A grey heron stood motionless amongst the bullrushes. The surrounding trees and bushes resonated with birdsong, the old swing creaking softly in the gentle breeze. Bella went towards it and perched gingerly on the weathered wooden seat. The swing had been there since way before she was born, and she wasn't sure how safe the ropes were.

'They look sturdy enough,' Will said, giving the rope a tug. 'There's no fraying I can see.'

'I'll trust you,' Bella said, with a smile. 'But if I end up in the pond, you'll feel my wrath.'

'Don't I know it,' Will grinned. He leaned against a tree trunk, hands in his pocket. Despite the bruised eyes, he was rather good looking, Bella mused, studying him surreptitiously under her lashes as she slowly swung back and forth over the sun–dappled water.

'I just want to apologize again for the way I behaved yesterday,' Will said. 'It was inexcusable. I never speak to people like that. I don't know what came over me. I'm sorry.'

Bella nodded. She closed her eyes, throwing her head back so that the tips of her long hair brushed the long grass at the edge of the pond.

'If you just get to know Arthur, you'll understand what an incredible person he is,' she said, savouring the feel of the sun on her face. She sat up suddenly, the swing shuddering beneath her as she brought it to an abrupt halt. 'If you ever say anything hurtful to him again, I will never speak to you again,' she said.

'I won't,' replied Will. 'It's beautiful here, isn't it?' he said, desperate to change the subject. He felt sick each time he recalled his words of the previous day. The truth was, he'd been so enthralled by Bella's bewitching beauty that he'd hit out at Arthur to deflect from his own feelings of inadequacy. He was heartily ashamed of himself. His grandmother had given him what-for, too. He'd had no choice but to admit the sorry incident to explain his black eyes.

'Isabella always was a little firecracker,' his grandmother had chuckled. 'It doesn't seem as though she's calmed down much in the years she's been away.'

'Are you free tomorrow afternoon?' Will asked, as they reluctantly made their way back. 'Grandma naps around the same time every day. We could come here again, if you like?'

'I'll bring Arthur,' Bella replied, raising a questioning eyebrow.

'Perfect. I'd like to get to know him properly.'

Bella regarded him sceptically. She hoped he meant what he said, because she was starting to quite like Will Mullens.

'That's a crested newt,' Arthur told Will, pointing at the small amphibian squirming in his net. He was crouched on the bank of the pond, his long fringe flopping in his eyes. He brushed it away with a flick of his damp hand. 'Ah, look,' he said in a loud stage whisper, pointing to an overhanging branch. 'A kingfisher.'

Shielding her eyes from the low sun, Bella followed his finger. Sure enough, a green and copper-coloured bird perched on the end of the swaying branch.

'It's a common kingfisher,' Arthur was explaining to Will.

'It's the only species of kingfisher that breeds in the British Isles.'

'You certainly know your stuff,' said Will, clearly impressed.

'Father has books on British wildlife in his library,' Arthur said, in his slow, melodious voice. 'I like to read them.'

It was Sunday afternoon. It was the fifth afternoon Bella, Arthur and Will had spent at the pond. And it would be their last. Tomorrow Arthur started his new job at Monk's farm and Bella would be spending the day preparing to start secretarial college on Tuesday.

'We can still see each other,' Will said, when Bella voiced this. He rubbed the bridge of his nose. His bruises had faded to a dull yellow. 'You'll be home in the evenings, and weekends.'

'The nights are drawing in,' Bella reminded him. 'It'll be too cold to meet out of doors soon.'

'Then we can go somewhere,' Will said. 'What about the cinema? We could go next Saturday afternoon on the bus.'

'I shall ask my father this evening,' Bella promised.

'He's better, then?'

'His headache has improved and he's hoping to join us at teatime. He was disappointed he wasn't well enough to take the service this morning. I thought the young curate did a decent enough job.'

'Do you think he will give his permission?' asked Will.

'I can see no reason why he would object,' Bella replied, flexing her bare feet.

'Do you fancy the cinema next Saturday, Arthur?' Will called, leaning back on his elbows, a stalk of grass protruding from between his lips.

'He'll be working,' Bella replied, when it became clear Arthur hadn't heard. 'He only gets Sundays off.' She watched as her brother carefully slid the newt back into the water.

'That's a shame,' Will said, secretly thinking it would be nice to spend time with Bella alone. While he had nothing but respect and admiration for her twin brother, he was hoping some time alone might move his and Bella's friend-ship up a notch. He was hoping she would consent to him courting her.

A gust of wind ruffled the water and Bella shivered. The sun was slipping behind the trees, casting long shadows across the grass.

'We'd better be getting back,' said Bella, reaching for her shoes and stockings. 'Arthur, it's time to go.'

'I shall miss our afternoons here,' Will said, as they gath-ered up their things and made ready to leave. 'But I shall look forward to next weekend.'

'Me, too,' replied Bella, meaning it.

Will walked with them as far as the vicarage.

'Until Saturday, then,' he said, as Bella pushed open the gate.

'Ah, there you are,' Alice said, bustling into the hall. 'Father is in the drawing room. Tea will be ready in about five minutes. You've both just got enough time to wash up. Did you have a nice time?'

'Yes, thank you, Mother.' Bella ushered Arthur towards the scullery where they both made themselves presentable.

'Hello, Father,' Bella said, leading the way into the drawing room. Her father sat at the table, his chair closest to the fire. He looked tired and gaunt, and Bella's heart went out to him. 'How are you feeling?' She slid her hands around his shoulders and kissed his cheek.

'Much better, my dear,' the Reverend Samuel Roberts said, smiling at his daughter. 'Have you both had a good afternoon?'

'Yes, thank you, Father,' replied Bella, taking her place beside him.

'I caught a crested newt, Father,' Arthur said, pulling out a chair. 'But I let it go again.'

'Good lad,' Samuel nodded, smiling indulgently at his son.

'Please start,' Alice said, coming into the room with the teapot. They always had a light tea on a Sunday afternoon. Mrs Wilson would leave after cooking the Sunday roast to visit her sister in Hedge End, and return first thing in the morning to prepare the family's breakfast.

Bella helped herself to a couple of cold roast beef sandwiches, idly listening to her parents' conversation. Arthur ate hungrily, his lapses in table manners earning him the occasional mild reprimand from his father.

It was so pleasant, all of them at the table again, laughing and talking, that it wasn't until her mother was handing round slices of Victoria sponge that Bella thought to mention her impending trip to the cinema.

'Mrs Hopwood's grandson, Will, has invited me to the cinema on Saturday, Father. May I go.'

Her father froze mid-chew. 'Who did you say?' he said, his voice dangerously low.

'Will Mullens,' repeated Bella, licking strawberry jam off her fingers. 'He's Mrs Hopwood's—'

'I know who he is!' Samuel thundered. Arthur's eyes widened and his bottom lip quivered. Bella reached over and squeezed his hand. Raised voices always upset him, he was such a sensitive soul.

'I didn't realize they were back?' Samuel muttered.

'Hannah's grandson has come back to look after her,' Alice said, evenly. 'Leah is unwell, herself and so couldn't come.' Samuel grunted.

'You're to stay away from that boy, Bella,' Samuel said, wiping his lips on his napkin.

'But why?'

'Because I said so,' her father said sternly.

'Darling,' Alice laid a hand on Samuel's arm. 'A trip to the cinema can't do any harm, surely?'

'Please don't contradict me in front of the children, Alice,' Samuel said. Alice sighed and removed her hand.

'You need to give me a proper reason, Father,' Bella said. 'You don't even know Will.'

'I know his family and they're not the sort of people I want my daughter associating with.'

'That's not fair!' exclaimed Bella.

'Isabella,' her father said, his tone warning her he would

brook no argument. 'You got your own way far too much when we were at Roaring Sands. The fault lies entirely with your mother and I, of course. We were too lenient with you, so, regretfully, it is time your unruliness was nipped in the bud. Instead of secretarial college, I should have enrolled you in finishing school. Your manners could do with some refinement.'

'Mother, please?' implored Bella.

'You must do as your father says, Bella,' replied Alice, her eyes relaying a plea to her daughter not to provoke her father any further.

'I thought you wanted me to make friends,' Bella said, throwing down her napkin.

'Not with the likes of him,' her father said mildly, helping himself to a second slice of cake.

Bella picked at her Victoria sponge, fuming silently as her parents discussed her mother's most recent letter from Bella's Great-Aunt Eleanor. Her father's reaction had surprised her. In Roaring Sands, a small hamlet surrounded by tobacco-growing farms, she and Arthur had made friends with many of the worker's children, most of them barely living above the breadline, so she found her father's reaction to her friendship with Will perplexing, to say the least.

CHAPTER FOUR

She was still smarting over her father's refusal to allow her to go to the cinema with Will the following day. She was cleaning her bicycle in readiness for cycling to secretarial college the following afternoon. Barney and Sybil lay nearby, noses resting on their paws, brown eyes sorrowful, missing their beloved young master.

Arthur had left for his new job just before six and wouldn't return until after six that evening. Bella found the house strangely empty without him, so it would be a relief to be away from home during the week, she mused as she wrung out the cloth to wipe down the muddy splattered spokes.

'Bella, may I speak to you, please?' Samuel stood in the doorway, wearing his black trousers and a white shirt, open at the collar, his clerical collar in his hands.

'Of course, Father.' Bella stood up, drying her wet hands on an old towel.

'In my study, please.' Bella followed her father through the vicarage to his study, the dogs padding at her heels. She felt a twinge of unease. If her father had wanted to tell her he'd changed his mind about her going to the cinema, surely he would have said so there and then?

'Take a seat,' Samuel said, indicating one of the two chairs facing his large walnut-veneered desk. Bella did so, as Samuel rounded his wide desk, and settled himself in his chair. Pushing aside a large Bible, open at Acts, he leaned back in his seat. Steepling his fingers, he regarded his daughter with a pained expression.

'Is something wrong, Father?' asked Bella, trying to quell the knot of anxiety building up inside her.

'As you know, your mother received a letter from Aunt Eleanor. It seems your mother's cousin, Benjy, is having difficulty employing a suitable governess for his daughters, Holly and Emily. This morning, I sent Aunt Eleanor a telegram offering your services.'

'What?' Bella sat bolt upright. 'I don't want to be a governess.'

'I was under the impression you loathed the idea of secretarial work, too,' her father said, with a wry chuckle. 'Half an hour ago, I received a telegram back from your great-aunt, saying Benjy is delighted and that you may start at your earliest convenience. You're leaving tomorrow morning on the nine-fifteen train.'

'Father!' Bella exclaimed in horror. 'I won't! I can't. I'm due to start college tomorrow.'

'You can and you will,' Samuel said, leaning forward, his hands splayed on the desk. The gold signet ring on his little finger winked in the pale sunlight streaming in through the window. 'I shall telephone the dean of the college this afternoon and explain. Now,' he said, pushing back his chair and getting to his feet. 'I must send a telegram to your aunt to advise her of your time of arrival so someone can meet you at the station. You will have to change at Clapham Junction.' Bella looked up him sullenly. He stared back stonily. 'You have some packing to do, don't you?'

Close to tears, Bella leapt from her chair and ran from the room, almost colliding with Mrs Wilson who was polishing the hall table.

'Lordy, girl!' she exclaimed, grabbing hold of a china shepherdess teetering on the edge of the table before it smashed to the floor. 'What on earth is the matter?'

'Where's my mother?' cried Bella, her cheeks flushed.

'She's in the drawing room, love, but . . .' Not waiting to hear any more, Bella turned and fled, the dogs racing after her, their claws skittering on the linoleum.

'Mother!' Bella burst into the drawing room. Her mother was sitting on the sofa, reading.

'Darling!' she cried, dropping her book and jumping to her feet. 'What is it?'

'Father is sending me away,' Bella blurted tearfully. 'Did you know?'

'What do you mean, sending you away?' Alice frowned. 'Come here, silly girl.' She smiled, as Bella fell into her embrace. 'I'm sure you're getting upset about nothing. Your father would never send you away. Whatever gave you such an idea?' She stroked Bella's long, dark hair.

'I'm to be governess for Holly and Emily,' Bella said, drawing back. Her mother studied her tear-stained face, her frown deepening.

'Pardon? Bella, what are you talking about?'

'I'm to leave tomorrow. Father is going to the post office to send a telegram to Great-Aunt Eleanor.'

'There must be some mistake,' her mother said, chewing her bottom lip in consternation. 'Your father would never make such a decision without consulting me. I shall speak to him. Wait here.'

Bella sank onto the lemon-yellow sofa, feeling hollow. She didn't want to leave her family, especially Arthur. She'd been dreading secretarial college but at least she'd be here to see Arthur in the evenings and on Sundays. How long did her father intend her to stay in London? She wracked her memory, trying to work out how old Emily and Holly would be. Six or seven, perhaps? The last time she'd seen them they'd been babies. She was sixteen. It would be five years before she could make her own decisions. She'd be an old maid by then, stuck in the schoolroom teaching the three Rs to her young cousins. She sighed angrily.

Getting to her feet she crossed to the door, aware of raised voices resonating from behind the closed study door. The hall was empty, the housekeeper having tactfully retreated to the kitchen. Leaning against the doorframe, Bella held her breath, straining her ears, but though she could hear voices, she couldn't make out any words. Sybil nudged the back of her knee, and she reached down to fondle the spaniel's long, silky ears. Barney lay against the study door, whining softly. Suddenly the door flew open, sending Barney scurrying to the kitchen and crashing against the wall, causing a painting of Salisbury Cathedral to slip sideways on its hook. Bella shrank back as her father came storming out, his face puce with anger.

'I will not have you questioning my authority, Alice,' he shouted, as Bella's mother appeared in the doorway of the study, her face white but for two angry red spots on her pale cheeks. Samuel snatched his hat and coat from the coat rack and, yanking open the door, stalked out of the house. The door banged shut behind him, making Alice flinch.

'I'm sorry, Bella,' Alice said, clearing her throat. 'There's no reasoning with him at the moment.' She crossed the hall, sliding her arm around Bella's shoulders. 'Perhaps once he's calmed down, I might try again.'

Bella shook her head. 'It's all right, Mother,' she said dully. 'He won't change his mind. I must resign myself to the fact I am going to London. It won't be too bad,' she said, attempting a smile. 'I enjoy my great-aunt's company.'

'And she shall be glad of yours, I've no doubt. I gather she's been rather lonely since your great-uncle passed away. She has Holly and Emily, of course,' Alice said, as she led the way upstairs. 'But I think they spend most of their day with the nanny and, as you know, my cousin works away a lot.'

'I shall miss Arthur,' Bella said, sinking onto her bed, as her mother began opening drawers and rifling through her clothes. 'We've never been apart before.'

'You'll be able to come home for visits,' her mother assured her. 'And if you're still there at Christmas, I'm sure Aunt Eleanor would love us to visit. Christmas in London is spectacular.'

They spent the next hour sorting through Bella's clothes, both chatting about inconsequential things, so neither had to dwell on the fact that Bella would be leaving in the morning.

'How will I tell Arthur?' Bella asked, snapping the catches shut on her trunk. She sat back on her heels. 'He'll be so upset.'

'He'll be all right,' her mother said, looking doubtful. 'He's got his job now. That'll keep his mind occupied.'

'But we've barely been away from each other in the past five years,' Bella objected. Her chest felt like it was encased in a lead band.

'That's another thing your father said,' Alice sighed, leaning her hands on the windowsill and staring down at the lane below. 'He feels you and Arthur are too dependent on each other. He feels some time apart will do you both good.'

Bella shook her head, incredulous. How could her father ever understand her and Arthur's bond? They were twins. They were meant to be together. She swallowed, blinking back bitter tears. She was dreading telling Arthur she was going away. She only hoped he could understand.

*

'But why can't I come with you, Bella?' Arthur asked for the umpteenth time, his expression so desolate Bella could barely hold back the tears.

It was evening and they were sitting in the kitchen. Mrs Wilson had banked up the fire and retired to her room, but not before telling Bella that things wouldn't be the same at the vicarage without her. Their mother was in the drawing room, pretending to read while staring unseeingly into the glowing embers. Samuel was closeted in his study.

Supper had been eaten in frosty silence. Even Arthur, sensing something was up, had sat hunched over his plate, head bowed, lip quivering. Only Samuel had cleared his plate, despite the meal being delicious as usual.

'I'm so sorry, Mrs Wilson,' Alice had said, mortified, when Ida came to collect the plates. 'We don't seem to have much of an appetite this evening.'

'Think nothing of it,' Ida had replied briskly, gathering up the plates. She gave Samuel a sideways glance then met Alice's gaze, her brows lifting slightly. Alice gave a wry smile. The housekeeper wasn't a stranger to Samuel's mood swings, but this was odd, even for him, Ida mused, as she carried the plates into the scullery.

'You can't, my love,' Bella said, her voice breaking in the face of her brother's abject misery. 'Farmer Monk needs you on the farm. You can't let him down. He's relying on you to do his deliveries now.'

Arthur nodded. He'd come home glowing from his first

day's work, chattering non-stop in his excitement. Until the strained atmosphere at the supper table burst his bubble.

'Will you write to me?' he asked, his beautiful eyes swimming with tears.

'Every day, I promise.'

A sudden gust of wind rattled the windowpane, causing the dogs to raise their heads. Sybil let out a low growl. Bella reached down and stroked her silky head. From behind the curtains came the sound of rain hitting the glass. It was turning into a miserable night, Bella mused, getting up to heat some milk for her and Arthur. Much like her mood, she thought darkly, going into the pantry.

CHAPTER FIVE

Cousin Benjy was waiting for her on the platform when her train pulled into Richmond station. He was a striking looking man, tall with lambchop sideburns and dark, wavy hair. He was smiling as Bella stepped off the train.

'Bella,' he said, stepping forward, hand outstretched.

'Hello, Benjy,' Bella grinned, putting her gloved hand in his. 'I wasn't sure you'd recognize me. I was a gangly eleven-year-old last time I saw you.'

Benjy's smile broadened. 'You haven't changed that much. Let me take your bag. Have you much baggage?'

'Just the one trunk.'

'I'll have my man collect it later. This way. The car's just outside.' With his hand resting gently on the small of her back, he led her through the milling crowd to the exit.

The sky was overcast, and it had obviously been raining. The pavement was wet, and water dripped from the eaves.

The street teemed with cars and horse-drawn traffic, wheels sending a spray of dirty water over passers-by.

Benjy led the way to a large black car parked alongside the kerb and opened the door. Bella slid into the passenger's seat, inhaling the smell of warm leather. Benjy stowed her bag in the boot and got in beside her. Soon they were weaving their way through the London traffic.

'I'm thrilled you agreed to take up the position of governess to my girls,' Benjy said, turning down a wide, leafy avenue. 'I was at my wits' end. I've interviewed numerous young ladies, but no one was suitable. Mother does her best, of course, but she isn't a natural teacher and she's far too indulgent.'

'Well, they are her grandchildren,' Bella laughed. 'Arthur and I could never do any wrong in my grandma's eyes either.'

'That's as may be,' her cousin replied drily. 'However, they need a firm hand and a decent education.'

'I shall do my best not to disappoint you.'

'I'm sure you will,' Benjy said, giving her a sideways smile. He turned the car into a street lined by tall Georgian townhouses. 'And here we are,' he said, drawing to a halt midway down the road. The black front door flew open, and Great-Aunt Eleanor appeared on the doorstep, her face wreathed in smiles.

'Bella!' Eleanor cried, as Bella got out of the car. 'Welcome to London.'

'Hello, Aunt.' The two women exchanged hugs and kisses, and Eleanor ushered her into the front parlour. 'I'll ring for tea. The girls are in the nursery. I shall have nanny bring them down in a minute. Sit down, please.' She rang a small bell and a uniformed maid appeared in the doorway. 'Maddox, this is my niece, Bella. Would you prepare the tea tray, please?'

'Will the master be staying for tea?' asked Maddox, as Benjy came into the hall carrying Bella's bag.

'Not for me, thank you, Maddox,' Benjy said, with a wave of his hand. 'I must get back to the office.' He set the bag at the foot of the stairs. 'Have this taken to Miss Bella's room, please, and ask Philip to collect Miss Bella's trunk from the station.'

'Yes, sir.' Maddox bobbed a quick curtsy and disappeared.

'I hope you settle in well, Bella,' Benjy said. 'I shall see you this evening at dinner.' He inclined his head towards Eleanor. 'Mother.'

'Oh, it's lovely to see you, Bella.' Eleanor said, once he'd gone. 'You look so well. So tanned, and so grown-up. You're quite the young lady now.' Eleanor seated herself on a chair close to the window which afforded a view of the grand house opposite.

As her aunt talked, bringing her up to date with the latest family news, Bella's gaze wandered round the room. It was tastefully furnished in creams and pale gold, with cream and gold embossed wallpaper on the panelled walls. There were ornaments on the mantlepiece above which hung a large portrait of Bella's great-grandfather. There were other painting on the walls, depicting well-known landscapes.

Maddox returned with the tea, after which Eleanor suggested she take Bella up to see the girls.

'They're very excited to meet you,' Eleanor said, leading the way up the stairs. 'I don't think Emily was quite a year old when you last saw her, was she?' she asked as she led Bella along the broad gallery.

'I remember her being not much more than a baby,' replied Bella, smiling at the sound of carefree laughter drifting down the stairs at the far end of the landing. 'Holly was just walking, I think.'

'There's only fourteen months between them,' Eleanor said, leading the way up another flight of stairs. 'I believe that's what killed their mother. Poor woman. She had barely recovered from the trauma of Holly's birth before she fell with Emily. It was too much for her.' Bella had been ten when her mother's cousin-in-law had passed away in childbirth, but she remembered her mother and father making the trip to London for the funeral.

'Anyway,' Eleanor said, shaking herself. 'Enough of that.' She paused outside a door, her hand on the handle. 'Are you ready to meet your charges?'

'I am,' Bella grinned. Eleanor pushed open the door. The laughter stopped abruptly as two dark-haired, brown-eyed little girls paused in their play to stare at the newcomer.

'Girls, this is your cousin, Bella. She's going to be your new governess. What do you say?'

'Good morning, Miss Bella,' the girls chorused in unison.

'Good morning, Holly, Emily. I am very pleased to meet you.'

'Pleasure to meet you, Miss Bella.' A tall, broad-shouldered woman with short, crimped hair stepped forward. 'I'm Nanny.'

'Nice to meet you.' Bella smiled. The woman had a pleasant face and Bella guessed her to be around fortyish.

'You both look so alike,' Bella said, smiling at the two girls. 'You could be twins.'

'People often mistake them as such,' responded Nanny.

'I'm a twin,' Bella told them. 'My brother and I look similar but not identical.'

She spent a few minutes talking to Holly and Emily as they showed her round the nursery, proudly showing off their dolls' house and other toys while Eleanor and Nanny discussed the week's schedule now the girls would be spending the bulk of their day in the school room.

'I think it's time for your walk, girls,' Eleanor said, clapping her hands.

'May Miss Bella come with us?' Holly asked, jumping up and down.

'Please, Miss Bella,' said Emily, her dark eyes pleading.

'Not today, girls,' their grandmother said, hushing them. 'Bella, I'm sure you'd like to see the school room? Then I shall show you to your room. You'll want to freshen up before luncheon.'

Nanny took the girls downstairs to bundle them into their coats and Eleanor led Bella along the corridor to the schoolroom. It was a fair-sized room, light and airy with two sash windows affording Bella a view of the houses opposite and a pewter sky. A pigeon groomed itself on the windowsill. There were two desks as well as a large table for Bella, a blackboard, and several bookshelves lined with classic novels. A Pear's encyclopaedia and a well-thumbed copy of the *Oxford English Dictionary* lay on Bella's desk. A large map of the world had been tacked onto the wall; the British colonies proudly pink in colour.

'The pins depict all the places Benjy has been on his travels,' Eleanor told Bella, as she showed her round. 'He's off to Cairo in a fortnight so that will be another pin for the girls to add.' She smiled. 'Now, let me show you to your room. Nanny sleeps on this floor, so she can be near the girls should they wake during the night, but I thought after a day in the school room, you'd prefer to be a little further away,' she said, leading the way. Bella followed her down the stairs and along the landing. 'You're just in here,' said her great-aunt, pausing outside a door that stood ajar, pushing it all the way open and standing back to allow Bella to enter.

It was a well-appointed room, elegantly furnished. The heavy furniture was made of dark teak, and the curtains, bedclothes and rugs were in varying shades of lilac and mauve. Bella's trunk sat in the middle of the floor and her small, travel bag had been placed on the bed.

'I hope you'll be comfortable,' Eleanor said from the doorway.

'I'm sure I shall, Aunt,' replied Bella.

Her aunt smiled. 'The bathroom is along the landing. Take your time. Luncheon is at one.'

Left alone in her room, Bella crossed to the window. Looking down at the wind-blown street, she leaned her forehead on the cool glass. Her change of circumstance had been so quick, she'd barely had time to process it. The train journey had passed in a blur, her emotions in turmoil. It had broken her heart to say goodbye to Arthur that morning and she resolved to write to him as soon as she'd unpacked. She'd thought a lot about Will, too. He would think her rude to have left without a word and she wondered what her parents would tell him when he called for her on Saturday, expecting to take her to the cinema. She would write to him, too, and explain. If she addressed the envelope care of Mrs Hopwood, the letter would certainly get to him. Strawbridge was so small, everyone knew each other.

She gave herself a shake. She was here now, and she resolved to make the best of it. Her aunt couldn't have been more accommodating, and her young cousins seemed delightful little girls. She was sure it wouldn't be too much of a hardship and, perhaps, in a few months she'd be able to return home, for a visit at least.

CHAPTER SIX

1939

'I have to tell you now,' the sombre voice of Prime Minister Neville Chamberlain resonated around the drawing room, 'that no such undertaking has been received, and that consequently this country is at war with Germany.'

'Well, that's that, then,' sighed Benjy. 'We're at war.'

Bella and her aunt exchanged worried glances.

'What will it mean for us, Benjy?' Eleanor asked, a slight tremor to her voice.

'I shall be spending more time in the City,' her son replied, sucking hard on his pipe. 'Maddox, Nanny, you may return to your duties.'

The two women nodded solemnly and left the room. Bella could hear them whispering in the hallway, no doubt wondering how this would affect their lives, and livelihood.

Benjy got up and closed the door. 'Bella, you are to return home and I'd be grateful if you took the girls with you and delivered them to my Aunt Lily. Mother, you should go as well. Your sister would be so happy to have you stay in Hedge End. London is going to be a very dangerous place from now on and I'd be happier if I knew you were all safely in the country.'

'Leave my home?' Eleanor said, as though the idea was the most preposterous thing she'd ever heard. 'Certainly not. I shall not allow that Hitler fellow to force me from my home.' She patted Bella's hand. 'Though I do agree Bella and the girls must go. I'm sure your mother is writing to you right now to insist on your return.'

Bella managed a watery smile. She felt a heaviness settle on her shoulders. They were at war. Fear coursed through her veins, and she felt bile rise in her throat. She swallowed it down and tried to concentrate on what her cousin was saying, but it was as though she were listening to him underwater.

There had been talk of war for months as Adolf Hitler's quest for power and territories continued unabated, but Bella, like the rest of the nation, had clung to the thin sliver of hope that he might withdraw his troops from Poland and war would be averted. Like her cousin Benjy had warned on numerous occasions over the past few weeks, there was no reasoning with a man like Hitler. He would only be stopped by force.

'I would prefer it if you would evacuate to the country, Mother,' Benjy was saying, when Bella managed to focus her attention on him. 'I shall have enough on my plate without having the added worry about you. Please think about it, at least. If you do decide to go, I shall close up the house. I've already decided to let Maddox and Nanny go.'

'Where will you live?' Eleanor asked.

'I shall stay in the City. I'll be working all hours so it will suit me. Bella, ask Nanny to have the girls ready to leave first thing tomorrow. I shall send a telegram to your parents advising them to expect you on the eleven o'clock train.'

'So soon?' Eleanor said, rising from her chair. Suddenly a loud siren pierced the air. Bella held her breath as her aunt turned pale and rushed towards the window. Benjy reached out and grabbed her arm.

'It's a drill,' he said, steadily. 'But even so, stay away from the window. If there was a real raid you'd risk being hit by flying glass, or worse.'

'Oh, my Lord!' Maddox burst through the door, her hands over her ears. 'Are the Germans here already?' she screeched, tears streaming down her rosy cheeks.

'Calm down, Maddox,' Benjy said, his voice firm but kind. 'It's only a drill.' She was followed by Nanny, Holly and Emily close behind. Now eleven and ten, the two girls hurried to their grandmother's side, their faces pale.

'Everyone calm down,' Benjy said, giving his daughters an encouraging smile. 'This is a drill,' he repeated. 'Listen, it's stopped.' A short silence was followed by another siren. This time the tone was steady, a marked contrast to the waxing and waning of the previous siren.

'That's the "All Clear",' Benjy said, as everyone heaved

a sigh of relief and the tension eased. 'Now, I must telephone my office. I shall be in my study and I'm not to be disturbed.'

He strode from the room, leaving the women staring at each other. No one seemed to know what to do next.

'Perhaps the girls and I should start packing,' Bella said. Her aunt nodded absently.

'Ma'am?' Nanny said, looking perplexed.

'Holly and Emily will be accompanying Miss Bella and then going to my sister's in Hedge End,' Eleanor said, faintly. 'Benjy believes the villages to be far enough away from Southampton to avoid any serious threat.' She straightened her back, her expression pained as she turned to address her employees.

'My dear Nanny, and Maddox,' she said, a hollow feeling in her chest. 'I'm afraid my son has decided to let you both go. He feels you would be safer away from London.'

'What about you, ma'am?' Maddox asked. 'How will you manage without me to do for you?'

'I shall be sensible and listen to my son's advice. I shall go with the girls to my sister's.'

'Can't Nanny come with us?' asked Emily, her eyes swimming with tears. She'd never known her own mother, who had died when she was born. Nanny had been like a mother to her.

'I'm sorry, sweetheart,' her grandmother said, gently.

The sight of the two girls' distraught expressions brought tears to Bella's eyes.

'Come on, girls,' Nanny said brusquely, her own eyes suspiciously bright. 'Let's do what Miss Bella said and start packing.' She smiled. 'Think of it as a holiday.'

'But you won't be there,' mumbled Holly, dragging her feet as Nanny coaxed her from the room.

'We can write to each other,' Bella heard Nanny reply as she ushered them towards the stairs.

Beside her, her great-aunt sighed. 'The first casualty of this new war,' she said bitterly. 'How many more heartbreaks must we suffer before this is over?'

A telegram arrived from Bella's father early that afternoon, demanding she leave London immediately, having obviously crossed Benjy's telegram advising her parents that she'd be home tomorrow.

She left it on the hall table and wandered out into the garden. There was a hint of autumn in the air. The grass was damp beneath her feet as she made her way over to the bench in a sunny corner beneath a canopy of late-blooming roses, inhaling the perfume of the peach-coloured petals.

It was almost four years to the day since she had arrived in London. In that time, she had been home on visits several times and her family had visited her. Arthur had been a great hit with Holly and Emily. She'd been pleased to hear that he was happy in his job, and that he'd been given much more responsibility by Farmer Monk. He was a man now, broad and fit from long hours of physical work, yet he still retained that boyish innocence. It had been several months since her last visit home and Bella was looking forward to seeing him again, despite the distressing circumstances.

'Ah, here you are, Bella.' Eleanor stepped out of the back door, her cardigan slung around her shoulders. 'It's all a bit much to take in, isn't it?' she said, as Bella shuffled along to make room for her on the bench. 'I know we've been half-expecting it for weeks but now it's a reality . . .' She broke off. 'I worry about our young men, Bella. My sister's boys will have to fight. I remember how awful the last war was. It's inconceivable that we're being asked to go through it all again.'

'We have to stop him, Aunt,' said Bella softly. With the sun on her face, and the sound of insects and birds all around, it seemed unbelievable that they were at war. Everything seemed so normal.

'Maddox has a cousin in Devon she can stay with, but she's decided to join the Women's Land Army. She's got three brothers who will be joining up, so she wants to do her bit. Nanny's devastated, of course. She loves Holly and Emily,' Eleanor said, with a sad shake of her head. 'I hope she finds some purpose in this damned war.'

'I'm not sure what I shall do,' Bella said bleakly. 'I could join the Land Army, I suppose. I'll need to do something.'

'You'll have time to think about that when you get home,' her aunt said. 'Now, are you all packed?'

'Just about.'

'I have asked Maddox and Nanny to join us for supper this evening,' said Eleanor, her eyes sad. 'It will be a wrench leaving here. I have so many happy memories of my life here. I came here as a new bride, my boys were born here.'

'God willing, you'll be able to come back one day.'

'I hope so,' her aunt said. 'Well, I shall go and discuss the supper menu with Maddox. We may as well push the boat out.'

Though everyone tried their best to make the supper a joyful affair, the jollity felt forced. Bella's throat felt too tight to swallow and although Maddox had surpassed herself with the delicious spread, no one could eat very much. They went to bed early, as they had to be up at first light to catch their train.

CHAPTER SEVEN

The station was heaving with evacuees. Children of all ages thronged the platform with their parents, as uniformed women walked up and down calling out names and organizing them into rows.

Bella clung tightly to Holly's hand, her gas box bumping uncomfortably against her hip. Her aunt followed behind with Emily. Both girls were red-eyed and blotchy-faced after bidding their beloved nanny and father an emotional farewell. They each carried a small suitcase; the bulk of their belongings would follow later.

Maddox had left in a taxi straight after breakfast. Benjy was going to drop Nanny off at her relations on his way into the city. He had already taken a room in a boarding house not far from the War Office. As the taxi had driven them to the train station, Eleanor had sat ramrod straight, staring directly ahead. She'd refused to look back. None of them could bear to see the house being shut up. Who knew if it would still be there once this madness was over.

'You wait here with the girls, Bella,' Eleanor said now, glancing round at the crowds. 'I'll go and find out which platform we need.'

Bella watched as she was swallowed up by the crowds of servicemen and civilians. The noise was horrendous. Children were crying, people were shouting or talking in loud voices. Whistles blew and steam hissed from the waiting trains. Her head began to ache.

'I need the lavatory, Miss Bella,' Holly whispered, her tear-stained face ghostly white in the gloom of the station.

'Oh, Holly,' Bella said. 'Didn't you go before we left? Your grandmother said to wait here. If we go looking for the lavatory, we'll get lost. It's chaos.'

'I really need to go,' Holly insisted.

Bella glanced round in the hope of spotting her aunt heading their way, but she could see nothing amongst the sea of waiting passengers. She bit her lip in a quandary. She didn't dare let Holly go on her own, and she could hardly leave Emily alone on the platform. They would have to all go together and just hope her aunt didn't return while they were gone.

She did one last desperate sweep of the platform in search of her aunt. Holly was hopping up and down beside her.

'Oh, come on, then.' Bella said. 'We'll have to be quick.' Gripping both girls tightly by the hand, she threaded her way through the milling throng to the public lavatory. She was rummaging in her purse for a penny when a voice called her name.

'Bella?' Turning, Bella found herself looking at a tall, dark-haired man in a long dark coat and hat. 'It's me, Will Mullens,' he grinned.

'Bellaaaa,' Holly groaned.

'Sorry, here.' Bella gave her the penny. 'Emily go in with her, and be quick.' She turned her attention back to Will. 'This is a surprise. How are you?' she asked, as the two girls disappeared into the lavatory, locking the door behind them.

'I'm very well, thank you. I've just enlisted in the air force,' he said. 'I'm on my way to Hatfield for flight training.'

'I'm just waiting for my aunt. We're leaving London.'

'Very wise,' Will said, nodding gravely. He looked leaner, his features more chiselled. 'How is Arthur?'

'He's well, thank you. Enjoying life on the farm.'

'We never got to go to the cinema,' Will said, with a wry smile.

Bella shook her head. 'I'm sorry. As I explained in my letter, which you never replied to, by the way,' she added with her own wry smile, 'my cousin was looking for a governess and . . . well, it was all very last minute. I'm sorry I never got to say goodbye.'

Will frowned. 'What letter?' he asked. 'I never received a letter. I called for you that Saturday and your father told me, rather brusquely, I might add, that you'd secured a position in London, and you'd already left.'

'My father can be difficult,' Bella apologized, her cheeks colouring in embarrassment. 'I wonder why you never received my letter. I wrote care of your grandmother.'

Will's frown deepened. 'Very odd. My mother had arrived by then, as well. She would have said if there'd been a letter for me.'

'Letters do go astray, I suppose,' replied Bella, with a puzzled frown. 'Perhaps I wrote the address wrong.'

'Unlikely,' responded Will. 'Everyone knew my grandma, so even if you'd only put "Mrs Hopwood, Strawbridge" it would have arrived.'

'I was sorry to hear that she'd passed away,' Bella said. 'She was a popular figure in the village. I remembered her from when I was little.'

'Thank you. It was a shock, but she went peacefully.'

There was a click behind her, the sound of a lock being disengaged, and the lavatory door creaked open.

'Well, I'd better go. My aunt will be looking for us,' Bella said, as Holly and Emily pressed up against her. 'Good luck.'

Will nodded. 'It was good to see you. Girls.' He nodded and touched the brim of his hat. 'Safe journey.'

Bella thanked him and, taking her cousins' hands, fought her way back to roughly where they'd been standing when they last saw Eleanor. When she glanced behind her, Will was gone, swallowed up by the crowd.

They'd barely returned to their spot by the station clock when she spotted her aunt making her way towards them.

'Right, girls,' Eleanor said, clutching their tickets in her gloved hands. 'We need platform two. We must hurry. Our train leaves in fifteen minutes.'

The train was crammed with evacuees and service personnel, but they managed to find an empty compartment. Eleanor sank wearily onto the upholstered seat. Bella stowed the luggage in the overhead racks before sitting next to her aunt, her gas mask resting on her lap. Holly and Emily sat opposite. They both looked scared, and Bella's heart went out to them. They were living in frightening times, but how much worse it must be for a child, she thought. Wrenched from everything they've known. Not knowing when they would see their father again. She smiled at them and got to her feet.

'Budge up,' she said to Holly. Holly scooted along the seat and Bella sat down between them. 'You'll love it at your Aunt Lily's,' she said, as the train slowly pulled out of the station in a cloud of swirling steam. 'You'll have lots of of young cousins to play with.' Holly regarded her in misery.

'I miss Nanny,' she said.

'We will all miss people, darling,' her grandmother told her kindly. 'We must be brave.'

Holly's bottom lip trembled, and she glanced out of the window. They were passing railway sidings and warehouses which soon gave way to rows of terraced houses.

'Let's play I Spy,' said Bella. 'It'll take our mind off things.'

The girls were reluctant to begin with, but as the city gave way to open fields, quaint villages and woodlands, they forgot their misery and became quite animated, exclaiming over herds of cows and flocks of sheep. By the time they had exhausted the game of I Spy, they had passed Basingstoke and were hurtling towards the south coast.

They had to change trains at Southampton. Even just pulling into the station Bella could tell that the city had changed overnight. Sandbags lined the fronts of buildings and there were military personnel and vehicles everywhere.

There was a sense of expectation in the air as Bella clambered aboard the train that would take them to Botley where her parents would be waiting for her.

It was comforting, seeing the familiar landscape rushing past the windows. Holly and Emily were in better spirits, their natural exuberance having come to the fore, and they crowded at the window, exclaiming over everything. It was a short train ride and barely forty minutes later the train pulled into the small station. Bella's parents and her grandmother were waiting on the platform, along with several official-looking women with clipboards.

Bella joined the throngs of children alighting the train, careful to make sure her cousins didn't get confused with the other evacuees.

'Bella,' called Alice, waving as she pushed her way through the crowd. There were so many passengers disembarking, the small station looked in danger of being overwhelmed.

'Mother.' Bella threw herself into her mother's arms.

'Oh. It's so good to have you home,' Alice said, hugging her tight. 'Even if it is regrettable circumstances.' She held

Bella at arm's length. 'You're such a young woman now. Not a girl at all.'

'She'll always be my little girl,' said Samuel, as Alice turned to embrace her aunt and hug her young nieces.

'Hello, Father.' Bella hugged him warmly. 'It's good to see you. Is Arthur here?'

'No,' Samuel replied. 'But you'll see him at supper time. Come along. Your mother thought it might be nice to have tea at the hotel before we head home.'

Disappointed not to see her brother, Bella hugged her grandmother, Lily, Aunt Eleanor's sister, and, with everyone talking at once, she followed them out onto the street. Buses lined the kerb.

'They're to take the evacuees to their billets,' Bella's father explained as they crossed the street to the hotel. 'I believe Isaac Whitworth is taking in several.'

'He has the room,' Bella said. 'I assume the Whitworths have left London, then?'

'They came down the day Hitler invaded Poland. Isaac still has contacts in the government. He knew war was in-evitable.' He glanced up at the sky before ducking his head to enter the hotel lobby. 'I feel we may not escape unscathed either,' he said, his voice low. 'Southampton is an important port. Hitler's bound to attack us.'

'Strawbridge and Hedge End should be safe, surely?' Bella asked, alarmed. 'They wouldn't have sent all these children if it wasn't.'

'Oh, I think we're as safe as we can be,' her father assured her, holding open the door to the dining room. 'There's always the risk of a bomb going astray, of course,' he continued, as they followed Alice and the others between the tables of early diners.

'I'm glad Arthur won't be deemed fit for military service,' Bella said, taking her place at the table. 'The thought of him having to fight, well, it makes me feel physically sick. Father?' Bella looked at her father in alarm as his face drained of colour. He swayed and had to catch the edge of the table to prevent himself from stumbling. 'Father, are you all right?'

Samuel nodded. 'Yes,' he said, looking confused. 'Yes, I'm well, thank you.'

'Samuel,' Alice half rose from her chair. 'Can I get you something? Water?'

Samuel shook his head. 'I'm well, thank you. Please, don't fuss.' He took his seat between his wife and daughter. Eleanor sat beside her sister, Alice on her other side, Holly and Emily between Bella and her grandmother, Lily.

Bella caught her mother casting worried glances at her father throughout the meal, but he appeared to have regained his equilibrium, and was animated and fun, making Holly and Emily laugh with his silly jokes. Alice smiled at him fondly. At times like this she regained the man she had married, before the trenches of France had taken their toll on his sensitive soul.

'I haven't had a chance to tell you yet, Bella,' Alice said, as the meal was ending. 'But we're taking in two evacuees.'

'Do we have room?' Bella raised an eyebrow.

'That woman from the Ministry of Defence seemed to think so,' her father replied drily. 'She insisted we could take at least two.'

'They're having Arthur's room,' Alice explained. Bella wiped her mouth with her napkin.

'Where will Arthur sleep?'

Her parents exchanged glances. 'Arthur lives in at Monk's farm now,' said Alice. 'He's happy there, Bella,' she added, as Bella opened her mouth to protest. 'He gets on with the other farmhands. He's made friends. You should be happy for him.'

'How long has he been staying there?' Bella demanded.

'A month. He has Sunday afternoons off when he comes home for his tea. He'll be over later to see you. Mrs Monk gave him permission.' Alice's face glowed with pride for her son. 'He's really settled in well there,' she said, her eyes pleading for Bella to understand. 'This is what we always wanted for him, Bella. Independence.'

'I know,' Bella agreed with a sigh. 'It's just that I expected everything to be the same when I came back.'

'Nothing stays the same, sweetheart,' her mother said, softly.

They lingered over tea, the conversation drifting on to the more serious subject of war. Grandma Lily imparted the news that both Bella's uncles had enlisted that morning along with her Aunty Caroline's fiancé.

'Your Aunty Martha's enlisting, too,' Grandma Lily said, sipping her Darjeeling. She spoke calmly but her hand shook, spilling tea on the pristine white tablecloth.

'But she could get posted abroad,' Alice exclaimed, worried for her headstrong sister.

'You know Martha, Alice,' Lily said. 'She's always known her own mind.'

'They'll need doctors here, too,' said Eleanor, stirring sugar into her cup. 'And perhaps the war won't last too long.'

'That's what they said about the last one,' said Lily drily. 'Over by Christmas, they said, didn't they? And how long did we have to endure? Four years. Four long years and none of us have been the same since.'

'Let's pray this one doesn't last anywhere near as long,' Samuel said, reaching for his wife's hand and caressing it gently with his thumb.

To Bella's delight, her brother was waiting on the doorstep when the bus pulled up outside the vicarage. Grandma Lily, Aunt Eleanor, Holly and Emily had continued on to Hedge End with the promise of coming back for dinner on Sunday.

'Arthur!' Bella shrieked, hurtling down the path to fling her arms around her brother. She hugged him tight, surprised again at how solid and muscular he was.

'Mrs Monk said I could finish early as it was a special day,' Arthur said slowly, his face glowing with unbridled joy.

'That was very kind of her,' said Alice, coming up the path. Samuel followed behind with Bella's suitcase.

'She gave me some butter and eggs,' Arthur said, linking arms with Bella as they made their way into the house.

'Bella!' Ida Wilson beamed, emerging from the kitchen in her pinny, her face flushed and shiny. 'Welcome home.'

'Thank you, Mrs Wilson. At least home hasn't changed,' she smiled, as a volley of barking heralded the arrival of Barney and Sybil. They barrelled into the hall, paws skidding on the linoleum flooring, tails wagging in ecstasy.

'Hello, Boy, hello, Girl,' cried Bella, dropping to her knees as the two dogs bombarded her with affection.

'I'm afraid they get rather bored with just us old folk for company these days,' Alice said, edging around the dogs to the kitchen. 'I know we've just had pots of the stuff, but would anyone like a cup of tea?'

'I'll have one,' Samuel said. 'I'll just take this up to Bella's room.'

'Thank you, Father. I wouldn't mind one, Mother,' said Bella, pushing the dogs aside and getting to her feet. 'So, Arthur, Mother tells me you're living in at Monk's farm now. Are you happy there?'

Arthur nodded. His face had that healthy, tanned look of a person who spends a lot of time out of doors.

'I sleep above the stables with Peter and Geoffrey,' Arthur told her, as they followed their mother into the airy kitchen. A pan bubbled on the stove, billowing steam, and the air smelled of stewed apples. 'They're my friends.'

'Are they nice friends?' Bella asked, her eyes narrowing suspiciously.

Arthur nodded. 'They took me to the cinema.'

'Did they?' Bella's brows rose. 'What did you see?'

'*Ask a Policeman*. It was good.'

'Arthur gets on well with everyone on the farm, don't you,

Karen Dickson

love?' Alice said, bustling about preparing the tea. 'But you seem to have an especially good relationship with Geoffrey and Peter. They're nice lads,' she added to Bella. 'We had them around for tea a few Sundays ago.'

Ida Wilson came in the back door from emptying the slop bucket in next door's pigpen. The dogs wandered over, tails wagging to sniff at the empty bucket, and she shooed them away. The doorbell clanged and the dogs started barking again, skidding across the slate floor in their haste to get to the door.

'That's probably Mrs Bradley with our evacuees,' Alice said, smoothing down her skirt. Bella followed her mother out into the hall. Samuel was just coming down the stairs, a slight frown on his face.

'Barney, Sybil,' he said sternly. The two spaniels fell silent, sitting back on their haunches, tongues protruding from their open jaws as Alice opened the heavy oak door.

On the doorstep stood a rotund woman with a stiffly lacquered helmet of iron-grey hair, and a ruddy, weathered complexion. She wore an olive-green tweed skirt and jacket over a cream blouse. A pair of spectacles hung around her neck on a silver chain. Two young boys stood beside her, one on either side. They wore grey shorts and shirts, and blue hand-knitted jumpers. The youngest boy's socks were at half-mast. They each had a gas mask slung around their necks and a luggage label pinned to their jumpers.

'Good afternoon, Reverend,' Mrs Bradley said. 'Mrs Roberts. These are your evacuees. Johnny and Jack Axe.

64

They're from Shirley. Mum put them on the list weeks ago. Dad's in the merchant navy and Mum's a nurse. They want them out of the city, for obvious reasons, but Mum will be wanting to visit.'

'Of course,' Alice said, smiling down at the boys. 'Come on in,' she said. 'Don't mind the dogs,' she added, as they sidled past Barney and Sybil, regarding them nervously, 'they're very friendly.' As if to prove the point, Sybil stuck out her tongue and licked Jack's hand. He giggled. 'Bella, take the boys to the kitchen. I'm sure Mrs Wilson will be able to find you a slice of fruit cake.'

At the mention of cake, both boys' faces lit up.

'Come along,' Bella said. 'This way.'

Johnny and Jack followed her in silence, their dark eyes swivelling anxiously as they took in their new surroundings.

Bella introduced the boys to Mrs Wilson and Arthur and they were soon seated at the large scrubbed-pine table, with a glass of milk and large slices of fruit cake. By the time Alice and Samuel joined them, Johnny and Jack had seemingly overcome their shyness and were talking ten to the dozen. They seemed particularly at ease with Arthur, who promised to take them to the farm some time and show them the cows.

CHAPTER EIGHT

'Father, Mother,' Bella said, coming into the parlour. 'I have some news for you.'

It was early October and Britain had been at war with Germany for just over a month. Recruitment offices had sprung up all over the place as young men and women hurried to enlist and do their bit for King and country.

'Oh?' Samuel looked up from his newspaper. Alice laid aside the socks she was darning. Johnny and Jack seemed to wear through an item of clothing at least twice a week. Having lived their entire short lives in the terraced streets of Shirley, the open fields and woodlands surrounding Strawbridge were a haven for adventures. Together with the other evacuees in the village, of which there were several, whenever they were not in school, they were out exploring and playing. Already they had gained weight, and their cheeks glowed with health that came from plenty of fresh air and good food.

'As I was on my way to enlist with the Women's Land Army,' Bella said, 'I passed a recruitment tent from the Air Transport Auxiliary.' Her parents looked at her, nonplussed.

'They're recruiting women,' she explained.

'Women!' her father said. 'Preposterous. Women can't fly in war time.'

'A Miss Gower is recruiting women pilots and I have applied to be one of them.' She held her breath.

'I absolutely forbid it,' Samuel said, folding his newspaper. He laid it down on the side table. 'You haven't flown a plane since you were sixteen and your uncle's small twin-engine is nothing compared to the planes they're writing about in the papers. You'd never be able to manage anything like that. No, Bella, you shall join the Land Army like you proposed. I shall hear nothing more about this flying nonsense.'

'Mother, please.'

'Bella, I agree with your father. It's too dangerous.'

'But I've applied.'

'I very much doubt they'll take you on,' her father said, turning on the radio in readiness for the hourly news broadcast. 'But if they do, you'll have to respectfully decline.'

Bella scowled and flounced from the room. Now she'd set her heart on flying, the thought of working the land had lost its appeal. She wandered out into the garden. The vicarage lawns and flower beds had been ripped up to make way for the growing of vegetables. At the far end of the garden stood the newly erected chicken coop where six plump hens scratched in the dirt. Close to the vicarage the foundations had been dug for the new Anderson shelter that was being delivered within the next few weeks.

She sank onto the bench under the kitchen window. There was a decided nip in the air, and she pulled her cardigan tighter around her. The surrounding trees were striking in their autumn colours and the air smelled of coal fires and decomposing vegetation.

Clouds scurried across a clear blue sky and from far away came the steady drone of an aircraft. Of course, Bella mused. They weren't far away from the airbase at Hamble. Shielding her eyes against the sun, she peered up into the sky, searching. Finally, she spotted it, a tiny speck way up high. It was coming closer. She watched as the speck grew bigger. Soon she could make out the wings and propeller. It dipped towards the earth, before swooping higher, tilting its wings. Its shadow ran across the garden as it disappeared over the house. Bella leapt to her feet as it circled around the village and came back, swooping low over the fields to finally disappear into the distance. As the silence settled around her, she felt strangely flat. With a sigh of resignation, she crossed the garden to the side gate which led to the churchyard, deciding she would walk over to Hedge End to visit her grandmother and Aunt Eleanor. She would pop into the Land Girls registry office on the way back.

'Bella, there's a letter come for you,' Alice called up the stairs three days later. 'It looks official.'

Bella came bounding down the stairs, her heart in her

throat. 'Thank you, Mother.' She took the official looking envelope and slit it open, her pulse racing. It was the reply she'd been waiting for. As her eyes scanned the neatly typed text, her spirits sank.

'It's from Miss Gower,' Bella said, her voice heavy with disappointment. 'She's turned me down.'

'Never mind,' her mother said, with a commiserating smile. 'It's for the best. You're due to join the Land Army next week, anyway.'

'Oh, no, wait,' Bella said, her quick gaze scanning the rest of the letter. 'She goes on to say that, although they have reached their quota for the time being, she is confident that they will be recruiting many more women pilots over the coming months and wishes to offer me a job on the ground in the meantime.' Bella's eyes shone with excitement. 'I am to report for duty at Chantry Fields airbase on the second of January.'

'Oh, Bella.' Alice bit her lip in consternation. 'I'm not sure I'm happy about this. And your father certainly won't allow you to fly.'

'I shall be twenty-one at the end of January, Mother,' Bella said gently. She touched her mother's arm. 'I really want to do this.'

Alice sighed. 'Your father's right. You've always been headstrong. I suppose you'll do what you feel is right, and I shan't stand in your way.'

'Thank you.' Bella kissed her mother's soft cheek. 'I must write back immediately and accept,' she said, hurrying up the stairs.

'I'm not happy about it,' Alice called after her, but she was smiling.

As predicted, her father did not take the news well. Bella waited until their midday meal to announce her plans.

'I thought I'd made myself perfectly clear,' Samuel said, laying down his knife and fork and regarding his daughter sternly. 'Flying with your uncle for recreation was one thing, taking to the skies during a war is another entirely.'

'But, Father . . .'

'Don't interrupt me, Isabella,' Samuel responded sharply. 'It may be that you'll be ground crew for the time being, but I know you. As soon as the opportunity to fly presents itself, there'll be no stopping you. It's not a ladylike occupation, and unbecoming of a vicar's daughter.'

'Is being a land girl anymore ladylike,' shot back Bella, earning herself a filthy look from her father.

'I'd rather you took work in an office,' he said, picking up his fork. 'I have to say, I regret my decision not to send you to secretarial school after all. Your cousin Benjy could have got her a job with the War Office, Alice. Perhaps he still could. There must be other jobs that don't require typing, like filing and such-like.'

'Filing? Father!' Bella pulled a face. 'While being a governess for my cousins was never my career of choice, I believe it was preferable to working in a stuffy office, and I certainly do not wish to spend the war filing and making tea.'

'Samuel,' Alice intervened gently, laying her hand on her

husband's arm. 'We agreed that we would always allow our children to make their own choices, remember.'

'Have you forgotten that I served in a war, Alice,' Samuel snapped, dropping his fork with a clatter. Under the table, Sybil gave a low whine. 'I don't want my children to suffer as I did.' His brow furrowed and his hands began to shake.

'I know, darling,' Alice said soothingly 'I feel the same. I would like nothing more than to keep them both under my roof forever, but we can't do that. Everyone is being asked to make sacrifices. Look at Johnny and Jack's mum. How must she have felt sending them to live with strangers? They're with her today,' she added to Bella. 'She had a day off, so they've gone to see the ships. She's talking about taking them back as nothing seems to be happening . . .'

'She'd be a fool to take them back,' interjected Samuel. 'Benjy told your mother that Hitler's lulling us into a false sense of security and that when he strikes, he will strike with a vengeance.'

'I'm sure he's right, darling,' agreed Alice. 'But that's by the by. As I say, we must all make sacrifices and, although I shall probably not know a moment's peace until this war is over, I know I have to let Bella go. You must see that, too, Samuel?'

Her words were followed by a deep silence, broken only by the soft panting of the dogs beneath the table and the creak of floorboards as Ida moved around overhead. Bella held her breath. Samuel looked at her, his eyes heavy with sorrow. She knew he had seen things during the Great War that she could never imagine, and her heart ached for him.

'Father,' she said softly, breaking the lengthy quiet. 'I have accepted Miss Gower's offer, and I will be joining the ATA in January, no matter what, but I should rather go with your blessing.'

Samuel sighed. 'You will be almost twenty-one by then,' he said, his voice gruff with emotion. 'So, even if I forbade you, it would only be a matter of weeks before you can do as you please, and I should hate us to part at odds with each other.' He reached for Bella's hand. 'Just promise me you will take every care of yourself?'

'Of course, Father,' Bella promised.

'What will you do about the Land Army?' Alice asked, refilling her teacup.

'I shall go and see them this afternoon,' Bella replied, reluctantly. It wasn't a conversation she was looking forward to.

'I must say, this is highly irregular, Miss Roberts.' The recruitment officer looked down her long nose at Bella. She was a tall, heavily built woman with short blonde hair and piercing blue eyes. Her olive-green blouse strained across her bosom, as she breathed in deeply, nostrils flaring.

'I'm sorry, ma'am,' Bella apologized, again. 'I realize this is an inconvenience but, as I'm sure you're aware, it is an honour to even be considered for the ATA and it's what I really want to do.'

The recruitment officer grimaced, as if she had little time for the notion of women pilots.

'I've read about Miss Gower in the paper,' she said, sitting down heavily behind her desk and pulling out a thick ledger. 'I can't see it taking off,' she said, flicking through the pages until she found Bella's form. 'Women aren't going to be trusted with an expensive aeroplane.' Bella smiled sweetly. She, too, had read a few of the derogatory comments in the newspaper, written, of course, by men who considered women to be inferior in every way, never mind in the air. The articles had made her so angry; she had forbidden herself to read anymore.

'Well, there we are, I have removed your name,' the recruitment officer said, regarding Bella with a look of acute disappointment. 'I wish you well,' she added, her tone belying her words as Bella turned to leave.

'Thank you, ma'am,' she said. Walking out of the office and down the draughty corridor, she felt a flutter of excitement. It might be a long wait, but in time, hopefully, she would be airborne.

CHAPTER NINE

1940

Bella shivered on the platform, buffeted by the cold January wind. Her eyes streamed and her cheeks were scoured red raw. Black clouds roiled ominously overhead, threatening more rain, and the road was awash with puddles. She'd already been splashed by a passing military vehicle, soaking her stockings and shoes.

Tugging the hood of her coat further over her head, she glanced each way along the street. She was supposed to have been picked up twenty minutes ago. She shivered, stamping her frozen feet, her gloved hands shoved deep into her coat pockets.

Despite her discomfort, she couldn't contain her excitement that she was here, at last. The weeks, while going slowly at first, had suddenly begun to race. Christmas had passed in a blur. There had been a big party at the manor house for all the evacuees and their host families, then on Christmas

Day itself, Bella and her extended family had all gathered at the vicarage where they'd been joined by Johnny and Jack's mother. Once the festivities were over, the days had rushed by in flurry of activity as Bella prepared to leave home. After an emotional farewell, she had boarded the train at Southampton for Gillingham in Dorset.

Now, as she stood on the windswept platform, teeth chattering in the cold, she was beginning to wonder if she'd been forgotten when an olive-green Jeep skidded round the corner, racing towards her. It came to an abrupt halt in front of her, sending an arc of brown rainwater into the air.

The window wound down and Bella peered in to see a pretty, freckled faced girl leaning across the passenger seat.

'Isabella Roberts?' she asked. Bella nodded.

'Gilly Ford,' the redhead said, with a grin. 'Dump your suitcase in the back and hop in.'

The Jeep door opened with a creak and Bella jumped into the passenger seat. It was marginally warmer inside the Jeep than out. Gilly ground the gears and they lurched forward.

'I'm sorry I'm late,' she said, pulling out into the street with barely a thought for any oncoming traffic. 'Welcome to Dorset, Isabella.'

'Thank you, and it's Bella.'

'Nice to meet you, Bella.' Gilly wrenched the steering wheel, and they sped round the corner, bouncing along the uneven tarmac as they left the small town behind and headed for the open country. Skeletal trees stood stark against a monochrome sky as the wind ruffled the grass verges.

'Are you a pilot?' Gilly asked, as they bounced along a muddy track.

'I haven't flown for about five years,' replied Bella. 'I'm being taken on as ground crew for the time being.'

'Me, too.' Gilly grinned, flicking on the wipers as the windscreen was lashed with rain. 'There aren't any female pilots at the airbase yet. And I should warn you that if you make any mention of your ambition to fly, the men will treat it with absolute derision.' She snorted. 'I reckon I could outfly any one of them, if I had the chance.'

'Where did you learn to fly?' Bella asked, with genuine interest.

'My father was a pilot. He taught my brother and me to fly.'

'Was?' asked Bella.

'Three years ago, he was flying some friends to Paris. They ran into bad weather over the Channel. His plane went down somewhere near the Normandy coast. No survivors.'

'I'm sorry,' Bella murmured.

'An occupational hazard,' Gilly said, slowing down to steer the Jeep through a wide gateway. Ahead of them were an assortment of buildings, scattered across the flat terrain. Military Jeeps, lorries and staff cars were parked haphazardly between the buildings. To the left of the camp was a large, corrugated metal hangar. Four aeroplanes were parked in front of its cavernous doors.

'That's the aeroplane hangar,' Gilly said. 'The landing strip is behind it and those long wooden structures are the men's bunkhouses. We're housed over there.' She pointed to a selection of small, shed-like buildings. 'They're close to the officers' mess and the kitchens. The warehouses are further back, where we pack the parachutes and such-like.' The Jeep bounced over the grass, Bella hanging on for dear life as she was jolted this way and that. 'We're getting our first batch of fighter pilots in this week. That should liven things up a bit. Right, here we are.' She hit the brake and the Jeep slowed to a halt outside a wooden hut, the word 'Office' burned into a slab of wood and hanging over the lintel.

'You need to report to Major Thompson. He's a bit of an ogre. Has no time for women pilots at all.' She gave Bella a wry grin. 'Take no notice of him.'

Heart racing in trepidation. Bella alighted from the Jeep and ran after Gilly through the pouring rain, up the wooden steps and into the office. The rotund major seated behind the large desk looked up in annoyance as the door banged shut behind them.

'Cadet Ford,' he snapped. 'Must you always enter a room like a force ten gale?' He shook his head, eyeing Bella belligerently over his spectacles. He had a ruddy complexion and thinning, greying blond hair. 'Cadet Roberts, I presume?' he said, shuffling through the sheaf of papers in front of him.

'Yes, sir.' Bella stood to attention, her pulse racing as the major read through her file.

'You're another one of these girls who think they can fly,' he snorted, shaking his head in derision. It was on the tip of Bella's tongue to reply that yes, she could fly, but as she caught Gilly's eye, she saw her give a subtle shake of her head. Sighing inwardly, Bella swallowed her protest and remained silent.

'Cadet Ford will show you to your quarters. After which you will report to the parachute packing shed. Dismissed.'

Tugging up her hood, head bowed against the driving rain, Bella followed Gilly across the sodden ground to one of the small huts on the perimeter of the airfield.

'You're bunking in with me,' Gilly said, pushing open the door. Bella stood just inside the doorway, dripping rainwater on the bare floorboards. The room was square and basically furnished. There were four narrow camp beds, each with a metal locker at the foot. On a table, under the single window, stood a washbasin and jug.

'That's your bed there.' Gilly pointed to the bed closest to the door. Folded on top of the olive-green blanket was her uniform. 'You can unpack later,' Gilly said. 'You'll meet Beryl and Amanda over in the parachute packing shed. They're our age, and good fun. Come on. Get changed and I'll take you over there.'

Shivering in the cold air, Bella quickly shed her civilian clothes and changed into the blue skirt, white blouse and jacket laid out for her. Pulling her sopping wet coat back on, she and Gilly made their way to one of the large sheds the size of a small warehouse. There were several aircraft parked outside.

'The men will be in the mess,' Gilly said, shouting to be heard above the howling wind and incessant rain. 'No one will be flying in this.' She opened the door and ushered Bella into the relative warmth of the parachute packing shed.

Several women looked up as they entered.

'Hi, everyone, this is Bella,' Gilly said, unbuttoning her wet coat.

'Hello,' said Bella, smiling round at the assembled women working at several long tables. Yards of silk parachutes were spread over the tables as the silk needed to be inspected for tears before nimble fingers deftly folded them into the neat squares that could be packed onto an airman's back.

'Cadet Roberts? Commander Joan Forrester. Welcome to Chantry Fields.' Commander Forrester was a short, slender woman with curly dark brown hair, dark brown eyes and an infectious laugh. Bella found herself warming to her immediately.

'As you can imagine, our work here must be of the utmost quality. If one of our brave pilots was to die because of a shoddily packed parachute, that would be unthinkable. Gilly will teach you everything you need to do.'

'Don't worry,' Gilly whispered, as she led Bella to one of the long tables. 'You'll soon get the hang of it.' She stretched out the parachute along the table. 'Firstly, you have to check for damage. The rigging lines need to be checked. I'll do this one, and then you can try.' Bella stood back, watching in amazement as Gilly deftly folded the twenty-four-foot canopy into neat folds. 'You have to be especially careful to make sure there are no tangles in the folds of silk,' Gilly said. 'We keep the folds in place with these bags of lead shot.'

79

Then Gilly showed Bella how the rigging, the lengths of nylon cord, had to be threaded through the parachute pack. 'Any tangle can be the difference between life and death for a pilot,' she told Bella soberly. Bella nodded, aware that she might, one day, have to rely on the conscientiousness of her fellow chute packers. 'It takes between twenty and thirty minutes to pack a parachute,' Gilly said, her tongue protruding from her mouth as she concentrated. 'There. All done. You have a go.'

Gilly lifted a freshly aired and checked parachute from its hanger and spread it over the table. Bella stared blankly at the yards of grey silk. She couldn't remember a single thing Gilly had shown her.

'I can't even remember where to start,' she said weakly.

'Spread it out,' Gilly said. 'Like this. Then you pull on the rigging, making sure it's straight.' With shaking hands, Bella followed Gilly's instructions. 'There you are.' Gilly grinned. 'That's it. Good job. You're getting it.'

By the fourth attempt, Bella finally managed to pack a parachute that Gilly didn't have to redo. 'Well done.' Gilly congratulated her. 'Do one more under my supervision and then I think I can trust you to get on with it yourself.'

'Remember,' one of the other girls cautioned her, laying her neatly packed parachute on the pile waiting to be collected. 'The lives of our airmen depend on us.'

Bella nodded. It was a huge responsibility and she made sure she checked and double-checked her work before she was satisfied with it.

By the time the dinner bell sounded, Bella's shoulders ached with tension.

'It gets easier,' Gilly told her, as they braved the torrential rain for the mess hall. She could hear the noise before Gilly pushed open the door. The room was packed with male ATA pilots and several of them wolf whistled as the girls entered, shaking rainwater from their hair.

At the far end of the room, three ATA girls were dishing out food to a queue of waiting men. Bella spotted Major Thompson and Commander Joan Forrester seated at a table with some other high-ranking officials.

'Come on,' Gilly said. 'Let's get our food.'

The men in the queue stood back to allow the girls to go ahead of them. There was a lot of laughter and joking between the men and women as they waited their turn to be served.

'It's all fun and games now,' Gilly told Bella in an undertone as they threaded their way back to a long table where several girls from the parachute shed were seated. 'But it's a different story when they find out you've got ambitions to fly.'

Bella put down her tray and slid onto the bench. The noise was indescribable, the cacophony of loud male voices interspersed by the clatter of cutlery on plates and the clangs from the kitchen. She glanced down at her watery mashed potato in dismay. One of the things she was going to miss most, she realized, was Mrs Wilson's cooking.

'Ah,' said Gilly with her mouth full, as two girls took their seats opposite her and Bella. 'This is Amanda and Beryl. Our roomies.'

'Cadet Amanda Chadwick.' The pretty, petite blonde stretched out her hand. 'Pleased to meet you, properly.'

'And I'm Cadet Beryl Hastings. Welcome to Chantry Fields. How did you find it this morning?' Beryl was as dark as Amanda was fair, with short, wavy black hair, dark brown eyes and olive skin tone.

'It was a bit hectic,' admitted Bella, spooning up a mouthful of insipid-looking beef stew. 'But I think I've got the hang of it.'

'The boys will rip you off something terrible,' warned Amanda. 'They always do with the newbies but take no notice.'

'I'd like to see one of them fold a parachute,' snorted Beryl.

'My Jonty would never dare tease me,' grinned Amanda, catching the eye of a nearby ATA pilot. 'Second Officer Jonty Castillo. My fiancé.' Bella turned to look. Jonty was a squat man with a shock of dark hair and laughter lines that crinkled when he grinned at Bella, giving her a mock salute.

'We met in Colorado last summer,' explained Amanda. 'My American father owns a ranch out there. That's where I learnt to fly.'

'You're American?' Bella asked, surprised.

Amanda shook her head. 'My father is. He and Mum divorced when I was little. I live with my mum and stepdad in Stepney, but I visit my American family every two years or so. Daddy pays my passage, of course.'

Over bowls of jam roly-poly and custard, Bella learned that Gilly had grown up in Kent, the daughter of a wealthy flying ace. After her father's death, her brother had taken over the one-man airshow until he'd enlisted in the RAF the previous November.

'I am descended from Russian Jews,' Beryl said, scraping the last of her custard from her bowl. She licked the spoon, savouring the last of the creamy mixture before retrieving a silver cigarette case from her inner breast pocket.

'Smoke, anyone?' she said, taking out a cigarette and passing it round. Gilly took one but both Amanda and Bella declined. 'My grandparents came to England as refugees in 1905 with their only surviving child, my mum. My three uncles, all under the age of ten, were murdered in the street.' Beryl paused, drawing deeply on her cigarette as Bella stared at her in horrified disbelief.

'But why?' Bella asked. Beryl shrugged.

'Because we're Jewish.' She let out a harsh, mirthless laugh. 'Ironically, neither of my grandparents were religious. I've never set foot in a synagogue.' She exhaled a cloud of smoke. 'And now it's happening all over again,' she said bitterly. 'My mother's cousin managed to escape from Germany in 1938. His wife, mother-in-law and three young children were due to leave on the Kindertransport on the third of September . . .' She ground her cigarette butt in the ashtray, as Bella slowly grasped the implication of her words.

'They couldn't get out,' she said soberly. Beryl shook her head.

'He hasn't heard anything from them since.'

'What about you, Bella?' asked Amanda, attempting to lift the mood. 'What's your story?'

'I'm a twin and the daughter of a country vicar.'

'A vicar's daughter, hmm?' Gilly said. 'I hope you're not going to be all strait-laced?'

Bella laughed. 'I'm anything but,' she replied. 'I spent five years living on a mission station in the Western Cape practically running wild with my cousins. My uncle taught me to fly in his Curtiss Robin.'

'I've flown the Robin a few times,' Gilly said. 'It's a nice machine.'

They spent a few minutes discussing aircraft before the bell went, signalling it was time to return to work.

The rain had stopped and the clouds had thinned, revealing patches of pale blue sky. But the January sun held no warmth and Bella shivered as she made her way across the boggy ground to the parachute shed.

CHAPTER TEN

Within a fortnight, Bella had become a dab hand at folding and packing her parachutes. She'd made friends with most of the women at the base, as well as some of the men. As predicted, the moment she mentioned her ambition to fly, she became the butt of their jokes, some good-natured and some not.

February arrived cold and wet. A bleak month at the best of times, it brought with it the disturbing news that Hitler had ordered a total U-boat blockade of Great Britain.

'We've already had our sugar, butter and bacon rationed,' moaned Beryl, as they made their way to the mess hall for breakfast one morning. 'What else will we have to cut down on?'

'Hitler's trying to starve us into submission,' said Amanda. 'But it's not going to work. My mum's only got a tiny patch of garden, but we had a glut of Brussels sprouts, cabbage and parsnips and she's already planting the spring veg.'

'Thank goodness the base has got its own chickens,' Gilly said, pushing open the door to the mess. 'At least we'll be able to have our fried eggs.'

The mess hall was as loud and noisy as ever, but today the numbers were swelled by the addition of twelve new ATA pilots who had arrived the previous evening. Bella swallowed the last of her scrambled egg, washed down with her last mouthful of tea, as the bell sounded calling everyone to their duties.

'Gosh, it's cold this morning,' Amanda said, rubbing her hands together as they left the mess. The wet weather over the last few days had kept most of the planes grounded but now the clouds had dispersed, leaving a bright, clear-blue sky in their wake and the mechanics were scurrying about preparing the machines for take-off.

The first group of pilots were already loitering at the entrance to the parachute shed.

'Morning, ladies,' they chorused. One or two whistled. The girls smiled back good-naturedly. Pushing past the pilots, Bella made her way into the shed to where the packed parachutes were waiting. Grabbing an armful, she carried them out to the waiting men.

'I hoped you packed that properly,' said a voice. With a flash of annoyance, Bella undid the straps of the last parachute and shook it out. There was stunned silence as yards of grey silk and rope tumbled out onto the wet grass.

'Pack it yourself,' she snapped. Turning on her heels, she strode back into the shed.

'Bella?' the familiar voice stopped her in her tracks.

'Will?'

She stood in the doorway, staring at Will standing sheep-
ishly in a pool of parachute silk.

'Do you know each other?' asked Beryl with a smirk, as
she handed Will another parachute pack.

'Er, yes,' he mumbled. 'Look, I'm sorry,' he said, looking
directly at Bella. 'It was a joke.'

'A joke I've heard almost daily for weeks,' replied Bella.
'Why are you flying for the ATA?' she asked, bending
down to gather up the parachute before Commander
Forrester spotted it. 'I thought you were going to fighter
training.'

'The eyes let me down,' Will said. 'Plus, I've got a bit of a
heart murmur. Nothing too serious but enough to keep me
out of active service.'

'Come on, Will,' one of the other pilots chided him. 'We
need to get our instructions from the control room.'

'You go ahead,' Will told him, as Bella straightened up,
yards of silk draped in her arms. 'Look, I'm probably not
going to be back until tomorrow but, well, do you fancy
meeting for a drink tomorrow evening? The lads said there
are a few decent pubs roundabouts.'

Bella regarded him thoughtfully. There was no denying
Will looked very handsome in his ATA uniform. And it
would be fun to go for a drink. She hadn't been off the base
in the five weeks since she'd arrived.

'That would be nice.'

'Great.' Will grinned. He nodded at the parachute in her arms. 'I'm sorry about that. It was a stupid joke, and I've made more work for you.'

'I shouldn't have overreacted,' Bella smiled back. 'But all this constant teasing does get wearying.'

'Mullens,' a voice shouted across the waterlogged field. 'Change of plan. Can you take the Hurricane to White Waltham, and pick up a de Haviland to take to Inverness?'

'Sure thing, Captain.' Will turned back to Bella. 'I've got to go. I'll see you tomorrow.'

'I'll look forward to it,' replied Bella. 'Take care.' Will nodded and, setting his cap on his short hair, strode towards the control office.

'How do you know First Officer Mullens?' Gilly asked, her voice laden with envy. 'He's gorgeous.'

'He looks like a film star,' said Beryl.

'We were friends for a while when I was sixteen,' Bella replied, walking over to her table. 'Before I moved up to London.' She'd told her friends how she'd acted as governess to her two young cousins but hadn't mentioned the brief time she'd spent with Will, nor had she elaborated on her father's rather bizarre behaviour. Hannah Hopwood had passed away later that same year. Bella hadn't returned for the funeral, but her mother had written to tell her that Will and his family had returned home immediately afterwards.

'And he wants to take you out for a drink, you lucky thing,' grinned Amanda.

'Don't let your Jonty hear you saying that,' Bella said, grinning back.

'Oh, my Jonty knows I love him to bits,' Amanda said, unhooking a parachute from its hanging and carrying it over to her table. 'There's a Valentine's dance at The Phoenix Hotel next Saturday. We should go.'

'I expect everyone on the base not on duty will be going,' Beryl replied. 'You'll have to see if your dishy Will is free.'

'He's not my Will,' Bella laughed. 'We're friends, that's all.' She stretched her parachute across the long table and tugged hard on the rigging to straighten it out. From outside came the sound of aircraft starting up and for about thirty minutes the air was filled with the sound of planes taking off. As the last one took to the skies a silence settled over the airfield. Placing her neatly folded parachute on the pile, Bella found herself gazing out of the window, across the wind-swept runway to the distant hills, and thinking of Will.

'How long have you been here?' asked Will, as the Jeep bounced over the rutted track. It was the following evening, and they were driving the short distance from the airbase to the town centre. It had been overcast all day and it had been touch and go whether Will would make it back, but at the last minute the cloud cover had risen enough to allow him the height needed to get back to base.

No stars or moon could penetrate the heavy clouds and the Jeep's dimmed headlights did little to dispel the thick darkness.

'Six weeks,' Bella said, straining her eyes against the darkness. It was almost impossible to see where they were going, and Will was driving as slowly as possible to reduce the risk of an accident.

'Enjoying it?'

Bella thought for a minute. 'I enjoy the company but the work's a bit monotonous. It takes an awful lot of concentration because one slip and it could cost someone their life.'

'It's a huge responsibility,' nodded Will. He followed a bend in the track and the feeble headlights picked out the corner of a building. They'd reached the town.

'How was your mission?' Bella asked, as they slowly traversed the dark, silent street. Not a chink of light was visible from any of the houses.

'I made good time to White Waltham yesterday,' replied Will. 'I met one of the female ATA pilots. A Joan Hughes. She was flying a Tiger Moth back to Hatfield.'

'Did you speak to her? What was she like?' Bella asked with a mixture of envy and admiration. She remembered Joan's name from an article she had read in the paper. A couple of months younger than Bella, Joan was one of Pauline Gower's 'First Eight'. She had been a flying instructor since the age of eighteen. Bella hadn't flown for five years, so it was understandable that she had been turned down for Miss Gower's initial eight. But she was hopeful she would get chosen for the upcoming refresher course and gain her wings.

'She seemed very pleasant,' replied Will. 'Friendly and

courteous. It's obvious the lads at White Waltham hold her in high esteem.'

'I'd love to meet her,' sighed Bella. 'And Miss Gower.'

'Maybe you will,' Will said, slamming on the brake as a cat ran in front of him. 'Damn, these dim headlights,' he said. 'Are you all right?'

'I'm fine,' Bella assured him. 'We weren't going fast anyway.'

'The pub's just along here,' he said, crawling slowly down the street and pulling up opposite St Mary's church. Switching on his torch, he leapt from the Jeep and, rounding the bonnet, opened the door for Bella.

She thanked him and they walked the short distance to the pub. The Red Lion was bustling with service personnel and civilians. Bella stood blinking just inside the door, the sudden brightness making her eyes water.

'What will you have?' asked Will, as they edged their way around the crowd.

'A shandy?' Bella said the first thing that came into her head. She seldom drank. The odd glass of wine at dinner or the occasional sherry with her grandmother at Christmas, but she knew Gilly and Amanda always ordered a shandy when they went out, so she thought she'd give it a try.

'You find a table while I order,' said Will, shouting to be heard over the noise. Bella nodded, glancing round at the occupied tables. She was making her way over to find one when someone tapped her on the shoulder. It was Amanda on her way back from the cloakroom.

'D'you and Will want to sit with us?' she asked, inclining her head to where Gilly and Beryl were sitting at a round table with Jonty.

'I thought you lot were going to the cinema,' Bella said, following Amanda through the haze of cigarette smoke.

'It was full, so we decided to come for a drink instead. It's packed in here tonight as well though.'

'I don't suppose there are many places to go round here,' replied Bella, leaning close to Amanda. 'Hello, Jonty, Gilly, Beryl.' She slid into the chair beside Beryl. 'Will's just getting the drinks.' She glanced over to the bar. Will was leaning against it, his back to the bar, his eyes scanning the crowded pub. Bella half-rose from her seat and waved. Will spotted her, his face creasing into a smile of recognition. He nodded and turned back to the bar. Ten minutes later, he was threading his way between the tables, holding a pint of ale and a glass of shandy aloft.

'Here you go,' he said, setting the glasses on the table and sliding into the seat beside Bella. Bella introduced Will to the girls. He'd already met Jonty in the flying pool. The two men shook hands warmly. They spent a few minutes talking about planes before Will turned his attention to Bella.

'How are your family?' he asked, sipping his pint.

'All well, thank you. I received a letter from Mother just this morning. Arthur is still enjoying his job on the farm. Farmer Monk has taken on a couple of land girls and Mother thinks he's got a crush on one of them. My aunt Martha has been posted to the Far East in charge of a large contingent of nurses. She's a doctor.'

'How does her husband feel about her being sent so far away?' asked Will.

'My aunt never married. My father and grandfather say it's because men don't like women who are cleverer than them.'

Will laughed. 'That old chestnut. My mother was certainly cleverer than my father. In common sense at least.'

'Was?' Bella frowned in sympathy as Will nodded.

'She passed away just before Christmas,' Will said. 'She'd been suffering from ill health for years.'

'I'm sorry. Were you close?' Bella asked. Her difficult relationship with her father had made her curious about other people's parental relationships.

'We got on all right,' he replied with a shrug. 'I was always closer to her than to my dad, which has led to some friction over the years, but he's proud of what I'm doing for my country. He served in the trenches during the Great War.'

'Is your sister still at home?'

'At the moment, but she's due to join the WAAF next month. Dad's still head gardener at Wilton House. It's been requisitioned by the army, so he's not allowed to talk about anything that goes on there. He was complaining the other week that they've put Nissan huts all over the grounds.'

'I suppose he must have taken great pride in his work before,' Bella acknowledged.

Will nodded. 'He did. All his prize-winning flower beds have been dug up to make way for food growing.'

'I understand why it has to be done.' Bella took a sip of her shandy. She grimaced. It certainly was an acquired taste. She took another sip, the bubbles popping on her tongue, and put down her glass. 'But it is a shame. My mother cried when the gardener dug up her rose bushes to make way for a vegetable garden and a chicken coop, and let's not forget the Anderson shelter,' she added with a wry smile. 'That took up all the hydrangea bushes.'

'With Hitler's U-boats attempting to cut off our imports, we don't have much choice,' Will said, raising his glass.

'We're going over to The Phoenix,' said Amanda, leaning closer. 'They've got a singer in. D'you fancy it?'

Bella looked at Will. 'I've got an early take-off tomorrow, so I'd better only have one more before I turn in. You're welcome to go, if you like?'

Bella shook her head. 'I'm happy to have another drink here and then head back to base. Another time, Amanda.'

'Sure. We'll see you later.'

Bella stood up as the girls gathered up their bags and hats, and readied themselves to move on with Jonty. He slapped Will on the back.

'See you back at base, Will.'

'I'm sorry,' Will said, once they'd gone. 'You could have gone.'

'I'd rather stay here with you,' replied Bella truthfully. 'Besides it's a bit quieter now.'

'Probably a lot have gone over to The Phoenix.'

'It's better,' grinned Bella. 'I can hear you properly now. It's so annoying having to keep saying pardon.'

Will laughed. He glanced at her half-empty glass. 'Another one?'

'Maybe just top this one up with lemonade,' Bella said, passing him her glass.

CHAPTER ELEVEN

'I think I've laddered my stockings,' Bella wailed, craning her neck to see the back of her calf.

'Let me have a look,' said Gilly, from the seat behind her.

'I'm sure I snagged it on the bus door coming up the steps,' said Bella as Gilly leaned down to get a better look.

'You're fine, Bella,' Gilly said, straightening up and patting her carefully crimped auburn hair. 'I can see a bit of dirt where you must have scraped your leg against the door, but it hasn't laddered your stockings.'

'Oh, thank goodness for that,' Bella said in relief. 'It's my last pair. I'd have hated having to walk into the dance with a huge ladder.' She sank back against the backrest. The base had laid on three buses to ferry them to the Valentine dance at The Phoenix hotel, two for the men and one for the ladies. It was a clear night, and the moon was full. Through her dusty window, Bella could just about make out the shape of the men boarding their buses. It was too dark to see their faces, so she couldn't tell whether Will was still milling about or if he'd already boarded.

Since their drink at The Red Lion four days earlier, she'd barely seen him. He'd left at first light on the Wednesday morning and had only returned that very afternoon, two hours earlier. Tonight would be the first chance she had to talk to him, and she was looking forward to it.

The bus was filled with laughing, chatting women, all looking forward to their night out, and the air was a heady mixture of perfume and cigarette smoke. Once everyone had found their seat, the door closed, and the bus rolled forward across the bumpy grass, casting a shadow in the ghostly moonlight.

'Jonty says the band's really good,' Amanda said. She was sitting beside Bella, half-turned in her seat, her back to the window. 'He saw them the other week at a pub in Shaftesbury.' She took her compact out of her bag and checked her appearance in the tiny mirror by the light of the moon streaming in the window. 'I'm so looking forward to tonight. I haven't had a good dance for ages.'

'I've never been to a dance,' Bella said.

'What, never?' Amanda said, closing her compact with a snap.

Bella shook her head. 'No. We didn't have dances at the mission station. And I was never invited to any in London.' She gave Amanda a self-deprecating smile. 'I hope I shan't embarrass myself.'

'You'll be fine,' Amanda assured her. 'Just take your cue from your partner. It's easy.'

Bella grimaced. That was easy for Amanda to say, she mused, a knot of anxiety forming in her stomach. She'd watched her three friends dancing to the radio in their room but, although they'd tried to persuade her, she'd never joined them, feeling too self-conscious. Now she wished she had. At least she had a vague idea of what to do with her feet and arms. She wondered if Will could dance, or indeed if he'd ask her. The other evening, she'd thought she'd detected a remnant of the spark that had ignited so briefly between them five years earlier, but with the availability of so many young ladies, she couldn't be too complacent.

The bus shuddered to a halt outside the hotel and Bella alighted to the sound of musicians tuning their instruments.

'Amanda,' Jonty called, jumping from the second bus. He was followed by Will. He waved at Bella, grinning broadly.

'I'm glad you got back safely,' Bella said. 'You must have run into some awful weather.'

'It was pretty hairy between Hamble and White Waltham,' he said. 'But I got the plane there in one piece.'

They squeezed through the door into the crowded foyer where they left their coats with the attendant before making their way into the function room. The band struck up a swing number and some couples took to the floor immediately.

'Would you like to dance?' Will asked.

'I'm not really sure how,' Bella replied, apologetically.

'It's easy. Come on.' Will offered Bella his hand. After a

moment's hesitation, she took it and he led her onto the dance floor. Will moved well on the floor, Bella noticed, feeling wooden and self-conscious as he swung her around. But he was an excellent teacher and she soon felt herself relaxing as the music touched her soul, and her inhibitions dissipated as she realized she was enjoying herself. Amanda whirled by in Jonty's arms, and Gilly was dancing with a tall, blond-haired soldier. Beryl was standing by the makeshift bar, drink in hand, talking to two ATA pilots.

She was panting and sweating by the time Will led her over to the bar. He bought her a shandy and a pint of local cider for himself, and they stood on the edge of the dance floor watching the other dancers, sipping their drinks in quiet companionship.

Will was looking particularly handsome tonight, she thought, watching him surreptitiously as he watched the dancing, raising his glass to his lips every so often.

'What?' he grinned, giving her a sideways glance.

Bella blushed, embarrassed to have been caught studying him. 'Nothing,' she said primly. Will's grin broadened. Hiding a smile of her own, Bella concentrated on the dancing. Suddenly the dancers began to move to the edge of the dance floor, and couples broke apart to stand and clap as Beryl took to the dance floor. Bella stared in amazement as her friend and partner, a tall, reed-thin soldier, flew around the room. With arms waving and legs that seemingly had a life of their own, Beryl danced and spun across the floor. There was a gasp from the spectators as her partner swung her up in the air and spun her around. As the music died, Beryl collapsed into his arms, her face flushed, her mouth stretched wide.

'I knew Beryl could dance but I didn't realize she was that good,' Bella said to Will, as the couple began to dance more sedately and other couples returned to the floor.

'She's very good,' Will agreed, leading Bella onto the dance floor. 'They both were.'

'I wonder who he is?' wondered Bella aloud as Will twirled her around.

'His name is Bob Marshall,' Beryl said, peering at her reflection in the cloakroom mirror and reapplying her lipstick. 'He's stationed at Blandford. He's here with his sister. She's a land girl over at Lox Lane Farm but they're both spending the weekend with their aunt here in Gillingham.'

'Have you only just met, then?' asked Bella, powdering her nose and cheeks, shiny from the dancing.

'Never seen him before tonight,' Beryl replied.

'Honestly, the way the two of you were dancing, anyone would think you've been dancing together for years.'

'Apparently he was a ballroom dancer like me.'

'Why have you never told us you're a ballroom dancer?' Amanda asked, fluffing up her hair with her fingers. Beryl shrugged.

'My parents liked holidaying in Blackpool. We used to go to the Tower ballroom, and when I was about fifteen, I decided I'd like to take lessons. I saved up my wages so I could pay for lessons over the summer.'

'Well, they certainly paid off,' Bella said, admiringly. 'You were fantastic out there.'

'Thank you.' Beryl grinned, as they left the cloakroom. The tempo of the music had slowed, and someone had dimmed the lights. Couples danced close together, swaying slowly to the music. Will held out his hand. Bella took it and he led her to the dance floor, pulling her close. The way he looked at her as they danced sent a shiver of excitement down her spine and she found herself wondering what it was about Will that her father had objected to. From what Will had told her about his family, they sounded perfectly respectable. She supposed she would have to put it down to just another facet of her father's unpredictable behaviour.

The tempo of the music slowed even more, and the lights dimmed further. It was the last dance of the night. Bella rested her head on Will's shoulder. With one hand resting lightly on her lower back, his other hand clasped hers tight, tucked under his chin. As they moved slowly around the dance floor, Bella felt she could certainly fall for Will. She had been on the cusp of doing just that when she'd been packed off to London. Surely it couldn't be a coincidence that they had ended up at the Chantry Fields

'What are you thinking?' Will murmured in her ear.

Bella raised her head. 'I was just thinking how strange it is that we both ended up at the same airbase.'

'It's fate,' grinned Will. Bella smiled back. As the last strains of the music faded away, he pulled her close and kissed her tenderly on the lips. The hall erupted in applause for the musicians, but Bella was oblivious. All she could think of was the sensation of Will's lips on hers.

'He kissed you?' said Gilly, with just the teeniest hint of envy as they boarded the bus to return to base. 'What was it like?'

'It was . . . nice,' Bella said.

'Nice?' repeated Amanda, leaning over her shoulder.

'All right,' Bella grinned. 'It was more than nice.' She sat back in her seat. How could she explain to her friends how her stomach had flipped over, or how her senses were still reeling from her very first kiss.

They kept up an endless stream of chatter all the way back to base. Bella had hoped she would get the chance to see Will getting off the bus, but Commander Forrester was waiting for them and ushered the women off to their beds before the men had even alighted from their buses.

'What a fantastic evening,' Amanda said, heating up a pan of milk for their bedtime cocoa. 'Jonty isn't much of a dancer, bless him. He's got two left feet. Not like you and that lance corporal of yours, Beryl.'

'Weren't they amazing?' said Gilly, leaning over Bella to grab her packet of cigarettes. 'You'll have to give us dance lessons in your spare time.'

'Are you seeing him again?' asked Amanda, spooning cocoa into mugs.

'He's taking me to the cinema next Saturday,' replied Beryl, casually inspecting her fingernails.

'Ooh,' sighed Gilly. 'Lucky you. I wish I could meet someone nice.'

'You weren't short of dance partners this evening,' Amanda reminded her, passing round mugs of steaming hot cocoa.

'No one invited me to the cinema, or kissed me,' she replied bleakly.

'You'll meet someone, Gilly,' Beryl said, sitting down on her bed, cradling her mug.

'There are over fifty men on this base, Gilly Ford,' Amanda reminded her, leaning against the wall, sipping her cocoa.

Gilly laughed, exhaling a cloud of cigarette smoke. 'I'm sure I will, but Bella, tell us about the gorgeous Will. He's so dashing. Why isn't he training to be a fighter pilot?'

'He failed the eye test,' Bella said, stretching out on her bed, her mug of cocoa cooling on the floor beside her. She lay back on her pillow, hands folded behind her head, staring up at the sloping wood roof, her friends' chatter washing over her as she relived Will's kiss over and over in her mind. She was definitely looking forward to seeing him again.

CHAPTER TWELVE

'Have you heard the news?' Gilly burst into the hut, looking troubled. 'Paris has fallen to the Germans!' She sank onto her bed, shaking her head in disbelief.

'We knew it would only be a matter of time,' Bella said, fear churning her stomach. With heavy hearts, both girls had watched the newsreels of the evacuation of thousands of Allied soldiers from the beaches of Dunkirk. With Hitler's armies just across the Channel, invasion was a frightening probability.

'I hope the prime minister can persuade the Americans to help us,' Gilly said, running a hand through her auburn hair. 'According to Jonty, most Americans don't want to get involved.'

'They must!' Bella exclaimed. 'We can't fight Hitler on our own.' She felt sick at the prospect of Hitler's army marching on London.

'What time is your train?' asked Gilly.

'Half past ten,' replied Bella. 'Will's driving me to the station.'

'Things are progressing well between you two,' grinned Gilly.

'They seem to be,' Bella blushed. Over the past four months she and Will had grown closer. They spent as much time together as their schedules allowed and Bella was close to falling in love. Gilly glanced at her watch.

'You'd better get a move on, then,' she said, getting up. 'Have a lovely time. I'll see you when you get back on Monday.'

'Thank you. Same to you. Have a good time in Bournemouth with Beryl. I would have come with you, but I really want to see Arthur and Mother.'

'Of course you do. We can do Bournemouth again next time.'

Once Gilly had gone, Bella packed the few things she would need for her short visit home, and, putting her hat on, went off in search of Will. She found him in the control office, perched on the desk, chatting to one of the two men who manned the telephone. All three men were smoking, and the open window did little to dispel the cloud of smoke that hovered over the cluttered desk.

'Bella,' Will said, with obvious pleasure, sliding off the desk. 'I was just coming to find you. Are you ready?'

'Cadet Roberts.' Both the men behind the desk nodded at her and she greeted them formally, as they were of a higher rank. 'Have a good leave,' the younger of the two said, cigarette clamped between his lips.

Bella thanked him. Will stubbed out his cigarette in the overflowing ashtray and they walked out into the warm June sunshine.

'Did you hear about Paris?' Bella asked, as they crossed the grass to the vehicle pool. Will nodded, his expression grim.

'It's the talk of the base. We knew it was inevitable, of course, but it does bring the war a bit closer to home.'

Despite the warm summer day, Bella shivered. Will stowed her small suitcase in the back of the Jeep and opened the door.

'Try not to let it spoil your visit home,' he said, climbing in beside her.

'It's difficult not to,' sighed Bella. 'When do you fly again?' she asked, as the Jeep bounced across the grass towards the track.

'I'm off to Inverness this afternoon, coming back tomorrow.'

'Stay safe,' Bella said, as she always did when Will was flying.

'I'll do my best,' he grinned, changing gear as the Jeep lurched over a bump in the road. With his free hand, he reached for Bella's, gripping it tight. 'I shall miss you.'

'I'll miss you, too,' Bella said, feeling her cheeks colour. Will turned to her and grinned.

'You look thoughtful,' he said. 'What are you thinking?'

Bella smiled wistfully. 'I was just thinking how peaceful it is here,' she said, her gaze taking in the tree-covered hills, the rolling fields with their herds of grazing cattle and bleating sheep, the buttercup meadows, the tall flowers waving gently in the breeze. 'It seems inconceivable that there's a war on.'

'I know what you mean,' agreed Will. They chatted about inconsequential things, driving along narrow lanes lined with waist-high cow parsley, buttercups and stinging nettles, humming with insects. Before long, they reached the town, sunlight glinting off tiled rooftops. Will slowed the Jeep to make room for a pony and cart coming the other way, and took the next turning, pulling up outside the railway station. He carried Bella's suitcase onto the platform where the train was already waiting, the carriages crowded with servicemen and women.

'I'll see you when you get back,' he said, kissing Bella on the lips, to the whistles of a couple of soldiers leaning out of the open windows. He grinned. Handing her suitcase to a nearby porter, Will saw Bella onboard. Despite the packed train, she managed to find a seat near the window, so she could wave as the train slowly pulled out of the station fifteen minutes later.

The journey to Southampton took just over an hour and a half. She had to change trains at Salisbury, boarding another, equally packed train. The main topic of conversation amongst the passengers was the fall of Paris. One WAAF Bella spoke to had cousins who lived just outside the French capital.

'My uncle is French, you see,' the WAAF, Nancy, told Bella as they shared a flask of weak tea just outside Salisbury.

'They moved there in 1938. The news will be hard for my dad. It's his sister, you see. They've got two young daughters.'

Another woman Bella spoke to, a nurse on her way to Brighton, had lost a brother at Dunkirk.

'My grandfather was lost during the evacuation of Dunkirk,' a young private interjected, leaning forward, skinny elbows resting on his knees. 'He answered Churchill's call to help and went over in his little rowing boat. He made it across and picked up two Belgian soldiers.' The private leaned back in his seat and scratched his nose. 'Grandad got them up alongside a Navy ship when they were hit by enemy fire. Grandad's boat capsized. The two Belgians were pulled to safety, but Grandad was lost.'

'I'm sorry,' Bella said. 'He was very brave. You must be so proud of him.'

'I am,' the private said, with a sad smile. 'Very proud.'

Bella leaned against the window, watching as the green fields and woodlands gave way to shunting sheds, warehouses and factories. Barrage balloons hovered over the rooftops, incongruous against the blue summer sky.

She stared out of the bus window at the ongoing work preparing the city's defences against the possible invasion. The pavements were lined with metal gates and some roads were blocked off by concrete structures. The bus trundled past a park where the newly formed Home Guard were practicing their drill, sending a chill down Bella's spine as she contemplated the very real possibility of invasion.

Her fears were brought even more into focus later that day by her mother.

She arrived at the vicarage just before one o'clock. Her mother was watching from the upstairs window and came flying out of the house as Bella pushed open the front gate. She was followed by Barney and Sybil, barking in welcome.

'Bella, darling,' Alice cried. She had been in such a hurry to greet her daughter, she hadn't bothered to change out of her slippers or take off her apron. Bella put down her suitcase and hugged her mother warmly. 'It's so lovely to see you,' Alice said. She took a step back, holding Bella at arm's length. 'You look very well,' she said approvingly. 'They're obviously feeding you well down in Dorset.'

'We have a lot of cream and butter,' Bella laughed, patting her stomach. 'I'm worried I'll get fat.'

'Nonsense,' her mother scoffed. 'You are one of those fortunate girls who seem to be able to eat as much as you like without putting on an ounce.' Bella picked up her suitcase and, with her mother's arm around her shoulders, walked up the path to the house.

'Bella,' Ida Wilson said, hurrying from the kitchen, wiping her hands on a tea towel. 'You're looking well. Doesn't she look well, ma'am?'

'She does indeed,' smiled Alice. 'Samuel,' she called, in the direction of her husband's study. 'Bella's home.'

'I'll put the kettle on,' Ida said. 'You're bound to want a drink after your journey.'

'Some elderflower cordial would be nice,' Bella called after her. 'If we've got some.'

'Of course,' Ida smiled. 'I'll get the bottle out of the pantry.'

'Bella, my dear.' Samuel emerged from his study. He was casually dressed in brown trousers, worn at the knees, a green and white checked shirt and a fawn cardigan.

'Excuse my attire,' he grinned, kissing Bella's cheek. 'I've been working in the garden.'

'It's nice to see you looking so relaxed, Father,' smiled Bella, giving him a hug.

'I thought we'd have luncheon on the terrace as it's such a lovely day,' Alice said. 'I'm sure you'd like to freshen up first so shall we say about ten minutes? It's only cold cuts and salad.'

'Sounds delicious,' Bella grinned. 'I'll be down in a jiffy.'

Declining her father's offer to carry up her suitcase, Bella made her way up the carpeted stairs to her old bedroom. Her mother had laid out a clean towel and there was a jug of warm water on the stand along with a new cake of her mother's favourite lavender-scented soap.

She washed quickly and ran her brush through her long hair. She was seriously thinking about having it cut. Most of the girls at the base had shorter hair and she envied them how much easier it was to look after. She wondered how her father would react, then reminded herself that she was a grown woman and quite able to make her own decisions regarding her appearance. She pinned it away from her face, making the firm decision to visit the hairdressers on her next afternoon off, and made her way downstairs. Her parents were in the garden, the dogs sprawled under the table. Johnny and Jack, the two evacuees, stopped their play to look at Bella shyly.

'You remember, Bella, boys,' Alice smiled. 'Come and say hello.'

'Hello,' they both mumbled.

'Hello, boys,' Bella grinned at them. 'What are you playing?'

The boys shyly showed Bella the lead soldiers lined up in the dirt in regiments. They were scuffed, some so badly it was hard to tell the colour of their uniforms.

'Are those Arthur's old soldiers?' asked Bella, sitting down on one of the wooden chairs, adjusting the yellow checked cushion behind her back, and stretched out her legs, crossing them at the ankles. The garden hummed with insects and the surrounding trees reverberated with birdsong.

'They are,' Alice replied. 'Your father dug them out of the attic. He keeps promising to paint them.'

'And so I will,' Samuel replied, a trifle testily. 'As soon as I get a moment.'

While the boys went indoors to wash their hands under Ida's supervision, Bella surveyed her surroundings. 'It looks so different,' she said, inclining her head towards the garden as she picked up her glass of elderflower cordial.

'I do miss my roses,' Alice said, passing Samuel the plate of cold, sliced chicken. 'But we must do our bit. You enjoy the gardening, don't you, dear,' she said to Bella's father as he helped himself to a slice.

'I do find it therapeutic,' Samuel replied. 'And the boys are a big help, aren't you lads?' He grinned at Johnny and Jack. 'We have carrots, beans, onions, cabbage, broccoli, you name it, we're growing it.' He helped himself to some lettuce and a spoonful of pickled beetroot. 'The Anderson shelter is a bit of an eyesore and I'm starting to wonder if it wasn't rather a waste of money. I mean, if we're invaded a shelter isn't going to do us much good, is it.'

'Samuel,' Alice implored him, her eyes heavy with anxiety. 'Not in front of the children.'

Samuel reached for her hand. 'Of course, my dear. I'm sorry. Not to worry, lads. You'll be perfectly safe here.' He took a sip of his cordial. 'So, Bella, how are you getting on? Your letters are very upbeat. It seems you're enjoying the work and you've made some good friends?'

'Yes, Father,' Bella nodded, helping herself to a spoonful of new potatoes. She wondered if she should mention Will but decided against it. Her father's behaviour last time had been so strange, she thought. Better to wait and see how their romance developed before bringing it up.

'I'm pleased you've forgotten all about this flying nonsense,' Samuel continued, buttering a slice of bread. Bella and her mother exchanged glances but said nothing. That was another thing Bella only needed to tell her father when, and if, it happened.

The rest of the meal passed in pleasant conversation. Alice

filled Bella in on the village news; the postmaster had lost a son at Dunkirk, and the owners of the big house were arranging a summer outing to the seaside for all the evacuee children in a fortnight's time.

'I'm going as one of the chaperones,' Alice said, refilling their glasses. 'I'm quite looking forward to it.'

'Can we get down now?' Johnny asked, swallowing the last of his stewed plums and custard.

'What do you say?' Samuel asked, amiably. Johnny beamed, his cheeks rosy in the afternoon sunshine.

'Please may we leave the table, Uncle Samuel?' the boy said, smiling angelically.

'Yes, you may,' Samuel replied, regarding the boy fondly.

'Me too?' asked little Jack, with a mischievous grin, a tuft of light brown hair standing on end.

'Of course,' Samuel nodded. The two boys scrambled from the table and disappeared off round the side of the vicarage, the dogs following joyfully in their wake. Samuel pushed back his chair.

'Right, I must go and work on my sermon for tomorrow,' he said, draining his glass. He dabbed his lips with his napkin. 'Will you be joining us at church in the morning?' he asked Bella.

'Of course, Father.'

'What time does Arthur finish work?' Bella asked Alice, once Samuel had gone inside and Ida had come out to clear the table.

Alice sighed. 'I need to speak to you about Arthur,' she said, her eyes clouding. Bella's stomach clenched with fear.

'What's happened?' she asked, with a deep sense of dread. 'Is he all right?'

'Well,' Alice said, pursing her lips. 'The thing is, my cousin Benjy came down the other weekend to see Aunt Eleanor and the girls. My mother invited Father and I for Sunday dinner, but your father wasn't well, so I went alone.' Alice's shoulders slumped. 'After dinner, Benjy took me aside and told me I should seriously consider sending Arthur back to South Africa.'

'South Africa!' Bella balked. 'Whatever for?'

Her mother regarded her bleakly. 'You know how the newspapers have been reporting that Hitler is sending Jewish people to special work camps? Well, Benjy says the Germans are doing the same to people with disabilities. They're sending people like Arthur, children even, to special camps. If we're invaded, Arthur will be taken away from us and likely sent back to Germany.' Her voice shook as her eyes filled with tears.

'Mother, that's awful. Surely, they can't do that?'

Alice shook her head. 'If Germany invades, Bella, they'll be able to do what they like. I'm seriously considering it. I haven't spoken to your father about it yet, but I think it's for the best. I couldn't bear it if anything happened to him.'

'Do you really think we will be invaded?' Bella asked, looking at her mother in dismay.

Alice shrugged. 'I don't know. But I want Arthur safely out of the way, just in case.'

CHAPTER THIRTEEN

Her mother's revelation had cast a pall over Bella's weekend home. She'd enjoyed spending time with Arthur, but the thought that this might be the last time she saw him until the war was over had weighed heavily on her mind and she'd cried when she'd left to catch the bus back to the railway station.

She arrived back at Chantry Fields late on the Monday afternoon. The bus dropped her half a mile from the base, and it was gone three by the time she trudged up the track towards it. She was almost at the gate when she saw Gilly running towards her.

'Guess what?' she shouted, waving, as she stumbled over the rugged ground. Despite herself, Bella laughed.

'What?' She stepped over a deep rut in the track, her suitcase bumping against her thigh. 'How was your week-end in Bournemouth?' she asked. Maybe Gilly had met someone, she mused, smiling at the look of sheer delight on her friend's face.

'Oh, never mind about that,' Gilly said, with a dismissive wave of her hand. 'Miss Gower and Miss Hughes are coming here tomorrow.'

'Really?' Bella's eyes widened with excitement.

'Commander Forrester told us herself,' replied Gilly. 'Isn't it exciting? I can't wait.'

'What exciting news to come back to.' Bella beamed as they fell into step together, chatting excitedly about the impending visit.

The airfield was bustling with activity. Mechanics were scurrying around the aeroplanes parked outside the hangars. A de Havilland Tiger Moth taxied along the runway, its propeller whirring, the loud drone of its engine drowning out every other sound.

'That's Will,' Gilly said. 'He said to tell you he'll be back this evening.'

Suitcase at her feet and shielding her eyes against the glare of the sun, Bella watched the plane taxi to the far end of the field and turn round so it was facing back towards them. For a few minutes, nothing happened, then the plane suddenly began moving forward. The engine roared as the plane gained speed, bouncing over the grass, sunlight glancing off its wings. The wheels lifted off the ground. As it rose into the air, Bella caught a glimpse of Will in the cockpit. He raised a hand in greeting as he soared over the airfield, slowly gaining height. Bella watched the plane clear the tree-line, climbing ever higher until it was just a speck in the clear blue sky.

Another plane was already taxiing along the runway while two more were being checked over by the ground crew. It was looking like it was going to be a busy day.

Bella was in the mess playing cards with Amanda, Beryl and Gilly when Will returned. The sole topic of conversation in the camp was Pauline Gower and Joan Hughes's visit the following morning. A lot of the men were mocking in their comments and looking forward to having their preconceived ideas about women pilots justified. Even the officers were of the opinion that a woman could not possibly handle a plane as well as a man, and were happy to voice their astonishment that the government would trust an expensive aircraft to someone who would be better off staying home and cooking her husband's dinner.

To Bella's relief, Will held no such chauvinistic views, and he appeared almost as excited as the four women as he pulled up a chair to join them at the table.

'Exciting day tomorrow,' he grinned, kissing Bella's proffered cheek.

'We were just saying, we can't wait,' replied Bella, shuffling the deck of cards. 'Will you play?'

'Sure.' Will nodded. 'Jonty not back yet?' he asked Amanda.

'There was low cloud forecast over Hatfield, so Major Thompson thinks it likely he'll stay over and fly back tomorrow.'

Beryl picked up her cigarette that was smouldering in the

ashtray and stuck it between her crimson lips, as she arranged her cards in her hand.

'I'm so excited about tomorrow, I can hardly concentrate on my cards,' Bella said.

'I thought you'd be over the moon,' he grinned, giving her a sideways glance. 'The ladies are due in at around nine-fifteen, weather permitting, and I believe every man on base will be out to watch them arrive.'

'I'm sure that won't intimidate Miss Gower,' Bella said primly.

'I'm certain it won't,' concurred Will, selecting a card and laying it down. 'How was your weekend? Your family are all well?'

'I had a nice time,' Bella replied.

'But?' Will asked, raising an eyebrow. He was astute enough to realize that beneath the excitement, Bella was troubled about something.

'My mother wants to send Arthur abroad,' she said, gazing round at her friends. 'He'd be in danger if we were invaded.'

'Is it safe for him to go abroad?' asked Amanda, frowning at her cards. She looked up, meeting Bella's eyes. 'What about Hitler's blockade? Isn't your mother frightened the ship will be torpedoed? That would be my main fear.'

'I feel sick just thinking about it,' Bella admitted, leaning back in her chair. All the way back to base, it had been all she could think about.

'Your mother has to weigh up the two evils,' said Will. 'A sea voyage would be fraught with danger, but how much worse would it be for your brother if he was shipped off to one of these labour camps your cousin was talking about?'

'At least he'd be safe with your uncle in South Africa,' Beryl said, inhaling a cloud of smoke. 'You can't guarantee the same thing if he stayed here.'

Bella shrugged. 'It depends on whether my father agrees to it,' she said.

'Don't worry about it tonight,' Gilly said. 'We've got Pauline Gower's visit to look forward to.'

Bella smiled. 'I'm trying not to. What do you think she's coming here for? Do you think it's to see us?'

Gilly shrugged. 'I have no idea but I'm hoping so.'

'Apparently Major Thompson has arranged a slap-up luncheon for them,' Will said. 'With the officers of course. It's not for the likes of us.'

'Ten minutes to lights out, ladies,' Commander Forrester called across the room.

'May I walk with you?' Will asked, as they concluded their game, drained their glasses and stubbed out their cigarettes.

'I'd like that,' Bella said, picking up her hat.

They followed the others out into the balmy night. The crescent moon hovered above the hilltop, though the sky was still light in the west. It would be midsummer's eve in a week's time. The longest day of the year. A solitary black-bird sang lustily in a nearby tree and from somewhere in the distance Bella heard the throaty roar of a motorbike.

'It's the perfect evening,' Will said, as they lagged behind the others so they could enjoy a few moments alone together.

He took her hand in his, his thumb gently caressing her skin, sending a shiver of pleasure up Bella's spine. 'So peaceful, it's hard to believe there's a war on.'

'It was different in Southampton,' Bella told him, as they gazed out over the airfield, listening to the haunting cry of an owl. 'Seeing the barrage balloons and the defences they're building really brought it home to me. For the first time since we've been at war, I felt properly frightened.'

Will gave her hand a squeeze. 'We're living in frightening times,' he said, grimly. 'I'd better let you go. You don't want to get on the wrong side of Commander Forrester.' He slipped his arm around her waist and kissed her. 'Goodnight.'

'Goodnight.' Bella slipped into the hut. Beryl and Amanda were already under the covers. Gilly was in her pyjamas brushing her teeth at the wash basin.

'I'm not sure I shall sleep at all,' she said, through a mouthful of toothpaste. 'I'm so excited.'

'Me too,' said Bella, unbuttoning her blouse. The four women chatted excitedly about the coming day, as Bella completed her bedtime routine and climbed into bed. Beryl extinguished the lamp, but they lay whispering in the dark until well into the early hours.

The morning of the 18th of June dawned fair and warm. By nine o'clock, everyone who could had assembled outside to await the arrival of Senior Commander Pauline Gower and First Officer Joan Hughes. An air of expectation hung over the airfield, as everyone kept scanning the sky for the first glimpse of the plane.

Far in the distance a tiny speck appeared. 'There she is,' squeaked Bella, gripping Gilly's arm. There was a stirring in the crowd, and a lot of mocking jeers from amongst the men.

The sun glinted off the fuselage, forcing Bella to squint as she tracked the plane's progress towards them. The drone of the engine was now clearly audible above the chirp of the birds and snap of the windsock in the breeze. Bella bounced on the balls of her feet, hardly able to contain her excitement.

The plane came in low over the airfield, to the jeers of the men. None of them would come in to land so fast. The pilot gave a wave. The wheels of the plane barely brushed the grass before, to everyone's surprise, it rose gracefully into the air.

'I knew she came in too fast,' one of the male pilots standing a few feet from Bella said, with a derisive snort.

'What do women know about flying a plane?' sneered his companion. Bella shot them a look of annoyance before turning her gaze back to the plane. It was climbing higher into the clear sky. Suddenly the engine stalled. From the ground came a collective gasp of horror. The silence from the sky was deafening. Bella clutched Gilly's arm, her heart thumping in terror as the plane went into freefall, tumbling towards the earth. One of the girls let out a shriek of horror. Bella had her hand over her mouth. She could hardly bear to watch but she couldn't tear her gaze away. When it seemed that the plane would crash into the ground, the engine kicked in and it soared over their heads, racing into the air once more where it performed a perfect loop-the-loop. The men had fallen silent, watching the plane with begrudging respect as Pauline Gower performed several feats of skill. The plane flew upside down across the airfield, disappearing beyond a bank of trees to return a few minutes later to land gracefully to resounding cheers.

The plane taxied to the hangar, followed by the entire camp. The engine fell silent, the propeller stilled. The cockpit opened and the two women clambered out, waving. They were both dressed in flying gear.

'Good morning,' said Pauline Gower, removing her goggles. She was a striking woman with curly light brown hair and a commanding presence. First officer Joan Hughes was smaller, barely more than five feet, with short, curly dark hair.

'Good morning, Senior Commander Gower, First Officer Hughes,' Joan Forrester said, pushing her way to the front of the crowd. 'Commander Forrester and this is Major Thompson.'

'That was some flying, ma'am,' Major Thompson said, with begrudging respect. He extended his hand.

'Good morning, Major,' Pauline said, shaking his hand. 'I like to make an entrance. It silences the critics.' She smiled. There was some embarrassed shuffling of feet amongst the men.

'Coffee in my office?' Major Thompson said, indicating the way with his hand.

'Coffee sounds lovely,' Pauline said. 'Thank you.' The

crowd parted to allow the two women to follow the major and Commander Forrester to the cluster of buildings on the edge of the airfield.

Bella returned to work feeling like the morning had turned into a bit of an anticlimax. The talk in the parachute packing shed was, of course, of Pauline Gower's amazing flying skills.

'The way she handled that plane,' Beryl said, in awe. 'It was amazing.'

'She certainly knows how to make an entrance,' chuckled Amanda. 'I've never seen the men so quiet.'

'I do hope we'll get to speak to her while she's here,' Bella said. 'Do we know how long she intends to stay?'

'She's leaving directly after the major's luncheon,' replied one of the women walking past with an armful of silk. Bella's heart sank in disappointment. The luncheon was only for the officers. As Bella's shift ended at half past four in the afternoon it was unlikely she'd get to meet her heroine at all.

Feeling rather disgruntled, she got on with her work, her thoughts flitting between troubled ones about Arthur's future and her disappointment that she wouldn't get to spend any time with the two women pilots.

From outside came the drone of an approaching engine. Amanda went to the door and peered out.

'It's Jonty,' she beamed, stepping outside and waving her hat as the plane touched down on the grass. 'It's always a relief when he's back,' she said, returning to her table.

There was a movement in the doorway and the women's

idle chatter died away as the imposing figure of Commander Joan Forrester filled the entrance, casting a shadow on the bare wood floor.

'Cadets Chadwick, Roberts, Hastings and Ford, you're to go to the major's office as soon as you're finished what you're doing.' The four girls exchanged glances.

'Are we in trouble, ma'am?' Gilly asked, tentatively.

'Quite the contrary,' Joan grinned. 'Senior Commander Gower wishes to speak with you all.' She chuckled at the four women's obvious delight.

Barely able to contain their excitement, the four friends hurried to finish their work. Bella had to force herself to stay focused. It was so tempting to rush through the job she'd done so many times she could do it with her eyes shut but, as the lives of the pilots depended on her attention to detail, she took her time, making sure every fold was perfect, every bit of the rigging was threaded through the loops correctly. At last she was done. She placed the neatly packed parachute on the pile and, together with her three friends, made her way across the sun-dried grass to the major's office.

CHAPTER FOURTEEN

Heart racing with trepidation, Bella straightened her jacket and knocked on Major Thompson's half-open door.

'Come,' he called, and she pushed it open, smiling nervously as the two women seated in the chairs in front of the major's desk rose to greet her.

'Senior Commander Pauline Gower,' said the taller of the two women, smiling and holding out a hand as the others followed Bella inside.

'I'm First Officer, Joan Hughes,' the shorter woman said.

The four women introduced themselves and shook hands. The major cleared his throat, and beckoned the four friends to sit down in the fold out chairs that were placed around the room.

A young clerk arrived with the tea tray and they made small talk while Pauline poured and handed round the cups.

'Now, let's get down to business,' she said, taking her cup

and saucer and returning to her chair. Bella leaned forward, eager to hear what the woman had to say.

'Cadet Roberts.' Pauline smiled at Bella. 'You said on your application form that you haven't flown for about five years.?'

'Yes, ma'am,' replied Bella.

'As none of you have flown within the past six months, I would insist on you undertaking refresher training.' Pauline leaned back in her seat and smiled round at the four women. 'Once you've completed that, I would like to welcome you all as members of my women's branch of the Air Transport Auxiliary.'

Bella stared at the woman. Had Miss Gower really just offered her the opportunity to fly? Gilly gave a whoop of delight, giving Bella the confirmation she needed and earning herself a glare from the major, who was looking rather put out.

'Welcome on board, ladies,' grinned Pauline. 'I have cleared it with the major here and your training will commence tomorrow, weather permitting. All being well, you should be ready to join the ferry pool by the middle of August.' She got to her feet. Realizing the meeting was at an end, Bella and the others rose too.

'A pleasure meeting you, ladies.' Pauline shook each of the women by the hand.

'Thank you, ma'am.' Bella said, her stomach churning with excitement. Tomorrow she would be in an aeroplane once more. She couldn't wait to write to Arthur and tell him. He would be so excited for her.

'You may return to your duties, ladies,' said Major Thompson, gruffly.

'Yes, sir. Thank you, sir.'

'I shall have the details of your training by eighteen hundred hours, cadets,' Commander Forrester said, as the four women made to leave. You're dismissed.'

'Yes, ma'am. Thank you, ma'am.'

'Senior Commander Gower, First Officer Hughes, if you'd like to follow me,' Commander Forrester continued, turning her attention back to her guests. 'I shall show you the Ops Room.'

'I can't believe we're actually going to be airborne as early as tomorrow,' Amanda said, as they made their way along the well-worn path to the parachute shed. 'I've got butterflies. I can't wait to tell Jonty. He'll be over the moon. He knows how long I've wanted this.'

'Me too,' said Bella, wrapping her arms around herself. She wished Will was around so she could tell him, but he'd had a flight first thing that morning delivering a Spitfire to the airfield at Hamble, before going on to White Waltham. All being well, he'd be back at Chantry Fields that evening.

Chattering excitedly, the girls returned to the parachute shed where their colleagues were waiting to pepper them with questions, eager to share in their co-workers' excitement. A few of the women expressed regret and disappointment that they hadn't been chosen to join the ferry pool yet, but were slightly mollified when, as they readied themselves to leave, Pauline stood on the steps of her plane and told the assembled crowd, to a hearty round of applause, that the Air Transport Auxiliary would be taking on many more women pilots over the next few months.

With a wave, she pulled on her goggles and settled herself in the cockpit, Joan Hughes seated beside her. She gave a thumbs up sign and one of the ground crew ran to remove the chocks while another started the propeller.

This time there were no snide remarks or jeers from the assembled men. As Pauline taxied along the field, several of them cheered and waved their caps. At the far end of the airfield, she turned the plane in preparation for take-off. The plane picked up speed, lifting off the ground like a giant bird. She flew low over the base, waggling the wings of the de Haviland before soaring into the summer sky.

'Well, there we are, then,' said Gilly, linking arms with Bella and Beryl as they watched the plane diminish into a tiny speck in the vast cobalt-blue sky.

'That'll be us soon,' Amanda said, her eyes shining. 'Oh, I wish Jonty would get back.' Her eyes searched the empty sky.

'Come on,' Bella said. 'We'd better get back to work. Do you realize,' she added, as they trooped back to the parachute shed, 'this is our last day working in here.'

'I'd suggest we go out and celebrate tonight,' Beryl said, 'But I don't want to risk being hungover in the morning.'

'I think an early night is in order,' agreed Amanda sensibly.

The afternoon passed quickly, with all four girls making sure their work was meticulous. No one wanted to suffer the guilt of having the death of a pilot on their conscience because of shoddy work. As she folded her final parachute, Bella was struck by the thought that, from tomorrow, she would be one of the recipients of the many parachutes folded and checked with so much care. Massaging the small of her back with her fingers, she took a long look around the large shed, taking in the concentration on the faces of the women and girls she'd worked with for the past six months. From now on, should anything go wrong while she was in the air, her life would depend on these women.

Commander Joan Forrester found them in the mess eating their dinner.

'Stay seated,' she said, as they made to rise. 'I just wanted to let you know your training schedule for the next few weeks,' she said, pulling up an empty chair. 'Here's the training rota. It's pretty intense but time is of the essence.' She gazed round at each one of the four women as they flicked through their itinerary. 'Let me know if there's a problem.'

Bella scanned her schedule. 'Trainer, First Officer William Mullens.' She raised her eyes, meeting Commander Forrester's gaze. Joan nodded.

'He's one of the best,' she said. 'A natural pilot. You'll be in good hands with him.'

Hiding her smile, Bella exchanged amused glances with her three friends. The thought of flying with Will only increased her excitement.

'I'll leave you to your supper,' Joan said, getting to her feet. She paused, her hand on the table. 'Miss Gower, Senior

Commander Gower, I should say, was very impressed by the four of you.' She leaned closer. 'It was quite amusing, really,' she said, lowering her voice as she glanced over her shoulder, making sure no one could overhear. 'But during the luncheon, the major was going on about how women have no business being pilots.' She smirked. 'Senior Commander Gower certainly set him straight on that score. The poor man. He turned beetroot red and didn't say another word for the entire meal.'

Bella chuckled. 'That will serve him right,' she said. 'I noticed the men were all quite impressed by her flying skills, too.'

Joan Forrester winked. 'About time these men were taken down a peg. Too full of themselves, some of them. I have some more exciting news for you, as well,' she grinned. 'We're going to have an RAF squadron based here, so there will be planes aplenty to keep you girls up in the air.' She bade them a good evening and returned to the head table where the rather subdued-looking major was tucking into his meal.

'Wow!' said Amanda, playing with her fork. 'That'll be something, having the RAF boys here. I wonder when they're coming?'

'Don't you go eyeing up some RAF pilot now, Miss,' scolded Beryl. 'You'll break your Jonty's heart.'

'Jonty knows he's the only one for me,' replied Amanda. 'But a little window shopping doesn't do any harm now, does it?'

'You wouldn't feel the same if it was Jonty casting his eye about,' Gilly said, giving Amanda a playful slap on the arm. 'Is he not back, yet?'

Amanda sighed. 'Nope. I'm starting to get a little worried, actually.' She looked towards the window. Bella followed her gaze. The sky was a clear blue. There was no reason why Jonty should be delayed. As all ATA pilots had to maintain radio silence, there was no way of knowing if he'd got into trouble, unless he managed to get to a telephone. If he'd crashed in a remote area, it could be weeks before anyone knew. She felt the first stirrings of unease in the pit of her stomach. Will wasn't back yet, either. There were so many things that could go wrong, not least pilot error. There was the unpredictable weather to contend with, sudden banks of low cloud, as well as the fact that some of the planes they ferried about the country were damaged. It was a risk the ATA pilots took every day. A risk that Bella herself would soon be taking.

They finished their meal in relative silence, letting the various conversations wash over them. Bella could see Amanda was worried. She glanced towards the window again. Dust motes danced in the shards of early evening sunlight, lighting up the floor. Concern for Jonty and Will had placed a damper on the women's excitement and they were quiet as they made their way back to their room. Beryl lay on her bed, scribbling a letter to Bob, her soldier over at Blandford. Amanda turned on her little radio. It was playing a song by Billy Cotton, 'There'll Always Be an England.'

'Fancy a game of cards,' Gilly said, reaching for the deck on the desk. 'It'll take your mind off Jonty for a bit.'

Amanda hesitated. 'All right. Bella?'

'Yes, I'll play.' The three of them sat cross-legged on Bella's bed. It was closest to the open window, affording them an uninterrupted view of the airfield, although they'd hear any approaching plane before they saw it. A warm breeze stirred the curtains. A fly crawled over Bella's hand, and she batted it away. She felt restless and unable to concentrate on the game. She looked at Amanda. Her friend's face was lined with worry.

'Do you think you should go over to the Ops Room and see if they've heard anything?' Gilly said, laying down her cards. 'Jonty might have telephoned to say he's held up.' She shrugged. 'It's worth a try.'

'Maybe,' Amanda laid her cards face down on the blanket and stretched. 'I'm sorry, Gilly. I can't concentrate tonight. I think I shall go over to the Ops Room. Bella, do you want to come? Maybe they've heard from Will.'

'Okay.' Bella stretched out her legs and groped under the bed for her shoes. She was just tying the laces when they all heard the distant drone of an aircraft. There was a collective intake of breath, and the four women hurried to the door, getting themselves wedged as they all tried to get out at the same time. Beryl and Gilly held back, and Amanda almost fell out into the late June sunshine, followed by Bella. Shading her eyes against the glare, Bella searched the sky.

'There,' she said, pointing to a tiny plane in the distance.

Only one plane. She bit her lip anxiously, walking a few steps forward as the plane came closer. Several other people were emerging from the various places, the barracks, the mess. A mechanic wandered out of the hangar, wiping his oil-stained fingers on a dirty rag. They were all staring up at the sky.

Amanda tucked her hand in Bella's elbow, as they both kept their gaze trained on the plane. As it approached the airfield, Bella gave a shriek. 'It's Will, and Jonty. They're both in there.' Amanda let go of Bella's arm and clapped her hand to her face.

'Oh, thank God,' she breathed, as the plane swooped low in front of their eyes, both pilots waving jovially as Will gently brought the plane in to land. There were a few cheers and whistles as the aircraft bounced along the grass, before coming to a halt in front of the building housing the Ops Room and Major Thompson's office. He stood on the step, his chest puffed out in importance.

Will and Jonty extricated themselves from the cockpit and clambered out of the plane.

'Where the hell have you two been?' barked the major. 'And where the hell is my other plane?'

Will only managed to blow Bella a quick kiss before he and Jonty were ushered into the major's office.

'Well, at least we know they're safe,' Amanda said, linking arms with Bella as they made their way back inside. 'I wonder what happened.'

'No doubt we'll find out later,' replied Bella, almost giddy with relief. Her growing fear for Will had left her in no doubt that her feelings for him were certainly growing. Dare she say it, she might even be falling in love.

'Jonty had quite a time of it,' Will said, taking Bella's hand and tucking it through his arm as they strolled along the narrow woodland path, lined with wild chamomile. Hazy sunshine streamed through the leafy boughs, dappling the path in front of them. A wood pigeon cooed in a branch above Bella's head and from further away came the hoot of an owl.

It was just after half past eight that evening. Will and Jonty had spent almost an hour being debriefed by the major and, after a quick meal which the cook had kept warming for them on the stove, they had come to find Bella and Amanda.

Amanda and Jonty had gone to the mess for a drink, but Will had said he'd prefer a walk, so they'd crossed the fields to the woods on the perimeter of the airbase.

'He hit low cloud and lost altitude somewhere near Inverness and came down, none too gently, I gather, in a loch. He almost drowned trying to get his harness off.'

'And the plane?' Bella asked, sobered by thoughts of Jonty's narrow escape.

'At the bottom of Loch Ness. He managed to swim to shore. The weather had closed in, so he holed up in a shepherd's bothy overnight and made his way to Inverness the next morning. He arrived at the airbase just after me. More bad weather came in, so we had to wait for a couple of hours.

We only had about a half hour window in which to take off, or we'd have been stranded for another night. The telephone lines were down, so we couldn't let the Ops Room chaps know.' He lowered his head. 'I'm sorry you were worried.'

'I wasn't until Amanda started to worry. But Jonty had been gone overnight, and as the weather here has been fantastic, we didn't think.' She gave a laugh. 'It's so easy to become anxious, isn't it?'

'It is. I had a few hairy moments myself going up to Inverness. At one point the cloud came so low, I thought I was going to have to land. Thankfully it lifted again so I was able to keep going.' He grinned. 'By the way, congratulations on making it to the ferry pool. Just don't go falling for your flight instructor. I hear he's rather dashing.'

'Silly.' Bella elbowed him in the ribs. 'Thank you. I'm so excited, and I'm so pleased you're training me.'

'I hardly think I'll need to do much,' replied Will, seriously. 'You knew how to fly before I did. It's only a refresher course. I know the major said six weeks, but I reckon you'll be ready to go within a fortnight.'

'You think so?'

'I'll tell you tomorrow,' Will grinned. 'Once I've been up in the cockpit with you.' He glanced at the sun, glowing orange through the trees. 'We'd better be getting back. I want you bright-eyed and bushy tailed tomorrow.'

'Yes, sir,' Bella said, giving Will a salute. His grin broadened.

'Just remember, until you earn your wings, I'm your

superior, in the air, obviously. I wouldn't dare to presume so on the ground.' He rubbed his nose. 'I still remember the thump you gave me. Not that I didn't deserve it, of course.'

'That's another thing I'm worrying about,' Bella said, pursing her lips. 'I wonder what my parents have decided to do about Arthur.'

CHAPTER FIFTEEN

Bella drew back the curtains to find the airbase shrouded in mist. Disappointed, she dressed and headed for the mess for breakfast and by the time she'd finished her second mug of tea, the mist had dissipated, and the airfield was bathed in brilliant sunshine. The sky was an unblemished blue as Bella and Will made their way across the dew-soaked grass to the Tiger Moth.

'Okay, Cadet Roberts,' Will grinned, handing her a leather helmet and a pair of flying goggles. 'Show me what you can do.'

'Yes, sir.' Bella grinned back. Gripping hold of the edge of the rear cockpit, she clambered up onto the wing and, straddling the side, which wasn't an easy feat in her skirt, carefully eased herself into the seat. Aware of Will settling himself into the cockpit in front of her, she pulled on her helmet and goggles, and strapped herself in. She took a few minutes to familiarize herself with the controls and, leaning over the side, gave Will the thumbs up.

She turned the fuel on and waited while the last-minute checks were completed. The prop swinger turned the propeller four times. Bella took a deep breath and set the trim and the throttle. She looked upwards, checking her fuel gauge. They had enough fuel for about two hours, Will had told her.

'Contact!' shouted the prop swinger. With shaking hands, Bella reached out of the cockpit and flicked her magneto on. The prop swinger pulled the propeller through, and the engine roared to life, sending a thrill through Bella's veins. Taking a deep breath, she signalled for the chocks to be pulled away and, keeping one hand steady on the throttle, used her other to unlock the slats ready for take-off. She pressed the rudder with her left foot, keeping the plane steady, as she checked her instruments again. The plane accelerated and she weaved along the runway, slowly increasing the pressure as they gathered speed. The wind rushed past her as she kept her gaze focused on the tree-line at the far end of the runway. As her speed reached 70mph, the plane seemed to levitate. She throttled back slightly, keeping the Tiger Moth steady as it cleared the trees easily, bouncing on thermals as it soared into the clear sky. She banked to the right, circling back over the airbase. Leaning over the side, she gazed down at the tiny planes lined up. The people were just dark specks below her. She straightened out, soaring over fields and woodlands. Far below a train raced through the Dorset countryside. She swooped low, feeling the old, familiar throb of exhilaration in her chest. The plane hit a bank of turbulence, and the machine shook violently. Bella held her breath, waiting for the machine to steady, then they were soaring smoothly through the empty sky. Wisps of cloud as light and fluffy as dandelion seeds drifted past her head. It was cold this high up and she was glad of her fleece-lined jacket and thick gloves. Will twisted round in his seat and gave her the thumbs up. She grinned back and turned her attention to her control panel. Performing a perfect turn, she steered the plane back towards the airbase, landing smoothly on the soft grass. She taxied slowly towards the hangar and brought the Tiger Moth to a halt.

'That was amazing,' she gasped, clambering down from the cockpit, her cheeks pink with cold. She snatched off her hat and goggles and flung her arms around Will. 'I'd forgotten just how exhilarating flying is.'

'Some decorum, Cadet Roberts,' Joan Forrester shouted.

'Sorry, Commander,' Bella blushed, immediately dropping her arms from around Will's neck.

Joan grinned. 'You looked good up there, Cadet. You should be proud of yourself.'

'You were brilliant,' Will said, as they walked across the grass to the Ops Room. 'It won't be long before you're cleared to fly solo.'

'Do you think so?' she asked hopefully. Will nodded.

'I know so.' He nodded at the door to the Ops Room. 'Good luck. I'll see you later.'

*

139

Bella spent the rest of the morning with the staff manning the phones in the Operations Room. One of the walls was covered by a map of the British Isles with pins depicting the airbases. On a large blackboard were written the names of the pilots currently in the air, where they were headed and when they were expected back. On the opposite wall was a notice board with the duty rosters. Two men sat at a large desk, littered with paperwork. There were two telephones. One of the operators had been on the telephone when Bella entered. The other man looked up from the papers he was paging through and nodded.

'Cadet Roberts?' He removed the cigarette from his lips, exhaling a cloud of smoke into the air.

'Yes, sir.'

'First Officer Neil Glover. Take a seat.' Bella sat down, tucking her legs under the chair. 'Right, this is the Ops Room,' Neil said, with a smile. He was a nice-looking man with short dark hair and a pencil-thin moustache. 'You'll report here every morning to pick up your itinerary. First Officer Harvey Bridgewater here . . .' Without a pause in his conversation, the fair-haired man speaking on the telephone raised his free hand in acknowledgement, '. . . will give you a rundown on the weather at the places you're headed. You'll never be asked to put your life at risk,' he continued, drawing long and hard on his cigarette. 'Even the men are allowed to decline a flight if they feel conditions are too unfavourable.'

'Yes, sir.' Bella nodded.

'Your name goes on the roster and as the calls come in, you take the order. There is some flexibility, of course.'

Harvey Bridgewater ended his call, grinning up at Bella as he replaced the receiver. 'Like Donald,' he said, giving Neil's shoulder a nudge. 'He's got himself a fancy woman over near Hamble, so whenever the call comes up to go to Hamble, he usually gets the designated pilot to swap with him. Especially if it means an overnight stay.'

Bella smiled. 'I understand.'

'Once the RAF lots move in, we're going to be a hell of a lot busier,' Harvey said, in his cut-glass accent. 'There'll be planes coming and going all the time. In the meantime, you girls have a lot to learn.' His eyebrows rose a notch. 'Think you're up to it?'

'Yes, sir. Definitely, sir.'

Both men smiled. 'I look forward to working with you, Cadet Roberts,' said Harvey. Both telephones rang and the men's attention was immediately on the callers at the other end of the line.

'Yes, sir,' Harvey said.

She spent the next two hours watching how the men assessed the various requests for planes and flights. On several occasions they had to turn down the request due to not having the relevant plane available.

She joined Gilly, Amanda and Beryl in the mess at dinner time. All three of her friends were buzzing about their flights.

'I didn't realize until I felt the joystick in my hands how

much I've missed flying,' Gilly said, as they queued for their food. 'How did you get on in the Ops Room?'

'All right,' Bella replied. 'The chaps seem nice.'

'I'm in there tomorrow morning after my flight,' Ginny said. 'I think Beryl's in on Friday and Amanda on Saturday.'

'What's that?' asked Amanda, eyeing the dollop of mash potato the cook plopped on her plate with some suspicion.

'When you're in the Ops Room?' Gilly replied. 'Saturday, isn't it?'

'That's right.'

'I'm not looking forward to ground school this afternoon,' she said, once the four of them were seated at their table.

'Neither am I,' said Beryl. A strand of raven-black hair had come loose from her ponytail, and she brushed it out of her face. 'I'm useless at map reading. Always have been.'

'I've never tried,' Bella admitted. 'You're not alone, Beryl. I haven't a clue, either.'

'We'd better keep an eye on the time,' Amanda said, glancing up at the clock on the mess wall. 'Jonty tells me Flight Lieutenant Walsh is a stickler for punctuality, oh, and he doesn't have a very high opinion of women.' She rolled her eyes. 'Especially women pilots.'

At precisely five minutes to two, the four women were seated at their desks in the draughty Nissan hut that served as the base's ground school, just before three older men came hurrying in.

'Hello, ladies,' they said jovially, taking their time finding a desk and introducing themselves as Matt Brown, Freddie O'Reilly-Smith and Dave Longden. They'd barely exchanged greetings when a loud cough just outside the door preceded the entrance of a tall, distinguished looking man Bella assumed to be about forty. He had short, dark brown hair, greying at the temples, a piercing gaze and a weathered complexion. He wore the royal blue of an RAF officer, and carried his hat tucked under his right arm.

'Good afternoon,' he said, brusquely, his gaze alighting on each of the seven candidates quaking before him. He walked to his desk, and laying his hat on it, he turned to face the class. 'I'm Flight Lieutenant Walsh,' he said, in a gravelly voice. 'You may address me as sir.' He picked up a sheaf of papers from his desk and flicked through them.

'Cadet Roberts?'

Bella swallowed. 'Sir?'

'You learned to fly in the Western Cape?'

'Yes, sir.'

Walsh grunted. 'I spent my formative years in Stellenbosch.' He flicked to the next page. 'Cadet O'Reilly-Smith?'

'Sir?'

'You lost the sight in your left eye in the trenches, I believe?'

'Yes, sir. Shrapnel, sir,'

'Well, the ATA will take anyone,' Walsh said dismissively. 'Apparently there's a chap with one arm.' He snorted. He spent the next five minutes going through the brief background of each candidate.

143

Bella learned that Matt, Dave and Freddie all had flying experience, and having all served in the Great War, they wanted to 'do their bit'. As they were too old to enlist, all being in their late forties, and with Freddie having the added impediment of having only one working eye, they'd opted for joining the ATA.

'Now we've got the pleasantries out of the way, we can get started,' intoned Walsh, striding across the front of the room, slapping his thigh with his wooden pointer. Bella and Gilly exchanged glances.

'You ladies had better be sure you really want to do this,' he said, his disparaging gaze sweeping across the room. 'Aeroplanes are expensive pieces of equipment. Why the government feels giving them to a woman is a good idea is beyond me but,' – he let out a long-suffering sigh – 'I've been tasked with bringing you up to speed, for my sins. So, listen up. Flying is dangerous. For obvious reasons, you will be flying without radio, you'll have no weather "actuals", no way of contacting the local RAF or weather station, no radio beams to home in on. In effect, you'll be flying blind. Which is why your map reading skills need to be second to none. Should you become disorientated, you will learn how to make use of railway lines and Roman roads to locate your position. You never fly above the clouds, but that's not to say you won't find yourselves suddenly engulfed in fog or a storm.' He glowered at the four women. Bella leaned back in her seat; her arms folded across her chest and stared defiantly back at the flight lieutenant to show him she wasn't intimidated by his words. He sighed.

'Okay, during your time in ground school we will be covering meteorology, map-reading, obviously, navigation and basic mechanics. If you have to land somewhere remote because of a malfunction, you'll need to know how to patch up the plane and get it airborne. You'll also be taught where to expect barrage balloons. You'd be surprised how easy they are to crash into,' he added in response to their shocked looks. 'Before you're allowed to join the ferry pool, you'll be expected to complete no less than thirty cross-country flights along fixed routes to familiarize yourselves with England from the air.'

Bella and her three friends exchanged glances. Amanda puffed out her cheeks and exhaled through gritted teeth. Bella got where she was coming from. It sounded daunting.

'Right, if you'll open your textbook on page one, we'll begin.'

After three gruelling hours of ground school, Bella was gasping for a cup of tea. She found Will in the mess, having just returned from an errand into town.

'How was it?' he asked, passing her the milk jug.

'Intense,' replied Bella, as they carried their mugs to one of the tables set up outside the mess. There were several servicemen and women sitting around, enjoying the balmy June weather. 'How did you find it?'

'Hard work,' Will admitted. 'I've never been one for book learning. I much prefer the practical side of things, but I got a pass.'

'I shall be spending a lot of my evenings studying, I'm afraid,' Bella told him, sipping her tea and gazing over the airfield where two swallows were swooping and diving, skimming the short grass in their pursuit of insects.

'It won't be for long,' Will assured her. 'We'll have plenty of time to go out once you've qualified.'

CHAPTER SIXTEEN

'Bella, what's up?' asked Beryl, walking past her on her way to the bathroom, a week later. The last week of June had been wet and windy and much of Bella's training flights had been cancelled. The four women had just returned from ground school but Bella's excitement at finding a letter from home awaiting her had turned to dismay as she read her mother's words.

'My mother and Arthur want to meet me in Salisbury on Saturday.'

Beryl frowned. 'That's good news, surely?'

Bella bit her bottom lip. 'No, I have a bad feeling. My mother wouldn't make such a trip unless it was necessary. I think she's coming to tell me they've decided to send Arthur away. She's bringing him to say goodbye.'

'Are you sure you don't want me to come with you?' asked Will, as Bella was about to board the train at Gillingham.

'No, thank you,' she replied. 'Like I said, if the reason for their visit is what I think it is, then it's better I go alone. Thank you, though. It's a nice gesture.' She leaned forward and kissed him.

'I'll see you this evening, then,' he said, seeing her on board and settled in a compartment.

'Thank you for bringing me to the station,' she said, giving his hand a squeeze. 'I could have got the bus.'

'I know,' grinned Will. 'But that would have meant I had less time to spend with you.' He caressed her cheek with his finger. 'Try not to worry too much.'

'Easier said than done,' said Bella with a wry smile.

The station guard blew his whistle, and, after one last kiss, Will disembarked to stand on the platform and wave as the train slowly pulled out of the station.

All through the forty-five-minute journey, Bella's mind revisited the thoughts that had been going around in her head since she'd first read her mother's letter. Though her mother hadn't been specific in what she said, being aware that should any hint of their plans fall into the wrong hands it could mean disaster, not just for Arthur, but for all the other passengers and crew aboard the ship, Bella was certain that was what her mother was going to tell her today. Arthur would be leaving, and her mother was giving Bella the chance to say goodbye.

It was just after a quarter to eleven when the train pulled into Salisbury railway station. The train from Southampton was due in ten minutes so Bella found a vacant bench and sat down to wait. Pigeons cooed overhead and strode up and down the platform, pecking at discarded cigarette butts. A cold wind howled through the station, and Bella shivered in her thin jacket. It was unseasonably chilly, considering they'd celebrated the summer solstice only five days earlier. The platform teemed with servicemen and women and the station building had been fortified with sandbags. Her train let out a shrill whistle and rolled slowly out of the station bound for London. Bella checked the station clock. Her mother's train was due in five minutes. It turned out to be a further twenty minutes before the Southampton train roared into the station, belching thick black smoke as it shuddered to a halt. The doors opened as it disgorged its passengers. Bella got to her feet, searching the sea of military uniforms for her mother and Arthur. The crowd thinned a little and she spotted her mother's pale face, her eyes anxiously scanning the crowd. Bella's heart gave a lurch as Arthur's beaming face swam into view. His hair was shorter, she noticed, pushing her way towards them.

'Bella!' Her mother's face registered relief as she held out her arms. 'It's so good to see you. You look well.'

'It's only been two weeks, Mother,' Bella laughed, giving Alice a hug.

'I know,' Alice bit her lip. 'But, well, with everything going on.'

'Hello, Arthur.' She hugged her brother warmly. Arthur wrapped his arms around her, squeezing her tight.

'You smell nice,' he said, sniffing her hair.

'Thank you.' Bella ruffled his hair. 'I like the new look. It suits you.'

Arthur ducked away. He'd always been averse to people touching his head.

'Right,' said Alice brightly. 'Shall we find a nice café and have some dinner?'

'I'm starving,' Arthur said, nodding enthusiastically.

'How have you been, Mother?' Bella asked as they made their way out of the station.

'All right.' Alice hesitated. 'Did you hear they bombed Dibden Purlieu?' she spoke. 'The church was totally destroyed.'

'I didn't, no,' Bella replied, frowning. 'That's a bit close to home, isn't it?'

'That's what prompted me to contact Benjy. If the Germans invade, Southampton will be one of the first cities they'll occupy.'

Bella's heart sank. She glanced over at her brother, who was avidly watching a passing convoy of army Jeeps. 'He's going, then?'

Alice nodded. 'This way, Arthur,' she said, lightly touching Arthur's arm. She indicated the pavement running underneath the railway bridge. They turned onto Fisherton Street. It was swarming with military personnel. Sandbags were piled against shops and offices, and steel gates lined the kerbs. The long road teemed with bicycles, olive-green army trucks and Jeeps, and buses. The Georgina Rose was situated halfway down the street, its brightly coloured awning casting a shadow over the pavement.

There were a few vacant tables available, and Alice chose one close to the window so Arthur could watch the traffic. He was fascinated by anything with an engine and had been in his element when Farmer Monk had invested in one of the new-fangled tractors. He'd even allowed Arthur to drive it on occasion.

A large, middle-aged woman in a pink floral apron bustled over, pencil and notepad at the ready.

'A pot of tea for three, please,' Alice said, scanning the handwritten menu on the blackboard above the counter. 'And I'll have the salmon mayonnaise salad. Bella?'

'Fish and chips for me, please.'

The woman looked up from her notepad, pencil poised. 'And what will the young lad have?' the woman said, looking at Alice. Alice stared at her, long and hard.

'He can answer for himself. Ask him.'

'There's no need to take that tone,' the woman retorted huffily, two rosy spots blooming on her plump cheeks. 'He don't look like he's the full shilling to me, bless him.'

'I'd like the Heinz baked beans on toast, please, ma'am,' Arthur enunciated clearly. Averting her gaze, the woman jotted down his order and marched back to the kitchen.

'When does he leave?' asked Bella in a low voice, as Arthur turned his attention back to the window.

'For security reasons, we'll only know a day or two before,' replied Alice. 'Benjy's been so helpful. I honestly don't think we'd have got permission to travel, if it wasn't for him.' She paused, her expression pained. 'The thing is,' she said, reaching across the table to take Bella's hands in hers, 'I'm going too. Arthur will need a chaperone on the ship anyway, and I'd feel happier if I was there to keep an eye on him.'

'Of course you must go,' Bella said, her throat thickening at the thought of losing not only her brother, but also her mother. How long might it be before she saw either of them again?

'What does Father say?'

Alice gave a wry smile. 'He's against the idea, of course, but I must put Arthur's safety first. According to Benjy's intelligence, the Germans are doing awful things to people with Down syndrome and the like. They're telling the families they're taking them to special schools and institutions when in fact . . .' Her mother broke off, her mouth trembling. Her eyes swam with tears. 'Bella,' she whispered. 'Benjy says they're killing them.'

Bella recoiled in horror. 'No! Surely not?' She glanced at the back of Arthur's head. He was quietly rattling off the makes and models of the vehicles making their way along Fisherton Street. 'They wouldn't do such a thing.' She turned back to her mother. 'That's appalling.'

They were interrupted by the arrival of the proprietor with the tea tray. Studiously avoiding eye contact, the woman placed the teapot and three cups and saucers on the table.

'Thank you,' Alice said, as the woman scurried back to the kitchen.

Alice poured the tea while Bella told her and Arthur about her training. The food arrived shortly after. It was hot and tasty but the knowledge that this would be the last meal the three of them would eat together for a long time had cast a pall over the meal, and Bella struggled to swallow much more than a few mouthfuls.

'Aren't you eating that?' Arthur asked, eyeing the remains of her plaice and chips.

'Feel free,' she replied, pushing her plate towards him. While Arthur tucked in with gusto, Alice and Bella chatted about mundane things, neither of them wanting to dwell on the reality of the impending goodbye.

They had two hours to kill before they had to catch their respective trains, so they walked along the High Street to the cathedral. The grounds were a popular place for civilians and servicemen and women alike. The thirteenth century Gothic cathedral was an imposing sight. Sitting on the warm grass in the cathedral's serene grounds, Bella gazed up at the spire, the tallest in England. She leaned back on her elbows, enjoying the sun on her face.

'I worry about you flying,' her mother said, with a sigh. 'I haven't said anything to your father, yet.' She rummaged in her handbag, bringing out a brown paper bag containing lemon sherbets. 'He's dead set against your flying, you know?' she said, offering Bella the bag.

'He's made it very clear,' replied Bella, unwrapping the sweet and popping it in her mouth.

Alice handed the bag to Arthur, who took one and sucked

153

it while stretched out on his stomach, his chin resting on his folded hands, watching a group of soldiers playing a game of cards a few feet away.

'Maybe you shouldn't mention it until you've completed your training. He'll only fret.'

'All right.' The pleasant surroundings coupled with the warm sunshine were making her feel sleepy. She stretched, a sudden thought occurring to her. 'What will happen with Johnny and Jack when you go?' she asked.

'They'll stay with your father and Mrs Wilson. The boys are very fond of her, and of your father. He's very good with them.' She sighed. 'They'll miss Arthur, though,' she said, keeping her voice low. 'Johnny was very upset when we told him Arthur would be going away. I know they only see him on Sundays when he gets his half day, but they've grown very close. He's ever so good with them both.'

'We'll all miss him,' Bella said. 'I'll miss you, too, Mother.' It was on the tip of her tongue to tell her mother about Will, but something made her hesitate. She hadn't felt her mother had been as set against him as her father, but it was seldom her mother went against her father's wishes. It went to show how desperate she was to get Arthur to safety that she was prepared to defy her husband and take him halfway across the world.

The time passed all too quickly and before long they had to make their way to the station. The platform was teeming with service personnel, the noise reverberating off the steel girders overhead.

'You look after yourself,' she whispered, hugging Arthur hard. He beamed at her, his arms wrapped tightly around her waist. Refraining from ruffling his short hair, she drew back, drinking him in. She was determined not to cry in front of him, knowing how excessive displays of emotion could upset him.

'Oh, Bella, I shall miss you,' Alice breathed, as mother and daughter embraced. 'No tears now,' she said, her voice trembling. Bella nodded, blinking hard with the effort not to cry. Neither woman wanted to upset Arthur.

'I'll write as soon as we're on board,' her mother promised, as the Southampton-bound train roared into the station. 'I can post it once we dock in Madeira. I won't be allowed to tell you the name of the ship, or any details, but at least you'll know we're on our way.'

'Give Uncle Charlie my love.'

'I will,' her mother promised. 'Take care of yourself, darling,' she said, giving Bella a final hug. 'Don't take any unnecessary risks.'

'I won't, Mother. Have a safe journey.'

The station master blew his whistle and the crowd surged forward. Bella stood on tiptoe, until her mother and Arthur were swallowed up in the sea of embarking uniforms. She searched the windows, hoping to catch a final glimpse of them, but the compartments were so crowded it was impossible to make them out. Soldiers hung out of open windows to snatch a final kiss from the girls they were leaving behind, even as the train began to pick up speed. Bella hurried along the platform, waving frantically in the hope that her mother and Arthur were able to see her. Eventually, she ran out of platform and came to a halt. As the train sped away into the distance, she finally let the tears come.

CHAPTER SEVENTEEN

It was the first day of August. The thin mist hovering over the airfield heralded the promise of another glorious summer day. Instinctively, Bella glanced up at the clear, cobalt-blue sky. For three weeks now the Luftwaffe had kept up their intensive bombing campaign along the south coast. Since early July Hitler's planes and U-boats had been targeting ships, and so it had come as a huge relief to Bella when she received a letter from her mother informing her that she and Arthur had docked safely in Simon's Bay on the Cape Peninsula.

For weeks, Chantry Fields had been teeming with RAF fighter pilots. When the call came to scramble, they streamed from the buildings in droves, dressed and ready to go. Within minutes of the call coming in, the Spitfires and Hurricanes would be airborne, heading for the Channel. A few times the fighting had moved further inland and everyone who could be spared from their duties would congregate outside, eyes shielded against the sun's glare to watch the deadly games being played out above their heads.

Now though, at just after six o'clock in the morning, the airfield was quiet. The Spitfires and Hawker Hurricanes stood in gleaming rows outside the newly erected hangars. Bella, Gilly, Beryl and Amanda crossed the dew-damp grass to the mess. For once they weren't chatting at ten to the dozen, as each of them was lost in their own thoughts. Today was to be their first day as fully-fledged ferry pool pilots.

The hours spent in ground school had been long and gruelling, but so worth it. While the various instructors had initially focused their attention on the three male cadets, it had soon become apparent that the four women were proving themselves equally as capable intellectually, and technically, as their male counterparts. Though Beryl had a few problems with her map reading in the beginning, the four women had aced their exams, Bella and Amanda scoring higher than any of the three men. Even Flight Lieutenant Walsh had to admit to being impressed, albeit somewhat begrudgingly.

Today they would take on their first mission. With the air battles raging over the south coast, the work of the ferry pool had increased phenomenally as planes were constantly being moved from one base to another.

They entered the mess to a round of applause from the men seated at the few occupied tables. Bella blushed. The derision and mockery of the past had largely been laid to rest for the four women's sheer determination and skill had not gone unnoticed by their male counterparts.

They took their seats at the usual table and ate their breakfast. Their conversation was stilted, and Bella found she didn't have much of an appetite. Her stomach muscles clenched anxiously. She gave herself a shake. She had hours of flying time under her belt now. Why was she feeling nervous about what was expected to be a routine flight? She played with her scrambled egg, forcing herself to swallow a mouthful. It stuck in her throat, and she reached for her mug of tea to wash it down. She wished Will was here. He'd know how to alleviate her first-day nerves, but Will was far away in Scotland.

The mess started filling up and most of the men and women came over to wish the girls well.

'I'm very proud of you, ladies,' Commander Joan Forrester said, pausing by their table on the way to fetch her breakfast. 'I wish you God speed.' She glanced towards the open doorway, her expression troubled. 'I'm sorry you're flying in such dangerous times.'

Bella fingered the cuff of her jacket. Every day the threat of invasion grew more real. Much as she would miss her mother and brother, she could only rejoice that they were safely out of harm's way. She glanced at Beryl, who was staring moodily into space. Hitler's hatred for the Jewish people was well known. What would become of her friend if they were invaded? In her wildest moments she imagined Beryl flying herself and her parents across the Atlantic to America. Perhaps, if it came to it, that would be an option. She could only hope and pray it wouldn't come to that.

'Good luck, ladies.' Joan gave them all a firm handshake and went off to the serving table. Bella glanced at the clock.

'It's almost seven,' she said, her scrambled eggs churning unpleasantly in her stomach. 'Shall we go?'

The others nodded and, pushing aside their plates, they got to their feet. Amidst calls of good luck, they made their way out of the mess and over to the Ops Room.

'Good morning, ladies,' Harvey Bridgewater said, as they entered. He leaned back in his seat, wafting away a cloud of cigarette smoke with his free hand. 'Have a seat. Nothing's come in yet, but I do have a telegram here.' The four women settled themselves in the armchairs arranged in front of the desk. There was a noise in the doorway and Freddie, Matt and Dave entered, exchanging greetings and nods.

'My,' grinned Harvey, cigarette clamped between his teeth. 'You're all mighty keen.' He waved to the two remaining chairs. 'Take a seat chaps. I'm just looking for . . . ah, here it is.'

Dave and Matt sat down. Freddie leaned against the wall; arms folded across his chest.

'I have a telegram here,' said Harvey, removing his cigarette and balancing it on the ashtray. 'From Senior Commander Pauline Gower.'

Bella straightened her shoulders as the four women exchanged excited glances.

'She writes, "Congratulations. Welcome to the team. God speed."' Harvey laid the telegram on the desk and smiled at the women. 'Well done, all of you. Ah,' he said, as one of the two telephones began to ring. 'Here we go.' He picked up the receiver. For the next few minutes Harvey was kept busy scribbling down planes and their destinations. 'Weather? One moment, sir.' Twisting in his seat, Harvey glanced out the window. 'Clear, sir, light breeze. Yes, sir.'

At that moment Neil Glover arrived. He raised his hand in greeting, remaining quiet while Harvey rattled off the information he'd been given to the caller from central control. Harvey replaced the receiver. 'Nothing like being thrown in at the deep end,' he grinned.

Neil took the list and went over to the large blackboard. More ferry pilots filed into the room, though most chose to congregate in the room next door where they could read a magazine and enjoy a mug of coffee while they waited for their itinerary.

The four women chatted quietly while Neil worked out the schedule amidst much head scratching and rubbing out.

'Right, that's the best I can do. Ladies, gents, good luck, and safe flying.'

Bella searched the board for her name. She was flying a Tiger Moth to Hamble where she was to pick up a Spitfire and fly it to Hatfield. She swallowed the nervous lump in her throat.

'I've never flown a Spitfire,' she whispered to Gilly.

'Don't worry,' said one of the more seasoned ferry pilots, having overheard. 'The ground crew will give you a quick rundown of how everything works. You'll be fine.' Bella managed a weak smile.

'Thanks.'

Bella, Amanda, Gilly and Beryl made their way outside. The mist had cleared, leaving a perfect summer's day in its wake.

'Well, good luck, ladies,' Beryl said, as they collected their parachutes. 'See you all this evening, God willing.'

The four women wished each other luck and made their way to their respective planes. The air throbbed with the sound of engines. Bella clambered aboard, settling herself in the cockpit. She studied her map and set her compass. Taking a deep breath, she took her time going through the familiar take-off sequence. Pulling on her helmet and goggles, she leaned over the side and gave the signal. She turned on the magneto and the prop swinger turned the propeller. The engine burst into life and she weaved left and right along the bumpy ground, leaning out of the cockpit as far as she could to make sure she didn't hit anything. It would be a disastrous start to her career if she were to damage the aircraft on her first official flight. Out of the corner of her eye, she spotted a spitfire taxiing up the runway in front of her and she eased off the throttle, giving the other plane the space it needed to complete take-off. Once she was certain the coast was clear, Bella increased speed. The wind rushed past her, buffeting the sides of the plane as she reached take-off speed. The plane lifted gently off its wheels, gliding effortlessly into the clear sky. She cleared the trees at the end of the airfield and circled back around, setting her compass to SE. Once she reached a cruising altitude of 3,000 feet, she glanced over the side, gazing down at the patchwork of fields below. A meandering river cut through the swathes of green, gold and brown like a silver ribbon. This was where she was born to be, she mused, contentedly, her cheeks tingling in the cold air. The sky around her was filled with other planes but she soon peeled away, setting course for Southampton and Hamble aerodrome.

Her landing at Hamble went without a hitch. Clambering from the plane, she removed her goggles and pulled off her helmet, fluffing up her newly cut hair with her fingers before making her way to the Ops Room.

'Hello,' she said, knocking on the door. 'Second Officer Roberts. I've just delivered a Tiger Moth and I'm to pick up a Spitfire?'

'Welcome,' said the older of the two men seated behind the control desk. He looked about sixty, with a craggy face, thick grey eyebrows above rheumy blue eyes and thinning greying hair over a shiny pink pate. 'Grab yourself a cup of tea in the canteen while you wait.'

Bella found the canteen. Two dark-haired women in flying trousers and shirts stood to one side, chatting. Bella poured herself a cup of tea and walked over to join them.

'Hello there. Marion Wilberforce,' smiled one of the women, thrusting out her hand. 'This is Gabrielle Patterson. Welcome to Hamble. How long are you here?'

'I'm picking up a Spitfire to take to Hatfield,' Bella explained. She sipped her tea. 'I'm a bit nervous. I've never flown one before.'

'You're lucky,' Gabrielle said. 'It's only recently us women have been allowed to fly anything other than a Tiger Moth.' She gave Bella an encouraging smile. 'You'll be fine.'

They chatted for a while about their interest in flying and their experiences until the younger chap Bella had met in the Ops Room came to find her.

'Your plane's ready,' he told her, handing her a piece of paper. 'Outside hangar number five.'

'Safe flight,' Marion said, as Bella drained her mug.

'It was good meeting you,' said Gabrielle. 'I'm sure we'll catch up again some time.'

Bella said goodbye and walked out into the warm sunshine. She was sweltering in her fleece-lined jacket, but she knew she'd be grateful for its warmth once she was in the sky.

She scanned the paperwork as she approached the Spitfire. Its paintwork gleamed in the sunlight. One of the ground-crew ducked from underneath the plane, wiping his hands on an oily rag.

'It's all ready for you, ma'am,' he said, eyeing Bella with admiration. 'If you'll get yourself settled, ma'am, I'll give you a run-through of the controls.'

Thanking him, Bella pulled put one foot on the wing and hoisted herself into the cockpit where her nerves increased tenfold. The instrument panel of the Spitfire was more daunting than the Tiger Moth's.

'It's not vastly different to what you're used to,' the man, whose name Bella later learned was Don, said, leaning into the cockpit. He ran through the various instruments and switches. 'Got it?'

Bella nodded. She took a deep breath.

'I think so.'

Don gave her the thumbs up.

He hopped down to the ground. Bella pulled on her helmet and adjusted her goggles. Heart racing, she did all the pre-take-off checks. On her signal the groundcrew removed the chocks and, keeping her eye on the radiator gauge like Don had warned her, she taxied towards the runway. She performed her final checks and gently opened the throttle, pushing the control column forward. The plane began to pick up speed. The tail lifted, as the wheels bounced across the bumpy grass. The hangars and buildings were a blur as the Spitfire raced down the runway. The needle on her speedometer reached 85mph and the wheels left the ground. Once she started to climb, she closed the cockpit hood and did another quick check of her instruments. Everything seemed in order. She kept her speed at the ATA regulation cruising speed of 250mph. She checked her compass and her map, glancing down at the scattered towns and villages below. A train raced along a track, tiny puffs of smoke drifting up below her. In ground school, she'd been taught to follow rivers and railway lines if she lost her way, and she did so now, knowing that Hatfield aerodrome was somewhere near London, and assuming the train was most likely destined for the capital, she kept the railway line in her sights as she headed away from the coast.

She made it to Hatfield without incident, and within thirty minutes she was back in another Tiger Moth, heading back to Chantry Fields.

She was cruising along at the regulation speed, relishing the familiarity of the controls, as she flew away from the sprawling capital city. She was thinking about Will, and how she was looking forward to seeing him later, when she saw a flash in the distance. Turning her head slightly, she saw it again, her brain recognizing it instantly as the flash of sunlight on metal. There was another plane heading her way. She calmly adjusted her speed and altitude to accommodate the other aircraft. She glanced up. The plane had disappeared from her line of vision. She frowned. Leaning over the side of the plane, she saw the plane was heading straight for her. What was it doing? Her frown deepened as she pulled the nose of the Tiger Moth up, intending to gain altitude to allow the plane to pass below her. With the wind rushing in her ears, she couldn't hear the sound of the approaching plane's engine over the roar of the Tiger Moth, but she knew it was close. She twisted in her seat in an attempt to see if it had passed her by. Suddenly something slammed into her plane. Twisting round, she stared at the puff of smoke rising from her right wing. Was that a bullet hole? Before her brain could make sense of what was happening, another bullet hit her plane. The Tiger Moth shuddered, stalled – and went into free fall. At once Bella went into emergency mode, managing to get the plane under control and levelling out again at ten thousand feet. She leaned over the side of her plane, anxiously searching the skies. Her breath caught in her throat as her blood turned to ice water in her veins. The other plane was coming straight at her, side on. She could see the gun aimed at her. She was going to die. She was surprised at how calm she felt. She saw a burst of fire from the guns but, by some miracle, the bullets missed their mark. She dropped the plane a few hundred feet.

Suddenly the sky around her was filled with Spitfires. Two of them went after the German plane. There was a flash, and the German plane began spiralling downwards, flames billowing from the fuselage. Bella watched in horror as the plane hit the ground and exploded. A Spitfire pulled up alongside her and the pilot signalled, asking if she was all right. She nodded, feeling sick. The pilot gave her the thumbs up and peeled away.

Within minutes Bella was alone again. She gulped a lungful of cold air, blinking rapidly to clear her mind of the awful image of the burning plane. She realized she was shaking. Taking several deep breaths, she pulled herself together and headed for home.

CHAPTER EIGHTEEN

1942

Bella gazed out of the rain-lashed window with growing sadness as the bus wend its way through the bomb-damaged streets of Southampton. She knew from her father's infrequent letters that the city had been badly hit during the Blitz in the winter of 1940 and there had been several minor bombing raids since, but his letters hadn't prepared her for the devastation she witnessed now. Empty buildings with their fronts missing. Houses with gaping holes where once a bedroom had been. A staircase leading to nowhere. All against the backdrop of a dark, sombre sky.

Thank God none of the bombs had gone as far as Strawbridge or Hedge End. So far, her family hadn't suffered any casualties. Unlike poor Amanda who'd lost her stepdad and her half-brother, Jimmy, who'd been home on leave from the Royal Navy when their house in Stepney suffered a direct hit. Her mother had been badly injured and had spent weeks in hospital. She was now staying with relatives down in Devon. Amanda had been down to see her just last week to cheer her up with the news of her engagement to Jonty. They were getting married in a fortnight's time.

Bella turned away from the window, unable to bear any more devastation. Thankfully, over the late summer and early autumn of 1940, the heroic RAF fighter pilots had put paid to Hitler's plans to invade. What was it Prime Minister Winston Churchill had said?

'Never was so much owed by so many to so few.' But that winter it had seemed as though Hitler might bomb the British people into submission. He'd reckoned without their determination and grit, though, Bella thought now, as the ruined city gave way to open countryside.

The bus rumbled along winding lanes, splashing through puddles. The overhanging trees dripping, the soggy verges awash with dandelions, cow parsley, nettles and buttercups. Bella stared out of the window, wondering what reception she might get from her father when she turned up unannounced. In the past two years, she'd been so busy flying planes all over the British Isles that she hadn't managed a visit home. She'd seen her father only twice when he'd visited Salisbury on some clerical business, where he'd criticized her short hair, and remonstrated to her about the foolhardiness of working as a ferry pool pilot. He'd appeared quite put out when Bella had refused, point blank, to resign her job and look for something less dangerous.

So, she was feeling somewhat apprehensive as the bus

pulled up outside the Glyn Arms pub and she disembarked. Unfurling the umbrella she'd borrowed from someone at Hamble aerodrome, she hurried down the lane to the vicarage. She pulled the bell rope and the door was answered almost immediately by Ida, who threw up her hands in amazement.

'Miss Bella! What a lovely surprise. Come on in.'

Bella stepped into the hall, dripping water onto the lino as she shook out her umbrella, laying it against the wall under the porch to drip dry.

'Come into the kitchen. I'll make you a hot drink. Is your father expecting you?'

'No,' Bella replied, following Ida into the kitchen. 'I'm grounded for the rest of the day due to the weather, so I thought I'd surprise you all. Is Father here?'

'He's in the parlour and so is ...' She was interrupted by a voice from the hall. Bella turned to see her grandmother standing in the doorway, her face wreathed in smiles.

'I thought I heard voices. Bella, darling.' She held out her arms. 'How lovely to see you.'

'Grandma Lily,' Bella breathed, hugging her grandmother warmly. 'Is Aunt Eleanor here, too?'

'No, she's not. But the girls are. They're in the parlour with Johnny and Jack. Your father's there too. He'll be over the moon to see you.'

'I'll bring the tea through in a minute,' Ida said, as Bella shed her wet outer clothing, draping them over the clothes horse in front of the range.

'You're looking well,' Lily said, as they crossed the hallway to the parlour. 'I do like your hair. It suits you, and I'm sure it's much more sensible when wearing a flying helmet.' The parlour door was ajar. 'Look who's here,' she cried, pushing it fully open.

'Bella.' Samuel rose from his seat. 'What an unexpected pleasure.'

'Hello Father,' Bella said, kissing his cheek. 'It's lovely to see you. Hello, boys, Holly, Emily.' She beamed at the four children seated at the parlour table working on a jigsaw puzzle. 'My, you're all so grown-up.'

'Bella!' Jack, now a sturdy nine-year-old, scrambled down from his chair to run at Bella and throw his arms around her neck. Bella hugged him tight. 'Look what I've got,' he said, pulling a diecast Spitfire from the pocket of his shorts. 'Mrs Wilson says you fly these.'

'I do indeed,' replied Bella with a smile.

'Can you take me up in one?' Jack asked, looking at her hopefully.

'I'm afraid not, sweetheart,' Bella said, straightening up. 'May I help you all with your puzzle?' she asked, to distract Jack from his disappointment.

'Of course,' Emily replied, pointing to an empty chair. 'We're stuck on the sky.' Emily was a slender, good-looking girl of thirteen now, her sister, Holly, a year older. And Johnny was a stocky twelve-year-old. Ida brought in the tea tray, along with a plate of homemade biscuits. 'They're not very sweet,' she apologized. 'Thanks to the sugar rationing.'

'I'm sure they'll be just fine,' Lily said, pulling her stool up to the table. She turned to her son-in-law. 'Will you join us, Samuel?'

'I think I will,' Samuel smiled. To Bella's relief, he seemed in an amiable mood and for the next hour they worked on the jigsaw puzzle, the children chattering ten to a dozen.

It stopped raining, but the sky remained grey and foreboding. Samuel suggested they stretch their legs in the garden. Lily chose to remain indoors, but Bella, Samuel and the four children changed their shoes and went outside. Everything dripped but the air was warm and humid.

'Here, you can feed these to the pigs,' Ida called to the children, holding up a bucket of vegetable scraps. Holly took the bucket and the four of them leaned over the wall, throwing the scraps to next door's pigs.

'It's a beneficial arrangement,' Samuel told Bella, as they strolled amongst the raspberry canes and tomato plants. 'We feed the pigs our scraps and every so often Mr Angus gives us a side of pork.'

'Good job Arthur's not here,' Bella said. 'He'd be very upset. He'd consider the pigs as neighbours.' Her father shook his head.

'I despair of that boy's emotional bond with animals. It's fortunate old Monk's a dairy farmer. Heaven knows how Arthur would have coped had he been tasked with taking the animals to slaughter.'

'He'd have tried to save them, somehow,' Bella responded

with a smile. How she missed her beautiful, sensitive, kind-hearted brother.

'I received a letter from your mother yesterday,' her father said, as they paused by the chicken coop to watch the hens scratching about in the dirt. 'They're both well.'

'I haven't had a letter this week,' Bella said.

'You may read it if you like. It's on the mantlepiece.'

'Thanks. I will when we go back in. And how are you keeping, Father?'

'My headaches have been getting worse,' he said, rubbing his temple as though to emphasize the point. 'The doctor thinks it's stress.' He gave Bella a pointed look. 'I take it you're still flying those blasted machines?'

'Yes, Father, I am. In fact I flew down here this morning.' A drop of water dripped from an overhanging branch, landing on her cheek, and she brushed it away. 'I have to admit,' she continued. 'It was pretty hairy in such low cloud. I've flown in worse though,' she added, remembering a particularly bad day last winter when she'd been caught in a sudden snowstorm. Blinded by whirling snow, she'd only just seen the hill rising steeply in front of her at the last minute. Thankfully she managed to pull the plane up just in time to avoid a head-on collision with the hillside, but her undercarriage had been badly damaged. Mercifully she'd escaped with a few cuts and bruises and a sprained ankle, but the plane had been a write-off. She hadn't mentioned that little incident in her letters to her parents.

'I'm not flying back until the weather improves,' she said

now, slipping her arm through her father's. 'So, may I beg a bed for the night?'

'Of course. I'll get Mrs Wilson to make up the bed in your old room.' He gave his daughter a sideways glance. 'I really don't like your hair, you know?'

'I do hope you don't put yourself in dangerous situations unnecessarily, Bella,' Lily said, holding her needle to the light and threading it.

'No one deliberately seeks danger, Grandma,' replied Bella, leaning back in her armchair. Barney and Sybil lay at her feet, snoring softly.

'How are your friends keeping? One got engaged, you say?'

'Yes, Amanda. They're getting married at the end of the month. And Beryl's got herself a new chap.'

'Oh?' Lily looked up from the sock she was darning. 'What happened to Bob?'

'Oh, Grandma,' Bella laughed. 'She's had several beaus since him. She's seeing one of the RAF pilots at the base. Frank. He seems a nice enough chap.'

'And what about you, dear?' asked her grandmother, studying her intently. 'Have you got anyone special? Only you never mention anyone in your letters.'

Bella felt herself blush. 'Actually, there is someone,' she said shyly.

'Oh, do tell,' Lily said, her eyes shining with excitement. 'What's his name? Is he very handsome? Is he a pilot?'

Bella laughed. 'His name is Will, he's very handsome and he is a pilot, but not a fighter pilot. He flies for the ferry pool, like me.'

'Have you been courting long?'

'Two years,' Bella replied.

'Two years!' her grandmother exclaimed loudly, causing both dogs to raise their heads and glance her way. 'Two years, and you never thought to mention him?'

Bella shrugged. 'He's Mrs Hopwood's grandson. Do you remember? He stayed with her the summer before she died. No, perhaps you don't.'

'William Mullens? Leah's boy?' Lily said, her brows puckered.

'His surname is Mullens, yes.' Bella nodded.

'Well, I never,' she chuckled. 'What a turn-up for the books, you courting Leah's boy. She and your mother were best friends when they were girls.' She shook her head sadly. 'To this day I don't know why they fell out. Your mother's never said, and I don't like to pry. Anyway, when do we get to meet this young man of yours?'

'That's the problem,' Bella said, twisting her hands in her lap. She rose slightly to peer out of the window. Her father was in the garden with the children, picking raspberries and strawberries for their tea. 'We got close that summer. It was not long after we came back from South Africa. Father's behaviour towards Will was very odd. He wouldn't let me be friends with him. That's why I got packed off to Aunt Eleanor's, to get me away from Will.'

175

'That sounds very strange indeed,' Lily said. 'I wonder if it's because of who Will's father is?'

'His father?' Bella raised her eyebrows. 'Why should who his father is have anything to do with it?'

'Well, he was a gypsy, you see. His great-grandmother, Pearl, was a fortune teller. Your father couldn't abide that sort of stuff. Said it went against what the church believed, and he couldn't be seen to condone such nonsense.' Lily's expression softened. 'I'm not saying Samuel was harsh with her. Quite the opposite. He did everything he could for Pearl and her granddaughter, Tilly. He was such a kind-hearted man, your father.' Her eyes grew misty as she gazed int the distance, remembering a long-ago time. 'It was the war that changed him.' She blinked and turned her attention back to Bella. She smiled. 'If your heart is set on this Will, your father will just have to come round, won't he?'

It was late the following afternoon by the time Bella circled over the aerodrome at Chantry Fields. The cloud cover had hung around all morning and it had been almost noon before she got airborne. She'd taken a Spitfire to a base in Somerset, where a crowd of RAF pilots had converged in front of the hangars to watch her land. She was used to an audience. At many of the bases they landed at, women pilots were still treated as an oddity by the men.

There she'd picked up the Hurricane, which she now brought in to land. Her wheels hit the ground and she bounced across the runway, decreasing her speed until she brought the plane to a halt in front of the hangars. While the groundcrew did their thing, she removed her goggles and helmet, fluffing up her flattened hair with her fingertips. Glancing over the side of the plane, she spotted Will leaning against the open doorway of the mess and waved. He waved back. As soon as she was able, she clambered down from the plane and ran across the grass towards him.

'Hello,' he grinned, pushing himself off from the door-frame. 'You missed a good film last night.'

Bella gasped. 'You went to the cinema without me?'

Will laughed. 'Of course not. I thought we could go to-night, if you're not too tired?'

'I'd like that. I've got to do my debrief. Shall I meet you for a cup of tea in ten minutes?'

'I'll be waiting.'

Amanda and Gilly were in the mess with Will when Bella got there fifteen minutes later.

'Will and I are going to the cinema later,' she said, once she'd fetched a mug of tea for her and Will. 'Why don't you join us?'

Her two friends exchanged glances. 'Er, no, sorry,' Amanda said, inspecting her nails. 'I think I'll pass.'

'Me, too,' said Gilly with an apologetic smile. 'You two go and have fun.'

Surprised, because she knew how much Gilly had been looking forward to seeing *Back-Room Boy*, Bella shrugged. 'Oh, all right. If you're sure.'

'We are,' Amanda said firmly. 'Glad you got back safely. We were quite worried when the weather turned yesterday.'

'It was just coming in when I landed. I spent the night at home, which was nice.'

'Better than spending it in the Ops Room of a strange air-base,' said Gilly. She grinned. 'Will was quite beside himself, weren't you, Will,' she said, giving him a sly smile.

'I was concerned,' admitted Will. 'Not because I doubted your skill, but flying blind is no mean feat, for anyone. It was a relief when we got the call from Hamble to say you'd landed and were grounded until further notice.'

Bella glanced at the clock on the wall. 'Right,' she said, draining her mug. 'I'd better go and have my bath if we're to make the early showing.'

'I'll see you in a bit,' Will said, kissing her cheek.

They both enjoyed the film, and it was still light when they emerged from the cinema, blinking as their eyes adjusted to the evening sunshine. They were a week off the longest day and the sky was clear. Out of habit, they both glanced up-wards. These long summer evenings were perfect for Hitler's bombers but for the moment the sky was empty.

They popped into the Red Lion for pie and mash, washed down by a glass of ale, before walking back to base.

Night was approaching as they reached the base. The sky was the colour of ripe damsons, the setting sun streaking the western sky brilliant orange. The base was quiet, the buildings dark shadows against the purple sky. The planes sat silent, like giant roosting birds on the grass. The windsock hung motionless in the still air. From the mess came the sound of muted laughter. In the shadows, Will pulled Bella into his arms and kissed her tenderly on the lips. He drew back, studying her face in the twilight.

'When the call came in that all flights to Hamble were cancelled because of the storm, I was terrified for you. I couldn't concentrate until we got the call that you'd landed safely. I thought . . . I was scared you'd crash in poor visibility, like poor Harold last month.'

Bella reached up and stroked Will's cheek. They had lost several members of the ferry pool over the past couple of years. Poor visibility, pilot error and mechanical failure had all played a part, and each loss was felt keenly by the whole base.

'I was safe, Will,' whispered Bella. 'I would never take any unnecessary risks, I promise. If I felt I couldn't outrun the storm, I'd have landed in a field somewhere and waited it out.'

'I don't know what I'd do without you, Bella,' Will said, kissing her again. 'I love you so much.'

Bella wrapped her arms around Will's neck. 'I love you too, Will Mullens,' she whispered. 'With all my heart.'

CHAPTER NINETEEN

'Bella, can you come outside, please? You need to see this.'
Gilly leaned against the door of the shower block, a dark
silhouette against the bright morning glare.

'What is it?' asked Bella, above the sound of water splashing to the concrete floor, as she zipped up her skirt.

'Just come and see,' replied Gilly, heading back outside.
Bella grabbed her jacket off the peg and, fluffing up her
steam-damp hair, hurried after her friend. After the humidity
of the shower room, the early June morning air was refresh-
ing. It was a relatively clear day, with only a few wisps of
cloud drifting along on the breeze. Gilly and Amanda were
standing in front of the mess, along with a handful of male
pilots. Bella walked over to join them.

'What's going on?' she asked, pulling on her jacket. There
were a few smirks amongst the men and shuffling of feet.

'Wait and see,' said Gilly, as she and Amanda exchanged

knowing looks. They were joined a few minutes later by Jonty, Beryl and her beau, Frank. Everyone seemed to be gazing towards the far end of the runway.

'Are we expecting someone important?' asked Bella, shielding her eyes from the sun's glare as she followed their gaze.

'Yes,' Amanda replied, shortly. 'Look, here he comes.'

Bella heard the drone of the plane before she saw it. The yellow Piper aircraft crested the tree-line, heading for the airfield.

'Who is it?' Bella asked, as the plane came flying towards them. When no answer was forthcoming, she was about to repeat the question when she realized the plane was towing something behind it. As it flew past, its banner streaming in its wake, Bella gave a gasp. Crudely painted in large black letters were the words:

'BELLA ROBERTS, WILL YOU MARRY ME? WILL'

'Oh, my gosh!' She clapped her hands to her mouth as a rousing cheer went up from the small crowd.

'It's Will,' Bella laughed. The plane reached the end of the airfield and circled back around. He flew over again, waggling his wings. Bella could see him clearly in the cockpit.

'Yes.' She cupped her hands around her mouth. 'Yes,' she shouted again, as the plane roared past her. She gave him the thumbs up gesture and Will gave her one back. She could see his grin. He roared off into the distance, the banner trailing behind him. Gilly, Amanda and Beryl gathered around Bella, hugging her and showering her with their congratulations.

'Well, congratulations Second Officer Roberts,' said Commander Forrester, having come out to see what the excitement was about. Bella noticed that the crowd had swelled significantly in the past few minutes, the sound of the aeroplane's engine having drawn people's attention.

The roar of the engine came again, and heads turned to watch as the Piper landed gracefully on the grass and taxied to the hangar. Followed by the crowd, Bella ran across the grass to where Will was clambering from the cockpit. Still wearing his harness and parachute, Bella flung herself into his arms.

'Yes, I will marry you,' she said, laughing as he swung her round, and kissed her long and hard on the mouth. They broke apart and Will was swallowed up by his colleagues, all wanting to clap him on the back and congratulate him.

'I wonder who painted the banner,' Bella said to Gilly, walking behind the plane and lifting the end of the long piece of cloth.

Gilly and Amanda exchanged smiles. 'We did,' Amanda grinned. 'We did it last night while you were at the cinema.'

'Ah, I'm touched that you'd go to that trouble for me.'

'You should be,' snorted Gilly. 'I missed out on an evening with Philip Friend to do this for you.'

'Take no notice,' said Amanda. 'We're going to see *Back-Room Boy* on Saturday with Beryl and Frank, and a mate of Frank's.'

'He's my blind date,' Gilly said, with a squeeze of her

shoulders. 'Apparently, he adores redheads.' She patted her auburn hair. 'So that's something in my favour.'

'Of course he'll adore you,' Bella said. 'Do we know his name?'

'Richard somebody-or-other,' replied Amanda. 'He's a doctor at the military hospital in Motcombe, near the POW camp.'

'A doctor, hmm? Impressive.' Bella gave Gilly a nudge. She smiled shyly.

'I do hope he's nice, and we get on,' she sighed. 'I would rather like to have someone special in my life.'

'Well, I wish you good luck,' said Bella. 'I shall cross my fingers for you.' She turned to see Will making his way towards her, swinging his helmet and goggles at his side.

'May I borrow my fiancée for a moment, please, ladies?' he grinned. Tucking his hand through Bella's arm, he led her towards a quiet corner. There, away from the noise and banter of the airfield, he drew a small black box from the pocket of his flying jacket. 'Now that you've consented to be my wife, it only remains for me to do this,' he said, lifting the lid to reveal the small diamond nestled in its pale blue satin bed. Taking the ring out, he shoved the box back in his pocket and, taking Bella's left hand in his, he gently slipped the ring onto her third finger.

'It fits,' she grinned in delight, holding her hand up to the light. 'How did you know the right size?' she asked, turning her face to his.

'I asked Amanda, and she found a signet ring in your drawer. I borrowed it and took it to the jewellers.'

'Oh, goodness, my old signet ring,' Bella laughed. 'I've never worn it. Some old friend of my mother's gave it to me as a Christening gift. How amazing that it's just the right size.'

'You mean, I might have got it wrong after all?' Will stared at her. 'And I thought we were being so clever.'

'Amanda wouldn't know I didn't wear it,' Bella said. 'I keep it in my trinket box with a few other things. Perhaps I shall start wearing it, now I know it'll fit me.'

'What are you thinking?' asked Will, as a puzzled frown appeared on Bella's face.

'I was wondering if my signet ring might have been a gift from your mother. I know our mothers were friends once. Grandma said they fell out, but she doesn't know why.'

Will was silent for a moment, then said, 'I would like to think you have something from my mother.'

'You must miss her so much,' Bella said, wrapping her arms around his waist. 'I know I do, and my mother is only abroad. At least I can write to her.' She let him go and stepped back.

'I do,' Will said, shoving his hands in his trouser pockets and looking down at his feet. 'I think you and she would have got on well. I suppose I should have written to ask your father for his permission. Thought it might have come as a surprise, as he doesn't know we're courting.'

Bella pulled a face. 'No, you're right there. I shall write and tell my mother of our engagement, and my grandmother, but I think I shall let Mother break the news to Father. I'll give him a few months to get used to the idea before I take you home to meet him.'

'I shall look forward to it,' grinned Will.

'Have you set a date?' asked Gilly that evening, as they prepared for bed.

'Not yet,' replied Bella. 'We're thinking some time in the autumn, September maybe. It'll be a registry office affair. I don't want a big do if Mother and Arthur can't be there.'

'You could always have a do later,' suggested Beryl. 'Once the war is over.'

Bella rolled her eyes. '*If* it's ever over.' She pulled back the covers and slid into bed. The wooden barracks room was perishingly cold in winter and hot and stuffy in the summer. 'I've written to my mother and my grandmother. They'll go in tomorrow's post.'

'I bet your mother will be happy,' Amanda said.

'I'm looking forward to meeting your mum at your wedding. It's only two weeks away!' Bella said. 'How's she doing now?'

'She's all right, I suppose. Still living with her cousin in Devon. She misses my stepdad and Jimmy a lot.' Amanda shrugged. 'It's hard, but she's got her job, and her volunteer work, so she keeps busy.'

'I sympathize,' Gilly said. 'You must miss them, too. I know I still miss my dad a lot. I worry about my brother every day. I'd be devastated if anything happened to him.'

'I do. My stepdad raised me from the age of two, and

Jimmy was my baby brother.' Amanda's smile wavered. 'I always looked out for him when we were children.' Tears sparkled on her lashes, and she groped under her pillow for her handkerchief. 'And now I've got two half-brothers I'm very fond of in Colorado old enough to enlist,' she said, blowing her nose.

'It's just so awful,' Beryl said, stretching out on her bed. 'I hate thinking about my Babushka in her little house in Bethnal Green. She refuses to leave, even when the bombs are raining down all around her. She said she ran away from tyrants before and she's done running. My mother is at her wits' end.'

'Old people can be so stubborn,' agreed Amanda. 'My grandparents live in Liverpool, and my nan refuses to go to the shelter. She prefers to sit under the stairs. Her philosophy is if she's going to die, she'd rather die in the house she's lived in all her life, than a tin box in the garden.'

'Why are we being so melancholy?' Gilly said, perking up. 'This is a day for celebration and look what I just happen to have lurking under my bed.' She pulled out a bottle of sherry. 'Brian in the kitchen gave it to me,' she grinned. 'He said we needed to toast the happy couple, so here we are.' She raised the bottle above her head. 'I'm sorry Will's not here to celebrate with us, Bella, but here's to the two of you, anyway. May your life together be filled with much joy and few sorrows. Congratulations.' She handed the bottle to Bella. 'There you go. You have the first swig.'

Laughing, Bella took a long swallow of the thick, overly

sweet liquid. 'Thank you.' She handed the bottle back to Gilly, wiping her lips with the back of her hand.

They spent the next twenty minutes passing the bottle back and forth, toasting Bella and Amanda in turn, laughing and joking until Bella, yawning loudly, suggested they all get some sleep. She snuggled under the covers as Gilly blew out the light. Even though it was probably still light enough to see by outside, it being not quite ten o'clock, the blackout curtains plunged the room into total darkness the moment Gilly extinguished the light.

Relishing the unfamiliar feel of her engagement ring on her finger, Bella soon fell asleep, and didn't stir until morning.

CHAPTER TWENTY

The morning of Amanda's wedding day dawned warm and sunny. She and Jonty were getting married at the Gillingham registry office at ten o'clock, followed by luncheon at The Phoenix Hotel. After which, they were having a two-day honeymoon in Dawlish.

Amanda had bought a lilac suit for the occasion and was preening in front of the mirror in the registry office cloakroom. Bella, wearing a powder-blue dress and jacket her grandmother had made for her before the war, stood next to the bride, holding her small posy of wildflowers picked specially from the perimeter of the airfield that morning.

'Have Will and my mother arrived yet?' Amanda asked, anxiously, setting her mauve hat on her head.

'If the train was on time, they'll be here,' Bella assured her, trying to quell her own unease. The trains were often delayed or even cancelled without warning. Amanda had pleaded with her mother to travel over from Ilfracombe the day before but she'd been unable to swap her shift at work, so had had to catch the first available train that morning. It had been due in at nine-thirty-five. It was now almost a quarter to. As the railway station was a mere stone's throw from the registry office, they should have arrived by now.

'I daren't go and look myself,' Amanda fretted, fiddling with the buttons on her elegantly styled jacket with its three-quarter-length sleeves and mauve trim. 'I can't risk bumping into Jonty.'

'Gilly will let us know the moment your mother arrives,' Bella reminded her. 'Try not to worry.'

Amanda adjusted her hat, her face set. 'I've had a feeling all morning that Mum won't make it,' she said, fiddling anxiously with the string of pearls at her neck.

'She'll be here,' Bella assured her. 'You look lovely, by the way,' she said.

'Do you think so?' Amanda did a little twirl. 'At least we're wearing real stockings,' she said, sounding more like her usual self. 'I should have hated to be married with gravy browning-stained legs.'

'It's a real treat,' agreed Bella, savouring the feel of the sheer silk on her own legs. There was an American airbase not far from Chantry Fields and the American airmen were a welcome distraction for the locals, with their seeming abundance of chocolate and silk stockings. Jonty had spent many an evening in the Red Lion with his compatriots and once he'd mentioned his upcoming nuptials, several of the men had insisted on plying him with packets of stockings. Practically all the women at Chantry Fields now boasted at least one pair, including Commander Joan Forrester.

The cloakroom door opened with a squeak and Gilly poked her head in. Her smile told Bella and Amanda all they needed to know.

'She's here?' Amanda breathed, her shoulders sagging with relief. Gilly nodded.

'Pulling up outside as we speak.'

'She's cutting it fine,' muttered Amanda, tugging her small, net veil into place.

'She made it,' Bella said, gripping her friend's arm as they left the cloakroom. 'That's all that matters.'

Will was escorting a petite, dark-haired woman up the steps. Even if Bella hadn't known she was Amanda's mother, she would have guessed. Renee was an older version of her daughter.

'Mum!' Amanda hurried over to her. 'Thank goodness you're here. I was starting to think you weren't going to make it.'

'The train was delayed,' Renee explained, offering Amanda her powdered cheek. 'There was a plane crash quite close to the track.' She lowered her voice, her tone sombre. 'Poor lads. It didn't look like any of them made it.' Her face brightened. 'But enough of that. Today is a day of celebration.' She smiled around at everyone. 'Will you introduce me to your friends?'

'Of course, Mum. You've already met Will, this is his

fiancée, Bella Roberts, and my two other friends, Gilly Ford and Beryl Hastings.'

'Amanda speaks about you all in her letters,' Renee said, once they'd exchanged pleasantries. 'It's nice to be able to put faces to the names.' She glanced towards the registry office doors. 'Jonty is already inside, I take it?'

'I hope so. I know it's only a civil do, but we wanted to keep it slightly traditional, so I haven't seen him at all today.'

'I can vouch for Jonty's presence,' grinned Will. He offered Amanda's mother his arm. 'Shall we?'

'Oh, thank you,' Renee replied, clearly touched. She hadn't relished the thought of walking into her daughter's wedding alone. How her Barry and Jimmy would have loved to have been here, she mused sadly as she took Will's arm. She hoped that they were somehow looking down on them today, wherever they were. Will offered Bella his other arm and the three of them entered the registry office. Commander Forrester was there, as was Major Thompson, looking bored in his dress uniform, as well as a few of Jonty's closest friends from the base. Jonty was standing at the front of the room talking to the registrar, a middle-aged man with wire-rimmed glasses and an ill-fitting toupee. He turned round and, excusing himself, came over, arms outstretched.

'Renee,' he said, gripping her gloved hands in his and leaning in to kiss her cheek. 'I'm so pleased you could make it.'

'I wouldn't have missed it for the world, love,' Renee replied, giving Jonty's fingers a squeeze.

'If everyone is here, perhaps we might get started?' said the registrar, wiping his glasses on a clean white handkerchief. A hush fell over the room as everyone took their seats. Seated between Will and Beryl, Bella turned to see Amanda standing in the doorway, looking resplendent in her lilac and mauve suit. She smiled nervously, her eyes locking on to Jonty's, as she made her way slowly down the short aisle towards the registrar's desk.

'You look beautiful,' Bella heard Jonty whisper, as he took Amanda's hand in his.

'Ladies and Gentlemen,' intoned the registrar. 'We are gathered here today to witness the marriage between Jonathan Benjamin Castillo and Amanda Jane Chadwick.' His bespectacled gaze swept the room. 'If anyone knows of any lawful impediment why Jonathan and Amanda may not be joined in matrimony, please declare it now.'

As expected, there was no objection and the proceedings continued. Fifteen minutes later, Amanda and Jonty emerged into the sun-baked street in a shower of confetti.

'Congratulations, Mrs Castillo.' Bella hugged her friend warmly. 'I'm so happy for you.'

The major and Commander Forrester offered their congratulations and headed off down the street together, both having declined the invitation to luncheon.

One of Jonty's friends snapped some pictures on his camera, and they walked the few blocks to the pub where they enjoyed a delicious meal. There were a few risqué jokes between Jonty's mates, causing Amanda to blush.

'Sorry, Renee,' Jonty called to his new mother-in-law from his end of the table.

'Nothing I haven't heard before, love,' Renee replied, waving his apology away with a flick of her hand.

All too soon it was time for the married couple to catch their train.

'My train's due about fifteen minutes after yours,' said Renee, as the couple said their goodbyes outside the pub. ' I'll walk to the station with you. Goodbye, Will, Bella, Gilly. Goodbye, Beryl. It was nice meeting you all.'

'Goodbye, Mrs Chadwick. It was lovely meeting you,' smiled Bella. 'Have a safe trip home.'

After another round of goodbyes, the newlyweds finally made a move.

'That was a lovely wedding,' Bella said to Will, slipping her hand into his as they watched the happy pair and Renee walking away arm in arm.

'We're going back in for a few pints,' one of the men said, motioning to Will. 'Fancy joining us?'

Will shook his head. 'No, thanks, mate.' The man nodded and disappeared inside the Red Lion.

'I don't feel like going back to base,' Gilly said.

'It feels like a bit of an anticlimax, doesn't it?' agreed Bella. 'Why don't we go to the cinema? Beryl?'

'Thanks for the invitation but Frank's got a few hours off this afternoon so I'm going to visit him.' She glanced up the street. 'The next bus to Motcombe will be along any minute.'

'I fancy an afternoon at the cinema,' Gilly said.

'The cinema it is then,' said Will. 'And perhaps tea at the Lemon Tree café afterwards?'

'Sounds good to me,' replied Bella.

They were just in time for the second showing of *Wuthering Heights*. The Pathé newsreel was playing as the usherette showed them to their seats. Bella settled herself in the seat beside Will as they soberly watched the report on the fall of Tobruk. Watching the images of war filling the screen was disheartening after such a joyful morning and Bella was grateful for the pressure of Will's fingers entwined in hers. The news ended and the film began. Bella had read the Emily Brontë novel when she was younger, so she was familiar with the dark, tragedy of the story. The film was atmospheric and it didn't disappoint, but it did little to lift her spirits and it was a relief to walk out of the dim cinema into the dazzling June sunlight.

'When you're flying, don't you sometimes wish you could keep going forever,' Bella asked Will, as they shared a pot of tea in the Lemon Tree café a short while later. Gilly had errands to run so she'd declined to join them, telling Bella she'd see her back at base later.

'It's a nice fantasy,' Will grinned, spreading strawberry jam on his toasted teacake. 'But eventually I'd run out of fuel and crash.'

'Well, fly to a deserted island then,' said Bella. 'I'd love to be able to fly away from the war.' Her shoulders slumped.

'What is it?' Will put down his knife and reached for her hand. 'You seem a bit out of sorts.'

Bella sighed. 'I am, a bit.' She sat back in her chair, looking Will straight in the eye. 'I don't know. I can't explain it.' She shrugged. 'Maybe it's because I've been looking forward to Amanda's wedding for so long that now it's over, well, it's like Gilly said. It's a bit of an anticlimax.'

'We'll have our wedding to look forward to soon,' said Will. 'I think we should set the date right now.'

Bella smiled. 'When were you thinking?' she asked.

'We've both got leave due at the end of August. What about Saturday the thirtieth?' Will suggested. 'That will give us enough time to have our banns read. Would you want to marry in Strawbridge? Your father could perform the ceremony, do you think?'

'I don't know,' Bella said, with a frown. 'I don't know if he even knows about our engagement. I still haven't heard from my mother, yet. And I think I would rather be married by someone other than my father, as I would like him to be my father, rather than my vicar, and walk me down the aisle.'

'We can go and see the vicar of St Mary's this week. We'll have to have our banns read here anyway, as it's our parish church, but if you want to get married in your home church, we'll have to have them read there too.'

'To be honest, I don't have a connection to the church back home,' Bella said slowly. 'I only attended occasionally once we returned from South Africa before I went off to London. I'm happy to be married at St Mary's.'

'That's settled then,' grinned Will, picking up his teacup.

'I shall call in and make an appointment to see the vicar tomorrow.'

'I just wish my mother and Arthur could be there,' Bella said wistfully.

'I know.' Will took her hand in his. 'And I promise you, once the war is over, we shall throw the party to end all parties and your mother and Arthur will be the guests of honour. In the meantime, we'll make sure to get some good photographs which you can send to them.'

Bella sighed. 'I suppose that will have to do.'

CHAPTER TWENTY-ONE

'Letter for you, First Officer Roberts.' The young cadet handed Bella her mail as she walked into the Ops Room.

'Thank you.' It was postmarked Southampton. She sighed, recognizing her father's handwriting on the envelope. With a hairgrip, she slit open the envelope and unfolded the single sheet of writing paper.

Dear Bella,

Your mother has written to me informing me of your engagement to William Mullens. Please do not think I am intent on spoiling your perceived happiness, but I must forbid you to marry this man. Do not ask me why. I have nothing against him personally, and I am unable to explain my reasons more except to say there is a good reason why you and Will cannot be married.

Yours faithfully,

Your loving father

Bella read the letter again, certain she'd misconstrued what her father was trying to say. There was a reason she couldn't marry Will. What on earth could he mean?

'Everything all right?' Gilly asked, frowning at her friend in concern.

'Yes,' Bella said quickly, shoving the letter in her pocket. 'Everything's fine.' She nodded at the blackboard. 'What have you got first thing?'

'Spitfire to Bicester. You?'

'I haven't had a chance to look,' Bella said, trying hard to concentrate. Her father's words were going around in her head. What on earth did he mean? She would have to speak to him. Whatever his reasoning, it was bound to be something out of nothing. Perhaps he was having one of his strange episodes. All the more reason to visit him as soon as she was able. Without her mother there to keep an eye on him, he could be prone to all sorts of erratic behaviour. Pushing thoughts of her father from her mind, she checked the board. Her first job of the day was to fly a Hurricane up to an airbase on the east coast. She was just ticking off her name when she felt a hand in hers and she turned to find Will standing beside her, his fingers surreptitiously brushing hers.

'Morning,' he smiled, keeping his expression neutral as he checked the board.

'Have you just got in?' Bella asked. 'I missed you at breakfast.'

'I was held up by low cloud over the Thames estuary,' he said. 'Took off an hour later than expected.'

'I'm glad you're back safe. I'm off to Little Snoring first thing.'

'I see I'm off to White Waltham. Stay safe and I'll see you later.' Will gave her fingers a secret squeeze as they parted ways.

Bella caught up with Amanda and Beryl by the hangar.

'Where are you off to?' asked Amanda. She still exuded the glow of the newly married as she tugged on her flying jacket. Bella told her. 'I'm not far from there. A place called Ludham. I'll probably be on your tail most of the way.'

Bella pulled on her jacket and grabbed her helmet and goggles. 'See you in the air,' she grinned to Amanda, as they both clambered aboard their aircraft.

Once she was airborne, Bella's mind wandered back to her father's letter. Keeping the plane steady, she retrieved it from her trouser pocket. Rereading it only served to increase her vexation with her parents, for her mother's response had been lukewarm at best, and Alice had even gone so far as to suggest Bella wait a while before setting a date. She had never thought of her parents as prejudiced, but she could think of no other reason for their reaction, other than Will's gypsy heritage. Sighing with frustration, she glanced out of the plane, smiling briefly as she spotted Amanda's Spitfire some distance to her starboard side. Amanda waggled her wings in acknowledgement. Bella checked her cruising altitude and her compass. Peering overboard, she lined up the river snaking through the gold and green patchwork of fields with her map. Satisfied that she was on course, she settled back in her seat, her mind going back to her parents. If she explained to her father that Will was a decent man, and that she was determined to marry him, no matter what, surely he would come round? And she was certain that once her father changed his mind about her fiancé, her mother would too. She decided she would visit her father as soon as she could.

Her flights for the rest of the week were uneventful. During the second week of July the airbase suffered its worst loss of life since Bella had been at Chantry Fields. The run of good weather had come to an end with endless rain and low cloud. One of the ferry pool pilots, Terry, crashed his Spitfire into the Thames after losing his way when he was engulfed in low cloud, and several of the RAF pilots had failed to return from a reconnaissance mission over the south coast.

So, the mood on the base was sombre that Friday morning in the middle of July as Bella and Will made their way across the water-logged ground to the lane to catch the bus to the railway station.

'Don't be nervous,' Will said, holding the umbrella over their heads as they waited for the bus. 'I promise I shall be on my best behaviour all weekend. Whatever your father's objections, I'm sure we can convince him otherwise.'

Bella smiled but remained unconvinced. She hadn't heard anything more from either of her parents since her father's letter two weeks earlier, of which she'd told Will the gist. She was hopeful she could make her father understand how much she loved Will, but if he refused to accept her choice of husband, then she would marry Will anyway, without her parents' blessing, she thought determinedly, as the bus rounded the bend and pulled up in front of them with a hiss of breaks.

They paid for their tickets and found seats halfway along the aisle. The rain was falling steadily, running down the glass. The green verges and hedgerows were a blur through the rain-streaked window as the bus snaked its way towards town, the heavy dark clouds a fitting reflection of Bella's mood.

After a lengthy delay at Salisbury, the rest of their journey passed smoothly, but by the time the bus pulled up outside the Glyn Arms pub in Strawbridge, Bella's stomach was a mass of butterflies. The fact that her father hadn't acknowledged that she and Will were coming to visit was a cause for concern and she was anxious as to the sort of reception they might expect. Surely her father wouldn't be openly rude to Will, would he?

Will picked up their two small bags and they alighted the bus. It was still raining as he took Bella's hand. Feeling sick with apprehension, she unfurled the umbrella, and they walked the short distance from the pub to the church.

As they passed the cottage where Will's grandma had once lived, he paused. There was a new family living there now, of course. A child's wooden hobby horse leaned against the doorframe and a teddy bear was propped in the upstairs window.

A gust of wind blew down the lane, rustling the climbing roses and sending a flurry of petals swirling towards them.

The drizzle turned to a deluge just as they reached the vicarage. Water poured from the overflowing gutters and two sparrows were enjoying a bath on the sodden lawn. Lowering the umbrella, Bella tugged on the bell rope, listening to the jangle deep inside the house.

'Bella,' Ida exclaimed, opening the door, her eyes widening in delight. 'What a pleasant surprise. The reverend never mentioned we were to expect you?' She ushered Bella and Will into the dim hallway, her gaze questioning.

'Hello, Mrs Wilson,' Bella said, unbuttoning her coat. 'This is my fiancé, Will Mullens.'

'Fiancé? Well, well.' She studied Will a moment. 'You're Hannah's grandson, aren't you? I thought you looked familiar. Welcome to the vicarage. Your father is at a parish council meeting.' Ida glanced at the clock on the wall. 'I'm expecting him back any minute. Will you be staying the night?' she asked, ushering them to the kitchen.

Bella hesitated. 'Erm, yes. I am. Will is taking a room at the Glyn Arms.' She frowned. 'I wrote to Father last week. I wonder why he didn't mention our visit.'

'It is strange,' Ida concurred, filling the kettle. 'You'll have tea, won't you?'

'Yes, please.' At that moment the back door burst open and Johnny and Jack spilled into the kitchen, accompanied by the two dripping wet dogs. With a delighted bark of recognition, Barney and Sybil leapt at Bella, covering her skirt with muddy paw prints.

'Down!' shouted Ida crossly, flapping at them with a tea

towel as Bella laughed, pushing them away with her hands. They turned their attention to Will, sniffing at him politely. He patted their damp heads before Ida shooed them into the scullery where they could dry off.

'Hello, boys,' Bella said, smiling at Johnny, who was taking off his wet coat. 'Are you enjoying your summer holidays?'

'Yes, thank you,' he replied, looking at Will shyly.

'This is my fiancé, Will. Will, our evacuees, Johnny and Jack.'

'Pleased to meet you, boys,' Will said, extending his hand. Both boys shook it.

'Are you a pilot, too?' Jack asked, brushing a strand of wet fringe out of his eyes.

'I am,' replied Will.

'Wow.' Jack pulled out a chair and clambered on it. He had a muddy streak on his cheek and his knees were scabbed. 'We saw a dog fight, didn't we Mrs Wilson?'

'We did, love,' Ida confirmed, carefully measuring out the tea leaves for the pot.

'I've got some shrapnel,' Johnny said, pulling something from his shorts' pocket. He held out his hand. To Bella, the misshapen metal shapes looked rather uninspiring, but Johnny was clearly extremely proud of them. 'They're from a German bomb.'

Will took the shrapnel, turning it over in his hands. 'This is a great find,' he said.

'I know. Billy Murray's jealous because he's the only one at school who hasn't found any.'

203

The parlour clock chimed four. Ida lifted the kettle from the stove and filled the teapot.

'You two had better go and wash,' she said, covering the teapot with a knitted tea cosy. 'The reverend will be home shortly.'

The boys disappeared into the scullery and Ida reached for the mop.

'If there's one thing the reverend can't abide, it's mud,' she said, wielding the mop across the slate floor. 'It's good to see you again, Will, and I'm thrilled for the pair of you.'

They were almost finished drinking their tea when they heard the front door open and shut. At the sound of her father's footsteps on the linoleum floor, Bella tensed. From the scullery came a low bark, then silence.

'Bella?' Samuel stood in the doorway. He was staring at Will, his face ashen.

'Hello, Father,' Bella stood up, her heart racing. 'Father, this is Will Mullens, my fiancé. Will, you remember my father, the Reverend Roberts.'

Will was on his feet. 'Pleased to see you again, sir,' he said, holding out his hand. Samuel continued to stare at Will as if he hadn't heard a word.

'Father?' Bella said, glancing at Ida. The housekeeper frowned.

'Reverend?' she said tentatively. 'Are you well?'

'What's wrong, Uncle Samuel?' piped up Jack. The child's voice seemed to snap Samuel out of himself.

'Bella,' he said again, worry forming deep ridges across his brow. 'I wasn't expecting you.'

'You didn't get my letter?' Bella frowned. 'I wrote last week to say we would be coming.'

'There's a war on,' Ida said, bustling off to make a fresh pot of tea. 'Unfortunately, letters do occasionally go astray.'

Seemingly at a loss as to what to do next, Samuel glanced at the clock. 'Have you done your chores, boys?'

Johnny and Jack exchanged glances. 'No, sir.'

'Off you go, then.' Dragging their feet, the two boys pulled on their damp coats and opened the back door. It was raining heavily, and the trees in the garden were bent almost double by the wind.

'Here you are, Reverend.' Ida set a fresh pot of tea on the table, and hurried to shut the door. 'How was the PCC meeting?'

'It went as well as could be expected,' Samuel replied, morosely, adding a splash of milk to his tea. 'We might just have enough in the coffers to fix the hole in the roof.' He lowered his gaze. He seemed unable to look at Will, and Bella's cheeks burned with mortification.

'I'm sorry my letter went astray, Father,' she said, clearing her throat. 'I had assumed you would be expecting us.'

'I'm sorry news of our engagement took you by surprise, sir,' Will interjected when Samuel didn't reply. 'I should have spoken to you of my intentions and asked your permission before I proposed. I apologize for not doing so.' He paused and gave Bella a sideways glance. 'I would like to hope we will have your blessing, sir?'

Samuel snorted. Bella looked at Will. Tears stung her eyes as she fought to control her emotions.

'We've set a date, she said brightly. 'The thirtieth of August in Gillingham.'

'Not here?' Samuel looked at her askance. Bella swallowed, her father's response igniting a spark of hope he might be coming round.

'It won't be a big wedding, and it seemed sensible to get married near the base,' she explained. 'I think I would feel Mother's and Arthur's absence more keenly if I were to be married in Strawbridge.'

'You don't think it prudent to wait until your mother can be here?' her father suggested, making eye contact with his daughter for the first time since his arrival.

'No, Father. This war could drag on for years. Who knows when they'll be able to come home?'

Samuel sighed. He pushed aside his half-drunk cup of tea. 'I shall be in my study,' he said, rising from the table. 'I am not to be disturbed.'

Bella and Will exchanged puzzled glances with Ida, who shrugged. In the seven years she'd worked for the reverend, she'd grown accustomed to his odd ways.

'Why don't you go into the parlour?' she suggested. The boys will be back from doing their chores soon. There are some board games on the bookshelf.'

'If you're sure we can't help with anything?' Bella replied.

'I've got everything under control here,' Ida assured her.

'Your father really doesn't like me,' Will murmured as they left the kitchen. 'I can't understand why.'

'Like I've told you,' said Bella biting her lip. 'He's difficult. If only Mother was here.' She sighed. 'I'm so sorry. I feel awful.'

She pushed open the parlour door and crossed to the window, gazing through the rain-lashed glass out at the windswept garden. She could see the boys in the chicken coop. The wind whipped the raspberry canes, and rainwater ran in rivulets down the path. It gushed over the gutters and spewed down the drainpipe.

'What a day,' she said, turning from the window as Will came to stand behind her. He took her in his arms and kissed her tenderly. 'I'm really sorry about my father,' she murmured, as he kissed her again. 'He's a damaged soul.'

'Shush,' Will whispered into her hair. 'I thought I detected a slight thaw in his attitude just now and I've still got tomorrow to woo him with my charms. He'll come around, you'll see.'

'I hope so,' Bella sighed.

The boys traipsed noisily into the kitchen and Bella heard Ida admonishing them for walking mud all over her freshly mopped floor and dispatching them to the scullery.

'I think we're about to have company,' said Will, kissing Bella one last time before the boys, hands scrubbed and wearing their slippers, trooped into the parlour, cheeks glowing, hair sticking up in damp tufts.

'Mrs Wilson said we can play a game,' Jack said, walking over to the bookshelf. 'What shall we play?'

They settled on Monopoly, and for a while Bella managed to forget her worries, as she was swept along by the boys' carefree laughter.

CHAPTER TWENTY-TWO

Samuel didn't appear for supper, so Bella and Will ate in the kitchen with Ida and the boys. The chicken casserole was delicious, but the food turned to sawdust in Bella's mouth, and she had to force each mouthful down her throat. Her father's blatant rudeness made her feel sick, and no matter how much Will assured her that he didn't mind, she knew she would never forgive her father for his behaviour. If only her mother was here, she mused miserably for the umpteenth time. Even in her father's darkest days, her mother had somehow been able to get through to him. Without her steady, calming presence, it was as if her father was sinking deeper and deeper into a dark hole, and Bella had no idea how to reach him. It was looking increasingly likely that not only would her mother and brother not be at her wedding, she thought miserably, but that her father wouldn't be there either.

The boys chatted throughout the meal, plying Will with

questions about aeroplanes, so Bella's silence went largely unnoticed, except by Will, who kept smiling at her encouragingly. She managed a smile back. How she loved him, she mused, watching as he interacted with the boys.

'Tell us about the time you nearly got shot down by a Messerschmidt, Bella,' said Jack, startling her out of her meanderings.

'I've told you the story before,' she protested.

'We want to hear it again,' Johnny agreed, resting his elbows on the table and earning himself a look of reproach from Ida. 'Please?' he said, shifting his elbows to his side.

Bella smiled. Laying down her knife and fork, she regaled the boys and Ida with her story.

'I wish I was old enough to fight,' Jack said. 'I want to fly Spitfires and shoot down Germans.' His eyes shone with excitement.

'Hopefully the war will be over long before you boys are old enough to fight,' said Ida drily, as she gathered the dirty plates.

They spent the evening in the parlour, listening to the wireless and talking softly while the boys read. Bella's ears were trained on the study, as she listened for the click of the door, but it remained firmly shut the entire evening. At half past eight Ida came to tell the boys it was bedtime. With much groaning and complaining they took themselves off to bed, leaving Bella and Will alone.

'I suppose I'd better get going soon,' he said, pulling her close. They were sitting together on the sofa, Bella's head resting on his shoulder.

'What time will you come back in the morning?' Bella asked, reluctant to move. She felt so at home in Will's arms.

'About ten?' suggested Will. 'Depending on the weather, perhaps we could take the boys out for the day.' He grinned. 'The atmosphere is a bit oppressive here.'

Bella rolled her eyes. 'You don't say?'

'I'm going to turn in now, Miss Bella,' Ida said, poking her head around the doorframe. 'I'll see you both in the morning.'

'All right, Mrs Wilson. And thank you.'

Ida smiled. 'It was a pleasure meeting you, Master Will.'

'Likewise,' Will grinned

Bidding them 'goodnight', Ida left the room, leaving them alone.

Bella and Will stayed snuggled on the sofa, talking in low voices until the clock struck ten.

'Now, I really must go,' Will said, reluctantly extricating himself from Bella. 'Guests have to be in by half past.' Taking her by the hand, he pulled her to her feet. She walked him to the door. 'I love you so much, Bella Roberts,' Will said, as he kissed her goodnight. 'I can't wait to be your husband.'

'I can't wait either,' replied Bella. 'I just hope my father comes around.'

'He will,' Will smiled. 'Trust me.'

Bella gave him a wry smile. 'I hope you're right.' They kissed again, and then she let Will out, opening and closing the door quickly to prevent too much light spilling into the darkness. She was contemplating heading up to bed when she heard the study door open

'Father,' she cried in alarm, startled by her Father's stricken expression. 'Are you ill? Shall I call the doctor?' She asked, hurrying over to him, His skin was pale, and he had a sheen of sweat on his brow. His hands were shaking violently.

'I'm not ill, Bella,' Samuel responded with a shake of his head. 'But I must speak to you. Come into my study.'

Puzzled, Bella followed him. 'Take a seat,' he said, closing the door behind her.

'This sounds serious,' Bella said, with a shaky laugh. Samuel didn't return her smile. Instead, he pulled up a chair close to hers and sat down, leaning forward so his elbows rested on his knees.

'Bella, you know I love you and the last thing I would ever wish to do is cause you pain, but as I said in my letter, you must not marry Will.'

'Father,' Bella sighed. 'Why don't you like him? Is it because of his Romany heritage? Grandma told me you disapproved of his great-great-grandmother's habit of telling fortunes.'

'It's not that,' Samuel said, rubbing his hand across his face. He sat back in his chair, a pained expression on his face.

'Then what is your objection?' asked Bella, an impatient edge to her tone.

'Just trust me when I say this, that if you two were to marry it would be a sin against the law of God and of man.'

'What?' Bella stared at him dismay. Her father was more ill

than she'd thought. 'Father, you're not making sense. Please, let me send for the doctor. You're clearly not well.'

'I am perfectly well, Isabella,' Samuel snapped. He let out a low groan and bowed his head as he massaged his temples. When he raised his head, his expression was one of abject sadness.

Filled with compassion, Bella got up and knelt by his chair. 'Father, please tell me what's troubling you.'

Samuel let out a long, shuddering sigh. 'My child, I had hoped to spare you the sordid truth, but I see I have no choice but to be completely honest with you.'

'You're really worrying me now,' Bella said. She sat back on her heels, her heart thudding painfully against her ribcage.

Abruptly, Samuel got to his feet and stood by the empty fireplace. Bella could hear the wind howling down the chimney. Rain lashed against the French windows behind the blackout curtains. With one hand resting on the mantlepiece, Samuel stared into the empty grate.

'You can't marry Will because ... because he's your brother.'

Bella stared at him, speechless.

'I'm sorry, Bella,' Samuel said, his face in his hands.

'No,' Bella whispered. 'It can't be true. Why are you saying such a thing? Father, you are ill. I insist on calling the doctor and ...'

'No!' Her father's shouted response stopped her in her tracks. From the look of self-loathing in his eyes, she realized with horror that what he said was true.

'How?' she whispered, clutching at her chest. 'How can it be true?' Her chest felt so tight, she feared she was having a heart attack. She sank onto the nearest chair, her breathing ragged.

'It was a moment of madness,' Samuel said, bleakly. Unable to look his daughter in the eye, he kept his gaze trained on the fireplace. 'I had not long since been discharged from the Army. Leah, William's mother, had recently lost her fiancé . . . I was ill . . .' He threw up his hands in despair. 'Like I said, it was a moment of pure madness and instantly regretted.'

Bella stared at him. Her mouth was working but no sound escaped her lips.

'I used to believe God allowed Arthur to be born the way he is to punish me. I know differently now, of course. Arthur's a wonderful person in his own right.'

'Does Mother know?' Bella croaked, her eyes hard.

'Pardon?' Samuel blinked.

'I said, does my mother know how you betrayed her? Leah was Mother's friend.' Samuel flinched.

'No, of course not. I never wanted to hurt Alice, Bella, you must believe that. There was no love affair between Leah and me. It was a stupid mistake, and I can't see that it would benefit anyone for your mother to discover my indiscretion after all these years.'

'Will obviously doesn't know,' Bella said morosely.

'No one does. I think Hannah may have suspected. She always looked at me strangely after Will was born.'

Bella sank back into her chair. Her mind was whirling as the truth of her Father's revelation crashed over her like a wave. She and Will were brother and sister. They could never marry. She had no choice but to break off their engagement. She let out a cry of pain. Why did she and Will have to suffer for their parents' sin? Life could be so cruel.

'When do you expect Will back again?' her father asked gruffly, embarrassed by his daughter's distress.

Bella regarded him with incomprehension. She shook her head, trying to think. 'In the morning.'

'Then you will have to break things off with him. Mrs Wilson and I shall take the boys to the pond for a spot of fishing. That should give you ample time to do what must be done.'

'What will I say?' Bella whispered, one hand clasped over her shattered heart.

'Anything but the truth,' Samuel said. 'I have my repu-tation as a clergyman to consider and you wouldn't want to break your mother's heart now, would you?'

Through her pain, Bella could only stare at her father with contempt. 'You're asking me to give up the man I love, my heart is breaking, and yet you're more concerned about your reputation?' She rose to her feet, her fists clenched at her sides.

'It's your mother I'm thinking of,' said Samuel hurriedly. 'And Arthur. Imagine what this would do to him.'

'Oh,' Bella said, choking on the realization. 'Will and Arthur are brothers. And they can never know it.' She shot her father a look of pure loathing. 'I shall never forgive you for this, Father,' she sobbed. 'Never!'

With that, she fled from the study. Taking the stairs two at a time, she ran to her room, and flung herself on the bed where she gave in to the well of emotions erupting inside her.

How could she face Will and tell him she couldn't marry him, she thought miserably some time later. The great tide of emotion had subsided. Now she just felt empty and deeply sad. Whatever excuse she gave him for calling off the wedding, Will wouldn't believe her. He'd take one look at her face and know she was lying. She rolled onto her back. Her pillow was sopping wet where her tears had soaked into the fabric. She pushed it to one side and folded her hands beneath her head. The rain had stopped and she could hear an owl hooting in the lane. As she lay in the pitch blackness, she realized what she had to do. Groping about in the dark, she found her candle and the matches. By candlelight, she made her way slowly downstairs to her father's study. Standing in the doorway, she lifted the candle, letting the light fall on the room where all her hopes and dreams had been reduced to a pile of ashes. With a heavy heart, she made her way to the desk and, rummaging in a drawer, pulled out a writing pad and pen.

My dearest Will,
    Please do not ask me why for I can't explain, but I cannot marry you. I'm sorry.
    Yours always,
    Bella

By the time she folded the sheet of paper and slipped it into an envelope, she was sobbing. With shaking fingers, she took of her engagement ring and slipped it into the envelope. She wrote Will's name on the front of the envelope and propped it on the mantlepiece where her father would be sure to see it in the morning.

Stifling her sobs, she crept back upstairs and collected her bag. She hadn't changed into her pyjamas, so she had no need to get dressed. She made her way slowly back downstairs and retrieved her coat. Quietly letting herself out of the house, she felt her way along the side of the building to the garden shed where Arthur's old bicycle was stored. Taking a deep breath, she wheeled it out into the lane. There was barely enough moonlight to see by as she straddled the bike and pushed off. The bicycle's headlamp was feeble, but at least it afforded her enough light to lessen the likelihood of an accident.

She kept her eyes resolutely on the road as she cycled past the pub, not wanting to dwell on the fact that Will was just a few yards away, and no doubt dreaming of her and the future they had planned. Choking back a sob, she pedalled on. Somewhere a dog barked in the darkness, and something shrieked in the hedgerows, causing the hairs to stand up on her arms. The next minute she had to swerve to avoid a fox slinking across her path, some small rodent dangling from its jaws.

It was slow going and dawn was already lightening the eastern sky by the time she wheeled her bike into

217

Southampton's bomb-damaged railway station. She had left a note for her father, telling him where he could collect the bike, and she propped it up against the wall near the ticket office where he would be able to find it easily.

The station was quiet. The first train wasn't due in or out for an hour, so Bella settled herself on a bench to wait. As the platforms filled up with an eclectic mix of military personnel, servicemen and women, and civilians, she was torn between the dread of Will turning up and the hope that he would. He wasn't due at the vicarage for another three hours yet. Bella would be almost back at base by the time Will made it to the railway station.

The first train rolled into the station at seven o'clock. Bella got to her feet. Picking up her bag, she boarded. She leaned back in her seat as the compartment filled up around her, and closed her eyes. She hadn't slept a wink, and her eyes were gritty with tiredness, but she knew she wouldn't sleep. Nevertheless, she kept them firmly shut, not wanting to engage with her fellow passengers. The train lurched and pulled out of the station. Letting the chatter of the compartment wash over, Bella turned her face to the window, eyes tightly shut, and tried to quell her tears.

Will walked jauntily down the lane. After the previous day's storm, the day had dawned warm and sunny. The sky had that fresh, just washed look about it, pale blue with fluffy white clouds scudding along in the breeze. He breathed deep, filling his lungs with the smell of damp earth. The strawberry fields were bustling with activity, and from the grounds of the big house came the shouted laughter of children at play.

He'd spent the night tossing and turning, unable to sleep as he'd wrestled with the problem of Bella's father. He wasn't overly bothered whether the man took to him or not; he was marrying Bella, not her father. But it mattered to Bella, and if the situation was making her unhappy, then he was determined to do everything in his power to fix it.

Whistling cheerfully to himself, he swung open the vicarage gate and strolled up the path. Samuel had clearly been watching from the study window for he had the door open before Will reached it.

'Reverend Roberts,' he said cheerfully, reasoning that he may as well start as he meant to go on.

'Will,' Samuel greeted him gruffly. 'I'm afraid Bella isn't here.'

'Oh,' Will said with surprise. 'I see. May I come in and wait?'

'That won't be possible. What I mean is, Bella went back to Dorset this morning.'

'Pardon?' Will leaned towards Samuel. He frowned, certain he'd misheard the man. 'I don't understand.'

'She left you a note,' said Samuel. He stepped back and picked up an envelope from the hall table. 'I'm sure there's an explanation.'

Will took the letter in bewildered silence. He couldn't understand why Bella would leave without a word.'

'Gooday to you, Mr Mullens,' Samuel said, firmly shutting the door in Will's face. He ripped open the envelope, gasping in shock as Bella's ring fell into his palm, and pulled out the sheet of writing paper, reading the single sentence in disbelief. It didn't make any sense. He scratched his head and reread the simple message but no matter how many times he read it, he couldn't make sense of why Bella was calling off the wedding. And not only the wedding but, given her sudden disappearance, it appeared that she was ending their romance as well.

He must go after her. Shoving the letter and ring in his trouser pocket, he turned and ran down the garden path and up the lane, the few people about regarding him with mild amusement. He dashed into the pub, taking the stairs two at a time to his room, where he hastily threw his belongings together. The next bus into Southampton was due at twenty past ten. He should just make it. To his relief, the reception desk was quiet. The stout, blonde woman behind the desk took his payment and, shouldering his bag, he hurried outside, just as the bus came rumbling up the road.

Filled mostly with housewives and youngsters, Will found himself a seat near the back. He stowed his bag on the floor between his feet and stared out of the window. His mind was in turmoil. What on earth had caused Bella to have such a change of heart? Was her father so dead set against Will that he'd managed to persuade Bella to change her mind? He exhaled impatiently. He couldn't wait to get back to base and speak to her face to face. Whatever the Reverend Roberts had said, Will would have to convince her otherwise. He closed his eyes, willing himself to calm down. Getting himself all hot under the collar wouldn't get him there any quicker. Better to relax and get his thoughts in order, and with at least two hours' travelling time ahead of him, he had plenty of opportunity to do that.

CHAPTER TWENTY-THREE

Bella climbed out of the bus. Her throat was raw from crying. She shouldered her bag and, wiping her swollen, red-rimmed eyes, she blew her nose and took a deep breath. The journey from Southampton to Salisbury had been stop-start all the way and there'd been a lengthy delay just west of Tisbury due to a landslide.

Taking a deep breath to regain her composure, Bella crossed the lane and made her way along the rutted track. The airbase gleamed in the late morning sunshine. Sunlight glinted on aeroplane wings and the windsock hung limply on its post. As she crossed the grass, veering between haphazardly parked military vehicles, she noticed that there was none of the usual banter amongst the ground crew. She walked past the mess without glancing in, keen to get to her barracks without having to engage in conversation with anyone. She was too miserable to speak to anybody right now. But as sad as she was, she couldn't help but sense the deep melancholy that had settled over the base. Gilly was sitting on the steps of their barracks, smoking a cigarette. As Bella got closer, she noticed her friends' eyes were red from crying.

'Gilly?' Bella quickened her pace. 'What's happened?'

'Oh, Bella,' Gilly hiccupped, exhaling a cloud of smoke as she got wearily to her feet. 'It's Jonty. He was killed yesterday.'

'What?' Bella's heart plummeted. 'Oh, poor Amanda,' she wailed, her own heartache momentarily forgotten. 'What happened?'

Gilly shook her head and took a long drag of her cigarette. 'A call came in during the storm,' she said, in a shaky voice. 'No one wanted to do it. Too risky, everyone said so, except Jonty. He took off for Sheffield around noon. He almost made it.' Gilly's voice quivered. Bella put her arm around her friend's shoulders. 'It's just conjecture but they think he tried to fly above the clouds and got disorientated. He ejected as the plane went down over a disused quarry. A group of Boys' Brigade lads were camping nearby. They saw Jonty hit the water. A couple of them ran to a nearby farmhouse to get help but by the time they came back he'd disappeared under the water. He never came back up.'

'Did no one try and save him?' asked Bella, blinking away the mental image conjured up by Gilly's description.

'Some of the lads tried but it was deep and freezing cold. One of them had to be treated for hypothermia. A rescue team turned up within half an hour but . . .' She shrugged her shoulders.

'Where's Amanda?'

Gilly jerked her head. 'Inside with Beryl. I just needed a minute, you know?'

'Of course.' Bella squeezed Gilly's shoulder. 'I'll go see her now.' Taking a deep breath, she pushed open the door to their hut. Amanda was curled up on her bed, shoulders shaking with silent sobs. Beryl sat at the foot of the bed, her back resting against the wall. She met Bella's gaze with a nod. If she was surprised to see Bella home a day earlier than expected, she gave no sign.

Bella crept closer to the bed. 'I'm so, so, sorry,' she whispered, crouching beside Amanda, and gently stroking her hair. 'If there's anything I can do?'

Amanda rolled over so she was face to face with Bella. Her face was pale, her eyes red and swollen. 'I begged him not to do it,' she said, between juddering sobs. 'He wouldn't listen. He promised me he'd be all right.' Her expression was bleak. 'Nineteen days, Bella,' Amanda whispered hoarsely. 'That's all we had as man and wife.'

Bella's eyes filled with tears as her heart broke for her friend. 'I'm so sorry,' she said again.

'They haven't found him, you know?' Amanda said, her expression haunted. 'I can't bear to think of my Jonty lying there in the cold and dark, Bella,' she sobbed, her shoulders heaving. 'I can't bear it.'

*

Bella had just finished her second cup of tea when Commander Forrester knocked on the door to tell them Amanda's mother had arrived.

'I never dreamed we'd be meeting again in such sad circumstances,' Renee said, as the three women filed out of the hut. 'My poor baby,' she said, her crimson lips wobbling as she tried valiantly to control her emotions. 'A widow at twenty-four.' She shook her head sorrowfully and climbed the wooden steps into the hut. At the sight of her mother, Amanda's sobs rose in volume. 'Oh, my love,' Bella heard Renee croon. 'My poor, poor love.'

A plane was coming in to land, and they watched it as it descended gently onto the grass. Bella felt sick. She wondered if they'd found Jonty's body yet.

'What are you doing back here?' Beryl asked, suddenly. 'I thought you were only due back tomorrow.'

Bella cleared her throat. How could she explain to her friends why she'd broken things off with Will without revealing her father's shameful secret?

'It's over,' she said, studying her hands. Beryl and Gilly looked at her blankly. 'Will and I,' Bella said, her chest compressing painfully. 'It's over between us.'

'Are you mad?' exploded Beryl. 'You two are the perfect couple. What could he possibly have done to upset you so much you'd break off your engagement?' She gasped. 'He hasn't been unfaithful, surely?'

Bella shook her head. 'No. Will would never do that.' She sighed. 'It's complicated.'

'Then explain,' said Gilly, wiping her nose with her handkerchief.

'Look, I can't explain, but I have my reasons, all right?' She felt as though her heart might explode, the pain in her chest was so great. 'I need you to do me a favour. I need you to keep Will away from me. Please? I can't deal with seeing him right now.'

Her expression softened. 'Whatever it is, can't you work it out?' Beryl asked gently.

Bella shook her head, tears in her eyes. 'No,' she whispered. 'Look, it's for the best. Please, will you help me? I just can't see him right now.' Bella looked at her friends pleadingly. She couldn't even begin to think of Will as her brother yet. She felt ill every time she contemplated the idea, and if she saw him, she doubted she would have the strength to resist him. More than anything in the world she wanted to wake up and find it had all been a horrible nightmare and for them to get married in six weeks' time like they'd planned.

Beryl and Gilly exchanged puzzled glances. Beryl sighed.

'All right.' She shrugged. 'I don't know what this is about but you're my friend. I'm on your side.'

'Me too,' said Gilly.

'Thank you.' Bella managed a half-smile. 'Poor Amanda,' she said. 'I wish there was something we could do to help her.'

'Bella! BELLA!' Bella's heart skipped a beat as she heard Will shout her name. Every fibre in her body screamed at her to turn around and run straight into his arms but she forced herself to keep walking, as if she hadn't heard him. Beryl and Gilly closed ranks around her.

'Won't you just talk to him?' whispered Beryl. 'He sounds genuinely upset.'

'I can't,' Bella hissed, fighting to hold on to her composure.

'All right,' Beryl sighed. 'Have it your way.'

Flanked by her two friends, Bella entered the ablutions block. Breathing in the smell of damp and carbolic soap, she sank onto a stool and buried her face in her hands.

'Look,' Beryl said, squatting in front of her. 'You obviously still love him, so why won't you just talk to him?'

'I do love him,' Bella said, bleakly. 'That's the problem. I have to keep my distance, or I'll give in and I mustn't. I can't.'

'None of this makes the slightest bit of sense to me,' Beryl said waspishly. 'When you think how short life is . . . I mean, God forbid one of you could end up like poor old Jonty. I just think that what with a war on and everything, you should grab any chance of happiness you can and not let some petty squabble . . .'

'It's not a petty squabble,' Bella snapped.

'Well, whatever it is, I think you're silly to let it rob you of your happiness.'

'We promised Bella we'd support her,' Gilly reminded her. Beryl rolled her eyes.

'And we will. What do you want me to do?'

'Ask him to leave me alone. Please?'

'Fine. Wait here.' Beryl strode out of the ablutions block to find Will standing near the entrance, looking devastated.

'Beryl!' he cried, the anguish in his voice clearly audible. 'Why won't she speak to me? What have I done?'

'Look, Will,' said Beryl, firmly. 'I don't know what this is about. I really don't, but Bella doesn't want to see you. I'm sorry.' She turned to walk away but Will grabbed her arm.

'Look,' he said, shoving the unfolded letter under her nose. 'She left me this. She called off our wedding with no explanation, nothing. She couldn't even tell me to my face. Please?' The anger faded from his voice and his eyes were pleading. 'I just want to talk to her. I have a right to know what I've done wrong and what I can do to fix it.'

Beryl nodded. 'I'll talk to her.' She inclined her head towards the airfield. 'You heard about Jonty?'

Will nodded grimly. 'Awful luck. If he'd bailed out over land, he'd probably have made it. How's Amanda bearing up?'

'Her mother's with her.'

Will nodded. 'Please pass on my condolences. And tell Bella, tell her I love her, and whatever the problem is, we can deal with it.'

Beryl waited until Will had disappeared between the hangars before returning to the ablutions block.

'You left him a note?' Hands on her hips, she glared at Bella, her eyes flashing angrily. 'I'd have expected you of all people to at least have had the courage to break things off with him face to face.'

'I couldn't,' Bella whispered. 'I'm not strong enough.'

'Bella, what the heck is going on with you?' sighed Gilly.

228

Bella sighed too. The urge to unburden herself was overpowering. Did her father deserve her loyalty? His selfish, thoughtless action had cost her a lifetime of happiness.

'I can't tell you,' she said miserably. 'I'm sorry.'

'Well, things are going to be fun around here trying to keep the two of you apart,' Beryl snorted. 'Come on. I'm hungry. Let's get some grub.'

'You go,' Bella said. 'I'm not hungry.'

'You can't sit in here all day to avoid Will. You'll have to face him some time.'

'Just not yet.'

Neither Beryl nor Gilly seemed inclined to want to leave Bella skulking in the ablutions block, but they eventually gave in.

'You'll have to come out of hiding tomorrow,' Gilly warned her.

'I know,' responded Bella gloomily.

Left alone, she allowed her thoughts to turn to Will. It would be impossible working from the same base as him. She would have to apply for a transfer. The tears came again. This time she was crying for Amanda and Jonty, as well as for herself and Will.

'Bella,' Will shouted across the space between the two aeroplane hangars. 'Bella, wait.' Reluctantly, Bella stopped walking. Slowly she turned to face Will as he ran towards her. 'Bella,' was all he could say as he came to a halt just a few feet in front of her. He splayed his hands. 'Why?'

'Please, Will. Leave me alone.' She turned to go, but Will caught her arm. His touch was like a shot of electricity shooting up her veins and she flinched.

'What happened, Bella?' pleaded Will. 'Is it your father? Is what he thinks so important that you're willing to throw away our happiness?' Will's face was haggard. He looked as though he hadn't slept in days. 'Please, Bella,' he implored her. 'I've kept my distance like you wanted but I need to know. What went wrong? You owe me an explanation, at least.'

'Will, please,' whispered Bella. 'I can't.'

'Can't or won't?' said Will, an angry edge to his voice. 'I can't believe you're doing this to me. To us.'

Bella shook her head, blinking back the tears threatening to spill over her lashes. 'I'm sorry, Will.' Will stared at her for a moment, his expression stony.

'All right,' he said, his voice rough. He shrugged. 'I won't beg. I've got my pride.' He gave her a wry smile. 'See you around, First Officer Roberts.'

Watching him walk away, it was all Bella could do not to call after him. As soon as he was out of sight, she fell to her knees, clutching her stomach, doubled over by the agonizing pain of loss and grief.

She allowed herself the luxury of tears for a few minutes, then, taking a deep breath, she pulled herself together and walked over to the Ops Room. As always when she walked in, the names of their deceased colleagues seemed to jump out at her from the board. Jonty's name was the most recent and she sent up a quick prayer that it would be the last, for a while, at least.

'Fancy taking a Spitfire over to White Waltham?' Neil asked, putting down the telephone. 'If the chaps get on with it straight away, you should be ready for take-off in around twenty minutes.'

'All right, thanks.' Bella took the sheet of paper Neil handed her and scanned the information he'd jotted down in his barely legible handwriting.

'All clear?' Neil asked, his hand hovering above the ringing telephone.

'As mud,' she grinned. She gave him a thumbs up and left the room. She had twenty minutes. Plenty of time for her to call in to see the major.

She made her way to his office. The past five days had been the hardest of her life. She caught her breath. Was it only five days since her life had been irrevocably turned upside down? Five days since Jonty was killed. His body still hadn't been recovered. Amanda had been granted two weeks' compassionate leave and had gone down to Devon with Renee. She inhaled nervously. She'd flown any number of aeroplanes in some hair-raising conditions and had taken it in her stride but there was something about Major Thompson that she found intimidating. Plucking up her courage, she rapped on his door.

At the barked command to enter, she turned the handle and stepped inside. The room hadn't changed at all in the two and a half years she'd been at Chantry Fields.

'Yes?' the major drawled, glaring at Bella from behind his broad desk.

'Sir, I wish to request a transfer to another ferry port.'

The major shrugged. 'You're a civilian, First Officer Roberts,' he said, looking bored. 'You can go where you like.'

'Perhaps you might put in a word for me somewhere, sir?' Bella persisted. Major Thompson sighed.

'Very well. Leave it with me.'

'Thank you, sir.'

The sun was low over the tree-line by the time she landed her last flight of the day and taxied over to the hangar. A member of the ground crew ran over to her as she climbed down from the cockpit.

'All good?' he asked, as she pulled off her goggles and helmet.

'No noticeable issues,' she replied, running her fingers through her hair. Shrugging off her flying jacket, she made her way towards the Ops Room. She was bone weary, hungry, and looking forward to a relaxing bath.

'First Officer Roberts,' a voice called. 'May I have a word.'

Bella stopped in her tracks. Major Thompson strode towards her, hands behind his back, chest thrust out, his buttons gleaming in the early evening sunshine.

'I've got you a transfer to Woodhead airbase in Derbyshire. Here are your coordinates.' He handed her a sheet of paper. 'You're to report for duty tomorrow morning at ten hundred hours.'

'Tomorrow morning, sir?' Bella scanned the list of typed instructions. Derbyshire. She smiled wryly. That was certainly far enough away from Will. There would always be the chance she might run into him at some airbase somewhere but that was a risk she'd have to take if she wanted to continue flying, which she did. Now that she'd lost Will, her love of flying was all she had.

'Luckily for you they're in need of a Spitfire. You can fly it up there first thing. Let the Ops Room know to assign it to you.'

'Yes, sir.' Bella thanked him. As she turned to go, she caught sight of Will standing by the mess hall. Even at that distance she could see the bewilderment and hurt on his face. Bella half raised her hand in a wave then thought better of it. With a leaden heart she turned away. Tomorrow she would be gone, and Will could move on with his life. As for herself, there would be no one else. Fighting back the tears, she made her way over to the Ops Room to organize her flight to Derbyshire.

CHAPTER TWENTY-FOUR

Bella gazed down over the purple moors and craggy cliffs. A large part of the Derbyshire moorlands were scorched black where returning German planes had jettisoned their leftover bombs, clearly mistaking the seemingly flat landscape for an airfield. Ironically, Woodhead airfield lay just a few miles south, nestled between the towns of Glossop and Buxton, close to the village of Chinley. Bella checked her map. If her coordinates were correct the airstrip should be just up ahead. She peered through her windshield. She was flying over a town. She could see neat rows of terraced houses far below. She checked her compass and her map again. Deducing the town to be Chapel-en-le-Frith, she nosed the plane due north, keeping her eyes peeled. Then she saw it, a row of stationary planes glinting in the sunshine. A collection of buildings and a stretch of smooth green amidst the hilly landscape. Bringing the Spitfire round, she circled the airfield, checking it was safe to land, and brought the machine down.

As she bounced across the bumpy grass, several ground crew hurried out of a nearby hangar to meet her.

'First Officer Roberts,' Bella introduced herself, tugging off her gloves. 'Which way to the Ops Room?'

'The open door on the left,' one of the men said, pointing to a row of prefabricated buildings on the edge of the airfield. Bella thanked him and made her way over. 'Hello?' she called, rapping on the open door. She was pleasantly surprised to see the two Ops Room plotters were women. 'First Officer Roberts from Chantry Fields,' she said, walking into the room. 'I'm joining you today.'

The two women seated behind the vast, paper-strewn desk looked up and smiled.

'Ah, yes,' said one, a pretty brunette around Bella's age. 'I'm Patty Bishop. Welcome to Woodhead.'

'Valerie Sinclair.' The other woman, a slender blonde with bird-like features, leaned forward to shake Bella's hand. 'Welcome. We don't get many female pilots up our way, so you'll certainly cause a stir amongst the men.' She grinned. 'Is that the paperwork for the Spitfire.'

'Oh, yes.' Bella handed it over.

'It's a quiet day,' Valerie said, shuffling some paperwork. 'The chaps are all in the common room, if you want to get acquainted, or I could show you to your quarters. You'll be bunking in with the two of us. Hold the fort for a few minutes, will you, Patty?'

'No problem,' replied Patty, with a wave of her hand. 'I'll let Flight Lieutenant Briggs know you've arrived,' she added, picking up the telephone.

'This way,' Valerie said, motioning to the door. 'I must say, I do admire your pluck,' she said, as they strode out across the airfield. A warm breeze drifted across, stirring the windsock and ruffling the grass. 'You may find some of the chaps a bit difficult to get on with. We've got a pool of eighteen, nineteen now you're here.' Her face fell. 'We lost two of our chaps recently.' Bella nodded in sympathy, thinking of Jonty. She'd asked Gilly to tell Amanda goodbye for her. Both Beryl and Gilly had been sorry to see her leave, but they'd promised to write and keep in touch. That's what Bella would do once she was settled, she decided as Valerie led her to a row of long, low wooden buildings. She would write to her friends and let them know that she had reached her destination safely.

'Here we are.' Valerie mounted the wooden steps and pushed open the door. 'It's pretty basic I'm afraid.'

Her footsteps echoing on the wooden floor, Bella followed Valerie inside.

'I see what you mean,' she smiled, gazing round the dormitory. It was a decent size, with six beds in two rows of three along each wall. A small window looked out over the airstrip, the blackout curtains pushed aside and tied with string. Each bed had a trunk at its foot, and a small bedside cabinet.

'For your personal possessions,' Valerie told her.

'You can hang your spare uniform and flying jacket on this rail here, and anything big you can shove under the bed.'

Bella dumped her bag on the bare mattress. A sheet and standard grey, military issue blanket was folded at the foot of the bed, together with a white pillowcase. A rather flat-looking pillow was propped against the iron headboard.

'It's all right,' Bella said, looking round. Valerie snorted.

'It's sweltering in summer and perishing cold in winter,' she said, with a grimace. 'It's draughty and the roof leaks.' She nodded at the tin bucket in the corner of the room. 'The women's shower block is just across the way. Hot water's something of a luxury I'm afraid. Still, the cook makes a decent cup of tea and his food's edible. And there's always the café in Chapel-en-le-Frith. Patty and I go there on our days off. You're welcome to join us if you're free.'

'Thanks. I'd like that.' Bella smiled.

'So, anyone special in your life?' Valerie asked, perching on her bed which was next to Bella's.

'No, no one,' replied Bella, hanging up her jacket. 'What about you?' she asked, unfastening her bag and shaking out her uniform before hanging it up.

'I have a fiancé, Tim. He's stationed out in Burma.'

'How long have you been here?' Bella asked, tugging off her flying trousers and changing into her skirt.

'I joined up in June nineteen-forty,' Valerie said. 'Patty joined about the same time. We were sent here after our training. Patty's brother and boyfriend were both killed at Dunkirk.'

'Oh, poor girl. One of my friends lost her husband recently. They hadn't even been married a month.'

'It's awful, isn't it?' sighed Valerie. 'Patty's walking out with a chap from Glossop she met at one of the dances, now. He works in the paper mill. Reserved occupation.'

Talking about romances inevitably brought thoughts of Will rushing to Bella's mind and a heaviness settled on her shoulders. As if sensing her change in mood, Valerie got to her feet.

'I'll leave you to get settled in,' she said. 'Flight Lieutenant Briggs will want to see you as soon as you're done. His office is the grey building directly across from the shower block. Someone will come to collect you.'

Thanking her, Bella returned to her unpacking, but the moment Valerie left the dorm and walked across the grass, she sank onto her bed, her face in her hands. How had she supposed that moving across the country would make missing Will easier. If anything, she felt more miserable. As well as feeling homesick for Chantry Fields and her friends, her heart ached with longing for Will. She had no idea how she would get through the rest of her life without him.

She was startled by a knock on the door. Hastily wiping her face with the back of her hands, she jumped to her feet, snapping to attention.

'At ease,' the airman leaning nonchalantly against the doorframe said, with a grin. 'No need to stand on ceremony. Apart from old Briggs, we're all civilians here.' He held out his left hand. 'Terry White. Pleased to meet you.'

'Bella Roberts,' Bella replied, shaking his hand awkwardly.

He was about thirty, she surmised, with a receding hairline, his blond hair cut short, blue eyes and lightly tanned skin.

'I've come to take you to see old Briggs. Don't let him intimidate you. He's very old school. Thinks all women should be indoors keeping the home fires burning.'

Bella pulled a face. 'Oh, dear.'

Terry flashed her a wry smile. 'He wasn't too keen on me to start with. Didn't think I was up to the job.' He held up his right arm and Bella was shocked to see it ended in a smooth, rounded stump just shy of where his wrist should have been. 'Lost it at Dunkirk. I was flying cover for the evacuation. A German bullet came straight through my windshield and took my hand clean off' he said, matter-of-factly, as if losing a hand was nothing more than a minor inconvenience.

Bella winced. 'I'm sorry.'

Terry shrugged. 'Don't be.'

Bella closed her trunk and straightened up. 'How did you manage to land your plane after being shot?' she asked, as Terry pushed himself off the doorframe and stepped down onto the grass, Bella close behind.

'With difficulty,' Terry grinned. 'I crash landed on the beach,' he said, as they walked between the prefabricated huts in the direction of Flight Lieutenant Briggs's office. 'Luckily for me there was a medical team nearby. They got me off the beach and onto a ship sharpish. I spent several weeks in hospital before being discharged. It was either spend the rest of the war sitting behind a desk on civvy street or join the ATA.' He pointed to a small, grey building in front of them.

The door was ajar and she could hear the sound of typewriter keys. Terry mounted the steps and peered in. The typing ceased as he announced, 'First Officer Bella Roberts, sir.'

'Very well,' came a deep voice. 'Send her in.'

Terry gave Bella a nod. 'Good luck,' he whispered, as he passed her on his way out.

After the bright July sunshine, it took Bella's eyes a few seconds to adjust to the dimness. Flight Lieutenant Briggs was a tall, weathered man with dark hair and eyes. He sat behind a large desk, leaning back in his chair, his large hands splayed on the polished wooden surface. In a corner of the well-appointed office a young airman, barely out of his teens, Bella estimated, sat with his hands poised over a typewriter.

'Carry on,' Briggs snapped, with a nod of his head to the young man and the typing started up again. Bella took a deep breath to calm her nerves.

'First Officer Roberts,' Briggs said, looking Bella up and down with his dark, brooding gaze. 'When Major Thompson asked me to take on one of his pilots, I wasn't expecting a female.' He brought his hands together. 'I don't hold with this nonsense of women pilots. An aeroplane is an expensive machine and shouldn't be trusted to the likes of a flighty girl.' He shook his head, as if despairing at the folly of the Ministry of Defence.

Bella kept quiet. Since joining the ATA she'd come across a lot of men like Briggs. Men who refused to believe a woman could fly a plane as well as a man. Major Thompson would have reported to Briggs that Bella had achieved higher marks in her exams than her male counterparts, yet by the man's attitude he clearly still felt her to be incompetent. In time, she would prove him wrong, though whether he would admit it was a different matter entirely.

'I can use you in the Ops Room,' he said.

'The Ops Room, sir?' Bella responded.

'Yes, I think that's where you'll be better employed,' Briggs replied, the corner of his lips lifting in a smirk. 'Leave the real work to the men.'

'But, sir . . .'

'That will be all.'

Crushed, Bella turned on her heels and descended the steps. She stood on the grass, a pleasant breeze wafting over her as she fought her disappointment. She came here to fly. She needed the distraction being in the air afforded her. Sitting behind a desk would give her far too much time alone with her thoughts. Despondent, she made her way over to the Ops Room.

Valerie looked up as she entered. 'How did it go with Briggs?' she asked.

'Not good,' replied Bella, morosely. 'He sent me to work in here. He said this is where I'll be best employed.'

Valerie gave a derisive snort. 'Well, fortunately for you, he doesn't get to say how best you're employed. Me and Patty, fortunately, do.' She held out a slip of paper. 'This just came in. They want a Hurricane taken over to a base near Sunderland. It's yours if you want it.'

'Yes, please,' Bella grinned. 'I'll go get changed.'

*

241

Twenty minutes later Bella taxied the Hawker Hurricane down the airfield. Most of the ferry pool had come out to witness her take-off. In her peripheral vision, she caught sight of Flight Lieutenant Briggs standing in the doorway of his office, face like thunder. Taking a deep breath, Bella calmly increased her speed. The runway at Woodhead was far shorter than at Chantry Fields, and surrounded by low hills, so she had to make sure she took off at exactly the right time or she'd plough into the heather-clad hillside. She swallowed, her throat dry, as the hill rushed towards her, a blur of purple and blue, then she felt the familiar sense of weightlessness as the wheels left the ground and the plane rose into the air. She cleared the hill with room to spare and circled back over the aerodrome, setting her course for Sunderland.

CHAPTER TWENTY-FIVE

'Letter for you, Roberts,' a thickset man in his mid-forties flung the envelope across the table towards Bella.

'Thanks, Ronnie,' she said, using her knife to slit the envelope open.

It was late September, and the weather remained mild. The mess windows were open to the breeze and Bella could hear the drone of approaching aircraft. After a quiet start to her time at Woodhead, over the past six weeks she had been busier than ever. It was rare for her to spend more than two or three nights a week at Woodhead as much of her time was spent at various airbases between the Midlands and northeast coast. In the eight weeks she had been flying out of Woodhead, she had earned the begrudging respect of most of her male colleagues. A few remained resolute in their assumption that a woman would be better off serving the war effort in a more sedentary role, and no one held that view more firmly that Flight Lieutenant Briggs. The man took every opportunity to spout his view on women pilots and he was always ready with a criticism or put-down. Bella did her best to ignore him but there were times it got her down. She knew she was a good pilot, better than some of her male counterparts, and it rankled that Flight Lieutenant Briggs had never flown under the difficult conditions that the ATA pilots coped with.

Now, she unfolded her letter, smiling to find it was from Amanda. She looked forward to her letters from her friends at Chantry Fields. Only once had Gilly mentioned Will, and only to say that he was working every hour God sent, that he would fly any plane, no matter its condition, and in any weather. She could feel their confusion coming off the paper in waves. But there was no way she could have explained without bringing her father's name into disrepute, or risk hurting her mother. Though she could never entertain a brother–sister relationship with Will, she did worry about him. That he was behaving so recklessly brought further pain to Bella's heart. Though her friends refrained from mentioning Will, she was sure they'd let her know if anything happened to him.

As she read Amanda's letters, she caught her breath.

'I have been assigned desk duties since the beginning of September,' she wrote, 'as I am expecting a baby next year.'

A baby? Bella read the words again.

'I've worked out that I must have fallen on our honeymoon. Oh, Bella, I'm so happy. I shall always have a part of Jonty with me. I just wish he'd lived to meet his son or daughter . . .'

The rest of the letter contained general chat. Bella read it quickly and refolded the sheet of paper, slipping it back into its envelope. Amanda was expecting Jonty's baby. She rejoiced for her friend, even while fighting her own deep-seated grief. She hadn't mentioned Will to Valerie or Patty, nor Terry, who had become a good friend over the past few weeks. What was the point? She stared at her empty plate, wondering what could have been. She and Will would have been married by now. Perhaps she, too, would be expecting a baby. The idea brought a fresh stab of pain to her heart, and she pushed it away. There was no point brooding over what could never be. She pushed back her seat and stood up.

The sound of aircraft hit her as she stepped outside. A Tiger Moth was coming in to land and several Hurricanes and Spitfires were being readied for flight. Groundcrew scurried here and there around the planes. With her flying jacket slung over her arm, helmet and goggles in hand, Bella walked over to the Ops Room. The common room next door was thick with cigarette smoke. Several pilots lounged on the chairs, discussing the weather and the plane they'd just flown. Most of them acknowledged Bella as she passed through to the Ops Room. One of them whistled. She gave him a weak smile and carried on through the door. There had been offers from the men, which she always turned down. Occasionally a visiting pilot would invite her to join him for a drink, but she always refused. The few times she'd gone into Chapel-en-le-Frith with Valerie and Patty, she'd been content to nurse her half pint of shandy while her two friends danced with American soldiers stationed nearby.

She knew a lot of the men thought her to be stuck-up, but the truth was she didn't want to get involved with anyone. Her heart, wrong as it was, belonged to Will, and she had no interest in anyone else.

'Hello, Bella,' Valerie said, looking up from her desk, telephone receiver in hand. 'Just had another call come in.' She nodded at Patty who was transcribing her notes onto the blackboard. 'Fancy taking a Spitfire to Dundee? They've got a Tiger Moth you can come back in?'

'Sure.' Bella nodded, as Patty scribbled her name next to the request. 'I'll be ready for take-off in a few minutes,' she said.

'Don't be late back,' Patty said, pausing in her writing. 'ENSA are coming tonight, don't forget. You don't want to miss the show.' There was always a buzz when ENSA entertainers visited the airbase, but the crew at Woodhead were particularly excited about this ensemble.

'I can't believe stars the likes of Emily Rose and Nellie will be bunking in with us,' Valerie said, with a swoon. 'My brother is dead jealous. I promised I'd get him a signed photograph.'

'Oh, that's exciting,' Bella grinned. 'Fingers crossed I shall make it back in time. When are they due?'

'Some time this afternoon, I think. The concert starts at seven. Be careful.'

'I will. See you later.'

Bella hurried outside. The sun was warm on her face. The surrounding hills were turning colour, the purples and greens giving way to dull brown. Sheep grazed up on the moors. Birds lined the telegraph wire, preparing for their long migration south. She chatted briefly with the two ground crew chaps who had been working on the Spitfire, and pulled on her jacket.

'You're good to go, miss,' said Bert, a stout, muscled man with greying dark hair and a swarthy complexion, handing her the chart. She studied it briefly, noting that there were no major concerns, and handed it back to him, with a nod.

'Thanks.' Placing one foot on the wing, she hoisted herself into the cockpit and strapped herself in. She pulled on her helmet and goggles and prepared for take-off.

Within minutes she was airborne. She gazed down at the base, watching it grow smaller as she flew over the hills, with moors and crags spread out below her. A train raced along below her, puffs of smoke drifting into the air. She flew over towns and villages, keeping her eye on her compass and her speed. Suddenly, the aircraft shuddered violently. Bella frowned and checked her instruments. Everything seemed in order. She leaned her head over the side of the plane, trying to see if there was any outward sign of damage, when the plane shuddered again. The engines began making a grating noise and the nose dipped. Swallowing down her fear, Bella checked her instruments again. She was losing altitude, fast. She pulled on the throttle, but the plane refused to respond. She wracked her brain, trying to remember what she'd learned in ground school, as she fought to keep the plane steady. Her chest heaved and she could feel the panic building up inside her. She had a matter of minutes before she lost control. She breathed slow and deep, forcing herself to concentrate as she fought against her rising panic. The engine sputtered and died. Bella stared in horror as her altitude plummeted with dizzying speed. With her heart in her throat, she fumbled with her harness straps. It was eerily quiet; the only sound was the wind rushing past her as the plane plummeted towards the ground. Feeling sick to her stomach, she pushed the door open. With difficulty, given the angle of the Spitfire, she eased herself up so she was standing on the seat. She clung to the windshield to keep her balance and prevent herself being flung out of the plane. She glanced downwards and closed her eyes, sending up a grateful prayer of thanks that the only thing below her was open moorland. Easing her trembling fingers from the windshield, she took a deep breath, closed her eyes, and jumped.

She felt suddenly weightless as she fell towards earth, the wind rushing in her ears. The crags and rough moorland hurtled towards her with terrifying speed, yet she felt strangely calm. If she was to die that day, then so be it. She was sorry she would never get to see her mother again, and Arthur. She hoped Arthur wouldn't take the news of her death too hard. He was so childlike and innocent that she wasn't sure how much he understood about death. Please God, let the parachute open, she prayed inwardly as she reached for her ripcord and pulled. For a terrifying moment she thought her premonition was right and it wasn't going to open, but suddenly she was jerked upwards, the huge silk canopy billowing over her like a giant umbrella.

It felt rather surreal drifting through the air, watching her plane tumbling below her. It slammed into the ground, disintegrating on impact.

She landed a short while later, hitting the ground at a run and jarring her ankle. Three dark-haired men came running across the field, shouting excitedly in a language Bella couldn't understand. They were followed by a group of children and an older man.

'Signor!' A dark-haired, olive-skinned man scrambled over the dry-stone wall. 'Signor? You are hurt?' he asked, his face registering concern. He and the other two younger men all wore similar clothes. Bella quickly realized that they must be a party of POWs working in the community.

'I'm fine, thank you,' replied Bella, unstrapping her parachute and ripping off her helmet and goggles.

'Ah, signorina!' the men exclaimed in surprise. The children came scrambling over the wall, followed at a more sedate pace by the older man. He had greying dark hair and walked with a stick. He leaned his frame against the wall, breathing heavily.

'Are you all right, miss?' he asked, taking a red and white spotted handkerchief from around his neck and mopping his brow.

Bella nodded. She put some weight on her ankle and, apart

from a slight twinge, it felt fine. 'Thank you, yes,' she replied. 'I'm afraid I can't say the same for my plane.' She looked ruefully at the remains of the Spitfire. It had broken up on impact and parts of it were scattered across the rough ground. A sheep bleated nearby, and Bella could only be grateful it hadn't crashed into the flock. 'May I ask where I am?'

The man grinned. 'You've landed on my farm,' he said. 'But the nearest village is Jericho Springs, just over yonder hill.' He held out his hand. 'Edward Wright.'

'First Officer Bella Roberts,' Bella said, giving his hand a shake.

'These are my children, Lenny, Simon, George, Milly, Bert and Lucy.' The children ranged in age from about ten to two. The youngest child, Lucy, clung to her father's leg, finger in her mouth, staring at Bella with open curiosity. 'Let's take a look at your plane, shall we?' Edward said. The children ran ahead, shouting excitedly. The prisoners, all of them Italians, the farmer told Bella, followed as they made their way across the rugged terrain to where the segments of the plane were scattered across the moorland. The children were exclaiming excitedly over one of the propellers that had embedded itself in the ground.

'Good job you managed to bail out,' Edward said, standing beside Bella as she silently surveyed the wreckage. She had a hollow feeling in her chest as she contemplated her lucky escape. Had she not bailed out when she did, she would be dead. There was no way anyone could have survived such a crash. The Italians crowded around the plane,

picking at bits of wreckage. The children were scrabbling
in the heather, searching for shrapnel. Suddenly one of the
POWs started talking quickly and making excited hand
gestures. One of them motioned to Bella, pointing at the
engine. Curious as to what they'd found, Bella walked over
to them. Stepping over the fuselage and trying to avoid
looking at the plane's crushed nose, she crouched down
beside two of the men.

Edward followed more slowly, leaning heavily on his stick.

'*Guarda, guarda!* Look, look!' One of the men said, pointing excitedly. '*Il volatile.* Bird.'

Bella frowned, and crouching lower, peered at where
he was pointing. 'Urgh!' she said, recoiling in disgust. The
inside of the engine was streaked with blood and feathers,
and she understood at once what had happened. She'd flown
into a flock of geese.

Bella brought her hand to her mouth in dismay. How had
she not seen them? Birds were one of the hazards they were
trained to watch out for.

'I didn't see them,' she whispered, mortified. Flight
Lieutenant Briggs would have a field day when she returned
to base and reported the incident.

'Don't fret yourself,' Edward said. 'It was an accident.'

Bella sighed. 'How far is it to the village? I'll need to find
a way to get back to base.' She wouldn't make it back by
evening, that was for sure.

'Where are you stationed?' asked Edward. The POWs
were helping the children in their hunt for souvenirs, their

carefree chatter drifting over to where Bella and Edward stood beside the mangled engine.

'Woodhead?'

Edward nodded. 'I've heard of it. My sister lives not far from there, in Glossop.'

He noticed her watching the way the POWs were interacting with his children. He chuckled. 'They're decent lads,' he said. 'Got caught up in a war they didn't support and ended up here, in a foreign country as prisoners of war. They've all got children of their own back in Italy. I trust them.'

Bella looked at him. 'It's sad how war makes enemies of people who might have been friends under different circumstances.'

'You're not wrong,' Edward said wearily. 'I've got a good friend, Günter Brockschmidt. Known him nigh on twenty years. One of the nicest, kindest men I know. He spent the Great War interned as an enemy of the state, and now he's been locked up again on the Isle of Man.' He shook his head. 'Still, we've got to beat this Hitler fellow, haven't we? He's run amok all over Europe. We've got to stop him, somehow.' He coughed and cleared his throat. 'Come on. You'd better come back with us. The constable will be along soon. Someone will have reported your plane coming down and he'll want to make his report. You're welcome to stay for supper.'

'Thank you. You're very kind. If you have a telephone I would like to call my base. I'll have to let them know what's happened.' She was dreading having to explain to Briggs that she'd managed to destroy thousands of pounds worth of aeroplane. 'They'll be expecting me in Dundee, so they'll report me missing soon.'

'I had a telephone installed in the farmhouse just before war broke out,' said Edward, signalling to the POWS that it was time to head back. 'You're welcome to use it.'

With the children chattering excitedly about their finds, they all walked back to the farm, Bella carrying her parachute. Back at the farmhouse she made the call to Woodhead, relieved to get Valerie, who once Bella had assured her that she was perfectly fine, promised she would notify Dundee and arrange her transport back to base.

The POWs returned to the fields and Bella spent a happy hour being shown around the farm by the children, who listened in awed excitement as she regaled them with stories of her flying endeavours.

'I'm going to be a pilot when I grow up,' Lenny, the oldest boy, said.

'Me too,' said George, skinny arms folded across his chest, chin jutting out in determination.

'I hope you do both get the chance to fly,' replied Bella, recalling how Johnny and Jack had said much the same thing. 'Though hopefully the war will be over by the time you're old enough.'

'Signorina!' She glanced up to see one of the POWs signalling to her from the house. He mimed using the telephone.

Extricating herself from the children, Bella hurried across the yard, sending the chickens squawking out of her way.

Edward was in the kitchen, holding the telephone receiver. Taking it, Bella thanked him.

'Valerie?'

'Unfortunately, not,' came Briggs's droll tone. Bella winced.

'Flight Lieutenant,' she said, clearing her throat. 'Thank you for calling.' She held her breath, waiting for the tirade she knew would come.

'Fortunately for you, I have a pilot bringing a Tiger Moth back from Sunderland. Apparently there's a place he can land not far from where you are. Take down the coordinates.'

'Yes, sir.' Bella glanced round, miming pen and paper. Edward handed her an empty envelope and a pencil. Nodding her thanks, she scribbled down the directions.

'He should get to you around fourteen hundred hours. Don't be late. Report to my office the moment you land, First Officer Roberts.'

'Yes, sir.' Bella put the phone down with a sinking heart.

'I take it he wasn't happy?' said Edward.

Bella shook her head. 'Not at all.' She gave him a wry smile. 'I suppose I shall have to face the music some time. May as well get it over with.' She glanced down at the envelope. 'Do you know where this is?'

'It's an airbase not far from here. I'll take you in the van.'

CHAPTER TWENTY-SIX

'Take care,' Edward said, as Bella pulled on her jacket and helmet.

'I will, and thank you for all your help.'

'It was my pleasure. Perhaps we'll meet again some day.'

'Perhaps.' Bella smiled. The pilot handed her a parachute and she strapped it on. She knew him vaguely from the ferry pool, but she'd never spoken to him. Jim, she thought his name was. Yes, Jim North. That was it. From his knowing smirk, she had a feeling he was one of the few who held little regard for women pilots.

'Thanks again,' she said, hauling herself up onto the wing and climbing into the cockpit. She pulled on her helmet and adjusted her flying goggles. Giving Jim the thumbs up, she strapped herself in. As Jim taxied the plane across the ground, she leaned over the side of the plane and waved.

Edward waved back. Once they were airborne, Bella sank

back in her seat, her mind on the reception no doubt awaiting her back at base.

'Do you know how much those planes cost?' Briggs bellowed at her, his face an angry red.

'Yes, sir,' replied Bella. She was standing in front of Briggs's desk, her hands behind her back. She looked him in the eye, her chin tilted defiantly.

'Thousands!' Briggs yelled. 'Thousands!' He shoved his chair back forcefully and got to his feet. 'This is the very reason I'm against women being in control of a plane,' he snorted. 'If I had my way you'd be grounded with immediate effect.' He perched on the edge of his desk, glaring at her. 'There will be an investigation, of course.'

'Of course,' replied Bella. 'The constable who inspected the scene was satisfied it was caused by geese becoming caught in the engines, sir.'

Briggs snorted. 'It would have to be a pretty big bird, Roberts. I'm thoroughly expecting a verdict of pilot error.'

'It was a flock of geese, sir,' Bella said, struggling to control her anger. Not once had the man asked after her welfare, or how she was feeling after her traumatic incident.

'We'll see,' Briggs said. 'I'll let you know as soon as the investigation is concluded. That will be all.'

'Sir.' As Bella left Briggs's office, she had to force herself not to slam the door.

'I wish I could slap that smug smirk off his face,' she seethed to Terry, who was waiting to escort her to the mess hall where the concert was due to start in just over fifteen minutes. 'He's an insufferable chauvinist pig.'

'I couldn't agree more,' Terry said. 'Don't worry about it. The investigation will find in your favour and that will shut him up. I'm just glad you escaped with nothing more than a mildly sprained ankle. How is it feeling?'

'It's fine,' she replied. She held on to his arm and flexed her ankle to show him. 'See?'

'Well, I'm glad you're in one piece.'

'I feel bad about the plane, though. I don't know how I didn't see the geese before I flew into them.'

'It's easily done if they're out of your line of vision,' Terry commiserated. 'Happened to me once. Only mine was a flock of starlings. I'd only just taken off. Came down in the next field. The plane was a complete wreck.'

Bella regarded her friend with a worried frown. 'Were you injured?'

'Two black eyes and a broken nose. They initially put it down to pilot error, so I got a bit of a rollicking from my commander, but I was cleared in the investigation. And you will be, too. Even if it did turn out to be pilot error, you're a civilian. You'll get a telling off and told to get on with the job.' He patted Bella's arm. 'Don't worry. It'll be fine, you'll see.'

He nudged her. 'Look, there's Emily Rose and Nellie. I'm going to get an autograph. Coming?'

'I'll grab a cup of tea and save us a couple of seats,' Bella grinned.

The mess was already filling up. Soldiers from the nearby

257

American base had been bussed over to enjoy the concert and the room was filled with loud voices and the sound of heavy boots on the wooden floor.

There were a few wolf whistles when Bella entered. She smiled good-naturedly as she threaded her way through the throngs to the refreshment table.

'Hear you had a bit of a day?' Chris, the cook said, pouring tea from a huge industrial teapot. 'You look like you came away unscathed.'

'I'm fine,' Bella grinned. 'Can't say the same for the plane.'

'Bet Briggs had a coronary,' Chris sniggered, handing her a mug of steaming hot tea. 'Milk and sugar are over there.'

'Thanks.' Bella took her tea and found seats for her and Terry in the third row. More men were filing in now. They came in pairs, chatting and clutching their autographs. Up on the makeshift stage, the musicians were tuning their instruments. Several of the ferry pool pilots came over to ask Bella if she was okay. It soon became clear, as she chatted to some of the Americans, that their view of women pilots differed from that of some of her English counterparts, and Bella spent a pleasant few minutes discussing various aspects of flying with three young American pilots, one of which had a sister in the ATA.

The mess was filling up now, the sign that the show would soon be starting. She spotted Valerie and Patty in the doorway, and she waved, indicating the empty seats in front of her. Terry came in behind them, and the three of them made their way over.

'What did Briggs have to say for himself?' asked Valerie as she took her seat. Bella shrugged.

'He wasn't happy.'

Valerie pulled a face. 'Take no notice of him. I got Emily's autograph for my brother.' She tucked the signed photograph in her breast pocket. Terry took his seat next to Bella.

'Did you get your signed photograph?' she asked him, as he crossed his legs and settled back to enjoy the show.

'I did,' he grinned. 'She's a sweet girl, that Emily. Nellie's nice, too. I think she's sweet on that musician fellow.'

Bella followed his gaze. The two singers had joined the men on the stage now and Bella agreed that Terry was right. There was something about the way the pair's eyes met that made it obvious they had feelings for each other. It made Bella think of Will. Her heart still ached for him, which was why she tried to keep herself busy. The lights dimmed and the musicians played the first strains of 'The White Cliffs of Dover'. They sang a lot of the popular songs which had the audience clapping along and even joining in with the singing. Some of the gentler melodies, speaking of lost love and bittersweet partings, had Bella welling up. A lot of the Americans were looking tearful, and Bella couldn't blame them. They were so far from home with no prospect of returning any time soon. She wiped away a surreptitious tear and caught Terry grinning at her. He handed her a handkerchief.

She whispered her thanks and wiped her eyes.

Emily and Nellie spent the night with Bella, Valerie and Patty, and the girls chatted until late into the night. Emily was due to tour the far east in the coming year. As she spoke, Emily Rose confided that she'd recently lost a man she'd been keen on. Bella's heart went out to her. No wonder her songs spoke so much about lost love. At least Will was alive, as far as she knew, though no less lost to her.

All five girls slept well, and after an early breakfast the ENSA troupe got on their way. They were touring all of the bases in the north of England and had several miles to go before their next stop.

Once they'd left, and the base slowly returned to normal, Bella was kept busy ferrying planes all over the north. She was happiest when she was flying, though during the long hours in the cockpit, it was difficult to keep thoughts of Will from her mind. It had barely been two months, she reminded herself one day when she'd been feeling particularly sad. She was bound to miss him for a long time.

November came and brought with it a band of cold, wet weather. The barracks leaked like a sieve and the wind shrieked across the bleak and drab moorland like a banshee.

She'd just come back from picking up a Lancaster bomber from the factory in Chadderton in the neighbouring county of Lancashire. Knowing she was the first person, apart from the test pilot, to fly it, gave her a quiet thrill. She was flying low, beneath the bank of thick cloud, and landed without incident. Flight Lieutenant Briggs was standing at his office window, scowling as usual. Bella gave him a wave as she taxied past. Much to Briggs's disappointment, Bella had been unequivocally cleared of any blame by the Air Investigations team and her record remained unblemished.

She clambered down from the plane and, ducking her head against the wind, ran through the freezing rain to the Ops Room.

'Glad you made it back,' said Patty, glancing up from the desk. 'We were wondering if you might stay overnight and see if the weather improved.'

'Not likely to, is it?' she asked, perching on the corner of the desk. She shared a bit of banter with the two pilots loitering near the window, watching the dark clouds swirling above the airfield.

'It's not looking good,' Valerie said, as the telephone rang. 'Sorry, no can do,' she said into the receiver. 'All our pilots are booked out for tomorrow. Thank you. Goodbye.' She replaced the receiver. 'There's a letter for you over there,' she told Bella, pointing to the post rack.

'Oh, thanks.' Bella hopped off the desk to retrieve the letter, wondering whether it was from either one of her parents, or the girls down in Dorset. To her surprise, the handwriting was unfamiliar. 'I wonder who it's from,' she said, ripping it open. She frowned. 'Edward Wright?' For a moment she couldn't place the name.

'Isn't he the farmer whose field you crashed in?' suggested Patty, as Bella read the letter. Her frown deepened. 'Yes, that's him,' she said, with a detached air. 'He's visiting his sister in Glossop for a few days and has asked if I'd like to join him for tea one afternoon.' She lowered the letter, meeting Patty and Valerie's gaze. 'What could he possibly mean by inviting me to tea? Oh, don't be silly,' she said, as Valerie and Patty exchange amused glances. 'He must be forty at least.'

'Age is immaterial,' said Valerie. 'Is he good looking? Rich?'

'He's attractive, in a way, I suppose,' Bella shrugged. 'As for his wealth, I have no idea.'

'I'd go if I were you. Have a bit of fun for once, Bella. You hardly ever leave the base.'

'What on earth are you talking about?' Bella laughed. 'I'm seldom ever here.'

'You know what I mean,' Valerie said pertly. 'You don't go anywhere when you've got time off. Write back and tell him you'd love to meet him for tea.'

Bella grinned. 'I don't think so.'

'Oh, Bella, why not? You might enjoy yourself.'

'I don't want to give him the wrong idea.'

The two girls kept up their badgering until Bella finally gave in and agreed to meet Edward.

'Just to thank him for his help that day,' she said, as Patty handed her a pad of writing paper. 'If you hurry,' Valerie said. 'You'll make the last post.'

Lying in her bed later, listening to the continual splash of water in the tin bucket, Bella wondered if she'd made a mistake in accepting Edward's invitation. She sighed and rolled onto her side. Both Valerie and Patty were snoring softly, but Bella couldn't sleep. It was in the depth of night when she missed Will the most.

CHAPTER TWENTY-SEVEN

The bus trundled into Glossop just after half past three on the following Friday afternoon. The rain had stopped, and hazy sunlight shone through the veil of cloud as Bella alighted the bus outside the Norfolk Arms. She adjusted her hat and straightened her jacket, smoothing the wrinkles out of her skirt, when the doors swung open and Edward emerged, a smile on his face and looking handsome in his brown suit.

'First Officer Roberts,' he beamed, leaning on his stick. 'Thank you for coming.'

'Hello, Mr Wright. Thank you for inviting me.'

'Our table is ready for us,' Edward said, offering Bella his arm. After a moment's hesitation, she took it and he led her inside. The interior was all dark wood panelling, patterned wallpaper and embroidered soft furnishing. Framed paintings hung on the walls and a thick carpet covered the floor. The air smelled of coffee, tobacco and stale beer.

Edward led Bella over to a small table overlooking the street. It was laid for afternoon tea with a white tablecloth and dainty, blue-patterned china.

He drew out a chair and Bella sat down, thanking him. She was still at a loss as to the nature of his invitation.

'Is your sister not joining us?' she asked, noting the table was only set for two.

'She's taken the children out for the afternoon,' Edward said, hanging his hat on the hook on the wall behind them. He looked up as a uniformed waitress approached. She was young, barely sixteen, Bella guessed.

'Tea for two, is it?' she asked.

'Yes, please,' Edward answered. 'And a selection of sandwiches and cakes.'

'They'll be with you directly, sir.' The girl smiled and hurried off towards the kitchen.

'I must thank you again for your help that day,' Bella said.

'It was my pleasure,' Edward replied. 'The children enjoyed meeting you. They couldn't stop talking about you all evening.'

Bella laughed. 'I'm pleased I made such an impression. I don't suppose you often get someone crashing their plane on your land. I was cleared of all blame.'

'I had no doubt,' Edward nodded. 'So, Miss Roberts,' he said, clearing his throat. 'Do you have a young man away fighting?' he asked, his cheeks colouring slightly.

'Er, no,' Bella replied, taken aback by his directness. 'There's no one.'

'Ah, I see,' smiled Edward. 'So, may I ask how you got into flying? It's an unusual career for a young lady.'

'There are actually quite a lot of women pilots,' Bella replied with a smile. 'My uncle is a pilot. He taught me.'

The waitress brought the tea and a tiered cake stand filled with daintily cut sandwiches and a selection of mouthwatering cakes. While they ate and drank their tea, Bella told Edward about her experiences growing up in the Western Cape, and her decision to join the ATA. In return, Edward told her he was a widow, his wife having died from complications following Lucy's birth.

'We were married nine years,' he said, helping himself to a cucumber sandwich.

'I'm sorry,' Bella said, thinking how incongruous the tiny triangle of brown bread looked in his large, work-calloused fingers. Edward popped the whole sandwich in his mouth and chewed slowly.

'I keep myself busy,' he said, once he'd swallowed. He shrugged. 'It helps, a little.'

Bella nodded. She understood what he meant. Hard work helped keep thoughts of Will at bay but didn't eradicate them completely. She could only hope that her pain would ease in time.

Over tea she learned that Edward was forty-one, and that his family had farmed for generations. He'd lost an uncle in the Great War and had two nephews serving abroad.

Her first impression of Edward had been that he was a nice man, and spending the afternoon with him did nothing to alter her opinion. He was easy to talk to, amusing, and seemed interested in what she had to say. The two hours flew by and Bella was sorry when the time came for her to leave.

'I've enjoyed myself,' Edward said, as she boarded the bus. 'I'd like to do it again, when I'm next in town.'

'I enjoyed it too,' Bella replied, meaning it. 'I'd like that.'

Edward lifted his hat. 'Take care, Miss Roberts.'

Bella found a seat, and the bus set off, winding its way up the Snake Pass towards Woodhead airbase. The views were breathtaking, the winter sun casting a golden hue over the rugged terrain. Sheep grazed at the side of the road and a stiff wind ruffled the bracken. Grey clouds roiled overhead, threatening more rain. In the valley below, a flash of silver caught her eye. A Spitfire was flying low across the valley floor. In the murky half-light, she could just make out the sprawl of buildings that marked out the airbase.

Had Valerie and Patty had been right about her needing to get out a bit, Bella mused as the bus rumbled down the steep incline. She had thoroughly enjoyed her afternoon. Edward was a nice man, but at almost twice her age, she did hope he wasn't thinking of courting her. She pushed the thought away. He'd told her he and the children were returning to the farm tomorrow and it would be some time before he could afford the time to visit his sister again, so it wasn't something she had to worry about now. She smiled. No doubt Patty and Valerie would want a detailed account of her outing. Though she wasn't yet as close to them as she had been with Amanda, Gilly and Beryl, she was grateful

267

for their friendship. Life at Woodhead would have been less enjoyable without them.

Barely a week had passed when she received another letter from Edward. In it he wrote how much he'd enjoyed their time together and how much he was looking forward to doing it again. After that, a letter arrived every week. Bella dutifully wrote back, ignoring Patty and Valerie's knowing smirks.

'He must really fancy you,' said Valerie, one freezing evening in early December. She was sitting on her bed filing her nails. ENSA were performing a pantomime in the mess that evening and the three of them were getting ready for what they expected to be a fun-filled evening.

'Don't be silly,' Bella said, taking her jacket off its hanger and slipping it on. 'He's nearly old enough to be my father.'

'My grandpa was fifteen years older than my grandmother,' Patty said. 'And they were happily married for thirty-three years.'

'I'm happy for them,' replied Bella, picking lint off her jacket sleeve. 'But I'm not interested in courting anyone.'

'Career girl, hmm?' Valerie teased. 'Are you going to devote yourself to a life of flying?'

'I might.' Bella sighed. 'Look, Edward seems a nice man. But I'm not interested in him romantically and it would be unfair of me to lead him on.'

'You could just have a war-time fling,' suggested Patty, studying her pretty face in her compact mirror. She snapped it shut. 'You don't have to marry him.'

'Not my style,' Bella replied. 'Right, are we ready? The show will be starting soon.'

'Is Terry keeping our seats?' Patty asked, putting on her hat.

'Of course he is,' Bella said, shivering as she opened the door. 'What would we do without our Terry, hmm? Come on, let's go.'

'What pantomime is it?' Valerie asked, donning her big coat as she followed the others out into the swirling snow.

'*Dick Whittington*, I think,' Patty said, through chattering teeth. 'Or *Puss in Boots*. Something with a cat, anyway. Crickey, it's freezing. Let's get indoors before we catch our death.'

CHAPTER TWENTY-EIGHT

1944

'What can I get you, love?' The blonde barmaid leaned across the polished bar top, giving Will an eyeful of her full breasts spilling over the top of her low-cut blouse

'A pint of bitter, please,' replied Will wearily, perching on the bar stool. It was loud in the Red Lion. Since December, the population of Gillingham had seemingly trebled by the influx of American troops and their tanks, lorries and Jeeps were a familiar sight in the streets. A group of GIs were playing a rowdy game of snooker in the adjoining room, watched by the crowd of local girls. There had been some jealousy-fuelled skirmishes between some of the local lads and the American interlopers, but generally everyone rubbed together well. The local children were in awe of the new arrivals, following them about shouting their familiar refrain of, 'Got any gum, chum?'

The GIs seemed to have an unending supply of silk

270

stockings, chocolate, candy and other luxuries the war-weary Dorset residents could only dream about. No wonder they were so popular, Will mused wryly, watching as a slender, pale-skinned red-haired girl flung her arms around the neck of a thickset, blond-haired GI.

'Here you go, love.' The pretty barmaid placed Will's pint in front of him, drawing his attention back to her. She leaned towards him, making sure he got the full benefit of her assets. She pouted, her crimson lips shining in the harsh lighting, twirling a lock of golden hair with her index finger, the nail of which was painted the exact shade of red as her lipstick.

'Thank you, miss.'

'It's Diane,' she said, smiling coyly. Will raised his glass.

'Cheers, Diane.' He took a sip, the warm ale sliding pleasantly down his throat.

'What's your name, then?' asked Diane, licking her lips suggestively.

'Will,' he said shortly.

'So, Will. You're a pilot?'

Will nodded. 'With the Air Transport Auxiliary stationed at Chantry Fields.'

'I know the place,' Diane smiled. She had a pretty face, Will acknowledged and, had he been on the lookout for a few hours of no-strings fun, she'd fit the bill perfectly. He sighed and took another sip of his beer.

'You new here?' he asked, sensing she was expecting some conversation. Diane let go of her hair and nodded, her golden curls bouncing attractively around her slender shoulders.

'It's only my second shift,' she purred, her wide, beguiling blue eyes never leaving his face. Will ran a hand across his chin, stifling a yawn. Apart from enforced periods of rest, he'd been flying practically non-stop for the past eighteen months. He relished the exhaustion. He was asleep at night as soon as his head hit the pillow. A deep, dreamless sleep. Anything to keep him from thinking about Bella. He'd been over it a thousand times. What had happened that weekend to bring about such a dramatic change of heart? What could her father have said to make her change her mind about marrying him? Many times over the last year and a half he'd contemplated going to see her father, thinking if he could just talk to the man ... But what was the point? If Bella had so easily let her father's prejudice against him alter her opinion, then perhaps she hadn't loved him as much as he thought.

Diane was looking at him strangely and he realized she appeared to be waiting for him to say something. 'Sorry.' He set his beer glass on the counter and flashed her an apologetic smile. 'I was miles away.'

'I said, my shift finishes in half an hour if you want to go somewhere a bit quieter. I only live across the street.' She batted her long eyelashes. 'My flatmate's working nightshift so we'd have the place to ourselves.'

Will shook his head. 'Thanks for the offer,' he said. 'But I'll probably just head back to base after this.'

Diane pouted. 'Suit yourself.'

'Oi, Di,' the landlord called. 'Stop your yakking. You've got customers waiting.'

'All right,' Diane muttered. 'I'm coming.' Shooting Will a look of reproach, she moved along the bar to where a group of five American GIs were waiting. 'Yes, chaps,' she said, thrusting her cleavage towards them and giving Will a sideways glance that clearly said, 'See what you're missing?' 'What can I get you?'

Will drained his pint and pushed himself off the bar stool. The air was thick with cigarette smoke and the cloying scent of cheap perfume. He pushed his way through the crowds and out the door. It was a clear night. Frost sparkled on the ground. From far away came the throb of aircraft engines. He held his breath, gazing up into the star-spangled sky as the drone of the planes came closer. They were German, he could tell by the uneven note in the sound of the engine. He searched the sky, wondering where they were headed. From far away came the sound of the anti-aircraft guns and he could make out the occasional flash of orange in the distance. Shoving his hands in the pockets of his heavy coat, he began the walk home. The moon was so bright he didn't need his torch. His breath billowed in front of his face as he walked, the frozen ground crunching beneath his feet. As always, when he was alone, his thoughts turned to Bella. His initial feelings of confusion and heartache had turned to anger. Why had Bella changed so suddenly? What had happened to make her leave her father's house in the middle of the night, and why had she refused to talk to him? He kicked at a stone angrily, sending it skittering into the hedgerows. He'd loved Bella since the day she'd punched him on the nose. He'd admired her spunk and the way she'd fiercely protected her brother. Even now, the memory of what he'd said that day filled him with shame. He sighed, wondering, as he often did, whether Bella was with someone new. Not only was she a strikingly beautiful woman, but she was also courageous, kind and intelligent. A woman like her wouldn't be short of admirers. He scowled, wondering why he tortured himself like this. Bella had made it clear she wanted nothing to do with him, and that was fine by him, he told himself sternly. He just wished his heart didn't hurt so much.

Bella reread Edward's letter with dismay. She'd met up with him a handful of times over the past sixteen months, always at the Norfolk Arms in Glossop for afternoon tea. She enjoyed her trips into town, and Edward was good company. She regarded him as a good friend, but now this letter changed everything.

'What's up?' asked Valerie, as she climbed into bed. 'You look like you've lost a pound and found a penny.'

'It's Edward,' she sighed, flopping back against her pillow. 'I noticed this in his last letter, he's starting to write to me as though we're romantically involved.'

'Aren't you?'

'No!' exclaimed Bella. 'He's a lovely man, but I don't feel anything remotely romantic for him. I enjoy his company.'

'But you've been seeing him for over a year.'

'I've been so careful not to lead him to believe there can

be anything between us other than friendship. Oh, dear. I shall have to write to him and explain.'

'He's obviously lonely and in need of a companion,' Valerie said.

'I know that,' Bella grimaced. 'Which is why I kept agreeing to meet up with him.' She sighed. 'Why does life always have to be so damn complicated?' She folded her hands behind her head, staring up at the wooden ceiling, the blankets pulled up to her chin. A cobweb swung from one of the beams, swaying in the icy draught. Brows puckered in a frown, she thought about Edward and his recent letter. From its tone, she was in no doubt that he was starting to think of her in a more romantic light. During their catch-ups, he'd often let slip that should he marry again, he would expect his wife to be a housewife and mother to his children. He'd also, on occasion, as they got to know each other better, expressed a slight disapproval of Bella's line of work.

'I'm surprised your father allows you to fly,' he'd said, on their last meeting just before Christmas. They'd been sitting at their usual table, a roaring fire burning nearby, the scent of charred pinecones filling the air. The hotel dining room had been busy with many of the tables taken up with GIs and their lady friends.

'He wasn't keen,' Bella had replied. 'I was over twenty-one when I joined the ATA so he couldn't forbid me.'

'I've always believed a woman should be obedient to her father, and to her husband,' Edward had said, calmly buttering his tea cake.

'A husband, yes to a certain degree,' Bella had replied warily. 'But these are modern times. Women are making their own way in the world.' She laughed. 'My father would have preferred me to remain as a governess or something equally boring. I need to fly. It's in my blood.' From the look of disapproval on Edward's face, her response had clearly not been the one he'd been hoping for. It had obviously not deterred him too much, though, she thought now, as Valerie turned out the lamp.

She lay awake fretting about Edward. She would have to write and put him straight. Though she knew she could never have a future with Will, her heart would always belong to him. It would be unfair to allow Edward to believe there might be something more between them. Bella had to be true to herself. After knowing a love like she felt for Will, she could never settle for anything less, and she wasn't ready to give up her flying. She would feel like a bird with clipped wings, she mused. Bella finally drifted off and was woken several hours later by the air raid siren.

Yawning and stumbling round in the dark, she found her torch and pulled her heavy coat over her pyjamas before following Valerie and Patty out into the cold January night. The base was a hive of activity as everyone hurried to the shelter. Once inside, the cook handed round mugs of tea. Bella clutched hers gratefully, wrapping her frozen fingers around the warm mug.

'I could have done without this tonight,' Patty grumbled, huddled on the uncomfortable wooden bench between Bella and Valerie. 'It's freezing in here.'

'Let's hope we're not here for long,' Bella agreed, rubbing her eyes. A hush fell over the shelter at the sound of approaching aircraft. Bella held her breath. Though they weren't an RAF base, as an airfield they were still vulnerable to attack. The drone of the planes was directly overhead now. The whole building seemed to shake with the roar of the engines. Patty reached for Bella's hand and squeezed. Bella squeezed back. Her heart thudded painfully against her rib cage, and she could hardly breathe. Fear coursed through her like ice water in her veins. Any minute now they could all be blown to Kingdom Come. The noise of the engines receded and there was a collective exhalation of breath before an almighty explosion made Bella jump out of her skin. It was followed by another, shaking the very foundations of the shelter.

'My God,' Patty clutched Bella's arm. 'That's close.'

'Too close for comfort,' Valerie added drily. Another explosion followed, then another, further away this time. Flight Lieutenant Briggs got up and went to the door. Opening it, he peered cautiously out into the night.

'They're bombing the moor again,' he said, in disbelief. He laughed and turned back to the room. 'Once again, the fools have got their coordinates wrong. '

The All Clear sounded and everyone surged outside. Teeth chattering in the biting cold, Bella stood amongst her fellow pilots and watched in horrified fascination as the moors burned. The skyline was a mass of orange flames, the likes of which would be seen for miles. Giant clouds of smoke billowed into the sky, obscuring the moon and stars. Even at a distance, Bella could smell the burning heather. The peaty soil could burn and smoulder for days. Thankfully, the wind was blowing in the opposite direction so the airbase was relatively safe, unless the wind changed direction, in which case they could be directly in line of the fire.

Briggs sent someone off to alert the local fire brigade and cautioned them all to be on high alert, ready to evacuate at once, should the need arise.

'That could have been us,' Terry said soberly, as he joined the three women watching the inferno. He was wearing a coat over striped pyjamas and boots and cradling a mug of tea.

'Yep,' replied Valerie, equally sombre. 'Thank God they got it wrong.'

'Do you think they'll come back this way?' Bella asked, hugging herself against the bitter cold.

'If they do, let's hope they've got rid of all their bombs,' replied Terry drily. Slowly they drifted back to the shelter where blankets and fresh mugs of tea were being doled out. Bella accepted a blanket gratefully and draped it round her shoulders. She hadn't realized how much she was shivering until she tried to grasp her mug of tea. The mug shook violently, sloshing hot tea onto her hand.

'Sit down,' Terry said, steering her towards a spare seat. 'You'll be fine in a minute. Probably a combination of the cold and shock.'

'Thanks.' Bella sat hunched over her mug. Her pulse was racing, and her heartbeat was erratic. Slowly she felt herself calming down.

All at once the air shook with the roar of aeroplanes over-head. A loud cheer went up from the men.

'They're ours,' Terry said, with grin. 'Good old chaps. They'll send Jerry packing with his tail between his legs.'

Stiff with cold and bleary-eyed from lack of sleep, the three women made their way back to bed.

'If we're lucky we might manage an hour or so before the bell goes,' Bella said, climbing into bed. Now that she'd re-covered from the shock of the unexpected raid and warmed up, she felt bone weary. Tired as she was, sleep eluded her. She couldn't get the pictures of the fire out of her mind. A few miles further west and the airbase would have been in the middle of the firestorm. The thought of how close she'd been to certain death sent cold tremors through her body, which was strange, considering how she took her life into her hands every time she climbed into the cockpit. But somehow, the thought of dying in a plane crash didn't seem quite as terrifying as being incinerated by an enemy bomb. She rolled onto her back. She wasn't going to sleep now, she thought ruefully, listening with some envy to Patty and Valerie's rhythmic breathing. She slid from under the covers and, feeling her way around her bedside cabinet, found her torch. Switching it on, she found her pad of writing paper and a pen and, crawling back under the blankets, so the light wouldn't disturb the other two, she penned a letter to Edward. When she'd finished, she bit her lip, hoping she hadn't been too forthright in what she'd said, but she had to set the man straight. She doubted there would ever be anyone who would make her feel the way she had when she was with Will, and she was not the sort of woman prepared to settle for second best. She sealed the envelope and addressed it and laid it on her bedside cabinet ready for the morning's post. She prayed Edward would understand.

'Hey, Will.' First Officer Neil Glover hailed him when he walked into the Ops Room a few days later. 'I've got a Lancaster needs ferrying from Lancashire to Portsmouth. You can take one of the Tiger Moths.'

'Sure.' Will ran a hand through his thick hair and checked his name off the board.

'Word's come through Jerry bombed miles of empty moorland just up from Woodhead. Luckily for our lads, they got their coordinates wrong, or they'd have been toast.'

Will's blood ran cold. 'Did you say Woodhead?' The piece of chalk in his hands snapped under the pressure of his fingers. Woodhead was where Bella was. He wasn't supposed to know that, as Bella had supposed he would have gone tearing after her begging her to come back. As if? He had his pride and she'd made it plain he meant nothing to her anymore. But that didn't stop him caring about her.

'You say they didn't hit the airbase? There were no casualties?' He held his breath.

'Pardon? What?' Neil looked up from his paperwork. 'Oh, Woodhead? No, no casualties. Jerry missed by a country mile. Excuse me,' he said, as the telephone rang. 'Ops Room, Chantry Fields. Yep, go ahead.' Neil grabbed a pen and scribbled something on a scrap of paper. Will took that as his cue to leave. He walked out into the cold January morning, muttering a prayer of thanks that the German bombers had been off course. He swore softly under his breath. He really must get Bella out of his system, he thought angrily, as he crunched across the frosty grass to the hangar.

CHAPTER TWENTY-NINE

'Telegram for you, Bella,' Valerie said, holding out the brown envelope. Bella's heart sank. With trembling fingers, she ripped it open, her shoulder sagging with relief as she read its contents.

MOTHER ARTHUR ARRIVE
HOME 14 APRIL 2PM

'It's from my father,' she told Valerie, who had been watching her anxiously. 'My mother and Arthur are coming home.'

'Oh, Bella,' Valerie said, her exhalation of relief almost matching Bella's. 'I was so worried it was going to be bad news.'

'Me, too.' Bella rolled her eyes. 'God knows, between us, we've had our fair share of it recently.' They were in the crowded Ops Room. Valerie was staffing the phones while

Patty plotted the day's flights on the board. A thick cloud of cigarette smoke hovered below the nicotine-stained ceiling. It was the first day of April and Bella was looking forward to the spring. February and March had been very bleak months for all three of them, she thought sadly, staring out of the window across the windswept runway. Bella's Aunt Martha had been killed when the hospital ship she was on was torpedoed and, barely a week later, her Uncle Jimmy had been seriously wounded in Burma, dying shortly afterwards of his injuries. Both Patty and Valerie had lost a close relative in recent weeks, and then, while they were still reeling from their losses, Bella's friend Terry had been involved in a tragic accident. He had been taxiing down the runway in a Tiger Moth when he'd struck another plane, shattering the propeller. Bits of broken propeller had been flung in all directions, mortally wounding one of the ground crew, a young lad just two weeks shy of his eighteenth birthday. His death had cast a pall over the airbase for days. Poor Terry had been beside himself with grief and remorse, despite being cleared of any wrongdoing by the Accident Investigations team.

'It's nice to have some good news for a change,' Valerie said, breaking into Bella's thoughts. 'You'll have to book some leave, so you can be there to welcome your mum and brother home.'

'I've got leave this weekend,' Bella reminded her. 'I'm going to Devon to see my friend. The one with the baby, remember?'

283

'Ah, yes, sorry. I forgot it was this weekend.' The telephone rang. Valerie raised her gaze heavenward and picked up the receiver. 'Woodhead, good morning. Yes, sir, no problem, sir.' Bella smiled and left her to it. She was picking up a plane from the factory at Blackburn in neighbouring Lancashire and flying it to Exeter. From there she was catching the bus to Dawlish to spend the afternoon and evening with Amanda. Her little boy, Jonty, was almost thirteen months old, and Bella had yet to meet him. From the photograph Amanda had sent her, she could see the little boy was the image of his dad.

She popped back to her dorm to pick up her flying jacket, helmet, goggles and her overnight bag, and headed for the vehicle pool. Dumping her bag in the back of the Jeep, she reversed out of its parking space and set off over the rough track. The sun streamed through the dust-streaked windscreen, and the sky was a clear blue. The verges lining the country lanes were awash with blue speedwell, stitchwort, cow parsley, yellow cowslips and primroses. The open moorland was dotted with sheep grazing amongst the wiry, brown heather stalks, their lambs frolicking in the spring sunshine.

Smiling wistfully at the signs of new life, Bella steered the Jeep through the rugged hills and valleys. She passed a sprawling farm which made her think briefly of Edward. He'd replied to her letter, expressing his dismay that the strength of her feelings had not matched those of his for her, and he'd tried to convince her to let time take its course, certain that they were a well-suited match. Bella had again, politely, declined. That had been over two months ago and, to her relief, she hadn't heard from him since.

She pulled into the factory car park just before half past ten. Coming here always gave her a thrill. Seeing the new planes lined up in the cavernous hangars, or on the runway awaiting their first test flight, sent waves of excitement coursing through her body. She left the Jeep and crossed to the reception where she was quickly dispatched to the airfield out the back.

'Bella,' Chris Jones, the chief test pilot called, raising his gloved hand in welcome as he loped towards her. He was a tall, rangy man with receding reddish, blond hair and a neatly trimmed moustache. 'Good to see you again. How did you get on with our girl last time?'

'It was an interesting flight. Quite heavy to handle.'

'The Lancaster is capable of carrying twelve-thousand-pound bombs,' Chris grinned, displaying a set of uneven teeth. 'It's going to be heavy. You handle it all right?'

'Oh, yes,' Bella grinned back. 'Much to the dismay of my flight lieutenant.'

'Briggs still giving you grief, is he?'

'I tend to ignore him now,' Bella replied. 'There's a rumour he's being moved on.'

'So you'll be getting someone new in command. Could be an improvement, or maybe not.'

'I know what you mean,' Bella said, with a wry grin. 'Better the devil you know.' She rubbed her hands together. A cold breeze was blowing across the open field. They weren't out of the woods yet, as far as the weather went. 'So, where is she?'

'This way.' Clutching his clipboard, Chris led her around the side of a vast metal hangar. The brand-new Lancaster was sitting on the grass, its wings gleaming in the mid-morning sunlight.

'She's a beauty,' Bella said admiringly.

'She is that. If you'll sign here, she's all yours.'

Bella scribbled her signature and, pulling on her jacket, clambered into the spacious canopy. There was enough room in the cockpit for the pilot and a flight engineer, with space in the back for the other who would make up the seven-man crew. She spent a few minutes familiarizing herself with the control panel before preparing for take-off.

The wind had dropped and flying conditions were perfect. Soon she was soaring over fields and towns, villages and rivers. As she headed south, the landscape below her became greener and smoother. She caught a glimpse of the River Exe on her left side, flat and smooth, sunlight dancing on the water like a million tiny diamonds.

She delivered the plane to the RAF base just outside Exeter and hitched a lift to the railway station. The train journey from Exeter St David to the picturesque town of Dawlish took over half an hour due to the many stops and starts. The sea sparkled in the late morning sunshine. The tide was out, the coils of barbed wire clearly visible on the damp sand. Troop ships and destroyers were anchored far out to sea. Peering through the salt-speckled window, Bella could make out the coast of northern France in the hazy distance. It always gave her a queer feeling in her stomach when she was reminded just how close they were to the enemy. A puff of smoke rose on the horizon, as the train pulled into the small station.

Bella gathered up her things and made her way to the door, smiling as she spotted Amanda pushing her way through the disembarking military personnel and families coming to spend a day at the seaside. 'It's so good to see you,' Amanda said, as they hugged each other warmly.

'You, too,' Bella replied, picking up her bag. 'You're looking well. Motherhood certainly agrees with you. Where is the little man?'

'He was napping so I left him with Mum. He should be awake by the time we get back. Come on, it's not far'

Chatting amiably, they walked through the quaint streets. While the town of Teignmouth, a mere three miles along the coast, had been bombed heavily, Dawlish had so far escaped unscathed. They walked adjacent to a pretty park where children played or fed the ducks on the little river. Daffodils and tulips nodded in the sea breeze and the smell of fish and chips hung heavily in the air.

'Here we are,' Amanda said, turning into a broad, cobbled street, and stopping outside a green door. The paint was peeling, and the number two hung slightly askew. 'Mum, we're home,' she called, pushing the door open and standing aside to allow Bella into the dim, dank hallway. The slender, dark-haired woman Bella remembered from Amanda's wedding two years earlier came out of the kitchen, wiping her hands on a tea towel.

'Hello, Bella,' she smiled. 'Welcome to our home.'

'Hello, Mrs Chadwick,' Bella smiled. 'Thank you for having me.'

'Jonty's still asleep in his pram outside, so why don't you show Bella where she'll be sleeping while I put the kettle on.'

'Okay, Mum, will do. This way.' Amanda motioned to the narrow set of stairs to Bella's right. Bella followed her up to a narrow landing. 'No bathroom, I'm afraid.' Amanda said, the landing creaking beneath their feet. 'We wash at the kitchen sink and the loo is just outside the back door and to the left.' She pushed open the first of the two doors opening off the landing. 'We're in here,' she said. 'Mum insisted Jonty and I have the bigger of the two bedrooms,' Amanda explained, as Bella stepped into the room. There was a double bed, covered with a pink candlewick bedspread, the dark-wood headboard pushed against the wall. The wallpaper was patterned with faded pink cabbage roses. A child's cot had been squeezed between the bed and the wall. A beady-eyed teddy bear glared at Bella through the bars. 'If you look carefully, you can just make out the sea between the buildings,' Amanda said, going to the window.

Bella put her bag on the bed and joined her friend at the open window. A sliver of silver-blue water was just visible between the buildings. Gulls squawked loudly on the rooftop opposite, and a brine-scented breeze stirred the curtains.

'If you want to hang anything up, there's space in the

wardrobe,' Amanda said, opening a door of the large, teak-veneered wardrobe. 'And I cleared out the bottom drawer for you.'

'Thanks.' Bella perched on the edge of the bed. 'So, how have you been? Really?'

Amanda sighed. 'I'm all right,' she replied, joining Bella on the bed, the mattress dipping. 'I mean, it's hard. I miss Jonty like crazy. He would have loved being a dad. Every time little Jonty does something new, I think how proud his dad would have been.'

'I'm sorry. It must be so difficult.' She reached for Amanda's hand.

'His parents keep in touch. Jonty's their only grandchild and they're talking of coming over to visit once the war's over.' Amanda snorted. 'God knows when that will be. They sent money at Christmas and for his birthday. It's hard for them, too. Jonty was their only child.'

'My grandmother lost two children in January,' Bella said. 'My mother lost a sister and brother. Oh, I haven't told you. I only found yesterday, but Mother and Arthur are on their way home. They arrive a week on Tuesday.'

'You must be so excited. How long is it since you last saw them?'

'Four years.'

Amanda winced. 'That's a long time.'

'Too long,' agreed Bella. 'And totally unnecessary, as it turned out.'

'Yes, but back then it really looked likely we'd be invaded.

And they probably fared better over there than here. No rationing for a start. The children of a friend of Mum's were evacuated to America and they're having the life of riley by all accounts. Plenty of food, lots of fresh air. I think your Mum made the right decision for Arthur.'

'I do, too, though I don't think my father has forgiven her yet.' Bella grinned. 'The same as he hasn't forgiven me for going against his wishes and joining the ATA.'

'Oh, I miss flying,' said Amanda. 'Not that I'd want to be without little Jonty, of course. Speaking of which, he should be waking up in a minute.'

'Oh, lovely,' Bella said, standing up. 'I'm excited to meet him. I can unpack later.'

Renee was setting out the tea tray when they went into the kitchen. 'I thought as it's such a pleasant morning, we could sit in the garden.'

'Good idea, Mum. Is Jonty awake?'

'He was still asleep when I checked on him a few minutes ago,' her mother replied, slipping a knitted tea cosy over the brown teapot. 'You two go outside. I'll bring the tray.'

Bella followed Amanda out into the small, secluded garden. Set in the middle of the daisy-strewn lawn was a weathered table and four chairs. The grass was overgrown, but the small vegetable patch in the shadow of the back wall appeared well-tended.

'And here he is,' Amanda said, leading Bella to a shady corner of the garden where a large pram was parked under a blossoming pear tree. 'My little boy.' Bella peered in at the sleeping child. He lay on his back, his dark hair fanning the white pillow, one little hand clenched into a fist, the other clutching the hand of a small, knitted rabbit. His rosebud mouth made little sucking motions as he slept.

'Oh, Amanda,' Bella breathed. 'He's adorable.'

'He is, isn't he?' Amanda said, beaming with maternal pride. 'He looks so much like his dad, don't you think?'

'I do,' Bella agreed. 'I thought so when you sent that photograph.'

'His dad looked just the same as a baby, apparently.'

'Isn't my grandson just the most handsome boy, ever?' Renee said, jovially, setting the cups and saucers on the table.

'He is, Mrs Chadwick,' Bella laughed. 'The handsomest baby I've ever seen. No doubt about it.' At that moment little Jonty began to stir. He opened his big, dark eyes, blinked a few times, and smiled. Still clutching his rabbit, he sat up and held out his arms.

'Hello, sweetheart. Did you have a nice sleep?' Amanda scooped the little boy into her arms, inhaling his warm, sleepy baby scent. 'This is your Aunty Bella. She's come to see you.'

Jonty regarded Bella solemnly for a moment before treating her to his big, toothy grin. He stretched out his arms and Bella took him.

'Hello, Jonty,' she said, jiggling him in her arms. He really was the sweetest boy, she thought, as he fidgeted and demanded to be put down. She set him gently on his feet and he toddled off towards a small toy wagon, dragging the rabbit across the lawn by its ears.

Renee spread a blanket on the grass and brought out a box of wooden blocks and a couple of toy animals. While Jonty played, chattering away to himself, Bella and Amanda joined Renee at the table.

'He's very good at amusing himself, isn't he?' Bella remarked.

'He's such a good boy,' Amanda agreed. 'Hardly ever causes a fuss.'

'But then, his father was such a happy-go-lucky sort of chap, wasn't he?' said Renee, pouring the tea. 'Nothing phased him, did it?'

'No, you're right,' Amanda answered, watching her son with a wistful air. 'I used to get frustrated with him sometimes because of his devil-may-care attitude. Perhaps if he hadn't been so gung-ho about taking risks, he'd still be alive today,' she said regretfully.

'Amanda,' scolded Renee, refilling her teacup. 'You can't think like that. When it's your time, it's your time. Now, what do you girls have planned for this afternoon?'

'I thought we might take Jonty for a walk along the seafront,' Amanda said to Bella, mustering a smile.

'Lovely,' smiled Renee. 'The fresh sea air will do you all the world of good.'

CHAPTER THIRTY

'Not too far, Jonty,' Amanda said, as the little boy toddled after a large grey and white seagull. The gull flapped its wings and squawked loudly, sending Jonty scurrying back to the bench to bury his face in his mother's skirt. He held up his arms, and Amanda lifted him onto her lap.

'He walks so well,' Bella said, stroking Jonty's chubby hand.

'He took his first steps at nine months,' said Amanda. 'And he hasn't stopped since.' Jonty squirmed to get down and Amanda set him on his feet. Immediately he toddled off towards the low wall that separated the pavement from the sandy beach. Spread along the shoreline were six-foot square concrete blocks, huge coils of lethal-looking barbed wire spread between them. Entry to the beach was strictly prohibited, with signs every few yards warning of the danger of mines. The waves hissed back and forth across the damp sand, leaving strands of seaweed tangled around the barbed wire.

Bella and Amanda watched Jonty toddle up and down the pavement. He found a shell and sat down, intrigued by its pretty conical design, his little brow furrowed in abject concentration.

'Not in your mouth, Jonty,' Amanda called. Jonty glanced over at her and grinned his toothy grin.

'Still nothing from Edward then?' Amanda asked, keeping one eye on her son, who was watching a large, shaggy dog coming towards him.

'Nothing, so I think he's finally given up on me.'

'There's no one else you're keen on?'

Bella shook her head.

Amanda frowned, shielding her eyes with her hand. 'You never told me what happened between you and Will,' she said. 'He was devastated when you left, you know?'

'I know,' Bella said, sorrowfully.

'I can tell you still care for him. So why did you leave? It was so sudden.' She brushed a strand of hair from her face. 'I was in bits myself because of Jonty being killed, but it was still a shock when I returned to base to find you'd transferred to Woodhead.'

'I can't tell you,' Bella said, biting her lip.

'Why not? What can possibly be so bad? Was he unfaithful? Did he mistreat you?'

'No, of course not. Will's not like that.'

'Then what? Come on, Bella. You can confide in me. I won't tell a soul. I promise.'

Bella sighed. 'Will is my brother.'

'What?' Amanda stared at her in disbelief. 'How is that possible?'

'My father and Will's mother had a fling. What makes it worse is that Will's mother was my mother's friend.'

'Oh my God,' Amanda breathed. 'Does she know?'

'I don't think so, although she was a bit odd when I told her about our engagement.'

'Goodness. Of all the things I imagined I have to say that scenario wasn't one of them.'

'Now do you see why I couldn't tell Will the truth?' Bella stared out over the silver sea. Several huge grey ships were anchored offshore, gun turrets gleaming in the sunshine.

'What a mess,' Amanda said, thoughtfully. 'Your father can never openly acknowledge his son, and Will will never know his true father. And you and Arthur can never acknowledge him as your brother.'

She sighed. 'You're right. It is a mess.'

'I don't suppose you'd consider telling Will in confidence, would you? Just to put the poor man out of his misery?'

Bella laughed mirthlessly. 'No. I can't have a brother–sister relationship with him. My feelings for him go way beyond that. It would devastate him to know his dada isn't his real father. I can't do that to him. '

'You still love him, don't you?' Amanda said softly. Bella nodded miserably.

'I can't help it. I know it's wrong to feel this way and I've tried so hard to forget him. I compare every man I meet to

295

Will. I can't help it.' She smiled sadly. 'That's why I have to keep my distance.'

'Poor you,' Amanda sympathized, tucking her arm through Bella's. She was quiet for a moment, then she said, thoughtfully, 'Do you think what you feel for Will might be your natural love for a brother, and you just mistook it for something romantic?'

Bella considered for a moment, then shook her head. 'I don't think so, no. Even now, knowing what I do, I can't think of him as a brother.'

They sat in silence for a few minutes, watching Jonty pottering. A blast of cold air wafted along the promenade, making them shiver.

'Ooh, it's turning chilly now the wind's picking up.' Amanda said. 'Shall we head back?'

'Yes, lets.' Bella got to her feet. White horses had appeared on the water, and the smaller boats moored close to the shore bobbed in the rising swell.

Amanda called to Jonty, who came running, still clutching his shell, and swept him into her arms. He grinned toothily at Bella, his cheeks pink from where they'd caught the sun. The salty breeze ruffled his dark curls and she was struck again by how much he resembled his late father.

'His father would have been so proud of him,' she said, as Jonty squirmed to be put down. Amanda set him on his feet and he reached for Bella's hand. She took hold of his chubby, sandy hand and, with Amanda holding his other hand, they set off for home, swinging Jonty between them.

Renee had tea all ready for them. It was too windy and cold to eat outside so they gathered around the kitchen table, Jonty in his highchair. With the radio playing softly in the background, so they could catch the hourly news bulletin, they tucked into Spam sandwiches and bread and butter pudding.

'You put your feet up Mrs Chadwick,' she told Renee.

The older woman smiled gratefully. 'If you're sure, love? I wouldn't mind a few minutes to myself.'

Taking herself off to the parlour with a cup of tea and the newspaper, Renee left Bella to the dishes. With her arms elbow deep in soapsuds, she gazed out at the garden. Two gulls preened themselves on the back wall and a yellow butterfly flitted across the lawn. From far away came the drone of aeroplanes and staccato beat of the anti-aircraft guns.

She could hear Amanda singing to Jonty upstairs and she sighed softly to herself as she reached for another dirty plate.

She was just emptying the washing up bowl out the back door when Amanda reappeared.

'He's gone off, at last,' she said, buttoning a navy-blue cardigan over her blue and white floral dress. 'It's really turned chilly, hasn't it,' she said, with a frown.

'It is only the first of April,' Bella reminded her, as Amanda stoked the embers in the stove.

'I suppose so. It was lovely earlier though, wasn't it? I think I've caught the sun. Jonty certainly has. His cheeks are quite red.'

'Me, too,' Bella said. 'Shall I make a pot of tea?'

'Please,' Amanda said, stifling a yawn. 'We can listen to the radio for a bit before we go up.'

'You go sit with your mum. I'll bring it through.'

Bella made the tea and carried it through to the parlour. It was still light outside, dusty sunlight streaming in through the window.

'Thank you, love,' Renee said, folding up the newspaper, and setting it aside. 'Just on that table there, would be lovely. Amanda, turn the radio up would you? The seven o'clock bulletin will be on shortly.'

Her daughter did as asked and the familiar voice of Vera Lyn filled the room. Suddenly their senses were assaulted by an almighty roar which rattled the teacups in their saucers.

'What the heck is that?' whispered Amanda, as she, Bella and Renee exchanged terrified glances. They jumped at the sound of gunfire. Before any of them could move, the room grew dark. The noise was deafening. The windows shook and the house trembled. Within a minute the shadow had lifted and the noise began to recede, leaving the three women frozen in place. For a moment there was a deathly silence. Then, from upstairs came Jonty's terrified scream.

'Jonty!' Amanda screamed, running from the room. Bella and Renee exchanged panicked glances before racing upstairs after Amanda.

They found her in the front bedroom, Jonty clutched to her chest. He was crying uncontrollably, his eyes wide with fear. For a moment Bella could only stare with incomprehension while her brain tried to make sense of the scene before her. Glass from the shattered window littered the floor.

'The bastard shot into the room,' Amanda said through teeth gritted in anger. 'Look.' Her eyes flashed as she inclined her head to the back wall. Renee let out a gasp of horror.

'Oh, my God,' Bella murmured, staring in disbelief. The cabbage-roses were pockmarked with bullet holes.

'Thank God Jonty was laid down in his cot,' Renee breathed, wiping tears from her eyes. 'If he'd been standing up like he does sometimes . . .' She shook her head, unable to voice the unthinkable. She went to her daughter and wrapped her arms around her and her grandson.

As she stood there, Bella became aware of the commotion in the street. Above the screaming and shouting the women heard a hammering on the door below.

'I'll go,' Bella said, turning and hurrying down the stairs. She opened the door to find an ARP warden on the doorstep.

'I'm Bill, from up the road. Just checking to see if you're all okay?' he said. He was a short, middle-aged man, his face creased with concern.

'We're all fine, thank you,' Bella replied.

'Ah, evening, Renee,' he said, looking past Bella to where Renee was coming down the stairs. 'The little lad?'

'He's terrified but unhurt. Thankfully he was asleep in his cot,' Renee replied. 'They went over him and hit the wall.'

Bill nodded. 'Not so lucky up the end,' he said, shaking his head in dismay. 'The young nurse who looks after Mrs Plumber at number six got hit in the head as she was helping the old girl into bed, and one of the lads at number eight took a bullet in the throat. He'd run to the window to see the plane.'

'Ah, they can't be more than eight or nine,' Renee said, coming to stand next to Bella in the doorway. 'Which lad was it?'

'It was the young one, Barry,' Bill said sadly. 'Just seven.'

Renee sighed loudly. 'Thanks for letting us know, Bill. We're all okay here, apart from a broken window. I'll go over and see Val. She must be devastated, poor love. She's only recently lost her husband, too.'

'Ah, it's a crying shame,' Bill said. 'I'll be along later and board up that window for you.'

'Thanks, Bill,' she said, with a grateful smile. 'You go be with Amanda while I go up the road to see Val,' she said, once the ARP warden had moved on to the house next door. 'I shan't be long.'

Bella found Amanda in the back bedroom, perched on her mother's bed.

'I'm too scared to leave Jonty in the other room,' she said, cradling her little boy on her lap as she gently stroked his head. 'What if there's another one?'

'I understand,' Bella said, joining her on the bed. 'What a thing to do. He must have known his victims might be children on their way to bed.'

'Thank God he wasn't any lower,' Amanda muttered. 'Have there been any casualties?'

'A young woman and a boy, Barry, I think the ARP warden said.'

Amanda winced. 'Oh, no, poor Barry. He was such a sweet boy.'

'Your mum's gone over to see his mother.'

Amanda nodded. 'Poor woman. She must be distraught.' She buried her head in Jonty's hair. He had calmed down now, his hysterical wailing reduced to the occasional sob. 'Would you mind if we all slept in here tonight? I couldn't bear sleeping in that room this evening.'

'Of course not,' replied Bella. 'We've all had a terrible shock.'

By the time Renee arrived home two hours later, Bella and Amanda had fallen sleep. Renee watched them with a sad smile. They were curled up the bed, little Jonty tucked safely between them. Careful not to wake them, she extinguished her candle and, not bothering to undress, slipped under the covers next to Amanda. Slipping an arm around her daughter's slim waist, she fell asleep.

The morning brought the news that the nurse, whose name Bella learnt was Avril, and Barry, were the only casualties, and that the plane had been shot down over the channel. The pilot hadn't survived.

The day had dawned overcast but dry and the children were playing outside, proudly showing off the bullets they'd dug out of their bedroom walls, all except for Douglas Boatwright, little Barry's brother. Barry and Avril had been taken away during the night, and nearly every upstairs window in the street was boarded up.

The curtains remained firmly shut at numbers six and eight and the mood amongst the adults was sombre.

'I feel awful leaving you so soon after what happened,' Bella said, as Amanda walked her to the railway station. Jonty sat up in his pram, hugging his knitted rabbit and taking in his surrounding with interest.

'I'll be all right. I spoke to Mum while you were feeding Jonty his breakfast and we're going to move the beds into the parlour. We'd both feel safer sleeping downstairs.'

'I don't blame you,' Bella said. She'd slept well but her dreams had been haunted by images of German planes shooting into civilian homes. Even now she felt cold at the thought of what could have happened if the noise of the plane had woken Jonty and he'd pulled himself up in his cot, as he usually did when he woke up.

'I'm going to call in to see Val later,' Amanda said, lifting the heavy pram up the kerb. 'I'm dreading it. I'll ask Mum if she'll have Jonty for me. I don't think it's right to take him with me.'

'No, it'll be upsetting for him, and for the poor woman, having just lost her own little boy ...' Bella shuddered. 'Awful. I feel so sorry for her.'

'So do I,' Amanda concurred with a sigh. 'Well, here we are.' She engaged the pram's brake outside the station entrance and gave Bella a hug. 'Thank you for coming. It's been lovely to see you. I'm only sorry it was spoiled.'

Bella shrugged. 'I'm just glad you and Jonty are okay.'

'Enjoy your reunion with your mother and brother, and

I hope you find someone one day. Someone you can love as much as Will.'

Bella chuckled. 'Maybe. Right now, I'm happy as I am,' she said, as a shrill whistle signalled the imminent arrival of her train. 'Take care of yourself, Amanda, and look after your little man.' She kissed the top of Jonty's head. 'I'll write soon,' she called, as she made her way up the steps and into the station where she was swept along on the tide of embarking passengers.

She settled herself in a carriage filled with brash American GIs. During the twenty-minute journey to Exeter St David, they engaged Bella in conversation and were obviously impressed to learn she was a pilot. In return, Bella discovered they were heading to the south coast.

'There's something big in the pipeline,' said a young, fair-skinned boy with short, white-blond hair.

'I reckon they're planning to invade,' said his companion.

'Shush!' scowled an older man with a severe crew-cut and bushy eyebrows. 'Loose lips sink ships, remember?' He nodded at the poster taped to the carriage door.

'Oops, sorry,' the boy said, looking chastened.

'Don't worry. I won't say anything,' Bella said, smiling at him. He was young, barely eighteen she guessed. For some reason he reminded her of Will. Perhaps it was his dark colouring, she mused. At times she could push her heartache deep inside but there were times, like now, when she missed him so much it almost drove her crazy.

She tried to concentrate on the GI's cheerful banter

as the sea flashed by the window, sparkling silver in the sunlight.

She wondered if what Amanda had said yesterday might be true. Were her feelings really a reflection of the natural bond between a brother and sister? She thought about it for a moment as the train pulled into Exeter St David. The platform was teeming with American and British soldiers. The GIs she shared her short journey with whistled and wished her well, and one carried her bag down onto the platform for her. Thanking him, Bella took it from him and, pushing her way through the milling crowd of olive green and khaki, she found her northbound train with minutes to spare.

By comparison, the Leeds-bound train was quiet. Bella entered the first carriage she came to. It was occupied by two middle-aged ladies, both dressed in black. One had clearly been crying. She clutched a screwed-up handkerchief in one hand and a rosary of ebony beads in the other. Neither lady spoke to Bella apart from muttering a brief hello. Settling herself by the window, Bella returned to her earlier thought. She loved her brother, Arthur, more than life, but her feelings for him were nothing like the love she felt for Will. Much as she wished her feelings for him could be put down to sibling affection, she knew in her heart that what she felt for Will went far deeper. She loved him with every fibre of her being. It was a sinful love, incestuous. No wonder her father had been so horrified when he'd realized she had feelings for him. She felt a flash of anger towards her father. Why had he been so selfish, so weak? If he'd never been unfaithful to her mother, she could be with Will now. Then the thought struck her, as the train wend its way inland, that had her father not strayed from his marriage vows, Will would never have been born, anyway. At least if he'd never existed I'd have been spared this heartache, she mused sullenly, resting her forehead on the cool glass.

It was late afternoon by the time she arrived back at base. Patty and Valerie were horrified to hear about the attack on Amanda's street.

'Thank God you're unhurt,' Patty said, appalled. 'The audacity of the man. What possessed him, do you think?'

'Just having a bit of sport,' Valerie said, drily. 'I've heard of that happening somewhere else. Bastards!'

'Until then, had you had a good time?' Patty asked, reaching for the telephone as it began to ring.

'Yes, thanks,' she mouthed. Patty gave her the thumbs up and turned her attention to the caller. 'Portsmouth,' Bella heard her say. 'Of course, sir. No problem.'

'We're getting loads of calls for planes to be ferried to the south coast,' Valerie said. 'I've got a request for a Hawker Hurricane just come in from RAF Hallows if you're interested. I mean, I know you've just got back but . . . ?'

'I'll take it,' Bella said, holding out her hands for the slip of paper containing Valerie's scribbled details. 'I'll unpack later.'

'Oh, and there's a letter for you,' Valerie said, reaching behind her and grabbing an envelope from a shelf. 'Sorry it's been opened. Everything's being checked and censored now.'

'Oh, okay. Thanks.' Bella recognized her father's

handwriting at once. She opened it on her way to the plane. Her spirit lightened as she read her father's brief note. Her mother and Arthur were due to dock at three o'clock on the eleventh of April and he wished to know if Bella would be there with him to meet them. Would she? Bella grinned. This was one reunion she wouldn't miss for the world. Feeling happier than she had for months, Bella strapped on her parachute and clambered aboard the plane. She went through the take-off drill and taxied onto the runway.

CHAPTER THIRTY-ONE

A stiff wind blew off the water. The crowd gathered on the quayside were dwarfed by the huge troop ships lining the docks. Anchored further away was the convoy of battleships and destroyers that had protected the troop ships during their dangerous voyage.

It was only now that Bella appreciated how fraught with danger her mother and Arthur's journey must have been.

'Do you see them yet?' her father asked, rocking from foot to foot as his anxious gaze scanned the disembarking passengers. Most of them were military and medical personnel. There seemed to be very few civilians.

'No, I can't ... oh, yes, there. I think.' Bella stood on tiptoe to see clearly over the surging crowd. 'Yes, there's Mother. Look.'

Drawing himself to his full height, Samuel craned his neck to get a better view of the disembarkation ramp. He clasped

Bella's arm to steady himself and it was all she could do not to shrug him off. She hadn't forgiven him for his indiscretion towards her mother, hating him for putting her in the uncomfortable position of having to keep his sordid secret. If he'd noticed her frostiness towards him, her father hadn't let on. She'd arrived late the previous afternoon. Johnny and Jack had been pleased to see her, though now a strapping lad of fourteen, Johnny was a little less enthusiastic in his welcome than his younger brother. Ida had complained that Bella was far too thin and promptly set about baking a meat and potato pie. Her father had appeared pleased to see her, and from his demeanour Bella correctly assumed that the abruptness of her departure two years earlier, and the revelation that had led to it, had clearly been swept under the carpet, never to be mentioned again.

Now, standing on the chilly quayside, dark clouds gathering over the Isle of Wight, Bella was filled with conflicting emotions. She was overjoyed at the prospect of seeing her mother and Arthur again after four long years, but she was dreading having to lie to them. And lie to them she must. Her mother had appeared matter of fact in her response to Bella's news of her broken engagement, but surely she would want to know the reason why? How could Bella look her in the eye and tell her a blatant lie? A fresh wave of anger towards her father welled up inside her, as she shielded her eyes against the light. She saw her mother pause midway down the ramp to scan the crowd.

'Mother! Over here.' Bella waved her arms. Standing beside

his mother, it was Arthur who spotted her. Bella saw him say something to Alice and her mother's head swivelled in Bella's direction. Even from this distance, Bella could see how her mother's face lit up at the sight of her husband and daughter.

'Excuse me, excuse me,' Bella and Samuel repeated as they pushed their way through the crowds. Alice and Arthur were doing the same and, suddenly there they were, face to face.

'Mother! Arthur! Bella shrieked, flinging her arms around her brother.'

'Hello, Bella, darling. Samuel.' Alice's face softened as she reached for her husband. 'Oh, my love,' she said, pulling Samuel close. 'I've missed you so much.'

As her parents embraced, Bella released Arthur.

He regarded her shyly. 'You've got short hair.'

'It's easier to manage,' Bella smiled. 'But look at your suntan. And those muscles.' She squeezed his arms playfully. Arthur laughed boyishly.

'We nearly got blown up,' he said, scratching his head.

'Did you?'

'Not really,' Alice said, breaking away from Samuel to hug Bella. 'Oh, sweetheart, it's so good to see you. It's been so long.' Her voice trembled.

'Yes, we did,' Arthur insisted.

'Our ship wasn't bombed,' Alice assured Bella. 'One of the other troop ships got hit but there was only minor damage. No one was hurt.' She tucked her arm through Bella's. 'It was a nerve-wracking trip though,' she said, her voice low. 'Took us much longer than it should have because we had to keep zig-zagging to avoid the German submarines. Oh, you don't know how glad I am to be on dry land.'

'Hello, son,' Samuel said, shaking Arthur's hand. 'It's good to have you home.' Samuel jangled his car keys.

'You've bought a car?' Alice gasped.

'I have,' Samuel beamed. 'I didn't tell you as I wanted it to be a surprise. Come on. It's parked down the street. Have you instructed the purser to have your trunks delivered?'

'I have,' Alice replied. 'Our own car.' She smiled at Arthur. 'How exciting.'

'Can I drive it, Dad?' asked Arthur. 'Uncle Charlie let me drive his truck.'

'We'll see,' was his father's noncommittal reply.

Bella tucked her other arm through Arthur's and together they followed Samuel across the quay to where his grey Ford Deluxe sedan was parked alongside the kerb.

Samuel opened the front passenger door and pulled the seat forward so Bella and Arthur could climb in the back. Arthur settled himself on the red leather seat, gazing round in awe.

'This is very nice,' said Alice, tucking her skirt under her knees as she slid into the passenger seat. 'Very smart,' she said, running her fingers over the shiny wood-effect dashboard.

'Obviously, with petrol rationing, I can't enjoy it as much as I'd like,' Samuel said, slipping into the driving seat and starting the engine. 'But it's convenient for visiting some of my parishioners who live a bit further away.'

'It's great, Dad,' Arthur said. 'And it smells nicer than Uncle Charlie's truck.'

As they drove, Alice was a little more forthcoming about their trip. They'd had to stay well away from the African coast, in case any U-boats were lurking nearby or in case of any mines that might have been left behind from the North African campaign.

'There were only three families on our ship. The rest were South African troops. There were some prisoners of war, too. Italians mostly. They were very friendly. You got on well with them, didn't you, Arthur.'

'They were my friends,' Arthur told Bella. 'So were the soldiers. One gave me his penknife. Look.' He reached into his trouser pocket and pulled out a small penknife in a leather sheath. 'He said I could keep it.'

'That was kind of him,' Bella said, admiring the little knife. 'You'll have to look after it.'

'I will.' Arthur slipped it back into his pocket and turned his face to the window. 'His name is Billy. I played cards with him in the library at night.'

Alice gave a quiet chuckle. 'You know how Arthur tends to wander? Well, I was so petrified he'd wander off at night and fall overboard, that every night I stacked empty cans just outside his cabin door, thinking that if he left his room, he'd knock them over and wake me up. It was days before I discovered he was meeting up with his friends in the library at night. You just stepped over the cans without making a sound, didn't you, Arthur?' She looked back over her shoulder, smiling at her son.

'I'm not an idiot, Mum,' he said, grinning back at Alice.

311

'I expect your mates looked out for you, didn't they, Arthur?' Samuel said.

'Yes,' Arthur nodded. 'The soldiers are my friends.'

There was a lot to say and they were chattering away, but it wasn't long before Alice fell silent.

'I hadn't realized how bad the bombing had been here,' she said sombrely, gazing out of the car window at the bomb-damaged buildings. They drove down a residential street where several houses had been reduced to piles of rubble, leaving huge gaps in the terraced row. Some were missing just the front of the building, with the floors and back walls still intact, complete with wallpaper and pictures.

'It's heartbreaking to see it like this,' Alice said, sorrowfully. 'Samuel, you never said it was this bad. I knew Southampton had suffered in the Blitz, of course. We got the newspaper out there and we listened to the BBC World Service. We knew you'd be a target, because of the docks, but still.'

'When they bombed the Spitfire factory, they hit the Cold Store,' Samuel said. 'I think I told you in one of my letters.'

'I remember,' Arthur said. He gripped his father's headrest and leaned forward so his head was between the two front seats. 'It was full of butter and the fire burned for two weeks.'

'That's right,' Samuel chuckled. 'Fancy you remembering that.' Arthur laughed and sat back in his seat. He started telling Bella about how much he'd enjoyed helping the farmhands on his uncle's farm. Bella listened with interest, pleased that their bond appeared undiminished by their long separation.

'I thought we might take a detour through the city,' she heard her father say. 'You'll be shocked by how much it's changed.'

'Oh, Samuel,' Alice murmured in dismay, as they drove through the middle of Southampton. Much of Above Bar, where Alice had often shopped and visited tea shops with her friends when she was younger, had been obliterated. 'It looks so different,' she said, wiping away a tear. 'Turn back, please. I can't bear it.'

'All right,' Samuel said, executing a quick U-turn in the wide road. They were quiet until they left the city behind.

'I wonder if Farmer Monk wants me to go to work to-morrow,' Arthur said, as they passed a field where a huge bay shire horse was pulling a plough, led by a young boy.

'You can pop down to the farm tomorrow and ask him,' Alice suggested, tensing as Samuel took the bend a little too quickly.

'Sorry about that,' Samuel apologized. 'I spoke to Farmer Monk the other day,' he told Arthur. 'He's more than happy to take you back. You can start Monday, if you like? That'll give you a week to get acclimatised to being back home. What do you say?'

'I'd like that, Father.'

'Tell me more about your voyage?' Bella asked her mother, as the car wend its way along the country lanes.

'It was as good as it could be given the circumstances,' Alice said, half-turning her head.

'Despite the anxious moments?' Bella said.

'The crew were very good at keeping us distracted with games and activities. And it was comforting to have all those ships around us. It was frightening when the other ship was attacked, though. It really brought the war home. For, of course, we'd been quite sheltered from everything for the last four years.'

'The submarine got sunk. They used a . . . a . . .' Arthur screwed up his face in concentration, 'a depth charge,' he said, remembering. It made a huge splash, didn't it, mother?'

'It did,' replied Alice, somewhat drily. 'I thought the wave might swamp one of the boats.'

'It doesn't sound like it was the jolliest of times,' Samuel remarked, changing gears as they reached a crossroad. He took the road to the left, signposted for Strawbridge.

'It wasn't,' Alice responded shortly. 'I'm glad it's over.'

Johnny and Jack were waiting for them in the front garden with the dogs, who let out a volley of barking as the car drew up outside. The spaniels were almost ten now, and no longer the youthful dogs they'd been when Arthur left. But though they hadn't seen their young master for four years, they flew at him with an exuberance that belied their age. Arthur crouched down, laughing as the dogs leapt all over him, licking his face and wagging their tails.

'Boys, how you've grown,' Alice said, staring at the two evacuees with astonishment. 'Johnny, you're a young man now.'

'Good morning, ma'am,' Johnny said, politely, extending his hand.

'Oh, don't be so formal,' Alice exclaimed. 'Let me give you a hug,' she said, embracing the gangly fourteen-year-old. 'And you, Jack. You're so tall. Goodness, you must be what, ten?'

'I'm nine, ma'am.'

'Enough of this ma'am nonsense,' Alice said, as she hugged him. 'You used to call me Aunty Alice. Have I been gone so long that you've forgotten me?'

'No, ma'am.' Johnny shook his head solemnly.

'They'll get used to you again in no time,' Samuel reassured her. 'You remember Arthur, don't you?'

Arthur pushed the dogs aside and stood up. Both boys regarded him warily.

'Hello, I'm Arthur,' he said, holding out his hand. Both boys shook it.

'I remember you,' Johnny said, shoving his hands in his pocket. 'You took us to the farm.'

'Mrs Roberts,' said a warm, familiar voice. 'And Arthur. Oh, you're a sight for sore eyes,' said Ida, bustling through from the kitchen. 'Welcome home, Mrs Roberts. I've got the kettle on. I'm sure you're gasping for a decent cup of tea.'

'Thank you, Mrs Wilson,' Alice smiled. 'It's lovely to see you, too, and yes, please, I'd love a cup of tea.' She patted the dogs and followed Ida into the house.

'Do you want to see our tree house?' Jack asked Arthur, who nodded.

'Yes, please.'

'Come on, then,' said Johnny. 'It's this way.'

315

'Be back in time for dinner,' Samuel called after them, as they headed down the lane.

'We will, Uncle Samuel,' Jack shouted over his shoulder.

Bella and Samuel watched them go, the dogs following sedately behind them.

'You won't say anything to your mother, will you?' Samuel said, as they turned to go into the vicarage. 'It would only upset her unnecessarily.'

'I won't,' Bella said, narrowing her eyes crossly. 'It's unfair of you to put me in this predicament,' she said, keeping her voice low so as not to be overheard.

'I'm not proud of myself, Bella,' Samuel said, curtly. 'But what's done is done. Come along. Your mother will be wanting to spend as much time with you as she can in the short time you've got together.'

Bella followed her father indoors.

'I've work to attend to in my study,' Samuel said. 'Tell your mother I'll see her later.' Bella nodded and made her way to the kitchen.

'It was such a shock seeing how much damage had been done,' Alice was saying to Ida. 'Ah, Bella, here you are. Come sit beside me.' She patted the chair next to her.

'Father's attending to something in his study,' Bella said, sitting down. 'He said he'll see you later.'

'Okay, thank you,' Alice said. 'Oh, Bella, I've missed you so much. I like the hairstyle. She stroked Bella's dark, chestnut-brown hair. 'It suits you short.'

'It's easier to manage,' Bella said. 'And more convenient.'

'I'm sure,' Alice said, wistfully. 'I've missed so much.' She shook herself. 'Sorry, I'm being maudlin.'

'You did what was best for Arthur,' Bella said.

Alice pulled a face. 'As it turned out . . .'

'You weren't to know. If we had been invaded and Arthur was taken, how would you have felt then?'

'It came pretty close,' Ida said, setting the teapot on the table. 'Those first few months after you sailed, everyone was expecting imminent invasion. You did the right thing, Mrs Roberts.'

'Thank you for saying so, Mrs Wilson.' Alice smiled. 'So, darling, what have you been up to?'

Both Alice and Ida were shocked when Bella recounted to her the terrifying events during her visit to Amanda.

'What an awful thing to do,' Ida said, indignantly, banging down the milk jug. 'He could see it was a residential street. His only intent could have been to cause hurt and distress to innocent civilians.'

They talked for a while more as they sipped their tea. Their letters back and forth were always censored and there were things, they, especially Bella, couldn't mention in a letter that might possibly be intercepted and fall into the wrong hands.

Alice visibly blanched at some of Bella's escapades, though Bella was careful not to recount anything too hair-raising, lest her mother side with her father and insist she cease flying at once. Alice picked up her teacup, looking thoughtful.

'I'm sorry about what happened between you and Will,'

she said, avoiding Bella's gaze. Bella sighed. It was the conversation she'd been dreading but, to her surprise, her mother appeared content to leave it there, changing the subject to ask,

'Have you met anyone else, apart from that Edward fellow you mentioned?'

'No. I'm too busy to think about romance,' Bella replied.

She cleared her throat. 'When are you intending to visit Grandma and Aunt Eleanor?'

'I shall go over this afternoon.' Alice's face fell. 'I was heartbroken to hear about Martha and Jimmy, especially with their deaths coming so close together, as well. Such a shock for all of us.' She squeezed Bella's hand. 'How long can you stay?'

'I'm expected back at base tomorrow,' replied Bella. 'So, we've got today and this evening. I shall be leaving on the eight o'clock train.'

'So soon,' Alice said, shaking her head sorrowfully. 'Well, we'll just have to make the most of the time we have, won't we?'

CHAPTER THIRTY-TWO

Bella was kept busy all the rest of the month and into May ferrying planes to the south coast. From her mother's letters, she learned that great forces of troops were gathering in Southampton.

'Every day we have convoys of American tanks, lorries and Jeeps rolling through Strawbridge,' she wrote, and Bella could only smile, knowing how excited Arthur must be to witness such a great manoeuvring of military vehicles.

There were rumours and counter rumours. It was obvious something big was afoot and all everyone at Woodhead air-base was talking about was whether the Allies were finally going to invade France. Bella was certain her Uncle Benjy would know exactly what was being planned but, of course, he wouldn't be allowed to mention it to anyone. Her mother had mentioned on several occasions, however, that Benjy was courting. She worked as a secretary at the war office and was a widow, having lost her husband in the first months of the war. Holly and Emily, now aged sixteen and fifteen, had yet to meet their father's lady friend but, by all accounts, they, and their grandmother, Bella's great-aunt Eleanor, were pleased Benjy had met someone at last.

As May progressed, Bella was flying five or six hours a day. She fell into bed each night mentally and physically exhausted. Patty and Valerie were equally busy in the Ops Room taking requests and planning the daily rotas.

In the middle of May the base was rocked by another tragedy when one of the newer ferry pilots, on only his third flight, flew into a hillside directly after take-off. He'd been a pilot in the RAF until he'd been medically discharged after being shot down over the east coast. His death cast a pall over the airbase, but in the middle of war there was little time to grieve and it was business as usual for Bella and the rest of the crew.

As she flew around the country, she witnessed for herself the mass gathering of troops all along the south coast.

She still thought of Will often, wondering how he was faring. Beryl and Gilly kept in touch, and she knew they would have let her know if anything had happened to him. They were still ferrying planes, and at the end of May Gilly and Bella happened to be at the same airbase at the same time. They'd managed to squeeze in a quick cup of tea together before they had to leave, in which time Gilly told Bella she was still seeing Richard, her doctor in Motcombe, and that

Beryl was hoping Frank would pop the question while he was on leave that week.

'Keep me posted,' Bella grinned, as the two girls parted ways.

The first few days of June brought strong winds and thick cloud. There was little flying due to the dangerous conditions, and the ferry pilots, Bella included, spent much of their time hanging around the Ops Room or in the Common room playing cards and listening to the wireless. Patty and Valerie were inundated with requests of planes which they couldn't fulfil due to the weather. All they could do was promise to get the planes delivered as soon as the weather improved enough for the pilots to get airborne.

On the morning of the sixth of June, Bella was eating her breakfast in the mess when a shout went up from a couple of the chaps seated at the far end of the hall.

'Turn it up,' someone shouted. The radio volume rose by several decibels and the mess hall fell silent. Bella sat with her spoon in her hand, listening with rapt attention as BBC reporter, Freddy Allen, reported on the BBC Home Services that Allied paratroopers had landed in France. A loud cheer went up amongst the men. The long-awaited invasion had begun.

'That's why Tim hasn't been allowed any leave, then,' Valerie said, her face white. 'They've been preparing for this. God, I hope he'll be alright.'

'It's always the paratroopers who go in first,' she said

morosely, glaring at the men who were talking loudly and animatedly. Bella guessed there were many of them who wished they themselves were over there in the middle of the action.

'You've got to stay positive,' Patty said, looking equally concerned. She had brothers serving.

Every radio on the base stayed on all day. At half past nine there was a newsflash and those who were on the ground gathered around the nearest wireless set to listen to General Eisenhower's rousing speech. His heartfelt words to the soldiers, sailors and airmen of the Allied Expeditionary Force as they embarked on their 'Great Crusade' left no one in any doubt that this would be the turning point of the war, and as he brought his speech to its conclusion, beseeching the blessing of almighty God on the 'great and noble undertaking', there was a resounding 'Amen' from the assembled men.

'Amen,' whispered Bella, thinking of Will. She'd heard via Beryl that Will had been flying planes to Europe and the thought of him being caught up in the conflict terrified her. Trying to put him out of her mind, she collected her rota from the Ops Room where Valerie and Patty were avidly listening to the radio while fielding the numerous telephone calls.

They both waved, and she headed outside. The sky was dark, but the cloud cover was high enough to allow the pilots to get airborne. She took off and circled back over the airfield, setting her course for RAF Warmwell, in Dorset.

*

As the month progressed, the hourly news bulletins brought encouraging news from France. Despite heavy losses during the first few days after the Normandy landings, the Allies were making good advances against the enemy and regaining territory. It also brought news of personal tragedies. Gilly wrote to Bella with the sad news that Beryl's fiancé, Frank, had been killed on D–Day. He'd been amongst the first wave of soldiers storming the beach and had been shot while still in the water. Flight Lieutenant Briggs lost two sons in the days following D–Day and another in the battle for the liberation of Paris in the August.

Sitting in a darkened cinema in Glossop towards the end of August, Bella, Patty and Valerie cheered along with the rest of the audience watching the Pathé news reels of the Allies and a convoy of French army vehicles marching triumphantly into Paris to be greeted by cheering, waving crowds.

Alice wrote to tell Bella that Johnny had left school at the end of the summer term, with his mother's permission, and was working with Arthur on Monk's farm.

Your father and I had discussed the possibility of Jack returning home after the summer, but what with these doodlebug attacks, we feel it's safer for him to remain with us for the time being.

My cousin Benjy married his lady friend, Camilla, last Wednesday in Westminster. They're coming down for a weekend as soon as he can afford the time off work. The rest of us are going along as well as can be expected. Grandfather

James had a narrow escape last week when a doodlebug landed a few streets from him. The explosion affected his hearing for several days afterwards.

I have decided to resume my volunteer work. I shall be doing hospital visits to start with. These poor young men are so far from home, and they get no visitors. Hopefully, I can help ease their loneliness a little.

Let me know when you're next able to visit. We had such a short time together; I feel I've missed out on so much. You were in London for such a long time, then we hardly had a few months before you were gone again, and I sailed to the Cape. You were a young girl the last time we spent any significant tome together and now you're a beautiful, accomplished young woman. I hope you know how so very proud I am of you. You have shown outstanding courage, and grit, as they say.

Bella could imagine her mother's wistful smile as she wrote these words.

Stay safe and God speed, my dearest girl,
  Your affectionate mother

Bella folded the letter and slipped it into her bedside cabinet with the others. She got up and pulled the blackout curtains across the window, plunging the room into darkness. She lay back on her bed, listening to the sound of the wind blowing under the eaves. Her eyes were heavy. She'd just returned from a marathon stint ferrying Tempests, Spitfires and Hawker Hurricanes along the south coast. This was the first day she'd been back at Woodhead in almost a week, and she was looking forward to a hot bath, but first she needed a nap

She'd just dozed off when there was a knock at the door. Patty poked her head into the room.

'Are you awake?' she hissed.

Bella grunted and rolled onto her back, blinking in the late August sunlight streaming into the room.

'This just came for you,' Patty said, coming into the room, holding out a small brown envelope.

'A telegram?' Bella sat up, instantly alert as her heart began to pound. 'Oh, God, what's happened now?' she murmured, her thoughts going immediately to her family in Strawbridge. Although they were a good five miles from the city, it wasn't inconceivable that one of Hitler's flying bombs had veered off course and hit the village. With shaking hands, she ripped open the envelope and scanned the words. Her heart stopped and the blood drained from her face.

'Bella, what is it?' Patty crossed the room to sit beside her.

'It's Will,' Bella murmured, her eyes filling with tears. 'He's been shot down. He's in the Royal Victoria Hospital in Netley, seriously ill.' She choked on the words.

'Is he a relative?' Patty asked, gently stroking Bella's back Bella shook her head.

'A friend,' she whispered.

'He obviously means a lot to you,' Patty said. 'You must go to him.'

'I don't know,' Bella said. She felt unable to form a coherent thought. 'Should I?' She looked at Patty with red-rimmed eyes.

'If he's seriously hurt, it might be your only chance,' Patty said, her eyes sorrowful. 'I'll clear it with Briggs. Pack what you need. I'll drive you to the railway station.'

Bella nodded. She felt numb as she threw a few things into an overnight bag. She was grateful for Gilly for sending the telegram. How badly was he hurt? Her insides churned as she crossed the grass to the carpool where Patty was filling out the paperwork for the loan of the Jeep.

'Hop in,' she said, grabbing Bella's bag and stowing it in the back. 'If we hurry you should make the five-fifteen train. They spoke little on the drive. Bella was too anxious to make conversation, and Patty, sensing Bella's need to be alone with her thoughts, stayed quiet.

'Good luck,' she said, dropping Bella off outside the railways station in Glossop.

'Thanks,' whispered Bella. She grabbed her bag and made her way inside. The platform was bustling with soldiers and civilian commuters heading home after a day at the office. Bella joined the queue at the ticket office.

'A trip home to see the family, huh?' the elderly man in the ticket booth said jovially.

'Something like that,' Bella replied, stiffly. She paid and, taking her ticket, made her way over to the train. It was a long journey with several changes and lengthy delays along the way. She tried to sleep but she was plagued with worry over Will and terrified that she would get there too late. What if he didn't want to see her? She knew she had hurt him and, even now, she had nothing to offer him. The only thing she was sure of, as the train raced through the night, was that she needed to see him.

It was gone half past ten by the time the train pulled into Southampton Central station. Wearily, Bella disembarked and followed the other passengers along the platform to the waiting room. It was too late to go to her parent's home, so she decided to spend the night at the station and get a bus to the hospital first thing in the morning. Surely, if Will was so badly hurt, they would allow her in, irrespective of whether it was visiting hour or not.

After an uncomfortable night on the bench, Bella had a quick wash in the lady's rest room adjoining the waiting room and made her way to the bus stop. The next bus to the hospital at Netley was due in twenty minutes so she bought herself a bacon sandwich and a cup of weak tea from a roadside vendor and settled down on the wooden bench to wait.

It wasn't yet eight o'clock but already there was a lengthy queue outside the butcher's. Heinz Jewellers across the street was boarded up. The sign above the door had been graffitied over as to be almost illegible and anti-German slogans had been daubed across the boards in black paint.

The bus arrived on time, and forty minutes later Bella was

getting off at the end of the long drive. Though Bella had always known of the hospital's existence, she had never seen it before, and for a moment she could only stand and stare in awe at the vast, palace-like building with its turrets and domes set in immaculate grounds.

Her feet crunching on the gravel, Bella made her way towards the main entrance. Though it was just gone nine o'clock, several patients were seated on the wide terrace outside enjoying the summer morning. Some were in dressing gowns, others in uniform. All were smoking. They nodded and waved hello to Bella as she climbed the broad steps.

'Your chap's a lucky fellow having a beautiful girl such as yourself coming to visit,' one of them said, exhaling a cloud of pipe smoke.

'Yeah, wish I could be so fortunate,' said another, giving Bella a wink. 'My girl's all the way up in Coventry.' He grimaced, as if in pain, and rubbed his legs which were hidden beneath a blanket. His hands, Bella noticed, shook violently.

She smiled at them all and entered the cavernous hallway. The air smelled strongly of floor polish and disinfectant. Doctors and nurses walked purposefully up and down the wide corridors. Doors banged and voices called out. From the bowels of the hospital came the haunting sound of someone screaming.

'Don't be alarmed,' a nurse said, pausing as she came hurrying down the corridor, arms full of soiled bed sheets. 'It's only one of the patients in the asylum.' The nurse was in her mid to late forties, Bella surmised, with wisps of greying blonde hair escaping from her white headdress.

Bella felt a cold shiver run down her spine. Her father had been a patient in the asylum during the last war.

'Are you all right, dear?' the matron asked, her blue eyes clouded in concern. 'You've gone a bit pale. Would you like to sit down for a minute?' She motioned towards one of the many wooden benches lining the corridor.

'I'm fine, thank you,' Bella said, composing herself.

'You're a bit early for visiting,' matron said, frowning. 'Who are you here to see?'

'First Officer Mullens,' Bella said. 'I know it's not officially visiting hour, but I think . . . I think he's in a bad way. Please, may I see him?'

Matron bit her lip, thoughtfully. 'Are you a relative?' Bella nodded.

'Sister.'

Matron sighed. 'Very well. It won't hurt for you to spend a few minutes with him,' she said, her voice kind. The sympathy in her eyes made Bella's stomach lurch in panic.

'Is he . . . is he . . . that bad?'

Matron gave her a sad smile. 'Where there's life, there's always hope,' she said gently.

'Nurse, one moment, please.' She motioned to a young nurse hurrying passed. 'Can you take this lady to Somerset Ward please. Bed three.'

'Yes, Matron.' The nurse gave Bella a tentative smile. She was around Bella's age, with mousy-brown hair and spectacles that kept sliding down her thin nose. 'If you'll follow me, Miss.' She inclined her head towards a flight of stairs. Bella thanked the matron and followed the nurse up the wide, curving Victorian staircase. Despite the August sun streaming in through the many windows, she felt cold. Dust motes swirled in the air, as nurse Collins led Bella along a wide, draughty corridor. Several patients were seated in the window seats gazing out over the hospital grounds, the silver-grey waters of the Solent glimmering in the distance.

'Here we are, Miss,' Nurse Collins, said, pausing outside a partially open doorway. She pushed the door all the way open.

A dark-haired nurse several years Nurse Collins' senior looked up from her desk. 'Yes?' she said, regarding Bella sternly.

'Sister, this lady is here to see the patient in bed three. Matron said it was all right.'

The sister had opened her mouth to object. Now she snapped her lips shut, glaring at Bella with annoyance.

'This is highly irregular,' she snorted. 'Very well. First Officer Mullens is very poorly. There's someone with him already but you may have five minutes with the patient and not a second longer.' She turned to glower at the young nurse. 'You may return to your duties.'

'Yes, sister.' Nurse Collins nodded at Bella, her smile laced with sympathy as she slipped out of the door.

Taking a deep breath, Bella took a few tentative steps down the ward. There were ten beds on either side of the long ward. Several patients were sitting up reading or just staring into space. Others were sleeping. One man, his face wreathed in bandages, was groaning softly to himself. Still others had the curtains drawn around their beds. Bed three was one of them. Bella hesitated. Her pulse was racing and she was dreading what she might find on the other side of the curtain. Gathering all her courage, she gently took hold of the faded blue fabric and pushed it aside. Though she had prepared herself for the worst, it was still a shock to see Will lying so still and lifeless. His face was the colour of day-old milk, and his breathing came in rasping gasps. She clung to the curtain, her gaze so transfixed on his face she didn't notice that someone was seated beside him.

'Bella?' Dazed, Bella turned her head slightly.

'Mother?' Her brow furrowed in confusion. 'What are you doing here?'

'I'm here in my role as hospital visitor,' Alice said, getting to her feet and offering Bella her chair. 'Here, sit down. It's a shock, seeing him like this, I know.'

'Is he . . . is he?' Fear kept her rooted to the spot.

'The doctor said he's holding his own.' Her mother said, gently. 'He's suffering from internal injuries. All we can do is hope and pray he'll pull through.'

'Oh, Will,' Bella whispered. A sob caught in her throat as she reached out and gently stroked his cheek. Apart from his colour, outwardly he appeared unhurt.

'His breath smells bad,' Alice said, as Bella leaned over him. 'That's because of the internal bleeding.' She stood behind Bella, resting a comforting hand on her daughter's shoulder.

'How did you know?'

'Gilly sent me a telegram. I came straight here from the station. One of the matrons gave me permission to visit for a few minutes.'

'That was probably Dora,' Alice said, with a smile. 'She's an old friend of mine. She and her family left Strawbridge when you were little, so you probably don't remember them.' Alice sighed, her smile fading. 'Their son, Frank, was killed in Normandy on D-Day.'

'I'm sorry to hear that,' responded Bella automatically. She couldn't take her eyes off Will. Her chest felt tight and for a moment she couldn't breathe. If Will died . . . A strangled sob escaped from her throat and she clapped her hand to her mouth, stifling the wave of emotion that threatened to engulf her.

'You are still in love with him, aren't you?' Alice said quietly. Bella nodded. 'Oh, darling.'

'Did the reason you and Will separated have something to do with your father?' Alice asked, breaking the short silence.

Bella's head jerked up in surprise, her tear-filled gaze meeting her mother's warm, brown eyes.

'Did he tell you Will is your brother?' asked her mother softly.

'You know?' Bella whispered hoarsely, her mind a whirling mass of conflicting emotions. 'If you knew, then why . . .' She swallowed. 'Why didn't you tell me?'

'Let's go and get a cup of tea,' Alice said, gathering up her gloves and hat. 'It's time we left Will to sleep,' she said, as Bella returned her troubled gaze to his bed. 'We don't want to provoke the wrath of Sister Cox by staying too long.' Her tone softened. 'You can come back later. Visiting starts at eleven.'

Reluctantly, Bella got up and followed her mother through the maze of corridors and down the stairs.

CHAPTER THIRTY-THREE

The canteen was relatively quiet at that time of morning. Just a few tables were taken up by medical staff grabbing a quick cup of tea between shifts. Bella followed Alice to a corner table, her mind racing as she tried to make sense of the fact that her mother clearly knew Will was her brother. Had she always known? Or had her father, terrified Bella might reveal his shameful secret, decided to confess all?

She clasped her hands together to stop them shaking while Alice went to fetch the tea. She couldn't stop shivering and it wasn't because of the draughty air.

'Here you are, love.' Alice set a cup of steaming tea in front of Bella. She watched the tendrils of steam curling into the air, making no move to take a sip.

Her mother wrapped her hands around her teacup, her face drawn. Bella thought how tired she looked, all of a sudden.

'When did you find out?' Bella asked dully.

'About your father and Leah? I've always known.'

Bella recoiled in shock. 'Why didn't you tell me?' she cried. 'Why did you let me fall for Will when all along you knew we couldn't be together?' 'Bella,' Alice said, placing her cup back on its saucer. 'Will is not your brother.'

Bella frowned. 'What do you mean . . .'

'Oh, he's your father's son, all right,' Alice said, her gaze focused somewhere over Bella's shoulder, as if she were avoiding Bella's gaze.

'I don't understand.' Bella's throat constricted so tight, she could hardly swallow. 'You're not making sense.'

'I knew the minute we heard the news that Leah had given birth,' Alice said, as if she hadn't heard Bella's question. 'Your father went snow white. He looked terrified and I knew in that instant that he was the father of Leah's baby boy.'

'Then, how can . . . ?' The blood drained from Bella's face as comprehension dawned. 'Are you telling me Father isn't my father?' She frowned, feeling sick. 'You were unfaithful, too?'

'No.' Alice said quickly. 'Bella, sweetheart.' Alice sighed deeply. 'This will come as a shock to you, darling, which is why I never wanted you to know the truth' She reached across and clasped Bella's hand. Bella snatched her hand away as if burned. Folding her hands in her lap, she glared at her mother. She was terrified of what she was about to hear.

'Your father was away when you and Arthur were born.'

For a few seconds Alice fell silent, her mind relieving the moment her two precious children became part of her life. 'Darling, you must understand, I couldn't love you any more than I do. I suffered several miscarriages. I didn't believe I'd ever carry a child to term.'

'What are you saying?' Bella whispered in bewilderment. 'That Arthur and I aren't yours?'

'Oh, Bella,' Alice said, her face a picture of anguish. 'It was an awful, stormy night when I gave birth to Arthur with only my housekeeper, Mrs Hurst, to help.' Alice looked at Bella, her eyes pleading for her understanding. 'Pearl, a local gypsy woman, turned up with this motherless baby girl.' Alice's eyes filled with tears. 'You were the most beautiful baby I'd ever seen. Pearl begged me to take you, to pass you off as my own. How could I say no? I was already in love with you.'

'Father doesn't know?' Bella said woodenly. Alice shook her head.

'Only me, Mrs Hurst and Pearl knew the truth.' Alice gave Bella a tentative smile. 'I'm sorry, sweetheart. This must be such a shock for you.'

'You're not my mother,' Bella said. Bile burned the back of her throat. 'Arthur isn't my brother.' The thought brought with it a stab of pain. 'Will and Arthur are brothers.' She massaged her temples. Her whole world had somehow tilted on its axis. 'Everything I've always believed is a lie,' she said, slowly raising her gaze to meet her mother's anxious face.

'Bella, please . . .'

'Why didn't you tell me?'

'I couldn't, darling. For a start, your father believes you are his. He dotes on you, Bella, you know that and . . .'

'And?' demanded Bella, regarding her mother coolly.

'And, I was terrified that if anyone found out the truth they would take you away from me.'

Bella glared at her mother. 'Bella, please,' Alice cried. 'Can you forgive me?'

'I don't know.' Bella pushed back her chair. 'I need to be alone. I'm going to walk in the grounds and then I'm going to see Will.'

'Will you be home later?' asked Alice, biting her lip anxiously. Bella shook her head.

'I'll book into a hotel. I want to be by myself. I need to think.'

'You've had a terrible shock, Bella,' Alice said, getting to her feet. 'But just know this, I've loved you as my own from the moment I saw you. Your father loves you, and so does Arthur. We're your family. Nothing has changed.'

'Oh, yes it has, Mother,' Bella said in a strangled voice. 'Everything has changed.'

Picking up her gasmask and her cap, she turned and strode from the canteen, oblivious to the admiring glances she was attracting from some of the male patrons.

Some time later, Bella sat at Will's bedside. There had been no change in his condition but the Sister in charge, a Sister

Phillips, a middle-aged nurse of about fifty whose cheery manner was in stark contrast to her dour predecessor, informed Bella that the longer Will hung on the better his chances.

Sitting beside him, holding his hand, Bella tried to get her thoughts into perspective. Finding out her parents weren't really her parents had come as a huge shock. But perhaps the worst of it was the knowledge that Arthur wasn't her blood brother. She loved him so much, it hurt. This man lying still on the bed was blood related to her brother. She studied Will's pale features curiously. Now she knew the truth, she could see the similarities between him and Arthur and her heart contracted painfully.

'Oh, Will,' she murmured. 'It's all such a mess.' She watched the rapid rise and fall of his chest, listening to the gasping, sucking sounds with every tortured breath.

'I'm so sorry I hurt you,' she said, a single tear trickling down her cheek. She brushed it away. 'I broke off our engagement because I truly believed it was the right thing to do.' She gave a harsh laugh. 'If you live, and please God, you will, I shall explain everything. I just hope you can forgive me for breaking your heart.' Another tear snaked its way down her cheek and suddenly she was sobbing. Great, gasping sobs that wracked her body and brought staff nurse Smith hurrying over, thinking that Will had taken a turn for the worse.

'There, there, love,' staff nurse Smith said, patting Bella between the shoulder blades. 'Don't upset yourself so. He's stable for the moment. Look, let me get you a cup of tea. That'll calm you down a bit.' She gave Bella an encouraging smile. 'Come on, love. It doesn't do to upset the patients, does it?'

Bella shook her head and wiped her eyes.

'That's better,' the staff nurse said. 'Now, I'll get that cup of tea.' She let the curtain drop. Bella blew her nose, as she heard staff nurse Smith say, 'First Officer Mullens? Yes, sir. He's just here.' The curtain was yanked aside to reveal a tall, well-built man that Bella guessed to be in his late forties or early fifties. His thick grey hair was pulled back in a ponytail and his skin was tanned and leathery. He held a wide-brimmed hat in his hands, a pheasant feather tucked into a leather band around the crown. He let out a short gasp, his gaze resting on Will lying in the bed. He ran a hand across his face, his eyes widening as he noticed Bella for the first time.

'Sorry, Miss,' he said, his voice gruff with emotion. 'I didn't mean to intrude.'

'Not at all,' Bella said, hastily tucking her handkerchief in her pocket. 'I'm Bella Roberts.'

'Joshua Mullens,' he said, with a slow nod. 'I'm Will's dad.' He moved closer and stood beside the bed, a thousand emotions flitting across his face as he watched his son fighting for every breath.

'Bella,' he said, at length. 'You the one what broke my boy's heart?' he asked, with no hint of anger. Bella lowered her gaze and nodded.

'Whatever your disagreement,' said Joshua slowly, 'it hardly matters in a place like this, does it?' He gave Bella a sideways glance. 'You obviously still care for my boy?'

'I do, sir.' Bella's voice faltered. 'I love him.' She turned her gaze back to Will. 'I never stopped loving him.'

'Here we are,' said a voice. The curtain flaps parted as staff nurse Smith appeared with two cups of tea. 'I brought you one as well, Mr Mullens,' she smiled. Thanking her, Bella and Joshua took their cups of tea. 'I'll leave you to enjoy your visit,' the staff nurse said, retreating behind the curtains.

Joshua fetched another chair and he and Bella sat in silence, listening to the sound of hushed conversation drifting from the ward beyond Will's bed. Someone was sobbing quietly.

Bella studied Joshua surreptitiously. She rubbed her forehead. She had so many questions that she needed answers to, but she had no intention of speaking to her mother any time soon. Her adoptive mother, she amended sourly, as a fresh wave of grief and disbelief washed over her.

'Will told me you're a pilot,' Joshua said, breaking the lengthy silence.

'Yes, sir,' replied Bella.

Joshua nodded. 'Good for you. I'm the gardener at Wilton House. It got requisitioned at the start of the war. My daughter, Tabitha, is stationed abroad. She doesn't know about Will . . .' His words petered out and he rubbed a large, course hand across his eyes. Bella could understand how he felt. The emotional stress was so exhausting that even just making small talk seemed too much effort. She, too, felt drained of all energy.

The curtains parted again, admitting a stern-faced doctor. He glanced at Bella, then turned his attention to Joshua, who stood up immediately.

'You're the father?' the doctor asked brusquely.

'Yes, sir,' Joshua said, clearly in awe of the other man. The doctor glanced down at his chart. 'I'm afraid your son has suffered a good deal of damage to his internal organs. Kidneys, liver, spleen are all damaged and there is significant internal bleeding which accounts for the substantial bruising.'

'What can be done?' Joshua asked, gruffly.

'Rest is the best cure at the moment,' the doctor replied, without any hint of compassion. 'We'll continue to monitor the situation. If we feel an operation would be in the patient's best interest, we'll reassess the situation then.'

'When will he wake up, doctor?' Joshua asked, his gaze straying back to his son.

The doctor shrugged. 'It's difficult to say. The patient suffered trauma to the head as well. He may never wake up. It's a waiting game, I'm afraid.' He nodded and took his leave, leaving Bella and Joshua feeling more anxious than before.

After a while Joshua got to his feet. 'I can't just sit here,' he said, shaking his head. 'I'll go mad just waiting for each and every breath,' he said, his voice hoarse with the effort to contain his emotions. 'It's quite a journey for me,' he said. 'I won't be able to come very often.' He laid a heavy hand on Bella's shoulder. 'If the worse should happen, well, it gives me some measure of comfort to know you'll be here for him.' His face crumpled and he turned away as he fought to regain his composure.'

'Goodbye, Miss Bella. I'm sorry we didn't meet in happier circumstances.'

'Goodbye, Mr Mullens.'

Bella turned back to Will, blinking back her tears, swallowing the huge lump in her throat. Her fingers closed over his. His hand was so cold. She rubbed it, willing some warmth into his cold stiff fingers.

She wasn't sure how long she would be allowed away from Woodhead. She had compassionate leave but they'd only allow her a week, perhaps two at a push before she'd be expected to resume her duties. The thought of leaving Will again filled her with dread and she refused to think about it now. God willing, he would wake up and be on the road to recovery before she had to think about going back.

She was making her way along the corridor at the end of the visiting hour when she heard footsteps coming up behind her. She turned to see the matron she'd spoken to earlier that day, smiling at her.

'Hello, you're the young lady who was asking after Flight Officer Mullens?'

'Yes, Matron,' Bella nodded.

'Then I'm glad I caught you.' The woman's eyes clouded and her smiled slipped. 'Will's mother was a dear friend of mine. Will and my Frank played together as babies.' She took a quivering breath, her eyes shining with unshed tears. 'I want to do whatever I can to help that young man and if your visits help him to recover then you may visit him as often as you like. I'll clear it with the ward staff.'

'Thank you, Matron,' Bella said, touched by the woman's obvious concern. 'I'm just on my way to the canteen for some dinner, then I'll go back.'

'Good girl,' Matron said, smiling. 'Talk to him. Let him know you're there. Who knows, he might be able to hear you.'

CHAPTER THIRTY-FOUR

Bella stayed at Will's bedside from first thing in the morning until late in the evening. The only time she left him was to spend a penny or visit the canteen. Towards the end of the first week, she'd been delighted to find Gilly and Beryl sitting at Will's bedside when she returned from grabbing a quick sandwich in the hospital canteen.

'It's so good to see you both,' she squealed softly, hugging her two friends warmly. 'You have no idea how much I've missed you.'

'Us too,' Gilly said, returning Bella's embrace. 'We figured you'd be here so we thought we'd come along to surprise you.'

'We wanted to see Will, too, of course,' said Beryl. They all turned their attention to the man in the bed.

'How is he?' asked Gilly. 'Has there been any improvement?'

'Not really,' Bella replied, deflating slightly. 'It's a case of wait and see, I'm afraid.' She fetched an extra chair, placing it close to Will's head, and sat down. 'Do you know what happened? I know he was shot down, but why didn't he bale out?'

Gilly and Beryl exchanged glances. 'He had a crew aboard,' Gilly explained. 'They were on a mission to fly supplies into France.' She pulled a face. 'Will volunteered. He had a crew of three on a De Haviland Flamingo, as well as four military personnel who were joining the fight. According to the official report, Will successfully delivered the military personnel and the supplies, and they were on their way back when they came under fire. They were hit pretty badly but they managed to limp back to England. This is the account of one of the chaps who bailed out. As soon as they were over the English coast, Will ordered them to bail out, which they did. All except Will. They were over Dover and he was worried that if he bailed out the plane could crash over the town, killing innocent civilians.' Gilly shrugged. Bella blinked back tears. She was clinging tightly to Will's hand.

'The air accident investigators believe it was Will's intention to fly the plane away from any built-up area and bail out when the plane no longer posed a threat, but the damage was too great. He'd just cleared the outskirts of the town when he lost control. Witnesses say the plane nose-dived and ploughed into a field. Thank God it didn't ignite, otherwise he'd have been incinerated before anyone could've got to him.'

Bella closed her eyes. The image of Will in the burning wreckage of his plane was too awful to imagine.

'It's a miracle he survived as it is,' Beryl added softly. 'The front of the plane was a mangled wreck. He was bashed up pretty badly.'

'I really hope he pulls through,' Gilly said.

'The doctors say every day he's alive is a positive sign. That and the fact he's breathing on his own.'

'You know you have all our love and prayers, don't you?' Beryl said, as they made ready to leave.

'I do know' Bella said, managing a small smile. 'Thank you.' She gave Beryl's hand a squeeze. Since the death of her fiancé back in June, Beryl seemed somewhat diminished. Even her letters to Bella had lost their wit and humour. Why was life so cruel? she wondered, as she hugged her two friends goodbye.

'Keep us updated on his progress, won't you?' Gilly said, pausing with the curtain flap in one hand.

'I will do.' Bella sank back into her chair, Will's laboured breathing loud on her ears. She gently cupped his hand in hers, contemplating the fact that she must leave him soon. Flight Lieutenant Briggs had confirmed her two weeks compassionate leave and her first week was already at an end. She sighed. How could she bear to leave him again?

She closed her eyes, letting the noise of the ward wash over her. She wondered if her mother was at the hospital doing her volunteer visiting. She hadn't seen or spoken to her since that day she'd dropped her bombshell. Bella had taken a room in Netley on the eastern shore of Southampton Water. Her window looked over the shingle beach to Hythe and Fawley.

She knew her absence would be hurting her mother, and her heart ached to see Arthur, but she couldn't bring herself to go home just yet. The hours she was spending at Will's bedside gave her ample time to think and her mother's revelation kept going around in her head. Right now, she was angry with both her parents. Her father had let her down by being unfaithful, but her mother had lied to her, her entire life. It was a betrayal she felt she might never recover from. What hurt more than anything was the realization that Arthur wasn't really her brother. Believing herself and Arthur to be twins, she felt closer to him than she had to anyone else and the sense of loss was almost too much to bear.

She was still struggling to get her head around the idea that Will and Arthur were brothers, she mused, blinking back tears of anger and self-pity. A feeling akin to jealousy tugged at her heart. If Will pulled through, and, once he knew the truth and formed a relationship with Arthur, would Bella always feel like she was on the outside looking in? With so many conflicting emotions racing around her mind, it was no wonder she was exhausted by the time she crawled into bed at night.

She lay in the darkness, listening to the distant guns and the waves pounding the shingle beach, anxiety over Will keeping her awake, despite the fact she was so tired she could barely stand upright. She was terrified he would die in the night and every morning; her nerves were in turmoil until she reached the ward and saw the reassuring smiles of the nurses she'd come to know so well.

*

It was the first week of September and there was a definite autumnal feel to the air as she walked the mile to the hospital. The shrubs were swathed in spider webs, the fine gossamer threads glistening with dew in the morning sunlight. A light breeze blew across the grounds, rustling the leaves that were already on the turn, and blowing faded rose petals across the damp lawn. Gulls screeched in a clear blue sky. The peaceful tranquillity was broken by the drone of approaching aircraft and she glanced up into the sky, shielding her eyes with her hand as the RAF fighter planes flew overhead, heading for France.

As always, the hospital was a hive of activity. Those patients able to leave their beds were wandering the wide corridors or sitting in the window seats smoking or playing cards. Orderlies brushed past her, pushing patients in wheelchairs and beds. Doctors barked orders and doors swung open and shut, snippets of conversations escaping momentarily to meld with the cacophony of the corridors.

Many of the patients were American servicemen and they whistled and chatted to Bella as she made her way to Somerset Ward. There was a different nurse on duty when Bella pushed through the doors, someone she hadn't encountered before.

'May I help you?' she said, looking up from her desk in surprise. She looked to be about thirty with a round, pleasant face.

'I'm here to see First Officer Mullens, bed three,' Bella said quickly. 'Matron Gardener gave me special permission to stay as long as I wish.'

'Oh, yes, I was informed.' She glanced down the row of beds. Following her gaze, Bella's heart lurched in shock. Will's bed was empty. It had been stripped down to the mattress. Feeling lightheaded with fear, she reached out to grab the back of a nearby chair before she fell. Yellow dots swam before her eyes. She was dimly aware that the nurse was speaking but she could hear nothing above the blood roaring in her ears.

'Are you all right, dear?' the nurse asked, with concern, rising from her chair. 'Can I get you a glass of water?'

The roaring noise cleared a little and Bella shook her head.

'If you're sure?' the nurse said, regarding her doubtfully. 'As I was saying, patient Mullens was moved to Wessex Ward late last night.'

'Moved?' Bella almost collapsed with relief. 'He's just moved wards? He's not dead?'

The nurse gave her a funny look. 'Dead? Oh, no, dear. Quite the opposite in fact. He regained consciousness last night so he's been moved to one of the neurological wards to assess whether he's suffered any damage to his brain.'

'May I see him?' Bella whispered, hardly able to grasp the unexpected, good news.

'Third floor, second door on the left,' the nurse smiled.

Bella thanked her and hurried up the flight of stairs to the third floor. This was where patients with varying degrees of brain and neurological injuries were brought. She paused on the top step. This would have been where her father would have spent his time at the hospital after the Great

War. Suppressing a shiver, she approached the door the nurse had mentioned and knocked. The door was opened almost immediately by a stout staff nurse with a lined, weathered complexion, and warm brown eyes. Tendrils of grey hair poked from beneath her cap as she regarded Bella quizzically.

'I'm here to see First Officer Mullens,' she stammered.

The staff nurse smiled. 'Of course. Matron told me you'd be along first thing.' She opened the door wider, affording Bella a view of the bright ward. It had the familiar layout with ten beds down either side but, instead of the patients lying silent in their beds, the majority of them were sitting up, chatting to their neighbour or reading. Two men, one with a bandaged arm, were seated at a small table playing cards. A wireless was playing softly in the background.

'Excellent timing, too,' the staff nurse said, stepping aside to let Bella through the door. 'We've just cleared away breakfast and it'll be a while before the doctors make their rounds. You'll find patient Mullens down the end, last bed on the left.'

Bella thanked her, but she hadn't needed the directions. She had spotted Will the moment she'd stepped onto the ward. He was sitting up, reading a paperback. Bella started walking towards him, the soles of her shoes squeaking softly on the scrubbed lino. The other patients smiled and said hello as she passed by the end of their beds. Will casually turned his head, and she saw the surprise register on his face as he laid his book face down on his bedside cabinet. His eyes never left her face as she walked the last few steps to his bedside.

'Bella?' he said, blinking as if he couldn't quite believe what his eyes were seeing.

'Hello, Will,' Bella said softly. For a few moments they could only stare at each other as she watched the conflicting emotions flash across Will's face.

'Did you visit me while I was unconscious?' he asked, his brow furrowed. 'My memory's a bit foggy but I thought I heard your voice.' He gave a rasping chuckle. His breathing still sounded laboured, but some measure of colour had returned to his cheeks. 'I thought I was dreaming.'

'It wasn't a dream,' replied Bella, softly drawing up a chair. 'I visited you every day.'

It's lovely to see you,' Will said, his brow furrowed. He winced. 'Sorry, I'm still a bit tender.'

'Have they said anything more about your injuries?' Bella asked, her mind whirling. How much of what she'd said to Will could he remember?

'I've had a lot of internal bruising, and I developed pleurisy caused by trauma to my chest wall, which is why my breathing is so bad.' He paused, wheezing loudly as he fought to catch his breath. 'Now I've regained consciousness, the doctor's satisfied I'll make a full recovery, though I'll probably be stuck in here for a while yet.'

Bella's eyes filled with tears. 'I was so worried I would lose you,' she said softly.

Will stared at her earnestly. 'Why did you come,' he said. Bella turned her gaze to the window. Southampton Water sparkled in the early morning sunlight. Two large ships were

351

anchored at the hospital jetty where ambulances were waiting to ferry injured soldiers back to the hospital.

Bella reached for his hand. 'Will, I need to explain …'

'You just cut me off without an explanation,' Will said, roughly. 'Why?'

'Bella sighed. 'This is going to sound crazy, but I thought you were my brother.'

'What?' Will stared at her, dumbfounded.

'That weekend we went to visit my father, he confessed to having an affair. He told me you were his son.' She looked Will full in the face. 'How could I have told you the truth and besmirch your mother's memory? I couldn't explain why I had to break off our engagement. That's why I left.'

'You should have told me,' Will said softly. 'It would have broken my heart, but at least I would have had an explanation. Just leaving me wondering was the worst. I kept trying to work out what I'd done wrong.'

'I'm sorry.' She inhaled. 'The thing is, I'm *not* your sister.'

'Will's brows dipped over his nose. 'What? I thought you just said …'

'Samuel isn't my father, nor is Alice my mother.' Bella shook his head. 'I know. I'm still trying to make sense of it all.' 'So,' Will said, rubbing his temples. 'We're not related after all?'

'No.' Bella replied with a rueful smile. 'I can't believe my mother lied to me all my life. She lied to my father, to Arthur.' She shook her head. 'I feel as though my whole world has fallen apart. Why didn't she just tell my father she wanted to adopt me? He would have agreed, surely. Why did she pretend I was hers? If she'd told me the truth from the start, we might have been married by now.'

'We would have been married by now,' Will wheezed. 'Arthur is my brother,' he said slowly. 'Wow!' His expression darkened. 'Your father is clearly not interested in acknowledging me as his son, which I'm not bothered about. As far as I'm concerned, my dad is my dad and always will be. He adored my mother and he's always been a good father to me. I'll never let on to him that I know the truth. It would break his heart.'

'I wonder if my mother.' She paused. 'Alice,' she amended, 'realized how much trouble her decision would cause in the future,' Bella mused.

'Bella,' Will said, gently. 'She's still your mother, and I doubt she'd have imagined it would ever have mattered.'

'I feel so deceived,' Bella said. 'And it hurts. My whole life has been a lie.'

'Look, Bella . . .' The rest of Will's words were lost in a coughing fit. He leaned forward, his chest heaving as he fought to draw breath, the hacking cough sending shuddering waves through his body.

'Let me get you some water,' Bella said anxiously, reaching for the water jug on the bedside cabinet.

A couple of nurses bustled over and several of the men in the beds nearby watched with sympathy. One of the nurses gently rubbed Will's back until the coughing fit gradually subsided.

'Thank you,' he gasped, taking the glass from Bella,

raising it to his lips with a shaking hand. His breathing was ragged and his face had turned the colour of a ripe plum but gradually his breathing became more regular, and his cheeks retuned to a more natural colour.

'Sorry about that,' he said, handing Bella his empty glass. She put it back on the table and sat back in her chair, her brow furrowed.

'That looked scary.'

'Will grimaced. 'It's not pleasant. I feel like my lungs are coming up my throat. This is only the second time it's happened. I had a bad coughing fit just after I regained consciousness. The doctor isn't concerned. He said it should settle down within a few days.'

'I hope it does. Poor you.'

Will grinned. 'How long can you stay?' he asked.

'One of the matrons gave me special permission to stay all day while you were so bad. Now that you're no longer at death's door, I expect I shall have to adhere to the visiting hours like everyone else.' Her face fell. 'I'm due to return to Derbyshire at the end of the week.'

'I expected as much.' Will said, with a rueful grin, as a nurse came over with a cup of tea for Bella.

'Time for your medication, First Officer Mullens,' she said jovially, handing him a small cup containing a several pills. 'Doctor will be doing his rounds in the next half an hour, Miss,' she said, giving Bella an apologetic smile. 'So I'm afraid I shall have to ask you to leave. Have your tea first, then you can come back later. Visiting is from eleven to twelve and again from two until four.'

'Thank you.' Bella shot Will an 'I told you so' smile. She drank her tea slowly, as they chatted, not relishing the prospect of having to leave him, even for a couple of hours.

'I'll be back later,' she said, when she got up to leave twenty minutes later.

'I'll be watching for you,' said Will, giving her hand an affectionate squeeze.

Bella hesitated, then gave him a quick kiss on the cheek. 'See you soon,' she said, walking away quickly before Will could respond.

CHAPTER THIRTY-FIVE

Bella spent every visiting hour at Will's bedside, and they soon fell back into their comfortable routine. The more time Bella spent with Will, the harder she knew it would be to leave him come the end of the week. She was dreading it.

At Will's request she'd sent a telegram to Joshua letting him know Will was recovering well and Will had written to him, hopeful that his father might manage another visit in the next few weeks, as it would be at least another month before Will was discharged.

Sometimes, some of the other patients would join them and they'd play cards and chat. The men were very impressed to learn that Bella was a pilot. There were two RAF pilots on the ward, Bill and Chris, and two Americans. All four had been shot down over France and had been evacuated back to England.

Troop ships laden with wounded servicemen continued

to dock at Southampton, and trainloads of the injured arrived at the hospital daily. At night, sitting in her room overlooking Southampton Water, Bella could hear the distant guns.

Now she woke to the familiar scream of the air raid siren. Groaning, she dragged herself from her bed and pulled on her dressing gown, feeling with her feet for her slippers that had slid under the bed. She could hear hurried footsteps on the stairs, and her landlady, Elsie Forward, calling to her husband to grab the cat.

Bella opened her bedroom door and joined the other residents on their way downstairs. The Anderson shelter was at the bottom of the garden. Elsie led the way, the moon lighting their path through the vegetable beds to the corrugated metal shelter which was half-buried with soil.

'Come on. Get inside, quick,' she barked, pushing the door open. With the siren wailing in her ears, Bella ducked through the opening, wrinkling her nose as her nostrils were assailed by the familiar damp, earthy smell. There was barely enough room for the four tenants, Elsie and her husband, James, a small overweight man who came panting down the path, carrying a large, ginger cat. They huddled in the dark, wrapped in blankets to ward off the damp chill, ears straining for the sound of approaching aircraft, or the dreaded doodlebugs.

Bella pulled her blanket tighter around her shoulders. No one spoke much. Outside the siren continued its high-pitched wailing. Pickles, the cat, purred noisily somewhere in the darkness. Elsie refused to light a candle in case any light escaped, giving them away to the planes high above their heads, so there was nothing to do except sit and wait.

Bella heard the drone of the planes above the siren, the telltale sound of German engines. She could almost hear their collective intake of breath.

'Please keep going, please keep going,' muttered Eliza Simmons, a young schoolteacher who boarded with the Forwards during term time.

The planes were overhead now. The stale air inside the Anderson shelter seemed to vibrate with the steady throb of the engines. Bella held her breath. Lately the planes had been ignoring Southampton and heading for London. As the noise of the engines dwindled, she exhaled, her shoulders sagging. Someone giggled nervously. They continued to sit in silence for another hour before the All Clear sounded.

Blinking in the moonlight. Bella made her way up the garden path. At the back door, she stared up at the star-lit sky, wondering whether there would be another air raid warning when the bombers made their way back to France.

'Excuse me, Miss Roberts,' Elsie said. 'You're blocking the doorway.'

'I'm sorry.' Bella yawned. 'I was just wondering if we'll have another warning tonight, what with it being so clear.'

'I hope not,' Cathy, one of the tenants, said grouchily. 'I'm exhausted. This is the third time this week I've had my beauty sleep interrupted.'

'Stay in bed next time, then,' said James, letting go of the cat. It shot between Bella's legs into the kitchen, disappearing up the stairs.

'I might just do that,' said the woman, haughtily. 'My old mum always said, if she was going to die, she'd rather die warm in her bed than in a cold miserable shelter.'

'She still going, then, your mum?' asked James as they filed up the staircase.

'She died in the Blitz,' Cathy replied, sombrely. 'She was sheltering under the stairs when our house took a direct hit. The ARP warden told us she'd have been killed instantly.'

'That's some comfort, I suppose,' said James dourly. Everyone parted ways on the landing, each to their own room.

Bella quietly shut her door and groped her way over to her bed. Throwing off her gown and slippers, she slid under the covers. She had two days left with Will before she was due to report back to Woodhead. She closed her eyes but she couldn't sleep. She was still struggling with her mother's deceit. She hadn't contacted her family since that first day, but she was missing Arthur, and her mother. Angrily she rolled onto her side. How could she forgive her mother? She'd been lied to every single day of her life. If Bella had never fallen in love with Will, would her mother ever have told her the truth? She doubted it. Her mother's deceit was like a dull ache in her heart that wouldn't let up. She thought about it all the time, even when she was with Will.

Dear Will. She smiled. He didn't seem at all phased by the fact that Samuel was his father. He'd been lied to as well, yet he didn't seem to care. As far as he was concerned, his mother had done what was best for him, and that was to allow him to believe Joshua was his dad. Bella couldn't understand how he could be so accepting of the situation when she was being driven mad by it.

She tossed and turned, unable to sleep. Some time in the early hours the air raid siren sounded again but was followed almost immediately by the All Clear, and she found out the following morning that the bombers had taken a different route home.

The milk she'd bought the previous day had gone off overnight, so, after washing it down the kitchen sink and rinsing out the bottle, she popped into a nearby café to order some toast and a mug of tea.

A group of workmen seated at a nearby table were talking about the recent V-2 rocket attacks on London, and Bella's thoughts went to her cousin Benjy. She hoped he was safe. She set her cup in its saucer with such force, tea sloshed over the checked tablecloth as she let out an involuntary gasp. Her cousin Benjy, Great-Aunt Eleanor, her Grandma Lily, none of these people were her blood relations. She pressed her fingers to her forehead, overwhelmed by a flood of nausea. Everyone she loved and cared for, and none of them really belonged to her. She felt sick. She pushed away her plate of half-eaten toast. Just the sight of it curdled her stomach. Pushing back her chair, she grabbed her cap and handbag and left the café, a sob riding in her throat. Walking quickly, she crossed the road, and onto the shingle. Bending double, she let out an anguished cry, gulping great breaths of salty air as tears threatened to swamp her. Huge, shuddering sobs wracked her body.

'Are you all right, Miss?' A postman called, pulling up on his bicycle. Bella held up her hand to ward him off. 'If you're sure, Miss?' the postman said, sounding doubtful. 'My condolences.'

He clearly thinks I've suffered a terrible loss, thought Bella, mopping at the tears streaming down her face, which I suppose I have. She sank onto the damp shingle, oblivious to the cool wind stinging her wet cheeks. She felt bereft and totally alone.

Wrapping her arms around her knees, she stared out through the coils of barbed wire at the grey water lapping up the beach. A seagull perched on a concrete block, eyeing her beadily. The waves lapping the shore were tinged with black and slick with oil. Several dead seabirds floated in the greasy foam. A thick mist was rolling in, shrouding the sea. The Isle of Wight had disappeared, engulfed by the fog.

'Oi,' shouted a voice behind her. 'Can't you read the signs? Get off the beach!'

Bella turned to see a stern-faced ARP warden striding towards her. She got to her feet, brushing sand and bits of broken shells from her damp skirt.

'I'm sorry,' she gasped, mortified.

The warden's expression softened. 'Had some bad news, have you?' he said, nodding knowingly as he took in Bella's swollen, red-rimmed eyes and tear-stained cheeks. 'Better get off the beach, love,' he said, kindly. 'You don't want to set off a mine now, do you? Get yourself off home, love,' he said, his tone laden with sympathy.

Bella nodded and blew her nose. It was still an hour until visiting time, so she took a walk along the sea front. The fog was moving in quickly now, obliterating everything in its path. She heard the blast of the foghorn through the swirling greyness.

At least the bad weather would keep the dreaded doodle-bugs away, she thought, popping into a newsagent's to buy Will a newspaper and a magazine. Now that his health was improving, his biggest problem was boredom.

The bus's headlights barely made a dent in the thick fog as it trundled along the streets of Netley to the hospital. It swirled around Bella, damp and cold, muffling her footsteps as she made her way up the gravel driveway. As always, the hospital was bustling. There must have been a new influx of patients from France, for the corridors were teeming with soldiers on stretchers and wheelchairs awaiting attention, while harassed-looking medical staff ran back and forth between wards.

Bella made her way up to Will's ward. Taking a deep breath, she composed herself and pushed open the door. Her eyes went straight down the ward to where Will's bed was, and she stopped in her tracks. A pretty nurse was leaning over him, her face animated as she gently brushed a lock of Will's dark hair from his forehead. Rooted to the spot in shock, Bella could only stare as Will reached up and grabbed her hand, laughing. Bella frowned, her brain refusing to accept what her eyes were telling her was true. Will had someone else. And why shouldn't he, screamed the rational part of her brain. She'd left him with no explanation. Of course he'd have found someone else. Will was a good-looking man. She had been a fool to think he'd still be free after all this time.

It was the last straw. She turned and pushed her way out of the door. She was vaguely aware of someone calling her name but she had no interest in waiting to hear Will explain, in the kindest possible way, that he'd met someone else and her hopes that they might be able to get back together were nothing but a foolish dream.

She ran down the stairs, her heart pounding in her chest, blood rushing in her ears. She would leave today. There was nothing for her here anymore. She had no family, no Will . . .

'Bella! Wait, please.' The woman's voice cut through the commotion in the corridor. Bella drew to a halt, and whirled round. It was Will's pretty nurse. Bella's heart sank.

'Bella, may I call you Bella?' the nurse asked, smiling. She had dark, curly hair and brown eyes.

Bella nodded dumbly.

'I'm Tabitha Mullens,' the nurse said. 'Will's sister?'

Bella stared at her, dumbfounded. 'Will's sister?' she repeated, wondering if she looked as stunned as she sounded.

Tabitha laughed. 'Yes. I'm on home leave. I docked this morning and came straight here to see my big brother before I head off to the station. He's told me so much about you.'

'I'm sorry,' stammered Bella. 'I thought . . .' she admitted with a self-deprecating chuckle. 'It's been a fraught couple of weeks.'

'Will you come back up? I know Will's been looking forward to seeing you.'

Bella nodded. 'Of course,' she said, embarrassed. 'You must think me very silly.'

'Not at all,' grinned Tabitha. 'Well, perhaps a little bit.'

Bella returned her grin. She was feeling rather foolish after her dramatic emotional display, and she blushed as she re-entered the ward but, to her relief, no one appeared to have noticed her rapid departure apart from Will.

'And it's only because I was watching out for you,' he said, as she sat down at his bedside and apologized for her behaviour.

'I can't believe you were jealous of my baby sister,' he crowed.

'Now, now, Will,' Tabitha reprimanded him with mock-sternness. 'Don't tease. How was Bella to know who I was?'

'I'm sorry,' Bella apologized again. 'I assumed . . . I mean, it's been over two years. It's understandable you would have met someone else in that time.' She smiled, her eyes begging him to tell her that no, there was no one else. Will took her hand, and she relaxed, knowing her prayers had been answered.

'There hasn't been anyone else,' he said, earnestly. 'Ever.'

Bella smiled.

'I don't know why you two broke up in the first place,' said Tabitha, filling Will's water glass. 'You were besotted with Bella, Will.'

'It was a silly misunderstanding,' said Will quickly, as Bella sought an explanation. One day, she and Will would decide whether to confide in Tabitha, but not yet.

'A misunderstanding we have now resolved,' she said, flashing Will a knowing smile.

'Well, I'm glad about that,' Tabitha grinned, her smile turning instead to concern as Will's chuckling turned into a coughing fit.

He held up his hand, his cheeks turning purple. 'I'm fine,' he gasped, his shoulders heaving. Bella got to her feet, her brow creased with worry as Will collapsed back against his pillow, panting for breath.

'Shall I call the nurse?' asked Tabitha anxiously. Bella glanced up the ward to where the two nurses were conversing quietly by the desk. Will shook his head.

'There's nothing they can do,' he wheezed. After a while his breathing calmed a little. 'Thanks,' he said, as Bella handed him his glass. 'I am improving. The coughing fits aren't lasting as long.'

'You're looking a lot perkier than you did at the start of this week,' Bella agreed. 'Last week was awful,' she told Tabitha. 'He was so still and quiet. Even the doctors didn't hold out much hope.'

'I know,' Tabitha replied, her mouth a thin line. 'Father wrote and told me. That's why I made the hospital my first port of call. I wanted to see my big brother in case ... well, you know?'

Bella nodded. She had felt the same way last week,

wanting to spend every minute at his bedside, terrified that every day might be his last.

'I'm disappointed you were all so quick to write me off,' Will grinned, lightening the moment.

'You have no idea how relieved I was to see you sitting up in bed,' Bella told him. 'Especially as I'd assumed the worst when I saw your empty bed on Somerset Ward.'

'I'm going to talk to that young chap over there,' Tabitha said, after a while. 'He doesn't have any visitors.'

'That's Barry,' Will said. 'He's American. His family are all back in Wyoming.' He nodded. 'Go ahead. I think he'll appreciate the company.'

Once Tabitha moved away, Bella pulled her chair closer. Most of the patients had girlfriends or wives visiting. A few of the visitors were older, parents or volunteers. One young woman with brass-coloured hair and bright crimson lipstick was sobbing softly into a handkerchief.

'Ken's being discharged this week,' Will told Bella, his breathing laboured. 'He's being sent back to France. That's his fiancée.'

'Poor girl,' Bella said, with a pitying glance. 'What will you do when you get out of here?' she asked. 'Will you go back to the ferry pool?'

Will shrugged. 'If they'll have me. I don't fancy a desk job.'

The turn of the conversation reminded Bella that she was due back at base on Saturday.

'Tomorrow's my last day,' she said, so quietly Will had to strain his ears to hear her over the hubbub of conversation.

'I know. I'm dreading it.' He reached for Bella's hand. 'I love you, you know that, don't you? I have since that day I met you and Arthur blackberry picking and I've never stopped. No matter how angry I was, I never stopped loving you.'

'I love you, too,' Bella whispered, her eyes filling with tears. How much time they'd wasted because of her mother's lies. Anger churned in her stomach. Right now, her wrath was directed more at her mother than her father. 'If only Alice had told me the truth,' she railed. 'We've wasted so much time.'

'Bella,' Will sighed. 'She's still your mother.'

'She's not, though, is she. I don't know who my mother is, nor my father, for that matter. I don't know who I am.'

A tear trickled down her cheek and she brushed it away angrily. She was determined not to waste another tear over the situation. She'd cried enough.

'You're you,' Will said gently. 'First Officer Bella Roberts, pilot extraordinaire and the love of my life.'

Will grinned.

'Pilot extraordinaire?' Bella giggled. 'I don't think so. But I'm glad to be the love of your life.' She leaned over and kissed Will on the lips. His hand snaked around the back of her head as he responded to her kiss. His lips were dry and chapped, and his breath still smelled slightly unpleasant, but Bella didn't care.

'Hey, Will, way to go,' shouted an American voice, and Bella drew back as Will released her, both laughing.

'About time, Mullens,' grinned the man in the next bed. His lady visitor smiled at Bella. Tabitha, seated across the aisle, looked back over her shoulder, her eyes meeting Bella's as she gave them both the thumbs up.

'I think we can honestly say we've got the approval of the ward,' Will said, his hard-working lungs making his chest heave.

'I believe we have.' Bella smiled. It was clear Will was well-liked by his fellow patients. The staff nurse was making her way down the ward.

'Visiting hour is over, ladies and gentlemen,' she said, as she passed each bed.

'I'd better go,' Bella said, reluctantly gathering her hat and her bag from the end of the bed. 'I'll be back later.'

'I'll be waiting,' Will grinned. 'Give Dad my best,' he said, as Tabitha came over to say goodbye. 'Tell him I'm doing well and I'll come over to see him as soon as I'm discharged.'

'I will do. It's been lovely to see you, brother,' Tabitha said. She wrapped her arms around Will's neck and hugged him. 'Get better quickly,' she whispered, resting her cheek against his.

'You take care, Tab,' replied Will, hugging her back.

Bella and Tabitha walked the length of the ward together, turning back every now and again to wave.

'I hate leaving him,' sighed Tabitha, once they were outside in the corridor. 'It's a comfort to know you'll be back to see him later.'

'Only until tomorrow, though,' replied Bella ruefully.

'I know. Such a shame,' Tabitha commiserated. 'We'll have to write to him often.'

They joined the throngs of doctors, nurses, orderlies, service personnel and civilians streaming down the wide staircases, heading for the exit doors.

'I'm so pleased to have met you at last,' Tabitha said, as they made to part ways.

'So am I,' nodded Bella. Will's sister was a pretty, bubbly girl, and she bore a slight resemblance to Will which, of course, she would. They were half-brother and sister, after all, Bella reminded herself. It was only she who was a cuckoo in the nest, she mused, her happy mood deflating like a burst balloon.

CHAPTER THIRTY-SIX

Will watched the door swing shut behind the two most important women in his life, then sank back against his pillows with a sigh. His chest felt tight from the effort of talking, and his breathing was coming in short, shallow gasps. He knew he'd overdone it but he hadn't wanted either Tabitha or Bella to worry unnecessarily. He was getting better. The doctors all said so, although perhaps not as quickly as he might like. His chest felt like it was on fire, and he closed his eyes, breathing slowly, in and out. His heartbeat steadied and the pain in his ribcage receded slightly. It was the pleurisy that was causing so much discomfort, but with luck, the medicine would soon sort that out. The doctors were satisfied his internal organs were healing well and agreed, to Will's immense relief, that there was no need to operate.

While he'd been unconscious, he'd been aware of various voices talking around him, doctors, nurses. At one point he was certain he was being given the Last Rites. He'd recognized Bella's voice immediately and he'd tried to open his eyes but it was as if a heavy darkness was pressing down on him, and he'd begun to feel panicky, thinking she would leave and never come back

He wasn't sure how he felt about learning that the Reverend Roberts was his father. He certainly didn't feel any affection for the man and it was clear Roberts had no intention of claiming him as his son. But, as he'd told Bella, the man who had raised him would always be his father. He thought about his mother. He'd idolized her and, while he had been shocked to the core to learn that she'd slept with her best friend's husband, he wouldn't allow that revelation to besmirch her memory. Of course he would never reveal the truth to Tabitha. Growing up, he'd always suspected Joshua wasn't his real father, so the revelation that he was the reverend's son hadn't come as too much of a surprise. But, he felt no need to upset Tabitha needlessly.

He could certainly understand Bella's animosity towards her parents but, where Bella's thinking was clouded by anger, he could understand the reasoning behind Alice's decision not to tell Bella the truth. Too many people would be hurt, including her husband. Why she had chosen to deceive Samuel, he couldn't be sure. Revenge, perhaps? Knowing that he had been unfaithful? Only Alice knew the reason, but he could understand that as time went on, the harder it would have been to tell the truth. The same with his parents. It had obviously made sense to his mother to let him believe Joshua was his father. Neither his mother nor Alice could have envisaged that he and Bella would fall in love. He sighed and massaged his temples. His head was throbbing with the beginnings of a headache. Wincing at the pain in between his shoulder blades, he reached for the painkillers on his bedside cabinet and swallowed them, washing them down with a mouthful of tepid tap water.

He leaned back against his pillows. The fog was beginning to thin and through the window opposite his bed he could make out patches of blue sky, though the foghorn continued to blare out its warning to the many troop ships sailing on Southampton Water.

'Hey, Mullens.' The chap in the bed diagonally across from him held up a pack of cards. 'Fancy a game?'

'Why not?' grinned Will. The man grabbed a crutch and eased himself off his bed and dragged his shattered foot across the floor to Will's bed.

'Cross, Anders? You boys want to join in?'

Several patients made their way over to Will's bed. Those that couldn't walk wheeled themselves in their chairs. And the young soldier Tabitha had been visiting with earlier was wheeled over in his bed. The nurse parked him as close to Will as she could manage and engaged the brake.

'Have fun, chaps,' she said, checking her watch. 'Dinner won't be for another twenty minutes yet.'

'Miss Tabitha said she'll write to me,' the young American GI told Will, lighting a cigarette with trembling fingers. 'She's a diamond, your sister.'

Will agreed that she was. One of the soldiers dealt the cards and the game commenced, amidst much ribaldry and teasing.

They broke for dinner at half past twelve. As Will watched the hospital volunteers handing out the trays, an idea came to him. It was a problem he'd been wrestling with over the past two days, and he wondered if, perhaps now, he might have a solution.

The volunteers paused at each bedside, engaging in a few minutes' conversation as they dished out the meals. They would post letters, send telegrams, run errands, pretty much anything they could to help make the patients' lives a little more comfortable.

'Hello, Will.' The volunteer who appeared at Will's bedside was called Nettie. She was youngish, early thirties, he'd say, with curly dark-blonde hair and bright blue eyes. Will knew her husband was serving in the Far East and that she'd moved to Netley to live with her grandparents after her parents' house had been flattened in the Blitz.

'How are we today?' she asked cheerfully, setting a tray of beef stew and steamed jam roly-poly on Will's bedside cabinet.

'Getting there,' replied Will, leaning forward so Nettie could rearrange his pillows. 'Better?' she stood back, regarding him with a raised eyebrow.

'Perfect,' Will replied, settling back against the pillows.

'Anything you need doing today?' she asked, one hand resting on her metal trolley. 'I expect your sweetheart's been in, has she?'

'She has, and my sister.'

'Oh, how lovely,' Nettie smiled. 'I suppose you got them to run any errands then, did you?'

Will hesitated. 'Actually, there is something,' he said, 'if you don't mind?'

'It's what we're here for,' Nettie reminded him. 'What can I do for you, love?'

Will told her and Nettie's grin widened. 'I shall do that with pleasure, Will. I hope it all works out for you. I really do.'

Giving him a wink, she pushed her trolley on to the next patient. 'Hello, Harvey. How are we today?'

Will stopped listening. He hoped Nettie would be able to do as he'd asked. His very future depended on it, he mused wryly as, picking up his fork, he got stuck into his dinner.

Bella made her way up the wide staircase. It was the following morning. She was catching the one o'clock train to Manchester so this would be the last time she'd see Will for several months at least. She stifled a yawn. There had been another air raid warning during the night, and she'd spent four hours in the shelter before the All Clear had sounded. Her eyes felt gritty from lack of sleep and there was a hollowness inside her brought on by the prospect of saying goodbye to Will.

At least this time she could console herself with the fact they were parting as friends. Well, she corrected herself as she pushed open the door, they were more than friends, they were . . .

Her train of thought was broken by a sudden cheering.

Bella stared round in bewilderment. The ward had been transformed. Pink and white bunting was strung between the light fittings and around the windows. Everyone – patients, visitors and staff alike appeared to be watching her. Bella looked over at Will, smiling uncertainly. She was surprised to see he was wearing his uniform jacket over his pyjamas, his cap perched jauntily on his head.

'What's going on?' she asked, smiling along with everyone. Apparently, she was the only one not in on the joke.

Feeling excruciatingly self-conscious, Bella walked through the ward. She could feel herself colouring under the intense scrutiny.

'What's going on?' she whispered to Will, taking her place by his bedside.

'Bella,' Will rasped, nerves taking their toll on his scarred lungs. 'I'm afraid I can't get down on one knee but, would you do me the honour of becoming my wife?' From underneath the bedclothes, he brought out a small box. Bella stared at it, remembering with sadness the first time they'd become engaged. If only . . . she pushed the thought away. This was no time for regret or recriminations. Will had opened the lid and Bella gasped. 'It's my ring?' she said, in bewilderment.

'I've kept it all this time,' Will said. 'Just in case.'

Bella couldn't keep the emotion from her voice. 'Oh, Will,' she sighed. 'Of course I'll marry you.'

The ward erupted in loud cheering as Bella lowered her face to Will's. He kissed her long and hard.

'Congratulations, Bella,' said a familiar voice.

'Gilly!' Bella flung her arms around her friend. 'What are you doing here?'

'I brought the ring,' she grinned. 'Flew down with it to Hamble yesterday afternoon.'

'I can't believe it,' Bella breathed, as Will slipped the ring onto her finger. As expected, it fit perfectly.

'We don't have any champagne,' Sister Cox said, beaming from ear to ear. 'But we've some bottles of elderflower cordial. Nurses, a glass for everyone, please.' She clapped her hands, briskly. 'We must toast the happy couple.'

Amidst much laughing and joking, the nurses handed round the filled glasses.

'Withing you both all the best,' Sister Cox said, raising her glass.

'Thank you,' Bella blushed. Will squeezed her hand. Beside her, Gilly was grinning like a Cheshire cat.

'How did you organize all this?' Bella hissed, once things calmed down a little and she and Gilly were seated at Will's bedside, slowly sipping their elderflower.

'I asked one of the volunteers to phone the airfield,' Will said. 'I'm sure Neil must have been quite surprised to get the call,' he said, with a chuckle.

'He was,' Gilly nodded. 'We'd been grounded due to the fog, so I was in the common room when he came looking for me. Beryl wanted to come too but she had a ferry call come through in the opposite direction.'

'The ring was in my bedside cabinet,' Will said. 'Obviously it's a different box.'

'It used to house a dress ring of Commander Forrester's,' interjected Gilly. 'She insisted I take it.'

'That's sweet of her,' Bella said, holding her hand to the light, admiring the way the diamond sparkled in the pale sunlight streaming in through the window. 'I must write and thank her.'

'You'll need to set a date,' said Gilly. 'Any ideas about when?'

Bella shook her head and looked at Will.

'Well, I want to get out of here first, obviously,' he said. 'Towards the end of the year, perhaps?'

'It'll just be a small wedding,' Bella said. 'Like we planned before.'

'But that was because your mum and brother were abroad,' cut in Gilly. 'Aren't they back now?'

Bella lowered her gaze so Gilly wouldn't read anything in her expression. 'What with everything going on, I think a small do would be best. I want you and Beryl there, of course, and Amanda, if she can make it.'

'Let us know when you set a date and we'll make sure to be there,' grinned Gilly.

She left soon afterwards, having to get back to the airfield at Hamble. Bella walked her to the end of the ward.

'Thank you so much for doing that,' she said, as they stood in the doorway.

'That's what friends are for,' Gilly replied. 'I never understood why you two split up in the first place. I'm just glad you've both come to your senses. You belong together. I've always thought so.'

'Thank you.' Bella hugged her.

'You're welcome. Any time.' Gilly raised her hand in farewell and was gone, the door swinging shut behind her.

'You look very dapper in your cap and jacket,' she said to Will, as she pulled her chair closer to his bed.

'Well, I could hardly propose in my nightshirt now, could I?' He grimaced. 'Do you mind if I take it off now. It's not very comfortable attire for bed.'

Bella laughed and got up to help him take it off. 'Ah, that's better,' he said, as Bella leaned over and kissed him. He drew back his head, searching her eyes, his expression earnest.

'What?' asked Bella, frowning.

'I want you to talk to your mother,' he said, gently stroking Bella's hand with his thumb. 'I don't want you at odds with her.' Bella withdrew her hand and sat back in her chair. 'Listen to me, Bella,' Will said. 'I don't want us to start our married life with a rift between our families. I know it came as a huge shock, finding out you're not who you thought you were but, listen to me, please,' he said, as she looked away, her expression mutinous. 'Your mother loves you. You know she does. I could tell by the way you used to talk about her how close you were. You don't want to throw all that away. Believe me,' he said, his expression clouding. 'One day she won't be around anymore and you'll miss her more than you can possibly imagine. Don't waste the years you've got left together, Bella. You'll regret it.'

Bella blinked back tears. 'I don't know,' she whispered. 'What she did, it hurts so much.'

'She did what she thought was best at the time,' Will said. He took Bella's two hands in his. 'No parent is perfect. Everyone makes mistakes. All I'm asking is that you talk to her, please? For me?'

'I'll think about it,' Bella said. 'But I'm not promising anything.'

'That's all I ask.' He looked at the clock on the wall at the far end of the ward. 'We've only got another ten minutes,' he sighed. 'But I shall be able to bear the separation much better knowing you're going to be my wife.'

'Who's responsible for the bunting?' Bella asked, with forced cheer. She was dreading walking out of the ward for the last time.

Wincing as he adjusted his position, Will glanced over at the bunting swaying gently in the draught. 'The nurses,' he replied. 'Apparently, it's been in a cupboard since the King's coronation. Sister Cox remembered it and got them to dig it out last night after I'd told her about my plan. I wasn't certain Gilly would even get here. I'd planned to use a curtain ring if not.'

'I would have loved a curtain ring just as much,' Bella laughed. 'Oh, I wish I didn't have to go,' she sighed, glancing up at the clock. It was almost twelve, the end of visiting hour.

'Just know that if you think of me, I'll be thinking of you.'

'Same here,' Bella said, reluctantly getting up from her chair. 'I shall write, every day.'

'Take care of yourself, Bella,' Will said, his fingers holding on to hers, as if he would never let her go.

Karen Dickson

'I will,' Bella promised, though they both knew any such promise was futile. It was war time. People were being killed every day. Chairs scraped on the lino as voices called goodbye. 'I'd better go,' Bella said, gently withdrawing her fingers. She kissed Will for the last time. Slowly she walked the length of the ward to the door. In the doorway, she turned and blew him a kiss. She managed to keep a smile plastered on her face until the door swung shut behind her, then she let the tears come.

CHAPTER THIRTY-SEVEN

'Letter for you Bella,' Terry called, flicking the envelope across the tabletop towards her.

Bella set down her fork and picked it up, her face brightening as she read the familiar handwriting. 'It's from Will,' she told Valerie, slitting open the envelope and unfolding the single sheet of writing paper. 'He's being discharged at last. He's being sent to Devon to recuperate before returning to work.' She glanced up, smiling as a gust of wind rattled the windows of the mess. The driving rain rendered visibility almost zero and snow was forecast.

It was two weeks before Christmas. Will had been in hospital for over three months, his discharge being cancelled after a fall during a therapy session put his recovery back by several weeks.

'Where in Devon?' asked Valerie, wrapping frozen fingers around her mug and lifting it to her lips. 'Gosh, it's freezing tonight.'

Bella shivered. 'I haven't been able to get warm all day,' she complained, tugging her scarf tighter around her neck. 'Thank goodness the weather's too bad for flying. We'd freeze to death in the cockpit.' She consulted Will's letter. 'A place called Paignton. He says it's only a twenty-minute train journey from where I'll be spending Christmas.'

'Oh, great,' grinned Valerie. 'You'll be able to visit while you're there.'

'I can't wait, sighed Bella. 'I've missed him so much.'

The predicted snow fell heavily overnight, leaving Woodhead airfield effectively cut off from the outside world. There were huge drifts up the sides of the hangars, and in the morning they were scraping ice off the inside of the window, and Valerie had to break the ice in the water jug before they could heat it up for a wash.

Bella spent the day playing cards with the other grounded pilots, listening to the hourly news bulletins on the wireless, and watching the snow swirl past the window as the wind howled under the eaves. She could only hope the weather improved by Christmas. She'd be brokenhearted if she missed the opportunity to see Will.

She was relieved he hadn't mentioned her mother in his latest letter. She still hadn't been able to bring herself to reply to Alice's frequent letters. She was pleased to learn that Arthur was doing well at Monk's and working well with young Johnny. The All Clear had sounded for the last time in November, and at the beginning of December, Jack had returned home to his mother.

Alice seldom mentioned Bella's father in her letters and Bella couldn't help but wonder whether things were a bit strained at home. She tried to tell herself she didn't care. She missed Arthur the most, of course. But she couldn't help feeling afraid things might be different between them now that she knew he wasn't really her brother.

Now, she crossed the mess to the window, staring out at the swirling whiteness. It was blizzard conditions out there and they'd been warned not to leave the base after several ramblers had got lost up on the moors. The news had come in by telephone when someone from the local constabulary had rung up to ask them to keep an eye out.

It was so perilous out there that a person could get lost just walking from the mess to their billet, and clothes lines had been strung between the buildings to guide people to the various places

In every letter her mother sent, she begged Bella to write back. It was clear from her tone that she hated the rift between them. Part of Bella longed to go back to a time before she knew the truth, but then she wouldn't be with Will.

'Oh, Mother,' she muttered now, her breath forming a cloud on the frozen glass. 'What a Pandora's Box you opened.'

'Everything all right?' asked Terry, glancing up from the newspaper he was reading. He sat in an easy chair, his feet up on the low coffee table.

'I'm all right, thanks, Terry.' Turning her attention away from the window, Bella came and sat in the empty chair opposite him. 'Just itching to get airborne again.'

'It's certainly a complete white-out,' Terry drawled, laying down his newspaper. 'How's the fiancé?' he asked, nodding at Bella's left hand.

'He's being sent to Devon to recuperate. Not far from where I'm spending Christmas, actually.'

'That's fortuitous,' said Terry. 'Give the lad my best, won't you,' he said, rubbing the end of his stump on his jumper. 'Bugger of an itch,' he said, noticing Bella watching him.

'You heading home for Christmas?' she asked.

'Nah, got nowhere to go,' he said, with a rueful grin. 'The boys in the kitchen will put on a good spread like always. I'll be quite happy staying here and listening to the King's speech in the afternoon then falling asleep in front of the fire.'

A high-pitched scream rent the air, killing all conversation. Bella was on her feet just in time to see Valerie fall to the floor in a dead faint.

'Oh, God,' said Patty, picking up the letter that had fluttered to the floor as Valerie fell. Four pilots had rushed to her aid and were lifting her up and helping her gently into the nearest armchair.

'It's from her fiancé's mother,' Patty said to Bella. 'Tim's been taken prisoner in Burma.'

'Oh no, poor Tim,' Bella sighed. 'Poor Val.' She crouched down beside her friend, who was sitting in the chair, her hands clenched, pale and wide-eyed with shock. 'Is there anything we can do, Val?' asked Bella, with genuine sympathy. Pathé news had reported repeatedly on the harsh conditions in which the Japanese kept their prisoners. Tim would need all his wits about him to survive his incarceration and Valerie would know that. No wonder she looked so devastated.

'I shall write to my mother,' Bella said, without thinking. 'She's a volunteer with the Red Cross, amongst other things. I'll see what she can find out.'

The sheer gratitude in Valerie's eyes nearly broke Bella's heart. Valerie grasped Bella's hands. 'Thank you,' she whispered.

'Here, drink this,' someone shoved a tumbler of brandy under Valeries's nose. She recoiled from the smell, but took the glass, her eyes dull. Grimacing, she drank it down, retching as she drained the glass.

'You're relieved from duties for the rest of the day,' Flight Lieutenant Briggs said. 'Not that you're missing much. The telephones are dead.' He glanced at the window. 'Not surprising. I doubt anyone's flying anywhere right now.' His gaze caught Bella. 'First Officer Roberts,' he said, lowering his voice. Keep your eye on WAAF Sinclair.' He gave Bella a pointed look which she understood immediately. A young WAAF cadet had killed herself recently on learning that her fiancé had been killed in action, and he was clearly concerned Valerie might be contemplating something similar.

She and Patty settled themselves next to Valerie, who sat staring into the glowing embers. The news had cast a pall over the mess. The ferry pilots were a family of sorts, and when one person received bad news, it affected them all. The men talked in hushed tones as they played cards or discussed the latest news story.

The storm continued to rage unabated all day. Late in the afternoon came the sad news that the four ramblers had been found frozen to death.

'They were huddled against a dry-stone wall clearly trying to keep warm,' said Flight Lieutenant Briggs, with obvious contempt. 'What sort of fool goes for a ramble,' he spat the word, 'in this weather?' He shook his head in disgust.

Valerie listened in silence. She had eaten no dinner and she had no appetite come supper time. Bella's every effort to tempt her was met with refusal.

'I can't eat, Bella,' Valerie snapped. 'Look, I'm sorry. I didn't mean to bite your head off, but I feel so sick with worry the very thought of food curdles my stomach' She bent forward, her arms folded against her stomach. 'Please write to your mother. I know I'll find out eventually through the official channels but if she could just let me know where he's being held and get word to him, I'd be ever so grateful.'

Bella nodded. Perhaps writing to her mother on behalf of Valerie would be a way of breaking the ice. Reluctantly, she fetched some writing paper and a pen from the desk in the adjoining Ops Room and sat down to compose her letter. She wrote about Valerie's predicament, adding very little personal news. She hadn't even told her family that she and Will were engaged again. She knew her mother would be disappointed by her cold, business-like tone but right now she didn't know how else to communicate. Her mother's revelations had left her a stranger in her own family.

Her mother's reply arrived a week later. The storms had abated and, though the snow still lay thick on the ground, the sky was a cloudless blue, and pale winter sunlight danced on the snow, so dazzling it hurts Bella's eyes to look at it.

> *My dear Bella,*
>
> *I was thrilled to get your letter. I'm so sorry to hear about your friend's fiancé and, of course, I shall do my best to discover where he is being held and arrange some Red Cross provisions to be sent to him immediately. Your friend should get a communication from the prison camp soon but, as you know, official communications can sometimes take longer than we would like.*
>
> *My dear, I hope you are well. I long to see you. Your brother misses you very much. I've told him how hard you're working to help win the war and he is incredibly proud of his beloved sister, and with good reason.*

Bella let out a disgruntled sigh. She could see exactly what her mother was doing here, emphasizing the fact that she still thought of Arthur as Bella's brother. 'But he's not, is he, mother?' Bella snapped, throwing down the letter. She was leaving for Devon the following day and she couldn't wait. She could have a good moan to Amanda before going on to Paignton to see Will.

*

Amanda was waiting for her at the railway station, little Jonty
at her side, so wrapped up against the cold all Bella could
see of him was his little face peeking out from the fur-lined
hood of his winter coat.

'It's so good to see you,' said Amanda, hugging Bella with
one gloved hand while keeping firmly hold of Jonty's reins
with the other. 'I was a little puzzled to hear about your engagement?' she said, with a confused frown.

'It's a long story,' Bella said. 'And I'll tell you all about
it later, but Will and I aren't brother and sister after all.'
Amanda's frown deepened. 'All right. I shall look forward
to hearing that story. Say hello to Aunty Bella, Jonty,' she
said to the little boy.

'Bella, Bella,' Jonty said, raising his arms. Bella put down
her suitcase and picked him up.

'Hello Jonty,' she said, giving his cold nose a kiss. His
cheeks were rosy from the icy wind blowing along the
platform.

'Come on, let's get home,' Amanda said, motioning towards the entrance. 'Mum's got the kettle on.'

'Oh, good. I'm frozen stiff.' Bella laughed, her breath
billowing in front of her face. The sea was grey and foamy,
a stiff wind blowing off the water. Her footsteps sounded
loud in the frigid air as they walked the few blocks to
Amanda's home.

Renee was in the steamy kitchen, a floral pinny over her
plain brown dress. Her hair seemed a little greyer than Bella remembered but she was still the same, warm, welcoming Renee.

'You sit yourselves by the fire,' she said, as the two younger women divested themselves of their coats. 'The tea's just brewing. Jonty, pick your toys off the floor, pet, before Grandma trips over them.' She placed a jug of milk on the kitchen table. 'How was the trip down, love?' she asked Bella.

'Long but uneventful,' she replied, stretching her stockinged feet towards the fire. Her frozen toes began to throb and tingle as they thawed. 'Thank you.' She took the mug of tea Renee handed her, wrapping her fingers around it and savouring the warmth. Jonty crawled around at her feet, gathering up the toy animals scattered across the worn carpet.

'So, tell me what happened with you and Will,' said Amanda, curling her feet under her and regarding Bella quizzically over the rim of her mug.

'Right, well, it came as bit of a shock and I haven't got over it yet but, it turns out that my mother and father are not my real parents after all.'

Amanda lurched forward. 'What?' she gulped, looking incredulous. 'You're joking?'

'Sadly, not,' Bella said. In between sips of tea, she spilled the whole sorry saga to Amanda, who stared at her open-mouthed.

'Wow!' she said, when Bella had finished. 'I wasn't expecting that.'

'It's sounds farcical, doesn't it?' Bella said, with a shake of her head. 'I feel like I've been cast adrift,' said Bella. 'Am I overreacting, do you think? Will says I should talk to my mother, but I can't bring myself to at the moment.'

'It's understandable,' Amanda said. 'I'd be devastated if I found out Mum wasn't really my mum. Gosh, what are you going to do?'

'I don't know.' Bella rubbed her forehead. 'I shall have to speak to her at some point, I suppose, though I'm not relishing it.'

'The thing is,' said Renee, thoughtfully. She was sitting on a kitchen table chair, Jonty nodding off in her arms. 'Your mother raised you. She'll love you as her own. Whatever her reasons for doing what she did, they obviously made sense to her at the time, and it's not that uncommon, believe me. Next door to us in London there was a young lad who believed his grandparents were his mum and dad. He thought his real mum was his older sister. People do what they think is best, and that's what your mum would have done. I just think you should give her a chance to explain.'

Bella gazed at her mug in contemplative silence. 'I know you're right,' she said at length. 'I just don't know what to say.' Her bottom lip trembled. 'What if I feel differently about her now? What if I can't love her anymore?'

'Do you feel you don't love her now?' asked Renee, frowning.

'I don't think so,' Bella admitted. 'I mean I'm angry and hurt, and disappointed and lost, yes, that's it. I feel lost. Like I said to Amanda. I feel like I've been cut adrift.'

'Oh, Bella,' Amanda said. 'You really need to talk to your mum.'

Bella sighed. 'I think you're right,' she said. 'I'll telephone her tomorrow before I go to see Will.'

'I think you'll feel better for it,' said Amanda, picking up her teacup.

'When Jonty wakes up,' Renee said. 'Why don't you girls decorate the tree with him? Young Bobby from next door picked one up for us this morning. It's outside.' She got stiffly to her feet, cradling her sleeping grandson to her chest. 'You take the little man and I'll go fetch the decorations out the attic.'

CHAPTER THIRTY-EIGHT

The Grand Hotel had been requisitioned early in the war and turned into a convalescent home for wounded servicemen and women. The tide was out and the wet sand gleamed beneath the pale December sky. Gulls circled overhead, their mournful cries echoing over Bella's head as she mounted the steps and pulled on the bell rope.

'First Officer Roberts,' the smiling nurse beamed, opening the door. 'Sylvia Moore. I'm the matron here. First Officer Mullens is in the library. I'll show you the way.'

Sylvia led Bella through an airy hall and down a narrow, wood-panelled passageway. The library door stood ajar, the hum of conversation drifting out into the passageway.

'Here we are,' Sylvia said. 'He's just in here.'

'Thank you.' Bella pushed the door open and stepped in the warm cosy library. The walls were lined with book-shelves and a fire roared in the large ornate fireplace, above which hung an oil painting depicting a Scottish Highland scene. There was a small artificial Christmas tree in the corner and coloured-paper streamers were draped jauntily across the high ceiling.

'Bella.' Will had been sitting in a chair near the bay window which afforded an excellent view of the beach below and the foam-flecked sea beyond. Now he got to his feet and hurried towards her. Taking her hands in his, he kissed her on the lips.

'Chaps,' he said, turning to the three men seated about the room. 'Meet my fiancée, Bella.'

There was a chorus of greetings. Two of the men had bad facial scarring, one wore a patch over his eye and the third was missing a leg. A pair of wooden crutches were propped against his chair. All the men were dressed in uniform, as was Will.

After a few minutes of small talk with the other patients, Will drew Bella to the nest of chairs by the window where they'd clearly been arranged to afford the occupants the best view.

'You look so well,' Bella said, as she sat down, her knees just touching Will's. It had been three months since she'd last seen him and the improvement in his health was heartwarming. His breath was still a little ragged and he admitted that his chest still pained him if he exerted himself too much, but his cough had cleared, and his internal injuries had almost healed.

'Another few weeks and I should be back on duty,' he

393

said. He leaned forward, taking her hands in his, and looked earnestly into her face.

'I've had a lot of time to think, as you can imagine,' he said, with a wry smile, 'and the thing is, once I'm back flying, we're going to be so busy we may not see each other for weeks. So,' he took a deep breath, wincing slightly, 'would you be willing for us to be married some time in January? That way we could spend a few days together before we must go our separate ways. I know it seems sudden, but I've never been surer of anything in my life.'

'So soon?' Bella said in surprise. 'How about the 27th? That's enough time to have the banns read.'

'What about a wedding dress?' Will asked. 'Will you have enough time to get something organized?'

'I don't need a proper wedding dress,' Bella said. 'I'll go into Manchester when I get back and buy something suitable. I'll get Patty to come with me. She's got a good eye for fashion.'

'We'll need to think about where we'll get married seeing as we live at opposite ends of the country.'

'Obviously it won't be at my father's church,' Bella said, pulling a face. 'Unless my mother has told him the truth, he'll believe we're committing incest and refuse to marry us.'

'You still haven't spoken to her?' Will's brows knitted together. 'Bella, come on. You need to get this sorted out. I don't want us starting out married life with this rift hanging over us.'

Bella sighed. 'I know. You're right. Amanda says the same

thing. I've promised her I'll phone Mum tonight, when I get back from here.'

'Good. Make sure you do. Now, ah, here's Matron with the tea,' he said, his gaze going past Bella to the doorway where Sylvia was wheeling in the tea trolley complete with a large fruit cake on a gilt-edged cake stand.

'Enjoy,' she said, backing out of the room. 'Dr Morely will be along about two this afternoon,' she said, smiling round the room, before pulling the door ajar behind her.

Bella poured the tea and handed round cups and slices of cake to the other convalescents before retaking her seat. 'So, where shall we get married?' she asked, taking a bite of fruit cake.

They decided to marry in Paignton. The vicar of St John's, the Reverend Derek Walmsley, visited the hotel regularly and he and Will had built up quite a rapport. Will would speak to him and book the date and get the banns called.

'We could have a small reception. The Inn on The Quay is nice. I've been there once or twice with some of the chaps. They've got a nice room upstairs we could book. How many guests were you thinking of inviting?'

'Not many,' replied Bella. 'Amanda and Renee, of course. Valerie and Patty, though I doubt they'll be able to come so far. Our families.'

'Tabitha won't be able to make it,' Will said. 'But I'd like to invite my dad.'

'There's a printer in Glossop. I'll pop in next week and get some invitations printed. If you can let me know about the venue before then?'

'The chaps and I are planning to go along to the pub this evening. I'll chat to the landlord then.'

'Oh, isn't it exciting,' Bella said, picking up her teacup. The only thing marring her happiness was the rift with her mother. When she and Will had first panned to marry, their joy had been tempered by the fact neither her mother nor Arthur would be able to attend, being away in South Africa. Now, she was still uncertain as to whether her mother would attend. The rift was like a dark cloud hanging over and robbing her of her joy. She sighed. Will and Amanda were right. She was going to have to sort things out with her mother if she was ever to be at peace again.

A stiff breeze was blowing off the sea when Bella alighted the train at Dawlish and made her way over to the telephone box next to the ticket office. Fishing in her purse for some change, she dialled the number for the operator.

'Strawbridge Vicarage, please,' she said, when the operator answered.

'One moment,' came the reply. 'I'm putting you through.'

As she listened anxiously to the distant ringing, Bella could imagine the telephone ringing in the hallway. Her chest felt tight and the hand gripping the receiver was clammy.

'The vicarage, housekeeper speaking,' answered Ida, sounding far away. Bella swallowed.

'Mrs Wilson? It's Bella.'

'Miss Bella, love. What a pleasant surprise. How are you keeping?'

'I'm well, thank you. Um,' Bella hesitated, her throat dry. 'Is my mother there, please?'

'I'm afraid she's not, love,' Ida said. 'Shall I get your father? He's in his study but I'm sure he won't mind being disturbed.'

'No, thank you, Mrs Wilson. I'll try again later. Thank you.'

'All right, love. And a merry Christmas to you, love.'

'And to you, Mrs Wilson.' Bella replaced the receiver with a feeling of anticlimax. She realized her hands were shaking.

The sky was a dark grey and the sea was the colour of tarnished silver, foam-crested waves pounding the small beach. Far out to sea rain was coming down like a sheet. Bowing her head to the wind, Bella briskly traversed the winding streets to Amanda's house. The first drops of rain were falling as she let herself in.

'Hello, I'm back,' she called, unbuttoning her coat as she went into the front parlour, and stopped dead, the blood draining from her face.

'Mother!' she blurted.

'Hello, Bella,' Alice said, getting to her feet.

'What are you doing here?' Bella frowned. 'I just spoke to Mrs Wilson. She didn't say you were coming to visit.'

'She didn't know,' Alice said softly, her eyes filling with tears. 'I didn't tell her I was coming here. I didn't tell anyone. Oh, Bella, I've missed you so much.' She held out her arms, her eyes pleading. Bella remained rooted to the spot, staring at her mother as if she couldn't believe she was actually standing in Renee's parlour.

'How did you know I was here?' Bella asked, her voice strained.

'I telephoned Woodhead,' Alice replied, her arms falling to her side. 'Your friend Valerie told me where you were, so I got the first train here.'

'Where are Amanda and her mother?' Bella asked, scanning the small parlour. The little Christmas tree twinkled in the corner. A few toys lay scattered on the hearthrug. A cup of tea sat untouched on the low table in front of the chair where Alice had been sitting.

'They took Jonty to visit a sick neighbour.' Alice smiled. 'He's a bonny lad, isn't he?'

Bella didn't answer. Instead, she shrugged off her coat and, draping it over the back of an armchair, sat down. Alice stared at her sadly before sitting down opposite her.

'Bella, I'm sorry you had to find out about your parentage the way you did. I never intended to hurt you.'

'You've robbed me of my family,' Bella said.

'No, sweetheart,' Alice said, looking pained. 'Darling, you couldn't be more loved. You must understand, darling, please. I'm begging your forgiveness. Everything I did was done with the best intentions.' She sighed. 'Your birth mother was called Tilly. She died not long after you were born. Pearl was her grandmother. She knew I was due to have a baby at any time and it was just by chance Arthur had just been born when she turned up, begging me to take you. Darling, I fell in love with you straight away. There was no hesitation on my part. I had to keep you. You father was away

398

at the time and I . . . well, I was afraid that if I told him the truth about you, he'd send you away. So, I lied.' She looked away, her gaze lingering on the logs burning in the small cast iron grate. 'I'm not proud of myself. I hated deceiving your father, but I felt I had no choice. I suppose I justified it with the fact that you'd have ended up in an orphanage. You and Arthur looked so similar; it was easy to pass you off as twins.' She raised her eyes, meeting Bella's stony glare.

'I'm sorry, Bella. I should have told you when you first got together with Will, and I truly regret not doing so. I kept quiet for your father's sake. I couldn't risk upsetting him. You know how fragile he is? At least you'll get to marry Will now.' She managed a sad smile. 'Yes, I know you're engaged. Dora told me on one of my hospital visits. 'I hold no animosity towards Will. Like you, he's an innocent in all this. I'm overjoyed for you, my darling.'

'Have you told Father the truth, or does he still think I'll be committing incest?' Bella asked, her tone chilly. She felt cold to her bones, despite the warmth of the fire.

Alice sighed. 'I've left your father.'

'What?' Bella sat forward, her mouth falling open in shock. 'Because of me?'

'Not really. I had to tell him about you, of course. As you said, with you and Will getting married, I couldn't allow him to believe you were embarking on an incestuous marriage. It would have been cruel. He ranted at me for deceiving him and said he never wanted to see me again. He shut up once I told him I knew he was Will's father.'

'Is it over between you?' Bella asked, sitting back in her chair.

'I don't know. Only time will tell. Alice sighed. 'What's done is done, Bella. The past can't be changed. I've made mistakes, of course I have. But I love you as if you were my own flesh and blood. I always have and I always will, no matter what.' She gave Bella a rueful smile. When no reply was forthcoming, she picked up her handbag and stood up. 'I've said what I came to say. It's up to you now. I'm at your grandparents' if you want to get hold of me.' She picked up her coat. 'Merry Christmas, darling.'

Bella couldn't move. Silently, she watched as her mother put on her coat and hat. Shoulders slumped, her face a mask of defeat, Alice walked out of the room. Above the crackle of the burning logs and the rain lashing against the window-pane, Bella heard the front door open and shut.

'Mother, wait! Bella leapt to her feet and ran into the dark hallway. She wrenched open the door. The rain was coming down heavily. It stung her face like millions of tiny needles as she ran into the street. Within seconds Bella was soaked through to the skin, but she was oblivious to the freezing rain as she ran along the slippery cobbles. By the time she reached the corner her clothes clung to her and her hair was plastered to her scalp. She saw Alice up ahead, her head bowed. 'Mother!' she shouted, blinking rainwater out of her eyes. Her mother stopped, then slowly turned around. Bella waved. 'Please, wait'

As she reached her mother, Bella realized she was crying.

Salty tears mingled with the rainwater running down her face as she fell into her mother's arms. They stayed like that for several minutes, rain beating down on them, oblivious to the curious stares of passers-by.

'You're frozen to the bone,' Alice said when they drew apart. 'Let's get you inside before you catch your death.'

CHAPTER THIRTY-NINE

'I'm so sorry, Bella,' Alice said, regarding Bella over her mug of cocoa, her eyes heavy with regret. 'But if I'm honest, I'd do the same again.'

They were sat in Renee's warm kitchen. Wind rattled the window frame and rain streamed down the glass. The gas lamp sputtered and flickered. It was already dark. Since the relaxation of the blackout rules, Bella hadn't got used to looking out and seeing her reflection, distorted by the rain, staring back at her.

'It was the shock,' she said, wrapping her fingers around her own mug. She was wearing Amanda's dressing gown while her wet clothes dried in front of the fire. 'Everything I believed about my life was a lie.'

Alice sighed and set her mug down. 'I know. Seeing it from your point of view, I can understand what an awful shock it must have been but, sweetheart, I did what I did with the best of intentions. I had to decide on the spur of the moment and once I made my choice, I couldn't undo it. Not that I ever wanted to.' She sipped her cocoa. 'Perhaps a part of me was pleased I had a secret of my own. Your father was unaware I knew about him and Leah, or that Will was his son. I didn't think about it at the time but, as I look back, I think that may have been one of the reasons I didn't tell him the truth about you. The main reason was because, as I said before, I was afraid he wouldn't let us keep you.'

'I feel so alone,' Bella said. 'One minute I was part of this large family and the next I have no one.'

'Bella, that's not true. We'll always be your family. As far as Arthur is concerned, you're his twin. I don't see that there's any need for anyone else to know the truth. Your father and I are the only ones who know the truth about Will's or your parentage, so there will be no awkward questions about you marrying him.'

'Won't Grandma and Great-Aunt Eleanor wonder why you've left father?' Bella asked.

'Everyone knows how your father has struggled over the years with his nerves. They'll just assume it became too much for me to manage. Arthur is happily settled at the farm. He took it in his stride when I told him I'd be living at Grandma's for a while.'

'Do you think you and father will sort things out?' asked Bella, sipping her cocoa.

'Like I said before,' Alice replied, biting her lip. 'Only time will tell.'

'How does he feel about me?' Bella asked the question she'd been dreading the answer to. 'Does he feel the same, now he knows I'm not his?'

Her mother's hesitation was all the answer she needed. 'I see,' she said quietly.

'Bella, I'm sorry. He'll come round. You just need to give him time. Like with you, it's a huge shock.'

'It will take time,' Bella agreed. 'For me, too. Mother, I don't want us to be at odds but it's going to take me time to come to terms with everything that's happened. Can you understand that?'

'Of course, I can, love. I know it's hard for you. I just don't want to lose you, Bella.' Alice's eyes filled with tears.

'You won't,' promised Bella, draining her mug. 'I'm getting married on the twenty-seventh of January, in Paignton,' she said, licking cocoa residue from her upper lip. 'We haven't worked out times and things yet, but I'd like you to come, if you can?'

'I'd love to be there,' Alice beamed, her eyes shining with tears as she reached out and took Bella's hands in hers. 'Thank you.'

At five minutes to eleven on the morning of Saturday the twenty-seventh of January 1945, Bella entered the church of St John's on her father's arm and prepared to walk down the aisle. She was wearing a pale mauve coat over a lilac suit, with a matching hat. As the organist struck up the opening bars of the wedding march, the handful of guests turned to watch as she and Samuel followed the vicar down the aisle. She was vaguely aware of passing the pews where her friends and family were sitting. Amanda and Renee were there with Jonty, Gilly and Beryl who had come down from Dorset. Her Grandma Lily had taken ill at the beginning of the year and was still too weak to travel and Aunt Eleanor had remained behind to look after her, but her mother was there, sitting proudly in the front pew, Arthur at her side, looking very dapper in his navy-blue suit. On the groom's side sat Joshua, looking uncomfortable in his old suit, reeking of mothballs, and two chaps from Chantry Fields Will was particularly friendly with. But all this Bella only noticed in passing. Her eyes were fixed on the altar where Will waited for her. He was in uniform, his cap tucked under his arm, staring at her with a look that could only be described as rapturous as he watched his bride walk towards him.

'Who gives this woman to this man?' Reverend Walmsley asked in his pleasant voice.

Samuel cleared his throat nervously. 'I do,' he stammered, running his index finger around his collar. Bella squeezed his hand and smiled at him. Samuel nodded and gave her a quick peck on the cheek before sliding into the pew next to Arthur.

Alice looked across Arthur and gave her husband an encouraging smile. It had been as she'd thought. Samuel's love for Bella was enough to overcome the fact that she wasn't his biological child and, when she'd written to ask if he would give her away, he hadn't been able to say no. Samuel met Alice's gaze and he returned her smile with a tentative one of his own. They were still living apart but perhaps, one day . . . mused Alice, turning her attention back to her daughter and soon-to-be son-in-law who were gazing adoringly into each other's eyes.

Oh, to be young and in love, Alice smiled, remembering her own wedding day, so many years ago.

Twenty minutes later Bella and Will emerged into the bitterly cold January sunshine to a flurry of confetti and good wishes.

'Happy the bride the sun shines on,' Amanda said, balancing Jonty on one hip as she hugged Bella. 'You look radiant.'

'Thank you,' Bella said, through chattering teeth. 'I just wish it wasn't so cold.'

'Gosh,' said Gilly, shivering despite her thick coat. 'Wasn't it cold in church. My feet have gone completely numb.'

'Let's get to the pub,' said one of Will's mates. 'A pint of ale will warm us up nicely.'

'You go on,' Bella said, noticing Alice loitering nearby. She was still clutching the damp handkerchief she'd used to mop her tears as her daughter and Will exchanged their vows. 'I'll catch you up in a minute.'

'Don't be too long,' Will said. 'We've only got a three-day honeymoon and I don't want to miss a second of it.'

'I won't, promise,' laughed Bella. As the guests made their way out of the churchyard, she walked over to where her mother was standing near a weathered gravestone. It was a child's grave, the stone weathered and covered with lichen, the inscription barely legible.

'Is everything all right, Mother?' asked Bella, taking her mother's arm.

Alice gave a shaky laugh. 'It's been an emotional day.'

'I'll say.' Bella held up her left hand, her wedding ring glinting in the weak winter sun. 'I'm Mrs William Mullens,' she grinned. 'Isabella Mullens, Bella Mullens. I quite like the sound of that. What do you think?'

'I think I like it very much,' Alice said. She sighed, her gaze on the small gravestone. 'I lost two babies before I had Arthur,' she said, as they started walking along the gravel path, leaving the little gravestone behind. 'They're buried in unmarked graves in the churchyard back home. I have no idea if they were boys and girls. I knew, when I had Arthur, that I should probably never have any more so, when I got the chance of having a little girl to complete my family, I was overjoyed, Bella,' Alice stopped walking and turned to face her daughter. The wind whipped at their hats, threatening to snatch them off their heads. 'You might be a married woman now, but you will always be my little girl. Don't ever forget that. I love you with every part of me, Bella, and I will until the day I die.'

'I love you, too, Mum,' Bella said, leaning in to hug her mother. 'Thank you.'

'What for?' asked Alice, dabbing at the corner of her eyes with her damp handkerchief.

'For loving me enough, for giving me a life other than the orphanage. I wouldn't have wanted anyone else for my mother, but you.'

'Oh, Bella,' was all Alice could say. Arm in arm they left the churchyard and walked the short distance to the Inn on The Quay. The sea was rough, boats bobbing wildly in the harbour. Waves slapped the quayside, sending up great showers of spray that sparkled in the sunlight. The salty air carried the scent of fish and oil. A large troop shop loomed on the horizon and gulls screeched overhead.

Someone whistled 'Here comes the bride,' as Bella entered the dim bar of the public house.

'Congratulations, Mrs Mullens,' the landlord said, rushing to take her coat.

'The others have all gone upstairs,' said Will, who was lounging against the polished bar, nursing a pint. 'I wanted to wait for you so we could go in together. What are you drinking, Mrs Mullens?'

'I'll have a lemonade, please, Mr Mullens,' Bella grinned.

'A lemonade, please, sir, and for my mother-in-law?'

Alice flushed. 'Oh, um, I think I'll have a lemonade as well, thank you.'

'I'll bring them up with the other drink orders,' the landlord said, his plump cheeks glowing in the firelight.

Alice went up ahead of them and, hand in hand, Bella and Will climbed the stairs to the upper room. A loud cheer rent the air when they entered and Will's two friend immediately launched into a badly sung rendition of 'For He's a Jolly Good Fellow.'

There was a lot of hugging and kissing and calls of congratulations as they seated themselves at the table. Bella found herself seated between Will and her mother. If Samuel felt uncomfortable seated near Joshua, he didn't show it. The two men appeared to have plenty to talk about, but Bella couldn't help but wonder how her father was feeling seeing his unacknowledged son marrying his adopted daughter. She'd never considered how never being able to claim Will as his son must have affected her father. She glanced across the table, meeting his eye. He smiled at her, his gaze warm and affectionate as he raised his glass in a silent, personal toast.

As the waitresses brought in the wedding breakfast dishes, she watched Arthur talking to Will and realized, with jolt, just how alike they were. She'd not seen them together since that summer she was sixteen, and Arthur had still looked like a boy. Now he was a man and the resemblance to Will was striking. She scanned the table and was relieved that no one else seemed to have noticed. Perhaps no one ever would, she mused, thanking the waitress as she set a plate of grilled fish in front of her. Dark hair and olive skin ran in her family. There was no reason anyone should ever make the connection. She knew her father certainly wouldn't want his affair being common knowledge. That would certainly put a stop to his aspirations of being made a bishop.

'What are you thinking, Mrs Mullens' asked Will, taking her hand in his and raising it to his lips.

'You look very contemplative.'

'I was just thinking how very happy I am. When I think how miserable everything seemed just a few short weeks ago, I keep feeling I need to pinch myself to make sure I'm not dreaming.'

'It's not a dream,' Will said. 'And we have three wonderful days before we have to go our separate ways.'

'Are you looking forward to joining the ferry pool again?' Bella asked. 'Gosh, this fish is good.'

'I am, and I'm not.' Will picked up his pint and took a sip. 'I'm looking forward to flying again but I'm not looking forward to being parted from you. It was bad enough these past few weeks when you had to return to Woodhead, but I knew I would see you again in a few weeks. Now,' he shrugged, 'goodness knows how long it will be until we're together again.'

'It will be hard.' Bella said, pulling a face. 'But we'll manage. We've been through so much, we'll just have to focus on the fact that one day the war will be over, and we'll be together, always.'

'That's all I think about,' Will said, with a mischievous smile. 'That, and tonight, of course.'

Bella blushed, thinking of the satin negligee she'd packed in the bottom of her suitcase.

'Ladies and gentlemen,' said Samuel, getting to his feet. 'I'd like to raise a toast to Isabella and William. Bella, Will, here's to many joyful years ahead of you.'

'Here, here,' echoed Joshua, half rising out of his seat. 'Wishing you all the best, lad, Bella.'

As a chorus of 'To Bella and Will,' reverberated around the table, Bella caught a flash of something cross her father's face as his gaze landed on Will, pride mingled with sadness for the son he could never acknowledge.

They were catching the two-fifteen from Paignton to Plymouth, so just before two o'clock, Bella and Will got into a taxi amidst a flurry of goodbyes, ribald jokes and knowing winks, and set off for the station.

The train was crowded and there were lengthy delays, as Bella had come to expect, so it was early evening by the time they reached their hotel overlooking the seafront.

Their room was small but adequate, with a decent-size bed and a bathroom down the hall. Bella was too anxious to eat much tea, so the seagulls ended up with the remainder of their fish and chips.

Now, she stood in the bathroom, staring at her reflection in the small mirror above the sink. It was raining again. She could hear it pitting against the bathroom window. She brushed a lock of hair from her face. She was wearing her new negligee. It was midnight blue satin, trimmed with lace. It clung to her shapely form, and she ran her hands down her sides, trying to imagine what it would be like when it was Will's hands caressing her body. The thought sent a shiver of delight through her body. Taking a deep breath, she pulled on her dressing gown to protect her modesty, should she happen to encounter any of the hotel's other guests, and opened the door. As she walked along the corridor towards her and Will's room, she forced herself to clear her mind of everything that had happened over the past few months, and the worry and anxiety of what the future might hold. There would be plenty of time in the days and months ahead to worry about the future and the past, she determined as she turned the handle and opened the door. Tonight belonged to her and Will.

EPILOGUE

1947

The June sun shone warm and bright over the little churchyard. Birds warbled in the branches of the surrounding trees
and butterflies flitted between the ancient gravestones as
Bella and Will emerged from the cool dim church.

'Wasn't she good?' crooned Amanda, gazing adoringly at
the baby girl she cradled in her arms. 'Not a single peep out
of her, the whole service.'

'She slept right through it,' Alice smiled, stroking the
baby's cheek with her index finger. 'Oh, look, Samuel,' she
said, turning to her husband, who stood at her side. 'She's
waking up.'

The baby blinked in the sunlight, her tiny forehead wrinkling as she frowned.

'Hello, little Elizabeth Anne,' Amanda said, jiggling
the cooing baby in her arms. 'I'm going to be the best
Godmother ever.'

'Oi, what about me?' interjected Tabitha, peering over Amanda's shoulder to smile indulgently at her three-month-old niece.

'Let's get a photograph of the proud parents and Godparents,' said Gilly, holding up her Kodak Brownie camera.

Bella gently took Elizabeth from Amanda's arms, smiling up at Will as he slipped his arm around her waist. She leaned against him, as the Godparents, Amanda, Tabitha and Arthur, crowded against them. Elizabeth cooed loudly, waving her chubby hands, her dark eyes and wavy brown hair in contrast with the frothy frills of her cream Christening gown. Her gaze found her uncle Arthur and she chortled, stretching her arms towards him. The adoration was mutual, and whenever Arthur happened to be home when Bella and Elizabeth were visiting the vicarage, uncle and niece were inseparable.

'Smile,' called Gilly, pressing the shutter, and catching Elizabeth and Arthur just as his large, calloused hand closed over her tiny little one.

'Everyone else now, please,' Gilly said, gesticulating to the guests standing around in the sunshine.

With lots of laughter Bella's family and friends gathered around her and Will, Alice and Samuel, holding hands. Alice had moved back into the vicarage a few months after Bella and Will's wedding. Their marriage wasn't perfect, but the two of them were happy enough, as far as Bella could tell. Both her parents doted on their baby granddaughter, as did Mrs Wilson. Bella had a drawerful of crocheted cardigans and bonnets the housekeeper had made. She joined them now, her face beaming. She couldn't have been any prouder if Elizabeth had been her own flesh and blood, a fact which hadn't gone unnoticed by Bella, and the realization had struck deep. The bond between a child and a parent wasn't based on blood, but on the love and nurturing they received.

She smiled at Amanda's fiancé, Jim, an architect from Exeter, Amanda had met him when he was demobbed after the war. He'd lost his wife and most of his extended family when his parent's house was bombed. The family had all been together to plan his younger sister's wedding. He joined them now, calling to Jonty as he took his place beside his wife. Four-year-old Jonty, looking very sweet in his little suit, came running over, his dark curls flying in the wind. The older he got, the more he resembled his dad. Jim grabbed him and swung him up onto his broad shoulders, the little boy chortling with delight.

Neither Valerie nor Patty had been able to make the christening. Valerie's fiancé, Tim, had survived his harrowing ordeal in a Japanese POW camp and the two were now happily married and expecting their first baby any day. After the war, Patty had remained in the WAAF and had accepted a transfer to Germany. She was currently seeing a British Army General and enjoying what seemed to Bella to be a whirl of social engagements.

Beryl was there, with her husband, Eric, as well as Bella's grandma Lily, and Great-Aunt Eleanor. Cousin Benjy and his wife, Camilla, had recently taken up a posting in

Washington, but Holly and Emily, now both young ladies aged nineteen and eighteen respectively, had come down on the train. Will's father took his place beside Will, looking every bit the proud grandfather.

'I'll take the photograph,' said Gilly's husband, Richard, walking towards her and holding out his hand. 'Then you can be in it with everyone else.'

'Are you sure,' replied Gilly, handing him the camera.'

'Why don't I take it?' said the young vicar who'd officiated in Samuel's stead. Stanley Warden, recently arrived from Portsmouth, would be taking over officially in the autumn when Samuel was ordained as Bishop of Winchester. Alice had already started packing for the next chapter in her life. Leaving Strawbridge would be a wrench, but Winchester was only a short train journey from Southampton where Bella and Will lived, so she wasn't too sad.

'That's very kind of you, sir,' said Richard, handing Stanley the camera. Slipping his arms around Gilly's shoulders, the couple hurried to join the happy group.

As she faced the camera, her daughter cradled in her arms, leaning against her husband, safe and secure in his embrace, surrounded by her beloved family and dearest friends, Bella couldn't have been happier.

'Say cheese,' grinned Stanley. There was a ripple of laughter, and he pressed the shutter, capturing the moment for all posterity.

ACKNOWLEDGEMENTS

First off, I would like to thank Clive Davidson from Henstridge Airfield for giving up his Saturday afternoon to give me a crash course on how to fly a Tiger Moth. I'd also like to thank my editors, Misha Manani and Molly Crawford, and all the staff at Simon & Schuster for all their hard work. Thanks also to Cassandra Rigg and Gillian Hamnett for their excellent copy-editing and proofreading, and pointing out my many discrepancies.

Thanks also go to my agent, Judith Murdoch, and to my family, for their continued support. And, last but not least, thank you to my readers. I hope you enjoy the book.

If you enjoyed *The Spitfire Girl's Secret*,
read on for a sneak peek of Karen's stunning
and heartfelt wartime saga.

The
Strawberry
Field Girls

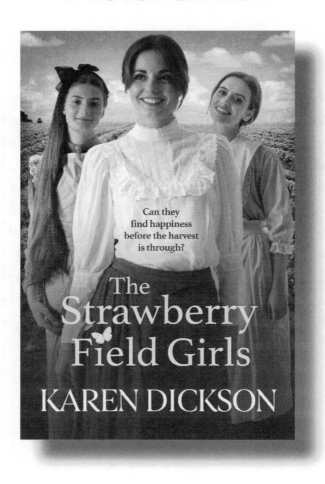

Can they
find happiness
before the harvest
is through?

The
Strawberry
Field Girls

KAREN DICKSON

CHAPTER ONE

1913

'Leah, Daisy. It's half past four. Time to get up.'

At the sound of her mother's voice, 16-year-old Leah Hopwood groaned and rolled onto her back. She stared up at the ceiling in the murky, pre-dawn light. From the lane below came the creak of wagon wheels and the slam of a cottage door. She sighed and nudged her 14-year-old sister. 'Come on, Daisy. Get up.'

Mumbling incoherently, Daisy rolled over, dragging the bedcovers with her. The gush of cold air on her exposed legs along with the rattle of the stove lid in the kitchen below was enough to spur Leah into action.

'Get up,' she said, giving Daisy's shoulder a shake. 'You can't afford to be late. Neither of us can.' She climbed out of bed and dressed quickly by the light of the pale dawn filtering through the thin curtains. Favouring their late father, William, Leah was tall and willowy with dark blonde hair and blue eyes while Daisy, three inches shorter with wavy, light brown hair and hazel eyes, resembled their mother.

As Leah twisted her hair into plaits, she couldn't help her gaze straying to the spot on the landing where Freddie's bed had once stood. She swallowed the lump in her throat. It had been four years since the diphtheria epidemic that swept through the tiny hamlet of Strawbridge had claimed the lives of so many. Leah's father, older brother and two younger sisters had all succumbed to the disease. Her strong, dependable father had been the first to slip away, followed by Freddie, three days later, dying on the eve of his sixteenth birthday. Mary and Sarah, just eight and five years old respectively, had passed away within hours of each other a few days later.

Forcing herself not to dwell on how noisy and happy the early summer mornings had once been with all five Hopwood children boisterously preparing for a long day in the strawberry fields, Leah hurried down the stairs.

The parlour was sparsely furnished. A single lead-paned window looked out onto the lane and the strawberry fields beyond. A large fireplace took up one end of the room, a brass coal scuttle standing beside the empty grate. Upon the mantelpiece, in pride of place, stood a framed photograph of Leah's parents, William and Hannah. It had been taken shortly after their wedding twenty-one years earlier. Beside it, between a pair of brass candlesticks, stood a photograph of the five Hopwood children taken two years before the epidemic.

Leah remembered the day it was taken as if it were

yesterday. It had been on a rare trip in Southampton. Dressed in their Sunday best, they'd dined at the Crown Hotel before visiting a photographer's studio close to the Bargate on Above Bar and there had been great excitement when the photograph had arrived in the morning post some three weeks later.

The sofa stood under the window, its faded upholstery hidden by a red and white crocheted blanket. Pushed up against the inside wall was the dropleaf table and four chairs. An oval mirror hung on the wall above it. On scuffed wooden floorboards were several handmade rugs. Above a small writing desk hung a watercolour depicting Salisbury Cathedral, its spire shrouded in mist, with the water meadows in the foreground. As usual, Leah paused to admire it. Her father had been inordinately fond of the painting, which he had bought off a market stall on a long-ago trip to Salisbury before he and Hannah were married. He had always promised to take them all to see the cathedral, a promise he could now no longer keep, and so the painting had garnered a certain poignancy for Leah.

Feeling the familiar tightening of her throat, she swallowed quickly and hurried into the warm, steam-filled kitchen where her mother stood at the stove stirring the porridge.

'Morning, Mum.'

'Morning, love,' Hannah replied, smiling at Leah over her shoulder. 'Is Daisy up?' Lifting the heavy-bottomed pan from the heat, she placed it on the metal trivet in the centre of the table.

'She was just stirring,' Leah said, pulling out a chair and sitting down.

'It was a mild night,' her mother said with a quick glance at the clock on the wall above the table. 'With a bit of luck, we've seen the last of the frost.'

'Let's hope so,' Leah said, ladling porridge into the waiting bowls. It was warm in the kitchen. Droplets of condensation ran down the misted-up window that looked out on to the back garden and the privy they shared with their neighbours. Theirs was the middle cottage in a row of three. The cottages that made up the hamlet of Strawbridge were grouped in twos or threes, sixteen in all, spread out between the Glyn Arms public house, the vicarage and St Luke's church.

Beyond the shared privy was a large chicken run and a flourishing vegetable patch, bordered by a hawthorn hedge, beyond which were the grounds of Streawberige House, home to the wealthy Whitworth family.

Blowing on her porridge to cool it, Leah looked up as footsteps sounded on the stairs and Daisy came bounding into the kitchen, her dark hair flying around her face. She dragged out a chair, its legs scrapping noisily on the slate floor, and was about to sit down when there was a knock at the back door.

'Who can that be?' Hannah wondered out loud. Setting the brown ceramic teapot on the table, she wiped her plump hands on her apron and opened the door.

'Morning, Mrs Hopwood.' The young man standing on

the threshold grinned cheerfully. He had a shock of black hair and olive skin that crinkled around his eyes when he smiled. 'I brought you something for your supper,' he beamed, holding up a brace of pheasants. 'And a posy for the lovely Leah.'

'You'll be for it if Mr Whitworth's gamekeeper catches you poaching, Joshua Mullens,' Hannah scolded, the smile in her eyes belying her stern tone. 'Come on in.' She stood aside and opened the door wider. 'There's porridge in the pot if you're hungry.'

'Starving, I am,' Joshua said. He handed Hannah the pheasants, pausing to remove his dirty boots on the mat before entering the kitchen. 'Morning, Leah, Daisy,' he said with a mock bow as Hannah took the pheasants to hang in the pantry. 'Flowers for the prettiest girl in Strawbridge,' he said, presenting Leah with a posy of early summer wild flowers.

She blushed. 'You're a fool, Joshua Mullens,' she chided him, but she couldn't help smiling as went into the pantry to find an empty jam jar to put them in.

'Will you tell me if you'll accompany me to the picker's ball, Leah?' he asked, as she placed the jam jar on the table and dished him up a generous helping of porridge. 'Or will you keep me in my agony of torment until I die of a broken heart?'

'You're silly,' Leah smiled, but her mirth was not reflected in her dark blue eyes. She was flattered by his attentions. Who wouldn't be? He was very handsome but ... She hesitated, reluctant to hurt his feelings. He was a good man, a little wild but his unruly ways hid a generous heart and, usually, she would have jumped at the chance to attend the ball with him . . .

Discover more from Karen Dickson

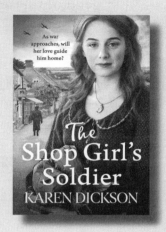

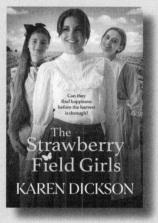

All available now

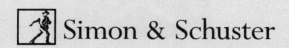
Simon & Schuster

booksandthecity.co.uk
the home of female fiction

NEWS & EVENTS | BOOKS | FEATURES | COMPETITIONS

Follow us online to be the first to hear from
your favourite authors

bc
booksandthecity.co.uk

@TeamBATC

Join our mailing list for the latest news, events and
exclusive competitions

Sign up at
booksandthecity.co.uk